DUCDAME

JOHN COWPER POWYS
DUCDAME

This edition first published in 2009
by Faber and Faber Ltd
Bloomsbury House, 74–77 Great Russell Street
London WC1B 3DA

Printed by Books on Demand GmbH, Norderstedt

All rights reserved
© Estate of John Cowper Powys, 1925

The right of John Cowper Powys to be identified as author of this work
has been asserted in accordance with Section 77 of the
Copyright, Designs and Patents Act 1988

This book is sold subject to the condition that it shall not, by way of
trade or otherwise, be lent, resold, hired out or otherwise circulated
without the publisher's prior consent in any form of binding or cover other than
that in which it is published and without a similar condition including this
condition being imposed on the subsequent purchaser

A CIP record for this book is available from the British Library

ISBN 978–0–571–24214–6

Our authorised representative in the EU for product safety is
Easy Access System Europe, Mustamäe tee 50, 10621 Tallinn, Estonia
gpsr.requests@easproject.com

**DEDICATED
TO
THAT SUPERIOR MAN**
KWANG–TSE OF KHI–YUAN

THE ONLY ONE AMONG PHILOSOPHERS TO BE AT ONCE RESPECTFUL TO HIS SPIRIT-LIKE ANCESTORS AND INDULGENT TO THOSE WHO, LIKE THE PROTAGONIST OF THIS BOOK,

> GO WHERE THEY ARE PUSHED,
> FOLLOW WHERE THEY ARE LED,
> LIKE A WHIRING WIND,
> LIKE A FEATHER TOSSED ABOUT,
> LIKE A REVOLVING GRINDSTONE.

AMI. What's that "ducdame?"
JAQ. 'Tis a Greek invocation, to call fools into a circle....

ACT II, Scene V, *As You Like It*.

DUCDAME

DUCDAME

CHAPTER I

SOME of the most significant encounters in the world occur between two persons one of whom is asleep or dead; and it might almost seem as if Rook Ashover had recognized this fact when he found himself standing by Netta Page's side on the night of November's fullest moon. Netta herself, before they went to bed, had drawn the curtain back and pulled up the blind; and she was now lying with her face illuminated and her soul, as it were, exposed. Rook looked at her with fixed intensity, as if he were striving to solve some long-withheld riddle; some riddle to which a night of this kind could alone bring the solution.

The effect of the moonlight on Netta's face was interesting. It was even complicated. It emphasized a certain haggardness, a certain battered, woebegone pitifulness in her; but it also endowed her with a touching and patient dignity.

She had never been beautiful; never even pretty; but as she lay now, with the breath coming evenly through her scarcely parted lips, there was something about her that would have arrested and held the attention of almost any onlooker.

It was perhaps an enduring softness that predominated in that immobile pose; a softness bruised, relaxed, passive; yet resistant, too, and singularly undefeated for all its helplessness. Rook Ashover continued to gaze at her face as it lay thus prostrate before him, unashamed in its unconscious exposure; but his eyes very soon fell to forgetting what he actually saw in the abstraction of his thought.

While he stood there, ready dressed to go out, the hands of the clock behind him pointing at two o'clock, he had the air of an intruder, almost of a stranger. When his thoughts did finally return to the figure in the bed, it was with a cold, remote, detached tenderness; the sort of tenderness that human beings feel in the presence of impersonal humanity.

It was a movement from Netta herself that broke the spell at last. She turned uneasily, as if conscious of his scrutiny, and the expression of her profile pressed against the pillow was less placid than it had been before.

Her movement made Rook vividly aware of the nature of his feelings; and a quick sudden anger against himself rose in his mind. What a fate it was to be made just as he was made, with this inhuman detachment always ready to fall upon him at every turn like a screen of coldly dripping gray-green water!

He left the bedside and walked to the window. The great "branch-charmèd" trees stood out there above the grass, motionless and hushed. The empty white road, the bridge over the river, the wide water meadows beyond the river, all lay before him transformed, etherealized. The liquid luminosity that filled the air seemed to emanate from something remoter and more mysterious than that round silvery disc floating in the high zenith.

Everything seemed insubstantial and dream-like. Shapes and shadows! Shadows and shapes! All the familiar things were distinct enough in that diffused pallor. But they seemed to him withdrawn, remote, intangible; as if he were regarding them from some solitary tower.

Rook Ashover stared across the fields as he had stared a moment before at the face of the woman.

The cold unearthliness of what he now saw found its response in what was occurring in his own mind, a response that went far to obliterate his self-contempt.

Out over those moonlit fields his spirit wandered, out over

the very brim, as it seemed, of our floating earth globe, thus rendered transparent and unsolid, out over the vast aërial gulfs beyond.

Between his soul and all this enchanted spaciousness there arose a reciprocity he could not analyze, a feeling that had the irresponsibility of despair and yet was not despair, that resembled loneliness and yet was not loneliness. It was almost as if, just behind all this etherealized chemistry, there really did exist something corresponding to the old Platonic idea of a universe composed of mind-stuff, of mind-forms, rarer and more beautiful than the visible world.

He left the window and stepping back to the bedside bent with exquisite precaution over the sleeper, touched her up-flung arm very gently with his lips; and then, opening and shutting the door as noiselessly as he could, ran hurriedly down the stairs and let himself out of the house.

Certain portions of the earth's surface seem, from the remotest past, to have responded in some particularly intense way to the influence of moonlight.

Among these predestined localities the strip of road and river and meadowland surrounding Ashover Bridge was one of the most susceptible of all planetary spots to the lunar sorcery.

This double-arched bridge, built of rough local stone, carries one of Dorsetshire's most traditional highways over the river Frome, at the point where Ashover Church on the one bank, and Ashover House on the other bank, give the place its historic significance. The bridge represents, for those who are travelling southward, the near approach of the parting of the ways between Tollminster and Bishop's Forley; but the milestone against the ditch opposite Rook Ashover's gate informs the traveller of the distance to London itself.

It was at this milestone that Rook glanced now.

London? The word had almost ceased to have any significance to him; though from his childhood it had touched that riverside road with a curious magic.

Arrived at the bridge he walked to the centre of it and leaned over the parapet.

It was hard not to feel as though this familiar stonework were strange and insubstantial under the indrawn breath of that immense silence.

The water itself as it swirled and eddied under the arches seemed to flow with a muted movement, as if it were not real water but phantom water.

It grew real enough, however, even as he watched it; for a great perch, at the bottom of what they called Saunders' Hole, rose suddenly to the surface with a splash that made Rook start.

To that big fish, too, it must have seemed as if there were more in this November night than a mere ordinary lapse of hours and moments.

Down to the depths of Saunders' Hole it sank again; and there, where the man's glance could not follow it, it moved rapidly to and fro as if under some lunar ecstasy; sometimes with great open mouth and huge iridescent gills turned upstream it lashed the water; sometimes with its sharp spine fins erect and its tail quivering it dug furiously at the river bed.

Leaning his elbows against the parapet Rook let his gaze wander from point to point of that well-known landscape. It was the same and yet how different!

To his left, as he overlooked Saunders' Hole, rose the square tower of Ashover Church, isolated among the water meadows.

Round the base of the tower he could make out a shimmering group of white objects, objects more congruous with the moonlight than they were with anything else in the world, except certain drifting gusts of gray slanting rain that came up with the west wind.

Among these tombstones of the generations Rook could distinguish even at this distance the one under which his father had been buried five years before.

All the rest of his house, from his grandfather back to Lord Roger, the Crusader, were very gently, century by century, becoming less and less distinguishable from the mouse-coloured dust that lay between the chancel slabs.

Turning to his right, away from the river, he could make out with hardly less difficulty the shadowy masonry of the house he had just left, standing in the midst of its ghostly lawn, between the branches of its two great trees.

Those trees looked more monumental than the house itself as he surveyed them now—especially the cedar. That was the tree he had had such trouble climbing as a young boy. He remembered how his grandfather—the one whose bones must still be intact, the bones of a life-weary octogenarian amid that mouse-coloured dust—had been forced to put a ladder to its trunk to bring him down.

The other tree was a lime, half of whose leaves had already drifted across the road into the ditch behind the milestone. But *that* tree Rook associated with later happenings, and all hurriedly, for he was loth to change his mood, he surveyed the house; the house of which he was himself the twenty-first possessor, as the guide books proudly put it, in the direct male line.

Ashover House had been a small house in the 13th Century. In the 17th it had been a spacious one. Now in the 20th Century it was a small house again; the mediaeval buttresses, the Tudor staircase, the Jacobean doorway, the Inigo Jones ceiling being the only portions of it that witnessed to its former dignity. For the rest it was a little, old-fashioned, lichen-covered building, dominated by two gigantic trees.

But small as it was, it had its own mysterious pathos to Rook as he watched it, so hushed and motionless there. Beyond the house his eyes followed the familiar kitchen garden with its high brick walls and well-kept out-houses. And beyond that, too, he looked; to where the trunks of the old apple trees weaving their twisted shadows on the long grass led to the thorn hedge where the yellow-hammers always nested; led beyond that to the rough sloping pasture, thick with mysterious knolls and hollows, which they called Battlefield; led, finally, to the high sentinel row of gaunt Scotch firs that guarded the top of Heron's Ridge.

Ragged, yet monumental, desperate in their abandoned gestures, yet sternly taciturn in their rooted immobility, these pine trees had been the background of his imagination as long as he could remember.

He turned away from them now with a sigh of unconscious distress, and, swinging clear round, gave himself up to the opposite quarter of that transfigured landscape.

Here he followed the road as it left the church gate and stretched away over the fields and ditches. There was a mile of it before one came to the hamlet, a mile of mud and reeds and floods and marsh fowl, out of the midst of which rose a second bridge across the river, a wooden one with white railings.

It was the forlornness of this unusual approach as much as the sturdy compactness of the place itself that made whatever view one got of Ashover village a thing extremely sensitive to atmospheric conditions, responsive to every varying shift of wind and weather.

At this particular hour its little mass of roofs and walls presented the appearance of a miniature city in some old steel engraving. Rook stared at it in half-ashamed sadness. How little he really knew, he to whom the place had given its name, of the actual thoughts, of the actual dramas, that went on under those projecting eaves and contorted chimneys!

Splash! An enormous water rat dived down from the bank into Saunders' Hole and proceeded to swim across the river.

Rook watched its course with curious interest, noting its sublime imperviousness to everything in the world except its immediate purpose.

There was something about the illuminated ripples that extended behind it, as it swam, that seemed in some way symbolical of all planetary movement. Vivid as quicksilver those ripples flashed, until the shadow of the bridge blotted them out!

No sooner had the rat reached its goal and vanished in the reeds than the great perch splashed out once more into the moonlight and sank, leaving a new circle of silver ripples, to live for a transitory moment.

Tired of seeing nothing but these reflected evidences of her power, Ashover leaned back against the stone coping of the bridge and stared up at the great luminary herself. Those queer hieroglyphs written across her face seemed as if they were on the point of revealing, to him alone of all the tribes of men, some incredible world secret. The immense silver disc grew nearer and larger and brighter as he gazed at it. It ceased to be a mere satellite of the earth, a mere mirror of an invisible sun. It became a round illuminated lake that drew him toward it, that drew him into it. The blue-black sky around it became a sloping, slippery shore, that held no ledge, no crevice, to which he could cling; nothing to break the swift, fatal, final slide into that magnetic gulf!

His neck grew stiff from the way in which he had twisted himself backward. But his fingers did not relax their hold on the stone coping. If some nocturnal bird had been circling above him the creature might easily have mistaken his face for some inanimate piece of whiteness, set up there as a mark in the night.

Still he remained motionless, spellbound, ensorcerized; and between the white face looking downward and the white face looking upward a strange correspondency established itself.

The spell was broken for him at last by the sound of feet upon the road. The footsteps were distant, but the silence of the hour caused them to be to him as though they were a few paces off. Rook crossed the bridge to the farther side and scrutinized the road that led to the village.

He had not long to wait. Emerging from the shadow of the clump of alders that hid the weir dam, where the sheep-washing pool was, came the figure of a man. The figure advanced in a way peculiar to itself. It advanced with difficulty, with a laboured, shuffling, dragging movement, and yet it advanced hurriedly and with a fixed intent. Rook remembered the unswerving preoccupation of the swimming rat.

The concentrated shuffle of his brother's feet, the monotonous tap of his brother's stick, had something about them that was primitive, subhuman, animal. They suggested the presence of an inbitten bodily hurt, the overcoming of which had become automatic, but could never become easy.

With rapid strides the elder brother hurried to meet the younger. They met at the church gate.

What Lexie Ashover saw was a tall, dark, massive-featured personage, bony rather than thin, clumsy rather than powerful, whose predominant facial expression was a sort of sullen, puzzled abstraction.

What Rook saw was an emaciated figure whose large fair head, covered with thick curly hair and out of all proportion to the leanness of his person, had been moulded, in some fit of divine whimsicality, into a startling resemblance to the well-known portrait bust of the Emperor Claudius.

Both brothers were bareheaded. Both were lifted at that moment above their ordinary level of feeling. But the excitement that was agitating them took in Rook the form of morose abruptness; in Lexie the form of nervous volubility.

It was a peculiarity of these two to display their affection for each other with a shameless freedom. They kissed each other now in the middle of the moonlit road as if they had been agitated conspirators, sealing some covenant of fatal complicity.

With his fingers twitching nervously at his brother's overcoat, Lexie began talking in a hurried eager voice, as if someone or something at any moment might interrupt him.

"I saw Nell last night; here at this very spot. Our priestly friend had stayed inside the church for some reason; and she had wandered out and was waiting for him just here. Rook, I know I'm right in what I told you about her. She's unhappy. She's very unhappy."

The elder Ashover's gaze transferred itself from his brother's face to the wall of the churchyard. "Unhappy," he repeated after a pause, and the word sounded like the splash of a stone that someone had thrown into a deep well.

"But, Rook, what a girl she is! What a girl! She feels things with her whole body. Do you know what I mean? She *thinks* with her body."

Rook turned his head still farther away.

"The brain is better for that," he muttered; but Lexie went on:

"I believe she's reached the point of absolute hatred for him. And shall I tell you what has done it? It's that book of his—that book." His brother emitted a sound that might have been a chuckle or a groan. "That book——" repeated Lexie. But the other remained silent.

"What do you do to all these women, Rook, to make them so fond of you? The thing's getting ridiculous. There's Cousin Ann—well! We all know what she and Mother are up to! And now it seems as if I've only to mention your name to Nell and she jumps out of her skin. Do you know what she said? She said you had a perfect right to live with Netta if you wanted to; and that it was outrageous of people to make such a fuss. She trembled all over like a bit of quaking grass when she talked about it."

Rook Ashover made no reply of any kind to this. His face grew hard. But Lexie rambled on without the least embarrassment.

"It's no use beating about the bush any more, Rook. You've got yourself into a pretty bloody predicament. No one can possibly tell what the upshot will be."

The elder man's sullenness did melt at this.

"The upshot will be that you and I will be the last of the Ashovers," he remarked grimly.

Lexie's resemblance to the least heroic of the Cæsars became strikingly marked.

"Mother hasn't said anything more, has she?" he enquired anxiously. "God! It was awful when she actually talked of you and Netta before Ann. Rook, tell me. Would you send Netta away and marry Ann if *I* went over to the enemy? Or would you hold out even against *me?*"

His brother seemed to regard this question as unworthy of any serious answer. He simply disregarded it.

"You're sure you do right in risking these walks, my dear?" He touched Lexie's forehead as he spoke and ran his fingers through the young man's thick hair as if he had been a woman.

"I can't help feeling," he went on, "that you *may*, after all, be sacrificing everything by not doing what that doctor said. As long as we're together you'll always be tempted to go beyond your strength; and I'm the worst person in the world for the business of reminding you. I can't realize things as I ought. I forget so."

Lexie had begun fumbling once more with one of the buttonholes of his brother's overcoat; but he dropped his hand now.

"I'm as fit as a badger in Field-Cover!" he cried. "It's when you talk like that——"

The malignant mechanism of chance stopped the words in his mouth.

He swayed a little and bent his head, poking automatically

with his stick at the mud under his feet which showed faint traces of frost marks.

Rook clutched at his shoulder.

"Lexie, don't! Lexie, what is it? You're not going to faint, are you?"

But the young man had already gained his composure.

"Let's go into the churchyard," he said, taking his brother's arm.

They moved together through the gate and followed the path that led to the base of the tower.

"Do sit down for a bit," pleaded Rook. "It frightens me when you get like that."

"Here? Near the old man?" and Lexie made a scarcely perceptible grimace in the direction of their father's grave.

"Yes; here."

And they sat down side by side on a flat tombstone, the name and date of which had been obliterated by many Novembers.

The rank autumnal grass in the uncut portion of the enclosure rose before them in the moonlight or lay in tangled swathes on the ground like the uncombed hair of a titanic skull.

The bent stems and rain-battered leaves of the hedge parsley that grew where the graves ended resembled now an enchanted Lilliputian forest through which some fairy beasts had trampled, leaving it outraged and desolate.

There was only one tree in that portion of the churchyard, a very old elm, lopped and beheaded and almost leafless, but with a trunk of such sturdy proportions and so deeply indented that it resembled the torso of a gigantic pillar, half buried in the earth but still bearing witness to its old obscure importance.

The two men contemplated this colossal relic, their attention drawn to it by a low sound that suddenly emerged from its headless jagged top and died away.

"Do you hear?" whispered Lexie. "What's that? There's no wind. There's something alive up there."

They both listened intently but the sound was not repeated.

"It's queer to think of these women—Nell, Netta, Cousin Ann, and our mother—all lying in their beds in the moonlight and all agitated in some way over you."

"Damn you, Lexie! Why over me? Why the devil not over *you?* With all this refusing to do what Twickenham tells you and all this walking too far, there's enough in your goings-on to keep every one of us awake at night."

He had hardly spoken the words when, with a wild tumbling of soft feathery wings, a couple of brown owls flew out of the headless tree. One flew straight across the water meadows; while the other, swinging round and rising over the heads of the two men, vanished behind the masonry of the tower.

"Netta is absurd about owls," said Rook. "She says that she must have been a field mouse once and owls ate her. I tell her that she was much more likely a great stoat who ate little owls. What are you laughing at, you devil? I suppose you think Netta hasn't the brain of a sparrow? And you think she can't appreciate the country? And you think I'm making an absolute idiot of myself by having her here?"

"We needn't go into all that now," responded Lexie. "Have a cigarette?" And with a series of movements that were concentrated in their punctiliousness he proceeded to light a match.

Rook shook his head. But he watched with curious interest the tiny Promethean flame lift up its eternal living protest between cold moonlight and cold mortality.

They were both silent for a space. Then Lexie suddenly uttered the words: "The left side would be better than the right."

Rook stared blankly at the little rings of smoke that followed one another into the phantasmal air.

"What on earth are you talking about? What left side?"

Lexie deposited a carefully preserved ash end upon the stone between them, where the little gray heap lay undisturbed, like the excrement of a wandering moon moth.

"Of the tree, brother Rook," he said, contorting the imperial ruggedness of his face into one of his humorous grimaces; "of the tree. And don't let the matter pass out of your forgetful mind! Mother's sure to want to bury me over there by the old man. And I don't want to be buried there. I want to be on the left side of the tree. Only for the Lord's sake let me lie deep. You know what elms are! It's one of those funny tricks of Nature; like the throats of whales. Monstrous trunks; and then silly little tendrils hardly bigger than turf-roots. I don't want to be exposed, brother Rook. So get that fixed in your mind. The left side of the tree; and *seven* feet down!"

The voice of the sick man died away into space; just as, a little while before, the fluttering of the owls had died away. Both sounds were now travelling, at a rate measurable to science, toward the moon. If the vibration of them survived the loss of the earth's atmosphere it would soon be reaching a point from which, if sounds had sight, the other side of the moon would be visible!

Some such fantasy as this passed obscurely through Rook's mind as he delayed his response.

In his abstracted fashion he sent his soul wandering over the wide expanse of water meadows, intersected by reedy ditches, which lay beyond the low wall of the churchyard.

He could actually feel the chill of those cold fields, of those flooded ditches, as if his mind had the power of carrying his senses with it on such a voyage. He seemed to himself to become a moving nebulous shadow, acting as sentinel to the very floor of silence upon which the world is built.

What he felt most conscious of at that moment was not the menace of mortality by which his brother was threatened, but the indrawn breath of multitudes upon multitudes of grass blades, full of the pallid greenish sap of that late season, that seemed answering the attraction of the moon with a conscious answer; just as the vast swaying sea growths are said to do under their fathoms of salt water.

"Why do you keep harping upon death?" he said at last. "Lots of people with your particular trouble live for years and years. You'll probably see *me* buried by the side of the old man long before they disturb the roots of your elm for you."

Lexie looked at him with the peculiar look that death-threatened people have in the presence of the ultimate treachery. The luminousness that surrounded them made it impossible that Rook could miss that look—a look that begged and pleaded, a look that howled, like a dog driven to its kennel.

"This is my last November," the look said, "and I love every moment of every hour of life!"

"Can't you see that I am sinking into absolute loneliness?" the look said. "Hold me! Clutch me! Save me!"

Rook glanced at his brother; saw the look; but still continued to allow his soul to wander over the fields. He wanted his brother to die least of all things in the world. He could not imagine life without him. And yet in some mysterious way, just because of the ghastly threat to the bond between them, he experienced an actual enhancing of the beauty of that night.

Something in the depths of his nature gathered itself together under his brother's words, focussed itself, roused itself to a strange pitch of exaltation. The white tombstones, the headless tree, the motionless shadow of the tower, the spellbound meadows, became so beautiful to him that death itself seemed hardly less beautiful.

Those pastures seemed to stretch away and away, until they crossed the borderline between death and life. They seemed to reach out to something dim and vague and wonderful; to some unearthly ghost garden, far from all human troubling, where nothing but solemn milk-white cattle moved up and down through a pearl-gray mist, licking every now and then with great languid tongues the drooping rims of huge moon mushrooms.

There must have been a long silence between the two brothers just then; for when Rook returned to himself it seemed that it was across an immeasurable gulf that his own last words returned to him.

By one of the quick simultaneous movements of thought that often occurred between them when they were alone together they both fixed their eyes upon their father's grave.

It was Lexie who finally put into words the thing that was in their minds.

"The old man won't like it if we're the last of his race. But I suppose that's nothing to you, Rook."

The face of the elder Ashover certainly did not at that moment suggest the passion of piety. Never had it worn more obstinately its characteristic look of truculent abstraction.

But Lexie was undeterred.

"Are you absolutely certain," he said, "that Netta can't have a child?"

Rook nodded.

"You'd marry her, of course, if she did?"

"I suppose so."

"And nothing any of us can do or say will ever make you get rid of her?"

Rook shook his head.

"Well, for God's sake, let's tell the old gentlemen inside that the family's done for, and see what *they* say!"

Lexie rose to his feet as he spoke and, hobbling between the graves, passed into the shadow of the tower.

Rook came slowly after him. There was an illusory chilliness within the shadow that gave to both men the sensation of crossing the mouth of a sepulchre. And in very definite sense this building *was* the sepulchre of their people.

They moved round to the south side of the church and followed the wall till they reached the east end. Then stepping close up to an unstained widow they peered straight into the chancel.

The moonlight streaming in behind them threw its ghostly light on everything there. The little church looked as if it had been illuminated for some nocturnal office.

The Norman arch, the carved mediæval niches, the brass lectern, the tall Puritan pulpit, seemed all of them emphatically conscious of some invisible ceremony. Was it an unending platonic dialogue they listened to, between nothingness and the dust of the generations? or did the living souls of all the animate creatures that were asleep just then—men and women under their blankets, cattle under their hurdles, wild fowl under their marsh reeds—gather together "on such a night as this," a queer, twittering, bleating, weeping, bodiless crowd, *animulæ, vagulæ, blandulæ*, and hold a secular consistory above those cold slabs?

There, at any rate, they all lay, the Ashovers of Ashover! Their two descendants, the fair one and the dark one, pressed their foreheads very close to the window and surveyed the well-known marble images and the brass inscriptions on the stone floor.

The most imposing effigy of them all was that of Benjamin Ashover, the 18th-century Deist, the friend of Voltaire.

The mortuary grandeur of this sturdy infidel threw all the rest into the shade. Clumsy classical cupids, with less resemblance to cherubs than to wine bottles, supported the plump pillow on which rested the well-shaped, supercilious head; nor could anything exceed the patronizing complacency with which this bewigged unbeliever contemplated his present surroundings!

Very different was the expression of Sir Robert Ashover, the cavalier victim of Oliver Cromwell.

Wistful and indignant, in lace collar and embroidered coat, this defender of old illusions stared out of his marble frame with an expression of melancholy surprise at the lack of gentlemanliness, or even of common decency, in "the ways of God to Man."

More different still from the philosopher's smirk was the impenetrable aloofness, stern and forbidding, of Lord Roger of Ashover, the Crusader.

With his mailed hands crossed, with his hound at his feet, with his unsheathed sword at his side, Lord Roger looked like a man-at-arms of Eternity, deep asleep, while the armies of Time trampled past him.

"*E la sua volontate è nostra pace*," his lips seemed to say under his pointed beard!

Rook and Lexie drew back together from the window and returned in silence to the gravel path that led to the gate.

Once outside in the road they both became conscious that the luminous mystery above them had worked some kind of sorcery upon their nerves, had vampirized in some perceptible way their life energy.

Every grass blade, every tree trunk, every gatepost, was still floating in a lovely transparent liquid trance.

But when the two men had parted from each other, and Rook, pausing on the bridge to listen to his brother's dragging footsteps and tapping stick, had become suddenly conscious that there was an alteration in the feel of the air, the echo of Lexie's final words returned to him.

"She has never been really friendly to the human race. Never really friendly! It's a shame we can't wait here together, brother Rook, until we can smell the dawn!"

CHAPTER II

THE rain lashed against the window panes of the dining room of Ashover House. Netta Page sat facing the window in a tall straight-backed chair.

She had finished her breakfast. She sat with her chin on her hands, her elbows on the table, her eyes staring in front of her.

There were no other people in the room. Rook and Lady Ann had breakfasted together earlier. Mrs. Ashover never appeared till midday. The same situation had repeated itself many times already; and these lonely morning meals were by no means distasteful to Netta.

As she sat now in that straight-backed chair her eyes were fixed steadily on the rain; but her thoughts were focussed on the figure of a little old lady in a black satin dress who had just passed her on the staircase.

It was not a nice experience to be looked through as if you were transparent and as if the balustrade on the other side of your body were requiring a new coat of paint; but it was a still more unpleasant sensation to be given a glance that resembled a sharp stinging smack on the cheek; and Netta, in recalling these incidents, was conscious that her resentment at them was something new; was something different from the weary habitual patience into which the buffets of life had beaten her.

But this sort of thing had been going on for a year; and she still could be quite happy at certain moments.

Not one single time, since Rook had brought her to the house, had Mrs. Ashover spoken to her, or smiled at her, or eaten at the same table with her.

The servants, too, old-fashioned and eccentric, had taken their cue from the old lady and had missed no opportunity of making the intruder feel her position.

Well! *that*, at any rate, was quite different now. The appearance of Cousin Ann upon the scene had changed all that. Netta did not quite understand Cousin Ann's kindness. But, on the other hand, she did not suspect it of any hidden treachery. She just accepted it as she had accepted so much else. And it certainly had made the whole difference as far as the servants were concerned. Lady Ann could not apparently coax Mrs. Ashover into a different mood; but she had forced her to retreat from position after position of overt contempt, and she had cast such a spell over the rest of the household that the girl no longer went to and fro among them like a convicted criminal.

Everybody in the place had felt the new influence. The worst of the village gossips, when they saw the daughter of Lord Poynings grow friendlier and friendlier with "the kept woman," had begun to wonder if it wouldn't after all result in Master Rook's marrying "the poor harmless body."

Even that formidable entity "the neighbourhood" showed signs of a certain restlessness under its own verdict. It was one thing to punish the impoverished Ashovers. It was another thing to be denied the pleasure of meeting Ann Wentworth Gore.

A tentative gesture, however, which was made from a certain quarter to propitiate Lady Ann without relaxing the proprieties, met with such an annihilating rebuff that it would have needed a bolder person than any who lived just then on the banks of the Frome to repeat that offence. The Ashover family was therefore left in peace to work out its own destiny.

Many other images besides those of the ungracious old lady and the friendly young one rose between Netta and the streaming window panes that November morning.

Rain more than anything else in the world carries the mind back to early associations, and Netta saw herself as a little girl in a starched pinafore watching it beat on the roof of the Black Dog at Portsmouth.

She saw herself as an overworked barmaid at the King George in Southampton, watching it turn the little stone gutter into a turbid flood.

She saw herself as the ambiguously protected "niece" of Major-General Sir James Caxton watching it drip, drip, drip from a Hammersmith waterspout upon a galvanized-iron roof.

She saw herself as a second-rate actress in a second-rate stock company watching it from the common dressing room as it changed the colour from yellow ochre to rusty brown of a Bristol alley wall.

She saw herself in a boat at Abingdon, watching it leap up in a million tiny water tongues from the surface of the great smooth river, the day when a Guy's Hospital student took her to Pangbourne. She could feel at that very moment the touch of his young feverish hand upon her body. She could hear the harsh-throated sedge warblers chattering in the reeds.

Netta loved these solitary interludes in the Ashover dining room.

She could dream things there and tell herself stories there, untroubled by any agitation. She could even think without hopeless regret of that rash proceeding that had for ever ruined her chance of having a child. She could even try to imagine what sort of child Rook and she would have had if things had been different!

So far off and so soothingly vague were Netta's thoughts that morning that she scarcely turned in her chair when Pandie, the red-haired housemaid, came in to set light to the fire.

"No, you'll never see no rain like our rain, miss, in all the countries you do travel through! 'Tain't in nature that water should fall from dry clouds same as from wet clouds, and there aren't no clouds this side of Salisbury Plain so wet as ours!"

Thanks to Cousin Ann, Pandie was always affable now; and the sound of her voice and the look of her sturdy broad back bent over the coals filled Netta with a delicious feeling of security.

Oh, how often in former times she had longed to be at once thoroughly idle and thoroughly respectable!

It was her craving for this particular combination that had betrayed her into the Major-General episode, the single one of all her experiences that she would have liked blotted completely out of her memory.

"I like your rain very much," she said softly. "Were you born in Ashover, Pandie?"

"Me, miss? Me, mum? The Lord love us! No, mum. I were born down Somerset-way at ween Tarnton and Durston. 'Twas fresh water, too, where Father lived. But 'tweren't Frome-water. 'Twas Parret-water; and there were big willow trees over'n and terrible black mud under'n. Corpses themselves would turn to water where I was born, miss; but that's not saying anything against these parts."

When Pandie was gone the crackling of the newly lit sticks increased Netta's content.

The effect of rain-lashed windows was to give to the light that filled the room a curious atmospheric quality; a quality that roused in the woman who sat there an indefinable feeling connected with a mysterious dream she had sometimes, the exact outlines of which, though repeated again and again, she invariably lost.

What the rain really did was to throw a greenish-gray shadow into the room, a shadow that was broken at this moment by spurts and splashes of redness coming from the grate.

She drank her remaining cup of tea in quick little sips, holding up the cup with a certain nonchalant air as she had seen Cousin Ann do, the little finger stiffly extended, the elbow resting on the table.

Over the fireplace was a portrait of Sir Robert Ashover, the unfortunate Cavalier; and the sad eyes and melancholy forehead of this picture met her gaze with penetrating sympathy.

From the very first she had taken a fancy to Sir Robert. She loved his carefully combed curls and his dreamy sensuous lips. She looked at him now with renewed reassurance. He was certainly the last person in the world to will any harm to a poor girl.

She found herself on the point of wishing that Rook was more like Sir Robert and less like his mother.

But Rook had something in him that separated him from all of them; from her most of all.

Oh, dear! She hurriedly jerked up her consciousness, like an entangled fishing line, out of *that* trouble; and threw it again, with a clear fresh swing, into less weedy waters.

How wonderful it was to be free from worry.

She had worried a great deal when she first came to this place. She wondered what her Bristol friends, Madge and Minnie, would feel if they were in her shoes.

She smiled to herself as she thought of such a possibility. They would be miserable. They would be pining for shops and picture houses and "boys." Why was it she didn't crave for any of these things? Minnie and Madge had always said she was a "funny one," and she supposed they were right. She remembered how even Rook had expressed surprise that she could go on like this, month after month, doing nothing at all and wanting nothing at all.

Cousin Ann was the only person who never seemed to get annoyed with her. It did not appear to aggravate Cousin Ann when she wanted to read stories in her bedroom instead of walking through the mud and rain. The young lady even chose books for her, just the ones she liked best, out of the jumble of volumes that filled the house.

Thinking of Cousin Ann she rose from her chair and went out into the hall.

Here she stood for a moment, very still and quiet, listening to the wind and to the voice of Pandie talking in the kitchen.

Then she gave a little jerk to one of her sleeves, glanced at her feet to see that her stockings were unruffled, and opening the door with rather a deprecatory softness, went into the drawing room.

Lady Ann was standing at a large rosewood table which she had covered with newspapers. On the table was a great rain-drenched heap of chrysanthemums, laurustinus, and a few marigolds, together with the wet leaves of certain other plants. Lady Ann was engaged in shaking the water out of these flowers and in arranging them in a row of tall vases.

She welcomed Netta with affectionate gravity, as one priestess might welcome another when engaged in something which implied an hieratic freemasonry.

Nor was their background at that moment unworthy of them. The chairs and sofas of the chilly room wore a kind of grand ghostliness in their chintz covers. They seemed to survey these two warm-blooded persons like so many wistful defunct nuns. The stately ornaments on the chimney-piece were all white and gilt; the landscapes on the walls were all in pale water colour or pastel. The whole room had the look of something that accepted Time and Change and Death as its lords and masters and yet refused to yield one inch of its own dignity and ceremoniousness.

Neither Lady Ann nor Netta spoke much as they went on with their work but they were both obviously very happy in what they were doing. Indeed, as they laughed and spread out fresh paper on the table and poured water from one vase to another one and arranged the cut stalks and the pungent-smelling leaves, it was as if all individual difference between them dropped away; while two depersonalized figures, as in some old faded print entitled "Women Arranging Flowers," substituted themselves for the real Ann Gore and the real Netta Page.

"Rook says that Lexie isn't so well."

These words, as soon as Netta had uttered them, sounded to her ears as if she had heard them long before, spoken by someone else.

Cousin Ann stared at her in obvious surprise.

"He didn't tell me that this morning," she said. "But of course he may have been too worried to talk about it."

She was silent for a moment, her large gray eyes staring in front of her, her full lips parted, her rounded chin raised.

Then with a sudden almost childish gesture of excitement: "Listen, Netta, I've got an idea. Let's go round there now, this very moment. Let's take him some of these flowers."

The blank look with which the older woman received this suggestion and her glance at the windows increased Cousin Ann's excitement.

"Yes, yes, yes," she cried. "That's what we'll do! We'll surprise him. There's heaps of time. I'll lend you my mackintosh and take my plaid cloak. Oh, you dear, how funny and frightened you look, Come on. I'll get Pandie to clear these things away. No, no. Of course I can't go alone. Oh, you dear thing. I do adore you when you look so scared."

In her impetuosity the young girl seized Netta's head between her hands and kissed her on the forehead. Then she dragged her out of the room and up the historic staircase.

The road between Ashover Church and Ashover village lay east and west. Between it and the water meadows there was nothing but a stretch of low white railings. Halfway to the village the road crossed a narrow wooden bridge where the river turned sharply to the south.

It was a road that had a distinct character of its own and no reforming county council had yet dared to meddle with that character.

The flooded ruts into which the two women kept stumbling might have been indented by the wagon wheels of Cromwell; and the rough ditch-side grass, now beaten flat by the weather, might have fed the flocks of Wolsey.

Cousin Ann's excitement seemed rather to increase than to diminish. Her thick boots and stockings kept her feet dry; while the water streaming down her cheeks heightened her eager colour.

Netta, on the contrary, was conscious that her feet were miserably wet, that the draggled ends of her hair were hanging loose, and that the rain was finding its way down her very neck behind the collar of her mackintosh.

Dead yellow leaves whirled past them as they struggled on. The willows bowed down toward the alders. The alders bent desolately toward the reeds. The reeds crouched and shuddered until they touched the surface of the swollen ditches. Tossed wildly on the rain came flocks of starlings, their awkward bodies carried up and down by the wind, their wings beating aimlessly.

The women arrived at last at the cottage of the Vicar of Ashover, a little whitewashed two-story building close to the road, where in former times had stood the turnpike toll-gate.

Lady Ann hesitated here a moment, pulling her cloak closer round herself and adjusting the mackintosh of her companion. She had made Netta wear a cloth cap of Rook's and the miserable patience of the rain-drenched face beneath it struck her now with a little twinge of remorse.

They were on the point of moving forward again when the door of the cottage opened and the figure of a young girl presented itself in the doorway.

"I saw you through the window," said this apparition in a voice so faint that the words hardly reached them. "Come in, won't you? Come in, please!"

They made their way through the tiny garden and entered the house.

Nell took them into her own sitting room and placed them on the sofa opposite the fire. She persuaded Netta to take off her shoes and hold her feet to the blaze.

They spoke of Lexie, how mysterious his illness was and how unwisely he treated himself, taking long exhausting walks when the one thing the doctor implored him to avoid was that kind of exertion.

And then quite suddenly, as she sat on a little stool by the side of the hearth, the visitors became aware that the girl was trembling from head to foot.

Shivering convulsive tremors ran through her slim frame. Her small head, whose wavy light-brown hair framed a face as shell-like in its transparency as an old miniature, straightened itself stiffly on its slender neck as if to defy some mortal weakness.

"What is it?" murmured Cousin Ann, laying her wet gloved hand on the young woman's knee.

The sympathetic voice and touch seemed to alarm the girl rather than quiet her. Curious twitching lines appeared on her face; and her mouth, which normally had a piteous twist, began to resemble the mouth of an unhappy little gargoyle.

She rose from her seat, biting her under lip, clenching her fingers in the palms of her hands, and stood by the mantelpiece.

Lady Ann also rose and for a moment remained hesitating. Netta, who kept glancing timidly from one to another as she stretched her feet nearer and nearer to the fire, was vaguely struck by something brusque and blundering in her friend's movement. She became conscious of a wish that Cousin Ann would turn her steady glance away from that troubled figure; and behind that wish she found herself feeling a faint, a very faint hostility to her dear friend.

Lady Ann had never looked more competent, more high-spirited, more kind. She seemed on the point of making some pronounced sympathetic gesture, perhaps even of taking the hysterical girl in her arms. Netta had a feeble inclination to cry out: "Let her alone! let her alone!" But all she could do was to wish herself out in the rain again, out in the road, in the fields, in the middle of Hangdown Cover; out anywhere, so as not to see—she couldn't tell quite what!

Thank Heaven! The door opened just then and the Vicar of Ashover entered. Netta had not been able yet to make up her mind whether she liked William Hastings or disliked him. He made her think of a picture of Napoleon that hung in the Major-General's bathroom and *that* association was horrible. But he also made her think of Monseigneur Tallainton, the little old French priest of the Catholic church in Bristol; and that association endeared him to her. She liked something compact and weighty about his rather corpulent body, and she liked his hands, which were very small and very white. It was a certain suppressed passion in his face which puzzled her and disturbed her. It was like a ship with its decks covered with great dark guns coming down upon her out of the mist.

The Vicar shook hands cordially with Cousin Ann and bending quickly over Netta herself prevented her from rising. It was while he was doing this that his young wife slipped silently around the outside of the group and escaped from the room.

It was not till after the conversation had begun that the girl's disappearance was noticed.

"Yes, I'm afraid she was upset by something," said Lady Ann, catching the Vicar's eye as it roved from Netta's outstretched feet to her cloth cap.

"It's the weather," said William Hastings. "She is always like this when it rains. Nell hates the rain."

"I think it was more than *that*, Mr. Hastings," said Lady Ann gravely. "But it's a pity the climate doesn't suit her, if you're going on living here."

"Dorsetshire suits us better than any other place when the wind's not in the west."

As if in response to the clergyman's words a great gust of wind shook the windows of the house and a splutter of rain came hissing down the chimney.

Netta thought she could hear a bed creaking in the room above them, and the sound troubled her more than the sound of sobs. She drew her feet away from the fire and began putting on her stiff half-dried shoes.

"Yes, we must be going," said Lady Ann, rising. "But I would have liked to ask you about your book. Is it coming on well?"

The Vicar's face changed its expression completely. "Seventeen chapters," he said with a look at Netta as if she and her troublesome shoe-strings were the eighteenth chapter. "But it is the old story with me, Lady Ann. I tear most of it up. It isn't a very cheerful book."

Lady Ann smiled as she wrapped her plaid round her. She had grown accustomed to this kind of thing from William Hastings and had ceased to take it seriously. No one but the man's own wife had ever seen this mysterious work, and for some reason or another Nell Hastings never spoke of it.

But Netta was on her feet now and gravely contemplating the faded carpet. Hastings and his book presented themselves to her mind as a great plump black crow carrying a little plump black crow in his claws. She fancied she heard that bed creaking again.

She pulled on her mackintosh with such rapidity that the clergyman was not in time to assist her. She was glad when they were out of the house. She was glad to feel the rain on her face again.

As for Cousin Ann the whole experience of that little room, with its grotesque antimacassars across the backs of mahogany chairs and its double row of daguerreotypes, seemed to sail off over the ditches like a bubble of froth. Her only remark, as the rain eddied and gyrated past them like a horizontal cataract, reducing the whole world to the grayness of a cadaver, was a remark that conveyed no meaning at all to the mind of Netta.

"Queen Elizabeth was right. There's something funny about it. They ought never to have allowed it."

The rain increased in volume. The village in front of them seemed completely to disappear. The plaid cloak soon became as wringing wet as if it had been flung into the ditch. The drops trickled down Netta's back in cold persistent streamlets that made her shiver. Her shoes were so full of water that they responded with gurgling swishing noises every time she moved her feet.

On and on they struggled, their heads bent, their soaked garments clinging to the curves of their figures like Pheidian drapery, their eyes blurred, the rain tasting salty in their mouths, as if it were the tears of some vast inconsolable Niobe.

It seemed to Netta as though their heavy progress would never end; as though all her troubled life had been only a fantastic preparation for a destiny that meant walking, walking, walking, by the side of a being whose thoughts she could never read, toward a goal that could never be reached!

And obscurely, through the clamminess of her clothes, through the gurglings of her shoes, she kept hearing that invisible bed in the upper room of Toll-Pike Cottage creaking, creaking, creaking, like the hinge of a gate behind a retreating assassin.

She began to fall into that mood of indignant pity about

Nell Hastings that used to puzzle the girls so when she displayed it over the affairs of poor Madge. Why did she always worry herself about people? Mrs. Hastings was nothing to her. She didn't want her pity. She did want *something*, though, and Netta wished she could give it to her.

She found herself giving it to her in her imagination, It took the form of a twenty-pound note, like the one which the manager of the Bristol Theatre gave to Minnie at Christmas. She saw that twisted mouth trying to thank her but she hurried away. . . . Why! They had actually turned down Marsh Alley and were at Lexie's very gate. "Never mind, dear. I expect we're both a little dazed." So Cousin Ann had been speaking to deaf ears! "I must stop fancying things," Netta said to herself as Lexie's housekeeper let them in and preceded them upstairs.

They found the invalid lying on a deck chair at the edge of his bookcase. On a little table by his side was a china mug and in the mug was a specimen of that curious plant, half fungus, half flower, which the botanists call broom rape.

Lexie sat up very straight and contemplated his visitors with wide-open eyes.

"We mustn't stay a moment," announced Cousin Ann. "Rook doesn't know we came. We've brought you these." And to Netta's astonishment, out of the deep pocket of her plaid coat the young woman produced a bunch of dilapidated chrysanthemums.

Lexie received the flowers, snuffed tentatively at them, remarked that they smelt like muskrats, and laid them down beside the mug.

He looked at Netta then, with something like a furtive appeal on his corrugated face.

"Do you want me to go and talk to Mrs. Bellamy?" Netta said humbly.

A glance of unconcealed irritation was her reward for this.

"You're both so thoroughly wet," he grumbled, "that I refuse to be responsible for keeping you a second. Thank you for coming, Ann. Thank you for bringing these. And now, for God's sake, clear off, both of you, and race home!"

He waved them away with both his hands and seemed seriously agitated. And yet Netta was once more aware that he was looking at her with that same significant expression. What did he want her to do? To go home alone?

"Why doesn't Ann stay to lunch with you and let Mrs. Bellamy dry her things?" she murmured.

"And leave you to go home by yourself? Can you see me doing such a thing?" cried Lady Ann.

There was an awkward pause between the three of them, during which Netta loosened the wet mackintosh from her throat and moved away from the support of a table lest her dampness should spoil Lexie's papers.

The drenched condition of the two women seemed to draw into that little room a desolate melancholy essence composed of fallen leaves, muddy cart ruts, and clammy mist. Toward the water that still clung to their bodies the great moving volume of water outside seemed stretching itself through the little window in irresistible attraction.

The red coals in Lexie's grate seemed to lose something of their power. The rosy glow reflected from Lexie's crowded bookcases seemed to fade. The little blue fire devil that danced like a demon butterfly on the top of the coals flagged and drooped. A great blind streaming face was pressed against the window—the gray featureless face of the rain. It was as if a corpse-cold cloudy arm, wavering and shadowy, fumbled and plucked at those two dripping figures; as though, drenched as they were, they belonged to the drowning fields outside and not to this warm human interior. Lexie himself, as he looked from the one to the other, felt conscious that something from those miles of soaked pastures, something beyond the mere drenched clothes and rain-draggled hair of the two girls, was separating them from him by an impassable barrier.

The thing made him petulant, querulous. It was always like this with women, he thought. They were so damnably absorbent of the chemistry of nature! They were so easily submerged by these elemental forces! When one wanted them to be especially rational and attentive, their bodies were drifting off, tissue by tissue, cell by cell, upon some long inhuman tide, leading God knows where!

He got up now with a painful effort, an effort that made Netta instinctively spring forward, while Cousin Ann fell back against the wall as if to ward off a blow.

"Do you know why she comes to me like this?" he said, leaning forward and addressing Netta.

Netta hurriedly withdrew the hand she had stretched out to support him.

"Don't!" she murmured, shaking her head. "Don't!" And then with a voice that gathered a sudden unexpected power: "Please sit down again, Mr. Lexie, and let me leave her here. Rook will understand."

The rugged-faced thin man leaned still farther forward. His hands pressed hard against the little table, shook it so that the broom-rape trembled.

"Rook!" he cried. "I should think he *will* understand! She comes to me to *square* me! Do you hear, you dear little fool? To square me! Did you think she came for anything else?"

His voice died away in his mouth like an echo in an open doorway; but his mouth still hung open, the under lip pendulous and quivering; and a drop of saliva ran down to the tip of his chin.

"Go! Both of you!" he cried hoarsely; and sinking back into his chair he turned obstinately toward the fire, hugging his thin knees.

Netta was conscious of nothing else but a desire to bend over that figure and press that heavy curly head against her breast; but Cousin Ann with a fierce little red spot burning on each of her cheeks had become completely mistress of the situation.

"Good-bye, Lexie," she said quietly. "Come, Netta."

They moved toward the door, but as they went out he turned again.

"Why don't you go to Hastings and square *him*? He'll give you reasons. But you'd better not read his book. Do you hear? Don't you dare to read his book! You have reasons enough without that. Ask Nell. She can tell you." His haggard profile and deep-set sombre-lidded eye seemed thrusting a pike into Cousin Ann's retreating figure.

"*It's all in the book!*" he shouted after them as they closed the door and ran down the stairs.

CHAPTER III

MRS. ASHOVER walked with a firm quick step. No one would have guessed, to see her little thin black figure making its way through the long grass of the orchard, that this was the seventy-third November the power of which she had defied.

The gate leading from the orchard to the sloping hill called Battlefield was a gate heavy on its latch. But it was a gate that Mrs. Ashover had manipulated as a young bride fifty years before and she was not to be daunted by it now. She rubbed her forefinger thoughtfully up and down its gray lichen-grown top bar. The sun was warm around her, a slanting autumn sun, and it fell pleasantly on the ancient gate and on the rough yellow patches of lichen which filled the crevices of that half-century-old plank. A piece of woodwork exposed to all the elements is a very different thing from a piece of woodwork protected within a barn or a church. Its life is five times as intense; its experiences five times as acute. That top bar by the time this particular afternoon sun reached it must have been, if vividness of experience were allowed to count, older than Dürer's famous Madonna in Nuremberg.

Mrs. Ashover looked from the gate to an old apple tree that grew beside it and from the tree she looked to the ground. A sprinkling of yellow apples had been left there, and many of them were half buried in the rank thick-bladed grass.

Mrs. Ashover tapped the gate with her knuckles. It was annoying that Rook was so careless and so casual in his handling of the place. In John's day good cooking apples such as these would have been gathered to the last rain-soaked pippin.

With a shrug of her shoulders and a fierce little sigh the old lady forced the stubborn latch and pushed the gate open.

When it was shut behind her she resolutely ascended the hill. She stepped carefully over the mole runs, avoided the patches of brown bracken and the mysterious hollow places that broke the ascent, and finally, a little out of breath, arrived at the summit of Heron's Ridge.

The horizontal sun threw her slim erect shadow along the close-cropped turf as emphatically as it threw the shadows of the Scotch firs. They were twice as old as she was, these trees; but she felt just then as if she were their contemporary. She prodded the trunk of one of them with her ebony stick. The gesture relieved her feelings; and she continued it till a piece of red-brown bark fell upon the ground.

With a flickering smile on her thin lips she left the tree and, moving to the farther crest of the ridge, looked down into the less familiar valley. A grassy slope, patched with bracken and furze, locally named Dorsal, led down to a narrow muddy lane. Beyond this lane a thick undergrowth of small oaks and hazels mounted up to a high leafy skyline called Antiger Great Knoll. There was only one human habitation visible between Dorsal and the Antiger Woods and upon this habitation she now fixed her eyes.

It was a small gamekeeper's cottage surrounded by pheasant coops and fowl runs. A footpath led down to it from where she stood; and an untidy vegetable garden, in which a bonfire of weeds was then burning, separated it from the lane.

Mrs. Ashover contemplated this scene for some moments in an attitude of intense thought. She knew every tuft of furze, every bracken patch, every grassy excrescence, every gravelly hollow, as well as she knew the furniture in her own bedroom.

There was the dead ash tree struck by lightning forty

years before, at the roots of which she used to sit and sketch and read, before Lexie was born.

There was the rabbit burrow, with the earth mould freshly disturbed and the little pellets of excrement freshly dropped, just as it had looked, with the sun falling aslant upon it, when she used to bring out her writing case and write long letters about her children and her husband to dear Edith, Cousin Ann's mother.

She could actually recall a certain sentence she had used, on one of these occasions, which poor dear Edith had commented upon and been greatly shocked by.

"I have washed all Wentworth blood out of me," she had written, "and gone over body and soul to John's people. John's gods have become my gods; John's dead, my dead."

Setting her face with renewed determination and clutching her stick tightly the old lady made her way down the hill to the back door of the house in the lane.

The gamekeeper and his wife were engaged in feeding the fowls, assisted by their idiot son. This child, whose half-articulate utterances and facial distortions would have been horrible in a city, fell naturally into his place among wilting hemlocks and lightning-struck trees and birds eaten by hawks and rabbits eaten by weasels.

Mr. and Mrs. Drool were thrifty, decent people who were able to increase their income very considerably by this fowl run of theirs; especially since Lord Antiger's agent had ceased to invite any one to shoot in those particular preserves and had gone to live himself in Bishop's Forley, five miles away.

"Mrs. Ashover! Well, I never!"

"The missus her own self! Well, I'll be jiggered!"

"Blub . . . blub . . . blub! Binnory good boy! Give Binnory summat."

"Don't drag at the missus, Binnory!"

"Don't 'ee mind him, Mrs. Ashover! Don't 'ee mind him! He do know who you be as well as he knows who we be! 'Tis a windle-wandle innocent; but you should hear'n holler to the hoot owls when sun be down. And he do know the gentry when he sees 'un as well as any God-fearing man."

Mrs. Ashover responded to these various voices with unruffled equanimity. She patted Binnory on the head and told him never to kill slowworms. She steered the conversation to Mr. Drool's pheasants and to Mrs. Drool's Wyandottes. She answered their questions about Rook and Lexie with becoming vagueness.

At the first pause in the conversation, however, she moved straight to her purpose.

"I want to see Mr. Richard," she said. "Is he in the house?"

"She wants to see Corporal Dick," repeated the woman, glancing with a certain obvious embarrassment at her husband.

"He be weed-burning in garden, mum," she went on. "It be a job he have always a mind for. He do like the smell o't and the flare o't. Joe and me have always marked it in him. He do look as eager for bonfire-time as 'twere for the King's birthday."

"May I go round and speak to him, Polly?"

"Certainly you may, 'm; mayn't she, Joe? Certainly she may speak to Granfer Dick. There's no reason why she shouldn't speak to the Corporal, is there, Joe?"

Mrs. Drool looked extremely uncomfortable as she uttered these words; and the gamekeeper's uneasiness was so great that without knowing what he did he picked up his corduroy coat from the clothes line and shook it in the air.

"Binnory'll take you to see Granfer Dick burnin' things. Binnory'll take you"; and the idiot tugged at Mrs. Ashover's skirt, uttering while he did so the peculiar inhuman sound represented by the syllables, "blub-a-blub . . . blub-a-blub."

Mrs. Ashover did not hesitate. Taking the boy by the hand she walked rapidly round the house, leaving the gamekeeper and his wife staring blankly at each other.

The reason of their embarrassment became quite plain when the strangely assorted pair reached the place. Granfer Dick, for some reason of his own, had stripped himself not only of his coat and waistcoat but of his shirt, too; and, armed with a pitchfork, was throwing weeds on the fire in nothing but a pair of old military trousers.

The Corporal was a man of gigantic size; and the sight of such an extremely old man in such scanty clothing surrounded by smoke and flame was certainly a thing calculated to disturb a stranger.

Mrs. Ashover was no stranger, however; nor did her appearance cause the least discomfort to the octogenarian. He leaned on his pitchfork and with a wave of his hand sent Binnory away.

"Well, sister Joan, what mischief brings *you* here this day of all days? You've only been three times to see me since John died and now you come on the very day he died."

The resolute little woman did not wince or draw back. She brushed a flying spark from her dress and pointed at the Corporal with her stick.

Between the fading November sunset and the clouds of blue smoke she looked like an aristocratic sorceress summoning up some great fire spirit. She was in one of her most reckless moods; but it was with a quiet affectionate gesture that she beckoned the old man to move nearer to her out of the smoke. Ever since her husband had first introduced her to this bastard brother of his she had felt friendly to him and free of her usual prejudices. She called him "Corporal" though now; and, as they fell to exchanging confidences, he did not repeat the "sister Joan," but addressed her without any appellation at all.

"I've no one to go to! I've no one to go to," Mrs. Ashover found herself saying. "Doctor Twickenham is a fool. William Hastings is mad; and Lexie is worse than mad where Rook is concerned. I told you a year ago, Richard"— "She drops the Corporal when she wants help," thought the old man—"where it seemed to me Ann Gore might come in. Well! I've had her with me for several months, and what's the result? I am besieged in my own house. That woman is everywhere. I meet her on the staircase. I meet her in the garden. I only *don't* meet her in the dining room and the drawing room because I stay in my own bedroom! I tell you the place doesn't belong to me any more. I am just an uncomfortable visitor, staying with my son and his mistress. That's how it must appear to all our neighbours; and that's how it is."

The Corporal threw his pitchfork away and led his agitated visitor back to the house. Opening the front door he took her straight into his own little room where there was a big wood fire. He placed her in a dilapidated armchair with the utmost courtesy and then began muttering and groaning while he fumbled for his best clothes in the chest of drawers.

"So Ann has gone over to the harlot? Ay, John. Ay, John. Ay, John. That I should have lived to see this."

"I've no one to go to," repeated Mrs. Ashover. "That's why I came to you. John always used to come to you. I can hear him saying it now—'I'll just run across and talk to Richard'—so, my friend," and she smiled almost wistfully at the wrinkled contorted features appearing under the upheld coat, "you must help us at this pinch or see us go right down to the bottom."

Granfer Dick pulled a chair to the opposite side of the fire, took his seat deliberately, and stared with concentrated intensity at his kinswoman.

"Smoke if you want to, Corporal," said the old lady. He

shook his head and continued to survey her with frowning forehead and screwed-up eyes, thinking many things.

"It's funny. . . . It's as funny as a bad dream," murmured the old woman. "But if something isn't done soon nothing will change it. Rook will get older and older till he dies childless; and the family will die out with him."

A fierce light came into the Corporal's pale eyes and the skin of his closely shaven face tightened itself over its bony framework like parchment that is pulled taut.

"What's that?" he cried. "Die out? The Ashovers 'die out'?"

"Certainly they will, if you can't think of how to help me. When once I'm buried and out of the way, things will go on exactly as they are now, till Lexie is dead and Rook is dead. That woman is certain to outlive them both; and then . . . Well! that'll be the end. There'll be nobody else."

The two old people looked each other full in the eyes and all manner of wild fantastic thoughts passed between them. They were like a pair of aged priests, servants for innumerable years at a venerable altar, who suddenly awake to the fact that the great god of their idolatry is stricken with a mortal disease.

Terrible with a kind of mad panic such priests might become. They might slaughter holocausts of sheep and oxen. They might steal the flocks from the shepherd and the swine from the swineherd. Nothing might be safe from their sacrificial depredations unless their god himself intervened.

But how could the shadowy god of Squire John's widow and Squire Ralph's bastard express its pleasure or displeasure?

Could the sad-eyed cavalier come forth from his gilt picture frame and say: "Let the family end!"? Could Sir Benjamin come forth with his marble smirk and say: "Let the family end!"? Could the Crusader uncross his feet, or

John Ashover lift the slab from his more recent dissolution, and cry with one united sepulchral voice: "Let the family be as though it had never been!"?

Without a word interchanged these two crack-brained old people, the elegant lady and the social outcast, let their wild fancies circle round the figure of Cousin Ann—Cousin Ann, who seemed dedicated by Nature herself to be a mother of distinguished offspring. It was incredible that a girl like that should really betray them. But what was she doing? It looked like callous, careless, cynical caprice. Girls *have* ways of getting hold of men. They have absolutely *sure* ways when they can be persuaded to sacrifice their pride.

The unspoken thoughts of the two fanatics grew queerer and madder every moment, as the November mist, blending with the smoke of the bonfire, darkened the windows of the room.

"What can I do?" murmured Mrs. Ashover at last, making a pitiful little movement with one thin arm toward her companion. But the Corporal had lifted himself up very straight now and sat bolt upright, his long fingers on the arms of the chair, his little eyes almost shut.

"With buck-rabbits who won't come to't, with buck-ferrets who won't come to't, with hound-dogs who won't come to't, 'tis only a matter of putting the right mate to 'em; shutting her up with him and taking yourself off. You know that and I know that. It's only a question of the hour and the maid."

The matter-of-fact gravity of the Corporal and the outrageousness of his suggestion so tickled the old lady's nervous fancy that she clapped her hands to her face and burst into a peal of hysterical laughter.

She laughed until the tears ran down between her fingers; but even then, deep down underneath her collapse, she was conscious that a set of fantastic possibilities, like blocks of erratic tesseræ, were forming themselves into a kind of pattern. It was all so mad and strange. But who could tell? She knew there were powers and forces in the world that would sometimes carry to a conclusion what was *imagined* when they refused to yield an inch to what was *willed*.

She was suddenly aware of a crazy desire to bring the Corporal upon the scene. It could do no harm for him to see Rook; it could do no harm for him to see Cousin Ann. It would gratify a perverse longing in her for him to see the intruding woman herself. Let the bastard deal with the mistress. There would be an ironic justice in that. She thought deeply for a minute, biting her lip and tapping the ground with her stick.

It couldn't do any harm; that was certain. Rook had always treated the old man well and Lexie, before he got ill, had been in the habit of spending hours with him.

She glanced at the clock on Granfer Dick's mantelpiece. How the days were closing in! It was only a quarter to five now. If they started together at once they might find the whole party still sitting over tea; and what was more natural than that she should have asked the Corporal to escort her home? Then he would see the woman. John was dead but John's brother would see the enemy in the house.

She felt like some beleaguered chatelaine who could bring up at need a trusty freelance ready for anything. The adventure appealed to the old woman's youthful spirit. It appealed to a vein of superstition in her, too. The Corporal was a queer character. Perhaps he had the evil eye! Perhaps he would strike God's own terror into the heart of the creature. Her mind ran off down a long avenue of wild conjectures. Perhaps John's brother would whisper such murderous threats into the wretch's ear that one of these fine days she would pack her things without a word and be off into the void!

The hands of the clock in that little empty room were still short of the hour of five when the mistress of Ashover, leaning on the Corporal's arm, was struggling up the slope that led to the Scotch firs.

"Tu-whit—tu-who! Tu-whit—tu-who!" came the voice of Binnory, and they fancied they could hear a long-drawn answering wail from the depths of the Antiger Woods.

It was getting very dark before they were halfway up the hill. The November night, rolling like a great brown-coloured wave across the earth, gathered up their human excitement into its own dark heart and diffused it over the misty woods and leaf-strewn lanes. The fatality of old age mingled with the fatality of vast dim vegetable forces moving to obscure dissolution.

Caw! Caw! Caw! came the cry of solitary belated birds, following their companions from the ploughed fields of the valley to the trees on Antiger Great Knoll; and the voice of the rooks became the voice of the night itself, that great primordial winged thing, woeful and yet undespairing, lamentable and yet consolatory; full of whispers and murmurs, of premonitions and memories, wherein the beginning of things reaches forward to the end of things and the end of things reaches backward to the beginning.

Mrs. Ashover's arm trembled as it rested on the Corporal's; and the old man himself had frequently to delay their ascent in order to take breath.

And yet something that was stronger than their decrepitude seemed to draw them both on. Was it that the actual flame of life in this man and this woman was leaping high and fierce just then because of some occult emotional understanding that was older and deeper than this present business? Had Joan Ashover from the very first felt more tenderly for this brother of her "John" than she herself had realized?

Perhaps some of these shadowy clumps of furze bush, dripping with wet white mist and smelling of dead wood and fungous growths, by the side of which they rested, were old enough to recall other encounters between these two, wherein the wild vagaries of the human heart had been fecund of astounding self-deceptions!

They were standing now beneath the great trunks of Heron's Ridge and both the old people drew into their lungs the chill, muddy, pungent breath of the distant water meadows as it came up to them across the flooded river.

Very old they both felt as they breathed that chilly breath! The little lady's outburst of adventurousness flagged, wilted, sank. The first coming on of the night, with its unsealings and releases, was a very different thing from the established nocturnal power that now sank its foundations into one abyss and lifted its ramparts into another!

She drew her arm stiffly out of the Corporal's and turned her face round to him. They could see little of each other's expression but John's brother was not surprised when she said in a faint querulous voice: "It's too late to-night. They will all have separated. I couldn't bring them together. That woman will have gone to her room, to my son's room. You'd better leave me here, Corporal. No! No! I couldn't think of taking you farther. You are older than I am, my friend. Good-night, Corporal!"

A few minutes later a slim figure with bowed head and weary limbs was descending the hill to the south through the rabbit burrows of Battlefield, while a gaunt figure with bowed head and weary limbs was descending the hill to the north through the rabbit burrows of Dorsal.

An electric current sent in a bee line through the clay heart of Heron's Ridge would have connected those two figures; but not for long.

Tu-whit—tu-who! Tu-whit—tu-who! wailed the owls of Antiger Great Knoll; but no one listened to them except the idiot; and he was too occupied with stamping out the ashes of Granfer Dick's bonfire to give them back their cry.

CHAPTER IV

WILLIAM HASTINGS sat writing at the window in the upper back room of Toll-Pike Cottage.

Pale watery sunlight, faint as though it had passed through fathoms of attenuating mist, spread itself out over his minute meticulous manuscript, over the bare floor, over the shabby bookcase, over the gaunt discoloured volumes of Philo, Iamblicus, Plotinus, Paracelsus, which stood like dehumanized, featureless ghosts between the melancholy milestones of his Latin and Greek theology.

The Napoleonic stomach of the man was pressed forward against the edge of the wretched little table which served him for a desk, while his white, plump ecclesiastical fingers held the pen with a suave ferocity.

It was not permitted just then to any living person to catch the expression on William Hastings's face as with calm, monotonous scrupulosity he formed word after word and punctuated them and dotted them and preserved their measured margins.

There happened to be two little crumpled-up dead flies upon the window sill before him, and it seemed as if some power inimical to life itself emanated from the movements of that white, plump hand. Was it an accident, a coincidence, that on the grass below the theologian's window a forlorn heap of frost-bitten feathers was all that was left of a seven-month-old sparrow?

Is there, perhaps, a power of destruction in human thought capable of projecting its magnetism beyond its own realm of immaterial ideas? Nothing moved in that shabby room except the hand that was writing, and yet there undoubtedly did mingle with the pale, watery light that filtered in something that seemed to make the more friendly of the volumes upon the shelves draw closer together, to make the print of Saint Jerome with his lion and his skull look unnaturally ghastly, and to make the black marble clock upon the mantelpiece tick like the heart of a condemned man.

But if the furniture in Mr. Hastings's room caught in such a troubled manner the vibration of his "not very cheerful book," there was someone in the house who received these mysterious emanations much more woefully.

The young woman down below kept wandering uneasily from parlour to kitchen and from kitchen to parlour. She presented the appearance of someone who struggled with an overpowering impulse to run out of the house, to run down the road, to run for miles and miles and miles.

At one point as the hours went on she did actually steal up to her bedroom and snatch her hat and cloak from the shaky cupboard; but she flung them aside when she came down and returned to her stove in the kitchen.

She was boiling something in an iron pot, and as she stood stirring this, she kept looking furtively round, holding herself very still to listen, her hand on the spoon and her head turned sideways.

Once she opened the back door a little and let the misty yellow light lie cold and comfortless on the gray flagstones and the smell of leaf mould mingle with the steam of her cauldron.

It was one of those days when the stillness is so absolute that it seems as if all the winds of the world had actually dropped out of the air, like great birds shot through the heart, and were now lying stone dead in remote lakes and ponds and backwaters out of all reach of recovery.

There was a small poplar tree behind Toll-Pike Cottage, and just because there were so few leaves left each one of them seemed to float in its own particular atmospheric circle; and as it floated, to be consciously holding its breath.

The very prevalence of pale yellow over every other colour gave to the fragment of space framed by the open door a look as of royal obsequies, as if all the land were covered, like a naked archaic corpse, with flakes upon flakes of chilly gold.

It sometimes happens, in an out-of-the-way country spot like this one, that even the most harmless and commonplace noises cease altogether, leaving behind them a silence so profound that it becomes ominous.

Such a silence, saturated like a great wet sponge with a watery yellowness that might have been washed from the golden body of some drowned idol, gathered closer and closer round the agitated girl.

She put her hands to her ears at last. She was afraid of hearing the scratching of a pen up there; but this gesture only had the effect of making her abominably conscious of the beating of her own heart.

Suddenly she decided to endure the thing no longer; and very silently, moving on tiptoe, she crept upstairs.

Pausing at her husband's door she found herself without the courage to open it and without the courage to descend. She just stood outside on the landing listening.

Ah! she was sure she could hear his pen now; and it seemed to her as if it were the beak of some obscene bird pecking at the throat of life. This monstrous thinking-machine was the only thing that was alive in that windless morning. By the chilly mortuary light of the same sun whose pallid gold made the leaves so yellow and the air so misty this infernal cerebral gimlet was boring its way into some undefended crevice in the foundations of human sanity.

She would have found it hard to say by what gradual means she had become so certain as to the nature of her husband's thought. But certain she was now; and if she had dared she would have rushed into the room like a madwoman and torn the abominable thing into a thousand fragments.

Why didn't she dare? What was there about this man that always paralyzed her? She leaned against the closed door and bowed her head upon her elbow. She seemed beyond the relief of tears, beyond the power of any decision.

It had all been so wonderful to her at first. To be loved by a recluse, by a thinker, by a person so different from the rest. And Aunt Martha had been so pleased about it before she died; so pleased that her nervous, troublesome niece had someone to look after her.

To look after her! What would the old lady have said could she have known? She recalled her feelings when she first fully realized that her ideal image of the man had been broken to pieces. But she mustn't think of that. Nothing that could ever happen would be quite as bad as what she went through then. Who was it who had told her once that cut flowers before they actually die suffer a spasmodic crisis and stretch themselves out with a palpable jerk, stark and rigid? That was just the way her romantic feeling for William had ended—given a horrible spasmodic jump, like a broken spring, and fallen in a dead heap!

And it was not only that the mainspring of her love was broken. There had taken its place another feeling about him, a feeling very difficult to define, a vague, mysterious terror of something within him that baffled and perplexed her, something that roused an agitation in her such as people feel in the presence of the supernatural.

It is true that this particular sensation came and went. It was at its worst at moments like this when something in the day itself played into its hands. But there were other days, when, in the ordinary exchange of little diurnal domestic interests, the thing subsided and died down. During these calmer interludes, though the romance of her love was dead beyond recall, she was not devoid of a certain quiet affection for him, strong enough to respond to his own attenuated, eccentric, spasmodic fits of tenderness.

But to-day that almost supernatural terror seemed at its very worst. Oh, she was at the end of her tether to-day and something would have to be done. She could bear the strain of it no longer. She began listening again with increased intensity. . . .

Ah, he had pushed his chair back in there and put down the pen. She could see him as clearly as if the wood against which she leaned had been glass. She saw how his white hands clasped themselves upon his stomach, just where the little gold cross hung down. Oh, loathing! Loathing! Loathing! What was this? She was downstairs now, pulling on her cloak. Bang! The door had shut behind her and she was in the garden. Click! The gate had swung behind her and she was in the road.

Where was she going?

It was not till she had walked some hundreds of yards down the road that she knew she was going to Lexie Ashover's. *That* was the last resort, then! That was what her feet would do with her when her mind ceased to act!

All the rest of the way she remained drugged and numb; and even at Lexie's door she was still too dazed to catch the look of disapproval with which Mrs. Bellamy regarded her, or to realize until she had removed her cloak in Lexie's room that she had forgotten to take off her apron.

Lexie had been more submissive to his doctor during the last week, and the girl was touched to see how this relapse into an invalid state had affected his spirits. He seemed to have lost something of his accustomed vein of humorous malice.

He removed a pile of books from the lap of a leather armchair and made her sit opposite him, scanning her face with a certain whimsical intensity as children in fairy books scan the faces of human-speaking animals.

The pallor of the day increased the natural pallor of her skin. Her oval forehead with the silky hair falling on each side of it seemed to carry more human sadness under its tender curves than any mere personal trouble could account for. Lexie's flickering fire threw softening lights upon this sorrow, without touching its lodged hurt.

His own cue, it seemed, was a low confidential tone of intimate gravity. "You know what happened after we talked in the churchyard that night? They came to see me . . . in the morning . . . just as you have come now . . . and Ann was more Ann than I've ever seen her. I couldn't stand it. It was too much. But whether Netta heard what I said, or understood what I meant, the Lord alone knows! They were both dripping wet and I packed them off. But I'm sure Ann understands. You know what I'm like when I get rattled, Nell. I don't beat about the bush."

A faint little smile crossed the visitor's face.

"What did you say to her?"

"I said she'd come to 'square' me."

"Lexie! Did you say that?"

"Why not? I believe in bringing everything right out into the air. I like to see the little horns protruding and the furry ears pricked up. I like to see the sharp claws under the velvet pads."

"But, Lexie, did Netta hear what you said? Oh, Lexie! How awful!"

"I tell you they were both so dripping wet that it was all very confused. It was like quarrelling in a laundry. You could smell their drenched clothes. You could smell their wet skins. Poor Netta stood on one leg like a rain-soaked heron, and Ann looked as if she didn't know her head from her tail. It was an entertaining scene, only I was too rattled to enjoy it."

"But do you really mean that Ann is trying to come between Netta and Rook?"

"Nell, I'm ashamed of you! Don't you know that women like that never come between people in that way?"

"In what kind of way do they do it, then?"

Lexie made a face at her as if he were playing at bears with a young child.

"They don't do anything," he said. "They just look on till it happens."

Nell raised herself very straight in her chair and met Lexie's grimace eye to eye.

"If she entangles Rook and makes Netta unhappy it'll be a cruel, scandalous, wicked shame!"

Her violent words had their effect. Lexie got up, shuffled to the mantelpiece, and leaning his elbow against the corner of it looked down with concern into her face.

"I suppose," he said solemnly, "it has never occurred to you that Rook may be thoroughly tired of both of them."

She frowned and tilted back her head to get the full significance of this, and the young man was aware of something more vibrant and tense in her manner than he had realized at first.

He began to wonder about the apron, too, which she had now untied from her waist and was mechanically folding upon her lap.

"Tired of both of them," she repeated; and then, avoiding his eyes and dropping her head—"He used to be very fond of Ann before he met Netta, didn't he?"

Lexie seemed to derive a mischievous satisfaction from delaying his answer to this question. He took his elbow from the chimneypiece and placed his hand upon the back of her chair.

She kept her head bent, but the next thing he did was done in so casual and natural a way that it was very difficult for her to take offence at it. He lifted up her chin with two fingers and kissed her lightly on the forehead.

"Did you say 'fond of Ann'?" he cried. "He used to make

love to her for whole summers. They used to stay out all night. My mother never knew half that went on. They were a fair pair; and I daresay Ann fell in love with him for ever and ever. She's certainly had endless chances of being married since, though she's only twenty-five—did you realize that, Nell?—only twenty-five now."

The girl sighed and, instead of returning his smile, looked abstractedly into the fire. Lexie suddenly remembered how Rook had grown remote and sullen when he rallied him in the churchyard.

"It's these two now," he said to himself. "I knew it." And then, lifting whimsically one of his heavy eyelids:

"I only hope," he thought, surveying the abstracted head and tilted shoulders beneath him; "I only hope the Reverend William will wear his horns with a good grace. For he'll have 'em. And good luck to him!"

Reluctant to break the spell of his companion's mood, thus scandalously interpreted, Lexie sank back into his armchair and rubbed his thin knees with outspread hands.

Oh, that he might only stay conscious, in this exciting chaotic world, three, six, ten, fifteen years longer!

The silence between them lasted for several minutes without a sound entering the room. Not a pulse stirred in all that sapless yellow world of vegetable mortality outside, from which the odour of accepted death mounted into the air.

Finally the girl came to herself and began to speak hurriedly and nervously, pinching the folded apron on her lap as if it were an object for sale upon a counter.

"I don't know why I should tell you these things—but there's no one else—I've got no one else—I don't think I can stand it any more.—It isn't that he's unkind to me or anything like that—he's always the same.—It isn't that he troubles me with questions—he doesn't notice anything—never anything! It isn't that he touches me"—she gave a little movement that made Lexie stop rubbing his knees—

"he's quite given up doing that. It isn't that he reads to me what he writes"—her mouth twitched and her forehead puckered—"it isn't that he talks to me about what he writes.—He never talks to any one.—It's just— Oh, Lexie!"—and she leaned forward with wide-open eyes and the apron crushed between her hands—"it's just the things he's thinking and the things he's writing——" She stopped short and stared wildly, as if looking at something behind Lexie's shoulder. "Do you believe in God?" she concluded with a funny jerk in her voice and a shuddering relaxation of her slim body.

Lexie's countenance had grown graver and graver while she spoke, and its expression, under his corrugated Claudian brows, more and more sympathetic. But at her final question, flung at him so unexpectedly and recklessly, his very soul seemed to draw back into some interior impregnable fortress, out of the little arrow slits of which he peered forth at her, over moat and portcullis, with a watchful and suspicious cunning.

"I don't see," he said slowly, "why you women have always to make such a coil. I'd like you so much better, Nell, if you just honestly told me you'd fallen out of love with that cold-blooded word-spinner of yours; that you hated him like a dead fish; that you'd adore giving him a shrewd blow in the gizzard!"

Two expressions overlapped each other, quick as thought, across Mrs. Hastings's tremulous face. The first one was sheer pain. The second was irrepressible childish amusement.

"Dear Lexie!" she murmured; and then in a calmer voice, "I expect I do seem to you silly. But it isn't as simple as you think it is. If you only knew, you wouldn't look at me as you're looking now. I'm not putting this on. I'm not playing on your sympathy. There may be quite natural reasons for these things; but I tell you William's a different person from what any of you dream. He's not an ordinary person at all. He's—he's—he's either *mad* or he's thinking—thinking something—that destroys—you know?—that destroys everything!"

Lexie withdrew even from behind the narrow aperture of his defensive tower. He withdrew backward, backward, till nothing was visible of him but a suspicious pair of fox's eyes blinking out of the darkness.

The girl sighed, but something seemed to drive her on to betray herself. "Don't you believe in good Powers and evil Powers? You must! You must! Don't you believe in people being obsessed?"

He made a movement with his hand as if to interrupt her.

"I could *make* you believe!" she cried, raising her voice. "I could *make* you!"

He came back again to the arrow-slit in his tower.

"Poppycock!" he murmured; and it was almost as if he had been a brutal schoolboy putting out his tongue.

She winced and fell back in her chair. A kind of bewildered anger seized her heart against all these men. She visualized the corrugated leathery countenance in front of her, smiling that superior smile, as if it were a burrowing badger, digging itself obstinately into its familiar hole when the sky was full of flaring comets.

"You don't believe in anything, then," she remarked faintly, "that doesn't happen under your very nose?"

"I don't believe in all these mystical fol-de-rols," cried Lexie; "and it would be a damned good thing for you if I could shake them out of *your* head."

The mere sight of her twisted mouth, quivering there before him as if he had struck it with the back of his hand, seemed to aggravate him to further abuse.

"The worst of you women," he began again, "is that you always find some mysterious fantastic reason for a perfectly legitimate and natural thing. You are thoroughly sick of that good man of yours; sick to death of him; and I don't blame you. Why don't you honestly say so, then, instead of dragging in all these metaphysical cantraps, and trying to make out that the poor devil's a bloody magician or God knows what?"

She turned away from him with a hopeless sigh and stared into the fire, her elbow on the arm of her chair, her long thin arm supporting her chin.

The reaction from his scolding tone, from his "beating her up" as he called it, caused a delicious warmth toward her to pass through his veins. Watching her sitting there, so much at his mercy, he experienced a sudden twinge of jealousy over his brother's prerogative. In the present sweetness of his feeling toward her, now that he had chastised her for her silliness, he felt greatly tempted to give his brother's monopoly a timely jolt.

His eyes narrowed under their heavy Cæsarean lids. She was a highly strung little wench. She would probably let him embrace her out of pure craving for sympathy, for refuge, for protection. The image of Rook's figure, as it had leant by his side at the moonlit window, the outline of that profile, high-cheekboned like a Red Indian, the shape of that closely cropped dark-haired skull, rose up irrelevantly, accusingly. And life was so short—so atrociously short—especially—*his* life!

He rose and came over to Nell's side. He laid his hand on the back of the girl's chair and caressed its polished woodwork with little jerky movements of his fingers. "Shall I touch her hair?" he thought, "or put my hand on her shoulder?"

He stood there very awkwardly for a perceptible passage of time while the girl beside him made herself more comfortable by a little indrawing movement. She seemed to be absorbed in a not unpleasant but very complicated piece of thinking.

"To the devil with these haverings!" he said to himself. "But why does a person's heart beat so absurdly at the mere thought of doing such a natural, such an inevitable thing? And why this sickening sensation in the pit of one's stomach?"

"You're not angry with me, Nell dear?" he asked. His voice must have had a quaver, a huskiness, a strained note in it, as quickly recognized by feminine nerves as the flick of a pike's tail is recognized by suspicious minnows. She gave him a scared sidelong look. But even in the act of turning her head toward him and meeting his gaze the fear went out of her face. There is always something pathetic and childish to a woman in a man's physical desire. To the man's own consciousness he may appear a veritable devil. To his would-be victim he is much more like a greedy infant.

Nell Hastings was not conscious at that moment of the least quiver of moral indignation. She just lifted her chin from her hand, pulled up her feet under her in the big chair and looked straight back at him with an understanding smile; a smile of more direct girlish happiness than had crossed her face for many a long month!

In the simple glow of finding herself desired by a man she respected, the nameless horror she had run away from receded and receded. What made Lexie's embarrassed overture the more touching was the very fact of his illness. He stirred something within her that had never been stirred before, her inborn protective instinct. She felt toward him what a lover of woods might feel who comes upon a rugged sturdy tree marked with a great staring notch and a chalk number. The last thing she had expected was that Lexie, as well as his mysterious brother, should look at her like that. Of course, it was different from what Rook made her feel. That was a thing by itself. She had not decided yet what that was. But she was far too grateful to poor dear Lexie for wanting her at all, and he so stricken and threatened, to

DUCDAME 57

fuss herself much as to how *this* situation dovetailed in with the other.

"Poor little Nell! Poor little Nell!" He had taken both her wrists now in one of his hands and had put the other lightly on her shoulder.

What she meant to do was to laugh affectionately and snatch her hands away, but instead of doing that she found herself standing by his side. Had he pulled her out of the chair or had she, to release herself from him, slipped out of it herself?

"Don't do that! No! No! Don't do that!" Her voice sounded calm and sensible enough, but what was the use of a calm voice when she was already in his arms and yielding to his agitated caresses?

Her mind raced about in all sorts of funny directions while she submitted to his love-making. She caught sight, over his shoulder, of a row of books entitled "Mermaid Classics" and she wondered what the girls in those books did when people took them in their arms. She found herself listening to see if she could hear Mrs. Bellamy moving about in the house. Then, in the midst of her feeble movements of resistance, she caught sight of a little bust of Voltaire on the mantelpiece. How benignly that malicious old man was watching her!

Suddenly she drew away from him and shook off his hands.

"Please don't, Lexie! I don't want it to be like this. I don't want it."

His face looked haggard as she pushed him back and she felt a wave of dangerous pity for him. How could he know that she had brought it to an end not because of indifference but because of the opposite of indifference? It was all right as long as she was a passive rag doll in his hands; but if she began to come to life—it wouldn't do.

In a moment she became stiff as a block of wood; and though she still smiled at him and displayed no shadow of anger against him, he felt that, for that day at least, he must be just the friend again, just the kind, disinterested friend.

They both moved to the window and looked out.

"Damn these niceties and nuances!" he said to himself. "She's in love with Rook and thinks it wrong to care for both of us. Yet she *does* care for both of us. Oh, when will human beings put all this business on a simple natural earthy basis?"

The look of the pools in the road reflecting the pale, chilly sunlight brought the girl's mind back to her immediate trouble.

"What am I to do now, Lexie?" she whispered. "It must be nearly time for his meal. He'll wonder where I am. He has to go to see Mrs. Drool this afternoon." She stopped and shivered. "I can't imagine what he says to these people or what he does. Think of seeing him sitting on a cottage chair!" And she suddenly burst into an uncomfortable laugh that made Lexie look at her very gravely.

"Nell, my dear," he said after a pause, "I fancy the only thing to do now is to go back and endure it as well as you can for a little while. One never knows! I tell you, my sweet Nelly, one never knows! The world is much more malleable than people realize. Go on as you are for a *little* longer: something's sure to happen."

She did not seem to be listening very intently. Her eyes had left his face and were gazing into the distance. A curious, inscrutable look came over her features and her twisted mouth quivered.

"Very well, Lexie dear," she said. "I will go back to him. Don't bother to come down. I can let myself out."

CHAPTER V

THERE was no reason why Cousin Ann shouldn't have tripped over a tree root during her walk with Rook and strained her knee. People *did* stumble over things and hurt themselves.

There was no reason why she shouldn't have answered Rook laughingly, jestingly, just as she *did* answer him: "I'd love you to do it for me!"

That was all. That was her way of flinging back his suggestion that he should "massage" the injured knee. It was natural enough. Nothing to complain of. They were old friends, old playmates from infancy. They met in a world totally outside *her* world. It was natural they should have their jokes. But it wasn't a very pretty joke this time. If Minnie or Madge had made it she would have cried: "Don't be vulgar!"

It was just that—just that Rook should make that sort of joke at all, that had driven her to make a scene. It wasn't jealousy, as Rook had said. She wasn't jealous of Ann Gore. It was only that she never could bear vulgarity. It made her sick in her stomach. And all men were like that, gentlemen and counter-jumpers, lords and bookmakers! They all loved to make vulgar jokes. But there was no need for Rook to get so angry. He ought to know that a girl doesn't always mean what she says; especially when her feelings have been hurt. But that was the way. Men were so stupid. They took things wrongly. They listened to your *words* instead of caring what you felt.

Netta's feet were on the fender of her empty bedroom grate

as these thoughts pounded and hammered in her indignant consciousness, making her head ache with the strain.

She had been too upset to ring for Pandie to light the fire. She did not want Pandie to see that she'd been crying. She did not want any one's pity, least of all that of a gossiping servant.

Mercy! How cold it was and how the wind howled round the house! It didn't feel like the morning, somehow. It felt like the afternoon; and yet it was only eleven—and all that trouble had happened since nine o'clock!

She rose stiffly to her feet and, though she was fully dressed, she snatched a cloak out of the cupboard and wrapped it round her neck like a shawl. Oh, what was that?—someone knocking at the door? A gentle knock; different from Pandie's; different from Rook's; who on earth was it?

She hurriedly hung up the cloak again and closed the cupboard. Then she glanced quickly round the room. Yes, it looked like a real lady's room: the vase of flowers on the dressing table; the pillows undisturbed; no stray petticoats lying about. "Come in!" she called in a firm, quiet, self-controlled voice; and rubbed her cheeks with both hands.

The door opened and was shut again, very noiselessly shut; and Cousin Ann stood before her. Cousin Ann looked very young and very girlish; not nearly so athletic and sportsmanlike as usual. This look was partly explained by the fact that she still wore her nightgown and dressing gown and had tied her hair back with nothing but a broad ribbon; but it was also due to a certain psychological softness brought about by her recent hurt. Cousin Ann limped as she moved to Netta's bed and sat down upon it. The other bed in the room, Rook's bed, seemed to take an unkind pleasure at that moment in emphasizing its presence. "Why doesn't one of you sit down on me?" it seemed to say. "I am here—Rook Ashover's bed—and this encounter interests me greatly!"

"I couldn't rest in that room," were the first words Lady

Ann uttered. "Pandie came and talked and talked; and Mrs. Ashover said she was coming; and so I thought I'd take refuge with you."

"It's very nice of you, Ann, I'm sure," murmured the elder woman, catching sight of herself, as she spoke, in the great gilt mirror and feeling dismay at the lack of youth in her own face. "It's very nice of you to come. Does your knee hurt you very much?"

Lady Ann glanced at the door. "Do you mind locking us in?" she said. The smile that accompanied these words had almost a schoolgirlish look of mischievous complicity.

Netta walked across the room and turned the key.

"I wish *you'd* massage me!" laughed Lady Ann, making a little half-playful groan of distress as she stretched herself out at full length on the bed.

"There, just there!" she murmured, struggling to rise on her elbow to draw her clothes aside.

"I see. I'll do it!" interjected Netta. "There! Is *that* where it is? I expect when it swells up it will stop hurting. It isn't swollen yet, is it?"

Lady Ann gave her a quick penetrating glance; but Netta's face was grave and sympathetic. "No," she said. "You can't see very much, can you? But it feels perfectly awful."

Netta sat down by the girl's side and moved her fingers gently across a knee that might have belonged to Artemis herself. She could not help a faint pang of envy at the extraordinary whiteness of the skin she touched. With a scarcely perceptible movement she rearranged her visitor's dressing gown and went on in silence, passing her fingers up and down the injured knee.

"How dark it is!" the younger girl cried. "And how the wind does howl! I fancy there must be a storm coming up."

"It's not so *very* dark," said Netta quietly, letting her hands sink wearily. "It's gray. I noticed it directly I got up. It's all gray, the sky, the garden, and everything. Rook said this was the sort of weather when you can see the wind! You know the way he talks! It's funny sometimes. It makes a person laugh."

Lady Ann smiled and let her fingers seek those of her friend. They both remained quite still for a time, listening to the rattling of the windows and the long-drawn moan that kept filling the chimney and then dying away again.

"Netta dear," said Ann suddenly, "are you very, very fond of Rook?"

The first effect of these words upon the woman sitting on the bed was a dull physical tremor, as if from a narrow path below a great mountain slope she had heard the beginning of an avalanche.

Wow ho! Wow ho! Wow ho! moaned the wind in the chimney.

Gathering up all her forces to deal with this crisis she extracted her fingers from Lady Ann's clasp and straightened her shoulders.

"Why have you waited to ask me that till to-day?" she said, in a low, flat, level tone.

She wanted to look Lady Ann straight in the eyes; but an indescribable timidity compelled her to fix her glance on the gray window.

"But are you, dear, are you, so *very* fond of him?"

Her lips made an effort to form the suitable words; but her throat seemed to be playing some tiresome trick upon her. It seemed to be necessary that she should keep swallowing.

"Because if you're not," Lady Ann went on, "I mean if you're not *very* fond of him, it's much easier to understand all you're doing."

"What—*do*—you mean? Oh, what *are* you saying to me?" stammered the troubled girl.

"Don't get excited, dear." And the aristocratic fingers sought the plebeian ones again. "There's no need to get agitated. I know well enough that nothing I say will make any difference. But it's like this, Netta. I sometimes think you don't quite realize, and never have quite realized, all that this means to Rook."

This time Netta Page did turn a scared, troubled face directly upon the beautiful head lying on her pillow.

"You've never spoken like this to me before," she said slowly. "Have I done anything? Is it because I got cross just now when he said—when he said that about your knee?"

Lady Ann folded her hands and closed her eyes for a moment. Her face in the gray light looked mysteriously lovely. Was she praying to her gods to give her strength to go through with the discomfort of acting the role of executioner?

"Have I done anything?" Netta repeated in a monotonous sing-song. "Have I done anything?"

"You've done this, my dear," said Cousin Ann gravely, opening her eyes and lifting her head a little. "You've made it impossible for Rook to have children—and if he doesn't have a child—if he doesn't have a son—there'll be no Ashovers left after he and Lexie are dead. And you know what Lexie's health is like? He's a dying man!"

Ah! The avalanche had begun to move. Thoughts and images pursued one another madly through Netta's bewildered brain. Fantastic images some of them were! One was the image of Cousin Ann herself—with her beautiful marbly limbs—lying on a bed like this, big with a boy-child of Rook's.

She said nothing for a long while. Her thoughts gathered about the knob of the bedpost above Cousin Ann's head. The bedpost marched in and out of her thoughts like a drill sergeant among shifty recruits.

Wow ho! Wow ho! Wow ho! moaned the wind in the chimney.

She kept forming words in the depths of her mind and then rejecting them.

One of these sentences got as far as the tip of her tongue.

"How do you know that *I* shan't have a dead?" it protested. But *that* sentence would have been a lie; a lie to her own heart; for she knew only too well that fate had written her down childless.

"Of course I understand it all perfectly," Cousin Ann's voice went on; "if you are not very fond of Rook. In that case you are naturally, as we say, out for your own hand. But what I find so puzzling is, how, if you *are* very fond of him, you can have the heart to blight his whole future and doom him to childlessness? *That* is what puzzles me, Netta."

Still the bedpost kept trying to play its part as the master of the ceremonies. But the convicted woman was not conscious any more of these little things. Slowly, with a thick woolly movement, blind and massive, the great avalanche was beginning to bear down upon her. Before the weight of it, before the reverberation of its descending, a landslide seemed to have begun that made the oasis in which she was living, with all its sweet earth and peaceful grass, rock and sway beneath her feet.

With the surface of her mind she was prepared to fight for every inch of her happiness; but, down in her soul, she felt conquered already. Something in herself betrayed her, with a dark subterranean treachery. Something called out: "I yield! I yield!" to the life-destroying whisper of this girl with these beautiful knees.

She found her tongue at last; but what she said was the merest froth of her mind's turmoil, the merest spindrift of the tragic turn of the tide.

It was a gross thing, too, a venomous, petty, poisonous thing—the thing a jealous chorus girl would say, quarrelling over some beau at the stage door.

"Did you really hurt your knee walking with Rook this morning?"

Cousin Ann lifted her arched eyebrows.

Netta was standing in the middle of the room now, her face a pitiable mirror of contesting feelings.

"Will you please go now?" she stammered helplessly; and then with a faint return of the ugly mood—"that's to say, if you can walk."

Cousin Ann rose up from the bed and certainly there was little evidence of lameness as she moved across the room.

"There's no need for us to quarrel," she said quietly as she unlocked the door. "I like you, Netta, and I am sorry for you. You're bound to suffer, whichever way things work out. One can't carry off a situation like this beyond a certain point; even *you* can't do that; though I do think you're rather wonderful!"

She was alone again; alone in that fireless room. The indent left by Lady Ann's head still remained in the pillow. The coverlet of the bed still showed the imprint of her body.

Netta walked to the window and looked out. The great lime tree was bowing and clutching at space under the wind's lash. High up in the air dark specks were being lifted and dropped, dropped and lifted, that once were green budding leaves.

There was a soughing noise in the bushes, as if some great invisible animal were panting there; and what she could see of the water meadows beyond the river looked dark and troubled as though under the persecution of some evil power the menace of whose purpose was still obscure.

The woman shivered, but did not leave the window. She found a certain comfort in sharing with so much helplessness and dumbness the concentrated malice of this invisible enemy.

Her nature had a peculiar passivity in it, an almost voluptuous inertness; and now, when her whole blind instinct was to put off the moment of thinking, there was a real relief in becoming part of these struggling trees and sullen, persecuted meadows.

The wind did actually seem to take on a palpable shape as she watched, a shape that *was* a shape, though it was chaotic, formless, wavering. And she could not escape the sense that in some definite malignant manner the invisible creature was directing its murderous violence against herself, against this intruder, this invader, this stranger within the gates!

She was still standing at the window when Rook, after a hurried knock, came quickly into the room. She glanced at him for one swift moment and then lifting up her arms, with a swaying staggering lurch forward, she flung herself upon him and clung round his neck.

"I am sorry. I am sorry. I am so sorry!" she moaned. "You *will* forgive me, Rook, my own? I ought not to have behaved like that. I know I ought not. I was mad, just mad!"

Rook answered her appeal with hurried soothing exclamations: "It's all right, little one. It's all right. It's absolutely all right. There! There! No, don't cry, sweetheart! I tell you it was nothing. Nothing at all! I've quite forgotten it. It's all over. You are my little Netta again—you are, aren't you?"

Feeling his arms so firm and tight around her and his lips upon her forehead Netta was sorely tempted to yield to an impassioned fit of desperate sobbing. Her whole nature craved for that relief. But long and bitter experience had taught her that men shrink from these abandonments, shrink from them and grow cold beneath their weight. So with an heroic effort she calmed herself and remained limp and exhausted but untrembling, unshaken, within his grasp.

At the first relaxing of his embrace she drew herself gently away, and all her endeavour was to retain the sweetness of his tenderness, without spoiling it by any blunder, without spilling a drop of its delicious security.

She pulled him down on the bed beside her, close to the pillows still marked by the imprint of Ann's head, and remained quite silent for a moment, holding tight to one of his hands and lifting it once—twice—three times—to her lips.

"Little Netta!" he kept repeating. "Little Netta!"

At last feeling his arm round her waist, feeling herself drawn close against him, she gathered up courage to speak again.

"I oughtn't to have acted like that, Rook. I know I oughtn't. I can't think why I did! You're not angry with me any more, are you?"

"Angry?" he repeated. "Angry? Good God! It's you who ought to be angry! Netta darling, listen—listen to me." His voice grew very quiet and resolute, the voice which she had come to associate with her happiest moments; the voice he had used when he first made her come with him to Ashover.

"Cousin Ann and I are very old friends. You do understand that, don't you? And when I say 'old friends' you do know what I mean? There's no danger to you, none at all, from what Cousin Ann and I are to each other *now*, you understand. It would be different altogether if we were meeting here for the first time. *Then* you might have had a right to be worried. But when people have known each other all their lives, there's a certain—oh, I don't know—a certain familiarity which to a person like me destroys all the thrill of—well! of love-making, to be quite frank.—Do you understand what I'm saying to you, Netta darling?"

The sweetness to her wounded feelings of the tenderness in his voice was all that concerned the woman at that moment. As to what he actually *said*, it just excited a vague wonder and amusement in her that her mysterious Rook could be so stupid, so blind. She felt he had not the remotest desire to deceive her, to pull wool over her eyes. But, mercy! what things men *could* think, what things men *could* say! An overwhelming wave of pitiful gentleness toward him, just because he was so funny, swept over her heart. She lifted up her chin and gave him a quick, sudden, passionate kiss.

"Oh, I know I was mad," she repeated. "I know I was mad."

His arm tightened round her in a reassuring hug. Then with a bound he was off the bed and hanging over the dead ashes in the grate.

"Why haven't they cleared this up?" he grumbled. "Why didn't Pandie light your fire?"

Wow ho! Wow ho! Wow ho! moaned the wind in the chimney above his head.

He moved to the side of the mantelpiece and rang the bell.

"Tell her to take the ashes away and bring some sticks," he said. "I've got to go round now and meet Uncle Dick. The old man's been hanging about all morning, they tell me. What he wants I can't think! You've seen him, haven't you, Netta? I told you about him. My grandfather was a rake in his time. I daresay I've got plenty of other relations hidden away somewhere if the truth were known."

Netta heard him as if his voice came to her through a dense volume of green, humming water. The wind began rattling the window again, as though its invisible fingers itched to get her by the throat.

"Uncle Dick?" she repeated vaguely. "Oh, yes, Corporal Dick! I know. Cousin Ann introduced me to him. He lives over there—beyond Battlefield. Yes, of course you must go if he wants to see you."

She got up and stood there, passive and hesitating. She would have given anything to be really loved just then—not petted and pitied but loved, so as to drown all her thoughts. But he moved straight to the door.

"Make Pandie light you one of her best fires," he said.

Rook Ashover found his poor relation waiting for him in the little nondescript place they had acquired the habit of calling "the Master's Study" since the time of Uncle Dick's progenitor. Perhaps that was the reason the Corporal always insisted upon being shown in there in preference to any more formal reception.

The old man was sitting on a high-backed chair, his long bony fingers crossed over one of his knees. His hat and stick and muffler lay on the table.

"Well, Uncle Dick, how goes it?" said the nephew, shaking his visitor cordially by the hand. "Sit down, sit down." And he drew up another high-backed chair and smilingly placed himself opposite him, with the look of one who deprecates an expected reproof.

"Wind rather strong to-day, eh?" went on the younger man. "Found it rough, I expect, coming across the hill? How are they all over there?"

The Corporal regarded the Squire of Ashover with an austere, quizzical eye.

"It's not about them, Nephew, that I've come so far to see 'ee."

"What is it for, Uncle, then? Just for old companion's sake and to tell me I've been neglecting you lately?"

"They tell me, down Dorsal, that Lexie be no better and that Doctor says there's no hope for 'n to see another year round."

Rook's smile died upon his face. "That's so, Uncle. I'm afraid that's so."

"Well, then, if that's so," returned the old man, uncrossing his knees and leaning forward, "how is it that you have the face, Nephew—you that be Squire and all that—to go and fix yourself up with a young woman that may be a decent body and such-like and I'm not saying she isn't, but one that makes your blessed mother feel lonesome and confounded in her own house, as if the whole world were turned higgledy-piggledy? 'Tisn't that I've anything against Miss Page here. She be a good-hearted young woman by all accounts. But, good or bad, we know that she isn't your lawful wife;

and we know that she be standing in the place of your lawful wife; and the long and short of *that* is—with Lexie being as he be—that when he's gone and when in due time you are gone, too, there'll be no more Ashovers on Frome-side. Young, old, rich, poor, that'll finish 'em! That'll be the end."

Having thus finished the longest consecutive utterance he had ever made in his life the Corporal crossed his legs, straightened himself out in his chair, and solemnly and gravely winked at his obstinate nephew.

Rook had shuffled uneasily more than once during this discourse, but by the time it was over he had taken his cue.

"Uncle Richard," he began, "I am very grateful to you for speaking your mind so frankly. Of course, I *do* see how unpleasant all this is for my mother. And I see exactly how you yourself must feel about it. Unfortunately there are certain questions in life that one cannot decide in consideration for other people's feelings; or even perhaps for one's own feelings. I don't think you'd wish me to behave badly, Uncle Richard. I brought Miss Page here to the house with my eyes fully open. She herself, I daresay, would have preferred to remain in seclusion. If I had known, of course, how my mother would take it, shutting herself up in her room and so on, I admit I might have acted differently. I fancied that time and habit would bring her round. They don't seem to have done so. And there it is! You must see for yourself that I cannot send Miss Page away *now*. It would be a dishonourable thing, a brutal thing, an impossible thing. No! No! Uncle; there are situations in life when a man must shift for himself. I fully understand your motives in coming to me like this. But it's no use. My mother is my mother and I am myself. As to the future, we shall see! Not even *you* can read the future, Uncle!"

The old man heard him to the end. Then with a stiff mechanical jerk he got up, straightened his shoulders to their full height, took his stick and hat and muffler from the table, and strode resolutely to the door.

"This is all I'm to get from you, then?" said he in a husky voice. "I'm an old man and a poor man; but this house and this family are more precious to me than my own life. You think I'm an old fool. Don't 'ee be too sure, Nephew; don't 'ee be too sure! There be some as can endure to see their hopes frustrated; and there be some as can't and won't. When a man's my age and has nothing to live for and nothing to fear, *he's dangerous*—that's what he is; he's *dangerous!* He's like a fox that's been half-skinned in a trap. He goes slow and he goes round; but he gets his goose in the end!"

Rook had risen to his feet and was standing with his body bent forward and his fingertips resting on the table. He might have been a bewildered parliamentarian watching the intrusion of some reckless bomb-thrower. He wished he had taken a different line with the old fanatic; been conciliatory, prevaricating, indefinite. Nothing more annoying than this could possibly have occurred—annoying and sinister. The old man's vague and obscure menaces were just the kind most of all calculated to worry a man's mind. The wildest, queerest thoughts whirled through Rook's brain as he watched his uncle turn round upon him once more, his hand on the door handle.

"You think because you were born legitimate-like and be Squire of Ashover and stand where your father stood and where my father stood, that you can do as you please. Do you know this place as I know it? Do you hear the voices of dead folks calling to you out of their graves? Do you see things in the woods, in the lanes, in the bartons, as I do? Things that do walk and wail o' nights, 'cause the Lord won't let un lie still? Hark to the wind now, young man, hark to the wind now! It's contrary to nature for the wind to talk to a man, but 'a do talk; I've a-heard un; day in, day out; and 'a do say such things as would turn a man's wits if he didn't know north from south in every copse and spinny o' Frome-side. But go your ways, Rook Ashover, go your ways! Drive our dead folks back where they belong! Be the black plague to your sacred mother! I've a-said my say and I be going. But I've not finished with this little job yet!"

To Rook's final astonishment before he disappeared into the hallway the extraordinary old man gave him a second portentous wink, the effect of which upon the aged face that made it was bizarre in the extreme. It was as if a judge, wearing the black cap, had suddenly put out his tongue at the condemned.

The agitated silence which followed the departure of Uncle Dick was interrupted by the familiar sound of Pandie ringing the hall bell as a signal for lunch. The noise made Rook think of the days when he and Lexie used to bolt up to their bedroom at the end of the passage to wash themselves clean of fish scales and river slime.

Oh, Lexie, Lexie . . . Ay! He would be content to go over the whole wretched business of his life again if only he could give his brother ten good years more of the existence he loved so well!

CHAPTER VI

DECEMBER had come; and with the coming of December there fell upon that country of pastures and orchards a warm trance-like stillness.

The earth seemed to lie back upon itself, relaxed and lethargic. The days slid by imperceptibly, each one resembling the one before it, in a heavy, damp, windless atmosphere, steamy and misty, with large sun-warmed, earth-brown noons followed by amber-coloured twilights.

On one of these rich mellow placid days, imperturbable and languid as a woman in bed with her first-born, Mrs. Ashover and Lady Ann sat in the former's luxurious room, enjoying afternoon tea.

Any one who could have peered into this privileged chamber would have displayed little surprise at learning that its occupant preferred to have all her meals brought up to her there.

The place was really an almost flawless work of art. It had the qualities of a drawing room and yet it was more delicate, more dainty, more personal, than any drawing room Lady Ann had ever seen.

Mrs. Ashover had a fire in the grate, but it was so warm that she had opened one of the windows, and the rich earth-heavy smell of ploughed furrows and mud-muffled lanes came floating in and hovered over the delicate bric-à-brac and over the Queen Anne chairs and tables.

It was perhaps because of the millions and millions of dead leaves that were dissolving back into the flesh of their great drowsy mother that, with this air from the woods and meadows, there came a perceptible savour, acrid and penetrating, of the very sweat of death itself.

It was the sort of day that has an especial appeal to the nerves of women, perhaps because the passivity, the inertness, the lethargy of the earth at these times, its preparturient *fallowness*, moribund and yet magnetic, self-absorbed and yet germinative, has something in it that answers to one of their own most profound and secret moods.

The land, thus lying fallow and immobile, might be said to have sunk down, to have sunk back, into some interior level or stratum of being, where it was unapproachable to the sun's generative warmth, and yet had a mysterious life of its own.

Hardly conscious of the systole and diastole of its faint breath, of the subterranean beating of its muffled pulses, the vast rain-soaked countryside seemed, during this placid winter solstice, to be in some mysterious way enjoying the ecstasy of its own virginal languor, of its own deep peace, as a "still unravished bride of quietness."

Something of this appeasement, of this self-amorous quiescence, must have floated in through that open window, must have worked its relaxing charm upon the old woman and the young woman, as they sat on the sofa side by side, their skirts touching, the supple athletic wrist in its tweed sleeve, the slender aged wrist in its lace sleeve, hovering over the little rosewood tea table, over the polished silver, over the Meissen china.

The influence of the day, the immense languid emanation that diffused itself through the room, endowed with a vague but very formidable power the subtle conspiracy, evasive, ambiguous, which rose like the scent of a sweet but poisonous flower from their intimate conversation.

"She is thinking over what I said," threw out Lady Ann, helping herself to another piece of thin bread and butter and lifting it to her finely curved mouth with the impetuousness of a greedy child.

"But what good will *that* do us?" murmured the old woman, flicking an errant tea leaf from the edge of her cup as if she would dispose of their enemy in the same more effective, more drastic way.

"No thinking that *she* does will take her off, switch her back to Bristol, or wherever it is he picked her up. That's what I feel about all this roundabout method of yours. It just doesn't get us anywhere! I told you from the beginning that the way you treated her would only give her a false impression; only make her settle down more snugly than ever in her warm nest. And now by giving her a jolt you've only made her suspicious of you. You haven't changed her. How could you change her? Why *should* she change?"

Lady Ann swallowed her bread and butter and stretched out her hand for another piece. She felt very hungry and for some occult reason very formidable. She moved her supple body inside her closely fitting clothes with a slow feline movement of muscular relaxation. "I'll go for a long walk after tea. I'll take Lion," she said to herself. And her mind visualized the enormous Newfoundland dog bounding over the gorse bushes and sniffing at the rabbit burrows. Between herself and this dog of Rook's a close attachment had sprung up. She had been shocked to find how little Rook cared for it. People who didn't understand dogs oughtn't to have dogs! They either neglected them heartlessly, or they corrupted them by ill-timed petting.

"How long will you give me, Auntie, to try out my method?" she asked, holding up her teacup and smiling, with the conquering smile of youth, at her companion.

"How long, my dear child? Goodness! I give you as long as you like! What else can I do? Nothing that *I* can say to the poor boy seems to make the least difference."

As the old woman uttered these words she thought within her heart: "Can't I make this proud creature see what our only chance is? Can't I make her see that our only chance is nothing else than her own reckless, unscrupulous beauty?" And the brutal game-preserving expressions of Corporal Dick, still redolent of rank weed-smoke, thumped and heel-tapped in her obsessed brain.

"She's been thinking a great deal lately," went on the younger woman, stretching out her long legs and sliding both hands into her jacket pockets. "She can't get what I said to her out of her mind. She's beginning to feel pricks of conscience. There's no doubt about that. And once get her to feel *that* sort of thing to a point of spoiling her illusion—well! there we are!"

Mrs. Ashover rose from the sofa and, impatiently pushing the tea table a little farther away, reached for her woolwork. Then sinking back by her companion's side she turned a querulous, anxious, disturbed face toward her.

"Spoiling her illusion? What are you talking about, child?" She sighed heavily and smoothed the lace cuff of one of her wrists with nervous fingers.

"I believe you have a sort of liking for the baggage!" she burst out.

Lady Ann lifted her eyebrows and regarded her with a mocking, slightly contemptuous smile. The daughter of a long line of courtly diplomatists, she began to feel a little irritated with her aunt. "It's the Gresham blood in her," she thought. "They always had a second-rate streak."

"Well!" she said slowly. "I don't feel that it's necessary to quarrel with people. One puts oneself on their level in that way, doesn't one? I daresay the poor little woman has had a hard enough time of it. If I could give her a good round income; a trim little villa down at Weymouth or somewhere; with a couple of servants and an old enamoured sea captain, shall we say, across the hedge—gracious! I would willingly do it!"

Mrs. Ashover's countenance expressed the sort of astonishment that she would have felt if Cousin Ann had suddenly kicked one of her neat shoes right across the room.

"You young people are too much for me," she murmured. "Too much for me. I suppose it's Rook who has put these ideas into your head," she added, with a quick glance of stealthy malevolence. "In my time designing minxes like that were not given incomes. They were given the stick!"

Lady Ann leaned forward and laid her strong young hand on the old woman's knee.

"Do you suppose, Auntie dear, that if I wasn't sure it would be all right, I should feel as happy as I do to-day?"

Mrs. Ashover's face cleared a little. There certainly did seem to gleam forth an overpowering confidence and assurance from the girl's limpid, mysterious gray eyes.

There was a tone of impassioned pleading in the old lady's voice as she murmured eagerly: "You give me your word? You *will* save him? You *will* save him from her?"

Ann Gore dropped her eyelids at this and a smile of deep, sweet, implacable power crossed her mouth, making her full lips, exquisitely childish in their perfect Cupid's bow, curve so divinely that her aunt leaned over and impulsively kissed her.

"We won't talk about it any more, child. I understand you. There! I expect you're wanting to get out now and have your walk. You mustn't give up the whole of a lovely afternoon to an old troublesome thing like me."

They both rose to their feet. The air from the open window, treacherous-sweet with the death smell of a world of dying leaves, flowed through them, rousing a poignant response in their deepest nerves.

The wide-stretching unsown plough lands, the patient indrawn leafless woods, the great inert, apathetic breasts of the earth, drew these women toward them in answering reciprocity. To the elder it was as if the strong invisible hands of the dead generations were urging her on, comforting her, sustaining her, in her struggle against her adversary. To the younger it was as if the very spirit of that hibernating countryside, lying fallow, secretive, implacable, were calling to her to share in some tremendous *waiting*, through rain, through frost, through everything—for the hour of the sowing of the seed.

They stood together for a perceptible space of time, caught, as two people often are, by the very beat of the wings of fate. Then all in a moment they became conscious that they were both listening, intently, absorbingly, to a sound in the garden outside.

It was the sound of a man's footsteps moving up and down, up and down, with irritating regularity, along the gravel path that ran parallel to the lawn.

They both felt instinctively that the man was Rook; and for that very reason they were each reluctant to go to the window and look out. Rook's personality had certainly hovered over their tea table, but neither of them was at all anxious for the intrusion of his actual presence at that juncture.

The situation was indeed, for one second, humorously disconcerting; one of those situations with which the clumsy gaucherie of men copes more easily than the finesse of women.

But Lady Ann kept her head, and soon proved herself a true daughter of the diplomatic Lord Poynings.

Without the flicker of an eyelid to indicate that she knew that both of them had heard those steps: "There's Lion!" she cried. "I'm sure he's dying for a run on Battlefield. Good-bye, Auntie! I've enjoyed my tea so much!"

The door was hardly shut behind her when Mrs. Ashover hurried to the window. There he was—her son the Squire—pacing abstractedly up and down, as if the little gravel path were the wall of a fortress.

Presently she heard the voice of Cousin Ann, a clear careless young girl's voice, calling: "Lion! Lion! Lion!" Apparently Rook Ashover also heard that voice; for he stopped suddenly in his abstracted walk, stood hesitating for a moment, looking nervously toward the sound; and then with a quick furtive stride and without so much as once glancing behind him, made off in the direction of the Frome bridge.

"Why doesn't she run after him?" cried the old lady in her indignant heart, tapping the window sill with her knuckles.

"Lion! Lion! Lion!" came the girlish voice from the stable yard.

"You fool! He's across the bridge! You stupid! He's across the river!" And the belligerent little woman positively shook the window frame in her impetuous annoyance.

Rook *was* across the river. He was not only across the river but he was also—very soon—across the churchyard and out into the water meadows behind it. He felt such an intense desire for movement, for action, for self-escape.

No doubt the peculiar quality of that pacing up and down the gravel path had been the outward sign of the rending and tearing within him of two opposite motive forces.

He had made a sort of half-appointment to meet Nell Hastings that afternoon; but something in Netta's mood, something illuminated, magnetic, had made him feel uneasy and perplexed.

Netta had seemed to escape him as she never had escaped him. She seemed to have acquired some mysterious independence. She had spoken to him and looked at him in such a strange, remote, exultant way! He felt piqued and confused. He found himself half-wishing that he hadn't made this appointment with Nell.

Rook did not realize how deeply the great goddess Artemis —the mysterious immortal whose love is for her own body— had come into her own that day. He did not realize that it was a day for the triumph of woman's nerves over man's nerves. On such a day, he ought to have told himself, had the dangerous thyrsus-bearing son of Semele come stealthily into the city of Pentheus. On such a day had the wild Bassarids and Mænads sent the gory head of Orpheus "down the swift Hebrus, to the Lesbian shore"! On such a day had the dogs and maidens of Diana torn the luckless Actæon limb from limb. It was a woman's day; a day that lay virginal, inscrutable, relaxed; yet with a magnetism in its inertness that could trouble a man's deepest soul.

And Rook Ashover hated the day. He felt a queer, nervous, reluctant uneasiness even about meeting Nell. He would have given anything for a hard, nipping black frost to get its grip upon these misty meadows, to turn all this clinging earth-flesh into frozen rock! He loathed the sodden, relaxed clay with its incense-reek of insidious mortality. He longed to escape from it all, into some clear, purged, bitter air. He felt homesick for the tang of the salt, unharvested, unfecund sea.

Blindly striding across the meadows—full of whirling, contradictory thoughts—he was suddenly brought to a standstill by a wide black ditch.

"Double-dyed ass! Of course there's no path over these cursed fens!"

He walked along the edge of the ditch, looking for a plank or a dam by which to cross.

No plank! No dam! Only another black ditch still wider than the one he was following!

He had a queer horrid moment; caught there, by those two black ditches. The reeds had been dead and rotten for some time and their brown stalks stood up like twisted feathers from some obscene bird's skull whose skeleton was mud-engulfed. One ditch was full of dead willow leaves. The other had a dead alder branch floating on its surface. And from both of them there emerged a heavy thick acrid odour that seemed as if it must be the very final exhalation of the dead flesh of a world.

Turning his heel in an angry desperation he caught sight of

a human figure emerging from the shadow of the church and moving hesitatingly among the graves.

His heart, in spite of himself, began to beat violently. She was earlier than he had expected!

Had there been some new trouble with that mad priest?

Well! Never mind the reason. She was there. And he quickened his steps to something approaching a run, fearful that she might take fright when she saw him and out of some crazy perversity elude him and vanish.

She gave no sign of retreating, however. She just remained passive—leaning against a tombstone; waiting for him. He scrambled over the low wall and strode straight up to her, holding his hat in his hand.

"I knew it was you," she said simply; and made room for him at her side; so that he could lean also against the monument to "Timothy Edward Foraker, yeoman of this Parish."

"I knew it was you," she repeated, letting her fingers remain clasped in his as they stared together across the misty expanse.

Rook did not speak a word to her for several minutes. His soul seemed divided into three separate beings. One of these beings was obsessed with a simple concentrated desire to get hold of the inmost fluttering identity of this passive creature. To get hold of that—to take it for his own—to make it his unresisting, helpless, abandoned possession.

Another being in him was full of nervous considerations that were tremulous with a thousand fears, like the quivering antennæ of moths, the agitated feelers of sea anemones, the twitching nostrils of horses; considerations that included Netta, Cousin Ann, his mother—Nell herself.

But the third being in him just looked on, with absolute detachment and indifference, at the whole turbid stream of his life. It hovered over both their heads, this third being, and over the gravestone of Timothy Edward against which they leaned. It hovered over the ragged, mournful trunk of

Lexie's elm tree. It voyaged out over the misty fens, over the gates and dams and poplars and ditches—over the rim of the horizon. And it was already out of its body, this third being, out of its malice-ridden, nerve-jangled body, drinking with deep, thirsty draughts the great calm under lake of hateless, loveless oblivion!

His first words to her came from the second being in him, the one with the twitching nostrils of a nervous animal. "Why did you come earlier than you said? It's only beginning to get dark now."

Even while he spoke, the first being in him was clutching her thin fingers more tightly, possessing itself of them more unscrupulously.

"Why didn't I wait?" she murmured. "It wasn't because I was in such a desperate hurry that I *couldn't* wait, Rook. Was that what you were thinking?" And she turned her head toward him with a faint little-girl smile, answering the pressure of his fingers.

"No, Rook dear," she went on. "It was because he is after all going to have vespers to-night. He told me yesterday he wasn't; that he had something else to do; and that's why I said to you to come to-night. But he *is*. So I came early; on the chance. I shall have to wait for him here," she added. "He likes me to be in the church."

Rook cast a slow, cautious glance toward the corner of the building. "But we've got a long time before vespers, haven't we?" he said.

"About an hour, I should think." And she, too, cast an anxious glance in the direction of the village. "Well, nearly an hour, anyway; but you'll go when I tell you, Rook, won't you? Sometimes I like to have you near me when I meet him. But not to-day. Oh, Rook! I saw Lexie this morning and he's worrying about himself. He says this damp weather'll kill him if it goes on. I thought he looked rather better, if anything. But he's worrying."

Rook dropped her hand and stood up. "Damn! I must go and see him," he said. "I haven't seen him for three days. I'll go straight over there to-night."

The girl got up, too. She felt only softly and gently sorry for Lexie. There was a queer exaltation in her that made it difficult to be more sorry than that for any one.

"He'll outlive us all," she said. "His mania for life is like the jump of that salmon trout I saw at Tollminster Mill. I told you about it. It jumped over the edge of the boat. It jumped over everything. And it got back, too, into the mill pond."

For some reason or other it gave Nell a peculiar satisfaction to think of Lexie as a silvery salmon jumping for his life. She felt that she would like to hold that struggling, arrowy, smooth-scaled fish tightly in her hand before seeing it go splashing back.

She became quiet and still, thinking of Lexie in this way; but in the end she wanted to stop thinking of him; for she suddenly recalled the particular look in the eyes of the animal in her childhood's Bible, entitled: "The Ram caught by its Horns." No fish, even with hooked gills, even with the tragic eye-sockets of the Dolphins of Scopas, could ever feel quite what that beast felt; and if a man felt more——

She found herself being led by Rook to the door of the church. The sun had been invisible for some time past; and now the whole scene was losing its distinctness, losing its familiar landmarks one by one as the night fell.

Gloom that drew its quality from dampness, a positive thing, was rapidly being replaced by gloom that drew its quality from darkness, a negative thing.

Rook pushed open the door of the church and drew her inside. It was like night within the building, a night that was faintly touched by a pallid greenish luminousness that seemed to have no connection with sun or moon.

As the heavy door closed behind them the girl felt she had

passed into a different world, a world smelling of some sort of chilly-fleshed fungous growths that had taken centuries to mature.

Rook took her by the hand and led her up the narrow aisle, past the brass lectern, under the Norman archway, to where the tombs of the Ashovers of old days lay in their pallid immobility. Standing behind her, while her knees touched the sleeping Crusader, he took her in his arms and kissed her cold cheek. Letting her head sink back and turning her face sideways she met his lips, while her slender body yielded itself to him.

She felt strangely and profoundly happy in his embrace. It was a different kind of happiness altogether from what she felt when Lexie kissed her on the day she had fled from her home. She had had Rook on her mind then, so that she could not lie back content upon the dark flood; but it was Rook himself whose desire was that flood now, and her whole nature was free to respond.

A queer remembrance came into her mind as she yielded to his caresses, the remembrance of a salt marsh by the Dorset coast, where the greenish-white light of a protracted sunset hung like livid phosphorus in the black pools, stained with pale blood. She remembered how a solitary heron with wide-stretched wings and trailing legs had descended into the water; and how she had felt that it was those livid pools in the black earth, rather than the darkened sky overhead, that offered an escape to her soul.

Here in the church with the man she loved she felt as if she were hidden safe away from all responsibility, from all pursuit. She felt as long as she could keep his desire concentrated upon her, that Time itself stood still; and a lovely, deep, enchanted Eternity substituted itself for the little poisonous rankling minutes that throbbed like evil ulcers.

Rook's mind also had its own obscure journeys to make. He was aware—as she never for a moment seemed to be—

of the presence of his dead people. He was aware of an angry menace rising from all that human dust under his feet, threatening him if he did not open the gates of the future to their race, cursing him if he barred and locked those gates in the selfish enjoyment of uncreative, unproductive emotion.

As he caressed her there in that dark church on that curious day he felt as though he were inflicting a definite wound upon the accumulated yearning, the gathered tension, stretching out into the future, of six long human centuries.

So many fathers begetting so many children; so many children begetting so many fathers; and all to end in his striking them back into the annihilating dark, with a mocking "Down, wantons, down!"

It was as if all the life energy of all that proud human tribe had been concentrated in one invisible gesture of intense creation, only to be derided, jeered at, spurned, by his flippant indifference.

Indifference? It was defiance; since he had chosen their very resting place to flaunt his sterile malice. Into this very shrine of their vitality, of their hope, of their unconquerable life urge he had come to parade his disillusionment, his alliance with emptiness, with nothingness, with the eternal *No* of the abyss!

He had come to fool them. How did the sentinel Crusader know that this girl he had brought with him was inhibited and disallowed; a mocking mirage to their hope? He had come to fool them. So at least that smirking infidel of a great-grandfather Benjamin seemed to guess as he leered at them over the plump cupids.

For it was against the very monument of the crafty Deist that the two were leaning now; and, as they clung together there, Rook felt he was taking a kind of revenge on fate itself.

He was certainly revenging himself upon the life lust of his own race. He was denying that race any future at all, He was saying to the vast dim company of future Ashovers, "Ye shall not live!"

It was a feeling of this kind, deep, cold, malicious, that made every caress he gave this girl a kind of flouting of the gods. Each kiss was a malignant sacrilege directed against the helpless invisible company of the Future.

He had decided to cut the living navel cord between these two. Let the one be totally forgotten! Let the other never be born!

Something of the viciousness of these thoughts must have passed into the very touch of his hands; but if it did, the girl neither regarded it nor was affected by it.

Rook was startled—as if it were something upon which he had not calculated—when he became aware of the spiritual exaltation of his companion.

The girl's white features, as he caught a glimpse of them in that spectral light, wore an expression of childlike beatitude. He knew there had been a mysterious attraction of some kind between himself and this woebegone little creature; but when he saw that illuminated look on her face, endowing her with an utterly unexpected beauty, he was conscious of a sharp secret pang, as if his nature had suddenly touched some "fourth dimension" whose superiority to his own level of existence shocked and troubled him.

Many months after this he remembered what he felt at that moment, when that white face swirled up to him as if on the crest of a dark wave, looking at him and through him and past him in an ecstasy of which he himself touched barely the fringe.

It was certainly in league with the nerves of women, the peculiar atmosphere of that December day.

Whether it was in league with the remorseless umbilical cord of those insistent generations was a different matter. Rook Ashover had only commenced his fatal struggle with *that* dark mandate!

The two companions found themselves back again at the door at last; the man troubled, anxious, perturbed, his mind abnormally alert to every shape and sound of the external world; the girl drugged, dazed, numbed, but unfathomably happy.

"It's like death to make love to you," he muttered when they were out of the church.

"Yes," she whispered. "I felt like that, too."

She lied with an entranced luxuriousness, careless of what he said or what she answered.

"I shall wait for William now without minding a bit," she added. "You go off quickly, Rook. No! No! No good-byes! I'll go back and light all the candles! You look when you get to the bridge and see if the windows aren't lit up! When you hear him ringing the bell you may think of me saying my prayers by those tombs! There! Go off quick——No! No! I won't say any good-bye!"

Rook did turn round when he reached the bridge; and sure enough, the windows were lighted up as he had never seen them lighted up before. It was a sort of heathen Candlemas; a twilight celebration of the tutelary Powers of that riverside, as they reassumed, with the fall of darkness, their ancestral domination.

The smell of the water washing against the mossy arches, the smell of the black mud in the banked-up ditches, the smell of miles and miles of damp grass sinking down, blade by misty blade, under the weight of the night, flowed like a palpable exhalation around the yellowish gleam of those Gothic windows.

He leaned against the parapet and listened intently. The air about him seemed supernaturally hushed; all the great gulfs of the night listening there, even as he was listening.

And then in a moment, with a suddenness that made Rook gasp, for he had heard no footstep upon the road, the great cracked reverberating bell rang out from the church tower.

Toom! Toom! Toom!

The very cattle and sheep must have stirred uneasily in their sheds and bartons. It was as if that heathen illumination had actually summoned forth out of the air the tangible presence of something that had been gathering upon Ashover since the dawn of the day.

Toom! Toom! Toom!

It was as if the gigantic feet of Cybele herself, *Magna Mater, Bona Dea*, were striding bronze-sandalled over the dark bedrock of Frome-side.

Toom! Toom! Toom!

CHAPTER VII

THE black frost prayed for by Rook came at last. It came a few days before Christmas, and on the morning of Christmas Eve it held all Frome-side in stark iron-bound rigidity.

The long-drawn-out dissolution of the leaves was over now. Except for a few holly bushes on the Tollminster Road and the line of Scotch firs on Heron's Ridge it might have been supposed that the whole phenomenon of foliage, of umbrageousness, had never existed upon the planet.

Brown and gray, gray and brown, the bare bushes, the bare branches, rose abruptly from the naked frost-bitten soil. In holes, in crevices, in rabbit burrows, under tree roots, in the bottom of ponds, in the minute tunnels of lobworms, certain shapeless nonentities that once vibrated to sun and moon and all the winds lay hidden, forgotten, annihilated, done for.

To any human being who loved form better than colour in material things the effect of this change amounted to positive ecstasy. Such an one was Rook; and the pleasure which he enjoyed hour by hour during these iron-bound days was beyond description.

An essential puritanism in his nature answered exultantly to this stark bleak time. To see the silhouette of the world gray upon gray; to see the stiff, constricted, sombre mornings pass abruptly into the space-dark, wind-bitten, frozen evenings; to see the hours between eleven o'clock and three o'clock blotted out, as it were, from the diurnal calendar—all this was like a deep, silent, magical satisfaction to his whole nature.

He was so happy that his happiness became a mesmeric tyranny over those who surrounded him. He seemed able to lift his hand against the very march of events; to keep fate itself petrified, immobile, suspended; harmless as the icicles that hung above the water under Frome Bridge.

He was especially happy that morning of Christmas Eve. He had had a long, shamelessly candid conversation with Lexie the night before, and the savour of Lexie's cynical sagacity was sweetening the taste of his early breakfast as he sat with Cousin Ann and Netta drinking cup after cup of tea and watching the reddening logs.

It was so dark that they had candles on the table; and the flames of these candles increased Rook's happiness, both by the way they drew their purity from the frost-bitten air and by something almost mystical in their quivering up-burning.

Netta, too, for some secret reason of her own, seemed in unnaturally high spirits. From where she was sitting she looked straight into the eyes of the melancholy cavalier; and if ever any particular atmospheric condition lent itself to the inner soul of a picture, this candle-lighted refuge from the black frost was the dedicated background for that of Sir Robert Ashover.

Cousin Ann was less in harmony with herself. She talked graciously enough. She kept her head. But her gaiety was of a conventional, external kind: a laughing curve here of her fine lips; a seductive glance there of her gray eyes; and all the while a little puckered frown that twitched and deepened between her arched eyebrows! She had, as King Lear would say, her "frontlet on."

If the mute gaze of the sad Sir Robert kept murmuring "a brave wench! a brave wench!" to the ex-actress from Bristol, something in the nerves of Cousin Ann responded to a chill of absolute isolation. She felt herself to be cut off from every support, human or inhuman. The frost had so petrified the rich life saps of the countryside, those sweet, rank, procreative forces that usually sustained her, that she had the sense of being separated from her gods by a glacial barrier.

Not that she relented in her purpose or relinquished one jot of her resolution. She continued to "steer right onward." But the mood that upheld her was a thing of blind human obstinacy.

As the hours drew on toward the birth of Christ the earth constricted itself in its primordial, inert malice; and against this tightening of brute matter round about her, the heart of the young girl hardened itself within itself, as if beneath bands of triple steel.

But even as this very thing went on, Cousin Ann's manner toward Rook became more coaxing and more provocative; her manner toward Netta more intimate and more disarming.

It was this exuberance in her that by degrees acted like an irritant upon the man's nerves and impinged upon his happiness. Something radiated from the girl that was alien to the temper of the day; alien to the frozen starkness in which he delighted, alien to that corpse-like rigidity that must be broken by a power beyond nature or not broken at all!

The atmosphere round their three heads, as they sat beneath the flickering candles listening to Lady Ann's chatter, began to grow intolerable to Rook. The very tingling in his blood, due to the electric contest going on between the burning logs inside and the frost outside, increased this feeling.

Finally he could endure the sound of that rich young voice no longer. He rose from the table abruptly, almost rudely, and muttering something about "giving Lion a run," went out into the hall.

No sooner was the door shut behind him than Netta also rose as if to follow him; but Cousin Ann laid her hand on Netta's arm and pulled her back into her chair.

The younger woman's heart was beating violently at that moment and a sort of dizziness like that which she felt on the hunting field when her horse approached an impossible jump made Netta's figure seem dim and wavering.

Having got her antagonist there before her, resigned and patient, it seemed as if the grand diplomatic stroke she had been meditating was infinitely more difficult than she had expected. The way, at that juncture, she clasped and unclasped her fingers may have reproduced on a smaller stage the very gesture with which her notorious great-grandfather, Lord Harry Poynings, had persuaded a crown prince to renounce his birthright.

"He *is* a dear, isn't he?" she murmured, in an impulsive tone which seemed signalling for an exchange of confidences. "There he goes, banging the kitchen door! Have you noticed how he always goes out through the kitchen? It's an old instinct, I expect. His father used to go out that way. He kept his guns there and used to meet the gamekeeper there. It *would* seem a pity, wouldn't it, Netta, if all these old ways died out? And of course they *will* die out if Rook doesn't marry."

The ex-actress did not wince. Her gaze remained fixed upon the melancholy face in the gilt frame. "Brave wench! Brave wench!" those sympathetic eyes seemed reiterating. But Netta stared back sadly enough at that sorrowful countenance.

An immense wave of weariness and disillusionment swept over her. Her exalted mood wilted and sank. The situation had been hard enough to bear when she first came to Ashover. Cousin Ann's appearance on the scene had relieved her from a tension that was becoming well-nigh intolerable. But now that her friendly rescuer had joined forces with the enemy she felt that the powers against her were more than she had strength to resist.

She could have resisted them, perhaps—for she was not devoid of the kind of stubbornness that passive natures of her quality possess—if it had not been for this fatal doubt in her own heart, this doubt which the blind humility of her love for Rook kept feeding with a sweet poison.

That love had assumed during these last days the form of a vague excited impulse, leading her she knew not where; ruffling the quiet of her mind with all manner of wild and wavering projects. She was only faintly affected by this matter of the Ashovers and their threatened extinction. The clamouring shadows from that crowded chancel might have beaten at her windows night by night and found her impervious to their entreaty. It was with Rook, and Rook only, she was concerned; and the gist of the excitement that had buoyed her up of late had been a desire to do something, something unexpected and new, that would make him know her as he had never known her before.

"If Rook *did* marry," Cousin Ann continued, "there's no earthly reason why he shouldn't go on taking care of you, Netta. You and he could find some delicious little place to hide away in; somewhere where you'd be quite free from the sort of thing that annoys you here."

Netta heard these words as if they were spoken in a dream. She withdrew her eyes from Sir Robert's face and let them rest upon her own hands folded tightly upon her lap.

"You *do* see what I mean?" went on the diplomatic voice. "Once get Rook safely married—married to anybody, Netta—to anybody!—and you and he need not be really separated."

She stretched out her arm and extinguished one of the candles which had begun guttering and hissing. She did this quite casually with her finger and thumb; and Netta could not help feeling as if she herself were that quickly despatched flame.

"Heavens, yes!" cried Lady Ann. "I can see you and me now, gossiping round some lovely little fire in Chelsea or Bloomsbury!"

Netta lifted her head at this.

"And the wife, too?" she said, with the shadow of a smile.

Ann received the retort in the spirit of a master fencer taking a well-directed thrust.

"Oh, the wife! Well! not quite *that*, Netta. Though these silly old embarrassments are fast breaking up. But, no! Not the wife, too, Netta. We'll leave *her* to the happy old lady upstairs. And we'll share Rook between us—as we're sharing him now."

The tone in which Cousin Ann spoke of "the wife" was really in the great manner of diplomatic badinage. It pulled Netta across some intimate threshold toward herself and thrust this poor imaginary lady into the outer darkness of conventional unimportance.

"The wife's affair," the girl continued, with a richly toned youthful chuckle, "will be to produce little Ashovers! Beyond *that* there's no need for any pathetic heroics. *I* should treat Rook just as I've always treated him, if he had a dozen wives!"

Netta looked past Cousin Ann's flushed cheeks, past the three still burning candles, to the gray square of the one unfrozen mullioned window. The naked boughs of the lime tree outside made a tracery of extraordinary beauty against this pane. And this tracery seemed to be actually reproduced in the mysterious frost marks which covered all the other windows with a lacework filigree.

It was as if that bitter weather had been an old German woodcarver, from Nuremberg or Rothenburg, outlining with his bony knuckles and iron tool a convoluted image of the very platonic "soul" or spiritual "eidolon" of some frost-benumbed growth of the Black Forest.

It was the impression she got from those mysterious frost marks and those knotted twigs, an old buried impression leaping suddenly into life, that created the resignation of her tone in what came next.

"Tell me what to do then—tell me—what to do—and I will do it!"

The words might have come from the clock above the chimneypiece, from the Cavalier's picture, from the ghost of the tree itself, so stern and faint and impersonal did they sound as they floated over the empty cups and over the charred logs.

Lady Ann heard these words with every sense she possessed. She heard them as a prick-eared fox might have heard the rustle of a plump guinea fowl settling down to sleep in a blackthorn hedge. She heard them with such a thrill of triumph that she rose instinctively to her feet. Whatever may have been the emotion of her great-grandfather when his royal victim capitulated it could hardly have surpassed what she felt just then.

The incredible good luck of this unexpected victory fairly took her breath away.

"You *will* give up? You *will*?"

Just for one flickering second there was a vibration in the air about them as if the excited girl were actually going to bend down and kiss her conquered antagonist.

But there must have been something in Netta's face that nipped in the bud any gesture of that sort.

The woman seemed to be collecting her strength very much as a person who had lost a lot of blood might weakly try to get up from the ground.

"Don't go yet," she murmured, misunderstanding Ann's restlessness. "Don't go away yet. It isn't as simple as you think. I must tell you something."

Cousin Ann moved across to the fireplace and relieved her feelings by striking one of the half-burnt logs a series of violent blows with the poker.

Returning to her seat she flung her plate and cup aside with a gesture more like that of a man than a woman and hurriedly lit another cigarette.

What she craved for at that moment was violent physical exertion. Her thoughts instinctively leaped from one blood-stirring activity to another. She saw the little white "scuts" of vanishing rabbits as she pursued them with her dog. She felt the blue-black ice crack beneath her feet as she skated over the Tollminster mill pond. She felt the kick of the gun against her shoulder as she shot wild duck with her father on Forley Marsh.

She would have liked to put the unhappy and wounded Netta "out of her pain" as she would have done to any other flying creature. She had "brought her down." But that was no reason why she should not treat her in a sporting manner. She wished she could finish her off as she would a moor hen dragged to her feet by Lion—wring her neck quickly and kindly, and then swing on over the frozen fields!

"Not as simple as I think?" she enquired brusquely. "It seems simple enough to me."

Netta appeared still to be struggling with a profound interior lassitude, as if out of the channel of some cut vein her blood was making a crimson pool on the floor. She uttered a little clicking sound in her throat. Then she spoke, exaggerating the genteel pronunciation of the words, as if what would really have relieved her feelings would have been to talk like a Portsmouth barmaid.

"One finds it difficult sometimes to make a person agree, you know, to accept one's decision. I *have* suggested the very thing you are now saying. I have *begged* Rook to take a room for me in Tollminster or Bristol. I have begged him not to let me be a drag on his life. I have told him I would perfectly understand his marrying; that I thought he *ought* to marry. I have said all those things to him, Lady Ann."

Ann's gray eyes scrutinized her coldly and critically.

"I expect you told him that you would not accept a penny from him after you left here and after he was married?"

Netta stared in surprise. How did this girl know that?

"Yes," she answered, "that was just what I did say."

A smile of malicious subtlety crossed Ann's beautiful lips. "And while you said it, of course, you knew that just that very thing would effectively stop him?"

The frowning bewilderment on Netta's face indicated without the defence of words her freedom from such elaborate guile.

But Cousin Ann went on: "I daresay it was all unconscious, the line you took. But I'm afraid we're responsible for these shifty moves, even though we don't realize it when we make them."

She was silent for a moment, tapping the table with her cigarette case.

"Damn it all!" she burst out at last. "You must pull yourself together, Netta, and *make* him realize you're serious. This offering to live without help, this offering to just disappear is only putting spokes in your own wheel. Of course he won't let you go off like that! What decent man could? When you take *that* line you leave him no alternative."

Netta's face showed quite clearly that this argument had gone through her like a sword.

"I thought——" she began; but even as she spoke the deadly implication of all that this meant stopped her words in mid-utterance. She sat staring at Cousin Ann with her mouth open.

That young lady's earliest playmate had been her father's gamekeeper. Missy Sparrow-hawk the old man used to call her. Certainly no raptorial hoverer over the wintry fields knew better the exact moment wherein to drop from the sky.

"One has to face the means to a thing when one wants a thing," said Cousin Ann. "You and I both care, I take it, for Rook's happiness above everything else. And Rook's real happiness, whatever he may *say*, is in carrying out his destiny. And his destiny, Netta, is in playing his part in life as his people have played it before him."

The ex-actress from the Bristol Empire closed her mouth, lowered her eyelids till it almost seemed as if her eyes were shut, too, and gave an imperceptible nod of the head.

"Rook must have a *son!*" added the excited girl, clenching one of her hands and beating it upon her knee as if she were annihilating the very possibility of female Ashovers. "And we've got to manage it. *You've* got to manage it."

What Netta was struggling to keep at that moment was the lovely vague impulse to do something wonderful and unexpected for Rook, some passionate effacement of herself, some act of desperate humility, that would bring him back to her in his thoughts, whatever became of her in reality.

The thought of something like that had been the last refuge of her weariness and her weakness. It had been a beautiful revenge upon them all and a complete escape from them all. But it was so difficult, when Cousin Ann talked in this way, to feel this any more. Cousin Ann made it seem as if she would be only tricking and fooling Rook. That was not at all what had been in her mind, filling her with this vague secret exultation.

"You mean that I should go off without his knowing?"

Cousin Ann indicated that she did mean just exactly that.

"But he'd come after me. Oh, you don't know him! You don't know him at all! You think it all depends on how little he cares for me. It doesn't depend on that! It depends on his own pride; on what he feels he has chosen to do, in defiance of everyone!"

Netta's voice as she went on became more and more careless and confidential. It became like the voice of a dying person confessing half-forgotten sins to a stranger priest.

"He would follow me and find me out wherever I went. To get some job somewhere and hide away from him would be absolutely impossible. He'd find me out. Nothing would stop him. He'd just bring me back here—and—and——"

Cousin Ann remained completely oblivious of the ricochet of pride in the woman's voice; pride that kept beating against her calm rational statement, like the wind against a beleaguered rampart.

"Don't you understand what I mean?" said Netta almost crossly. And then a sudden smile of irony, irony deep and simple as the earth itself, passed over her haggard face.

"No!" repeated the other. "Tell me, quick! What would he do then?"

Netta looked her full in the face.

"He'd insist on marrying *me* then!" she said.

"Ah! he would, would he?" cried Cousin Ann, making an attempt to return Netta's smile with appropriate playfulness.

The attempt was not a very successful one. The response hung in the wind a bit. For the pulse beat of a second the victory was with the late mistress of Major-General Caxton. For once in her proud hoverings Missy Sparrow-hawk blinked and swerved. That nuance of irony on her rival's face became something she could not discount or deal with. For a couple of ticks of the great dining-room clock Lady Ann Poynings was no better than a baffled barbarian.

The result of this momentary defeat, however, was to add a fiercer momentum to her next stroke, which certainly did not miss its mark.

"Then there's only one thing left for you to do if you're serious in what you said just now."

The strange illuminated look came back into Netta's eyes.

"You mean—to do away with myself?" she whispered.

Lady Ann gave a spontaneous start of surprise at this. Among the various issues she had projected for her campaign, the suicide of her victim had, so far, taken no place.

"Good Lord, Netta Page! What must you think of me! Of course I wasn't dreaming of horrors like that!"

Once more there came into the other's countenance the same disconcerting smile.

"I don't think you'd dream of anything for many nights," she said. "But what is this one thing left, if it isn't killing myself?"

Plumb-down, like a falling meteorite, came Missy Sparrowhawk this time.

"A woman can always," she whispered savagely, "kill the illusion which a man builds up about her or about himself in connection with her. And when that's done, there is nothing left."

The deadliness of this stroke was promptly proved by a curious case of obliteration. What was obliterated was the unearthly eagerness in Netta's eyes; that exaltation which had carried their struggle to a level of emotion outside the scope of a winner of "scuts" and "pads" and "brushes."

The look did not merely fade from Netta's face; for that would imply a process. It sank and was extinguished. *It went out* It disappeared as completely as the light in a ship's stern disappears when the ship sinks into the sea trough.

"Nothing left but just disgust with the whole thing," added Cousin Ann, driving the stroke home with ferocious finality. "They don't hang on as *we* do, Netta Page. We've only to let ourselves drift and drop our form a bit and they're off! They're awfully fastidious, men are. You'd think sometimes that they'd never seen anything born or anything die!"

Netta's face expressed a comprehension so bleak and stark that every vestige of beauty seemed frozen out of its haggardness.

"You mean that I should make him hate me?" she said humbly.

"I'm not dictating to you," breathed the other, with a deep sigh of relief and leaning back in her chair. "It's you who will have to do it. I'm not impertinent enough to suggest how it's to be done. I only know, Netta, that if you don't do just that, nothing that you do will make any difference."

Why should it have happened that at that critical moment, in place of glancing at the gentle Sir Robert, Netta's eyes fell upon the one unfrozen pane of the Elizabethan window, across which the lime tree stretched its branch? However it happened, the sight of that branch, motionless and benumbed in the leaden-coloured air reminded her of those drab wintry days when Florrie would bring back to their room from the Turk's Head, hidden under her cloak, a bottle of Gordon's gin.

She seemed actually to hear Florrie's voice at that moment; and there was a branch across the frozen window there, too.

"You get quite like the other girls when you're squiffy, Net!"

It was in that room that she had vowed to herself, one sickeningly gray morning, that she would never, never, never be "like the other girls" again!

She felt a sudden overpowering necessity to be quite alone. She felt that whatever happened it would be a heavenly relief, like the cessation of physical nausea, not to see Cousin Ann's brightly flushed cheeks and clear gray eyes any more!

Rather stiffly, for the frost seemed to have got into her bones, she rose from her seat and stood quite still, looking straight down at her enemy.

Cousin Ann felt as though she were riding an unknown horse without spur or bridle or bit. She experienced a sense of abominable embarrassment. She felt as she had felt once when her father caught her stamping on a slowworm. She felt more clumsy than cruel, more thick-skinned than victorious. She felt a fool.

This feeling was not diminished when her rival gave her

what seemed to resemble the melancholy shadow of an ironic curtsey. It remained when, with a movement that could not have been more dignified if it had been the exit of the betrayed crown prince, the friend of Florrie and Minnie bowed herself out into the empty hall.

CHAPTER VIII

NETTA never forgot the final hour of that Christmas Eve as she watched from their bed the figure of Rook standing in his dressing gown by the window. He was as one who reports to his companion from some solitary Childe Roland Tower the signs and portents of a world dark with mysterious travail throes.

So as not to chill her with the night air as she sat up erect in the bed, her brown hair hanging loose over each shoulder and her eyes big with her hidden purpose, he did not open the window, though he longed to do so; but since their only light was the last flicker of their fire, the great hollow spaces of the hushed midnight gave up their secret to him.

"There's a thaw beginning," he said, half turning toward the bed.

"Does that mean that it'll rain to-morrow?" she asked in a low voice as if she were afraid of disturbing something, afraid of interrupting some deep dark purpose of nature, as sacred and hidden as her own.

"It means a white Christmas—that's what it means," replied the Squire of Ashover. "I can't see one single star. Wait a moment! Cover yourself up, will you? And I'll open the window."

Netta obediently sank down on the pillow and pulled the bedclothes close under her chin. Lying warm and quiet there she closed her eyes. In spite of everything she felt strangely happy.

Rook opened the upper window sash and leaned out, inhaling great breaths of dark damp air.

"There are clouds over everything," he reported. "And they're not rain clouds, Netta. I can smell the snow coming."

"Can you really smell the snow?" whispered the woman; and as the night air swept in about her she, too, was conscious of an indescribable presence there in the great brooding spaces, a presence like that of some enormous, formless, feathery body, the approach of which did actually send out some vague impalpable essence, recognizable by human senses—the smell of the snow!

Netta lay for several minutes in silence, giving herself up to this mysterious elemental process that was going on out there in the vast night.

Then suddenly she was conscious of a vague uneasiness. Why did not Rook close the window and come back into the room?

She raised her head. He was still leaning out, staring into the darkness, motionless as a sentinel, and she became conscious from the very pose of his head that he was absorbed in watching something or listening to something. Was he listening to the relaxing of the crust of the earth as it yielded to the thaw?

All at once he closed the window and turned round.

"Did you see anything?" she asked.

He looked at her in surprise. "How did you know?" he returned. And she saw by his face that he had received some kind of shock.

He came and sat down on the bed, taking the hand which she thrust out toward him.

"What was it, Rook?" she whispered.

He fixed her with his eyes, seeing her and yet not seeing her, like a man who is recreating in his mental vision some disturbing image.

"Rook!" she repeated, this time with real concern in her voice; "Rook! What did you see out there?"

His natural and somewhat morose humour came back into his eyes.

"There's no point in making a secret of it," he said. "There's someone out there with a lantern, standing by the shrubbery, behind the trees. He moved off when I opened the window and slunk into the bushes. My dear, I don't like it! It's nearly midnight. Who the devil would be in our garden in the middle of the night?"

Netta drew away her hand and sat up very straight, staring at him with wide-open eyes.

"I believe I know who it is, Rook!" she cried excitedly. "It's Corporal Dick! Pandie was rambling on just now about him. Oh, Rook, do you think he's gone mad?"

Rook leapt to his feet and strode to the window.

"Whoever it was he's disappeared now," he said, coming back to the middle of the room and hesitating there with a puzzled frown, his hand on the chair where he had laid his clothes.

"I wonder if I ought to dress and go out and see—I don't *want* to make a fuss—but if it is Uncle Dick—— What did Pandie say about him?"

"She said he'd been behaving queerly all day; hanging about the garden with a gun and asking her questions."

Rook gave a perceptible start. "*What?*" he cried out. Then in a calmer voice: "I don't see anything very mad in that, Netta! Pandie's always getting the jumps about something or other. Uncle Dick was no doubt wanting me to go shooting with him. Good Lord! I can't see the old man wandering round here with a lantern in the middle of the night."

Netta shook her head. "But you said you saw someone. Did the man you see have a gun, Rook?"

He did not answer, but began pacing up and down the room, cursing under his breath: "The Corporal! Damn the Corporal!"

Each time he came to the chair where his clothes had been thrown, he stopped and picked up his shirt or his vest. Then he would throw the thing down and start walking and muttering again.

Nothing could have been more disagreeable to him than the idea of playing hide-and-seek at that confounded hour with a problematical Uncle Dick.

The unpleasant notion that if it *was* his uncle he might have to lock him up for the night, or even escort him back home over Battlefield and Dorsal, made him extremely unwilling to begin the business of dressing. And yet something ought to be done!

But perhaps it wasn't Uncle Dick at all—just some predatory night wanderer from the village on the way to his rabbit snares. A nocturnal chase after a poor devil of that kind would be worse than the other possibility.

Rook decided to let the matter rest. He became conscious of a superimposing weight in the atmosphere that made nothing seem more desirable than to take Netta in his arms and fall fast asleep.

He flung a shovelful of coal on the fire to keep it alive till morning, and throwing the window wide open to the now absolutely untroubled night, got straight into bed.

It was Netta and not he who stayed awake long enough to count the strokes, when the solemn Queen Anne timepiece in the hall downstairs, an object brought into the family by one of the sagacious marriages of great-grandfather Benjamin, struck twelve of the clock.

Rook was still fast asleep, as fast asleep as if he had spent the night drinking wine with Monsieur Voltaire, when Netta awoke to her first white Christmas at Ashover.

An extraordinary sensation, that sudden consciousness of the fact that the window ledges were thick with a soft feathery muffling substance, and the dark woodwork of the window a mere frame to the falling, falling, falling of heavy silent flakes!

A miraculous intrusion, this mysterious whiteness, so different from all terrestrial or solar elements; as if some vast meteoric moon, virginal and immaculate, had actually collided, in its mystic orbit, with our motley guilt-stained earth!

Netta glanced at the fire. It was still warm and glowing, while a light that seemed to proceed rather from the snow itself than from any remoter luminary filled the room with a faint bluish mist.

Very noiselessly she slipped out of bed and began hurriedly putting on her clothes. It was a little after seven and she knew that there was a service at eight in Ashover Church.

She had secretly resolved the night before that she would go to this service. Mrs. Ashover always went to the more popular one at eleven o'clock; but Netta had helped Nell Hastings to set up a little straw-thatched manger, overarched with holly, in that famous chancel, and she was filled with an eager desire to see how it looked with the lighting of the candles Cousin Ann, she felt sure, would go rushing through the snow with Lion if she went out at all. In fact, the chances were that there would be no human being at this queer ceremony except the disastrous Mr. Hastings and his equivocal wife.

She took her heavy cloak and muffler, drew a pair of goloshes over her thickest boots, pulled low down over her head a young girl's tam-o'-shanter that had accompanied her through all her vicissitudes, kissed her hand at the figure in the bed, and let herself out.

She left the house by the kitchen door, greeting Pandie and the cook, who were enjoying a cup of early tea over the stove, in so happy a voice that when she had gone Pandie remarked to the other: "These here actressy gels do love a bit of white Christmas, same as decent-living folks, then; seems so! Her be gone to hear Parson Hastings say his 'shed-for-you' by snow-shine I reckon! Will the poor deceived man give the like o' she the sacriments, do 'ee suppose?"

Martha Vabbin opened the top of the stove with an iron hook and shifted the kettle.

"Maybe he will and maybe he won't," she replied. "But I heard tell that when Corporal Dick askit for a sup o' them things in bygone days the Reverend that then was talked terrible straight to the poor hedge-dropped lad."

Netta's experience of snow in the real country was so slight that she felt an extraordinary sensation of awe as her steps broke the feathery whiteness that covered everything. A cart of some kind had entered the drive gate since the snow-storm began; but apart from this, everything was virginal and unstained.

The purity of the new-fallen snow made all the various little objects that displayed themselves in their shameless browns or yellows look more than just dirty; look in some queer way *degraded*, as if Nature had tossed them out in a fit of disgust. Every single twig or gatepost or tree root which *did* dare to assert its identity, bore upon its face the look of being subjected to a kind of penitential exposure, as if the self-respecting reticence with which it had concealed all the little birthmarks, deformities, and discolorations upon its poor skin were being held up to scorn.

Netta had passed round the corner of the house and was making her way through the little shrubbery path bordered by laurels and laurustinus, when she became aware of a sudden rustling and stumbling in the bushes behind her. She stopped and turned round. Could it be that Rook had found she was gone and had followed her? The moment she stopped and remained motionless, the person or animal behind her did the same thing; and so instantaneous was the sequence of silence upon sound that it was almost as if the steps of this mysterious pursuer were only an echo of her own.

Something kept her from retracing her way; perhaps a vague fear that it might be Cousin Ann; but each time she advanced and stopped again, the same phenomenon repeated itself. In the end she began to run, stumbling over the hidden roots and shaking the snow down from the smooth leaves of the laurels.

Just at the moment she emerged from the shrubbery near the drive gate and caught sight of the lighted windows of the church on the other side of the river, she tripped up over a dead branch and fell headlong to the ground.

Simultaneously with her fall two sharp reports rang out behind her and two volleys of leaden gunshot rattled against the gate.

She scrambled up on her knees, her face in the direction from which the shots had come. With a rapid movement of thought she wondered if she had been hit; and as she wondered, she was distinctly conscious of a delicious wave of relaxation and relief.

Her brain had never been clearer, her thoughts never more clairvoyant.

If only she *had* been hit, how lovely to die just here; especially if Rook came to find her when she was dead! It was with a queer detached observation, almost as if she had been an irresponsible onlooker instead of a muffled-up white-faced woman kneeling in the snow, that she watched the tall form of Corporal Dick emerge from the bushes.

Seeing her kneeling like this and gazing at him with great staring eyes, it must have crossed the crazed wits of the Ashover bastard that the contents of both his barrels had lodged in her body.

With a gasping cry he flung his gun away and stood panting, like an animal that has killed its quarry but has burst its own heart in the exhausting pursuit.

For the space of three or four seconds the woman's eyes and the man's eyes remained spellbound, entoiled in that peculiar and unique complicity—unlike anything else in the world—that unites a hunter and his victim.

Then in one swooning moment the effect of his twelve-hour vigil in the falling snow darkened the old man's senses. He reeled like a tree that has been cut with an axe, threw up his arms, and fell heavily on his face.

His fall and the sight of his outstretched figure lying before her broke the spell of Netta's paralyzed nerves. She staggered to her feet and moving toward him knelt down by his side. At first she thought he was dead; but as she turned his gaunt frame over, she felt his heart beating under his snow-dampened clothes.

With some effort, for Corporal Dick's tall figure was massive-boned though skeleton-lean, she dragged him along the snow to the nearest tree and there propped up his head on her muffler and tam-o'-shanter. Then she took off her cloak and spread it over him; and after standing for a second to see whether the tree trunk kept the snow from falling on his face, she started back at a run toward the house; crossing the lawn between the lime tree and the cedar.

As she ran she heard the church bell begin to ring. It rang unevenly, and she surmised that either Nell herself was ringing it or that Mr. Hastings had got some village boy to help him.

By good luck Rook had heard the report of the gun and was already half-dressed when she reached their room.

"Shot at you?" he kept repeating; and he hugged her with more warmth than Netta had experienced for many a long month. "Shot at you? Corporal Dick shot at you? Ay! What a race we are!"

He seemed to Netta to be actually exhilarated by the event. She heard him humming "Good King Wenceslaus" as he pulled on his boots. This was a tendency she was never quite able to fathom in him, this tendency to detach himself from things that happened and to enjoy them in a sort of inhuman trance, as if they were insubstantial dream pictures!

Netta felt obscurely piqued by his mood, in spite of the warm hug he had given her. It seemed odd that he should hum "King Wenceslaus" like that, when she had just been shot at as if she had been a pheasant or a rabbit!

She could not help the tears coming into her eyes as she thought how easily she might have been lying now just where the Corporal was lying.

It was through a vague self-pitying humour, not devoid, however, of a certain sweetness, that the domestic agitations that followed reached her mind as if through a mist made of fine-drifted snow.

It all seemed to mingle with the snow, this whispered, murmured agitation; Pandie's voice offering wild conjectures; Mrs. Ashover's voice issuing contradictory commands.

It mingled with the snow; it mingled with that sudden glance she had had of the lighted windows across the river; it mingled with the tune of "King Wenceslaus"; it mingled with a few floating fragmentary words from that old ditty, about "bringing meat" and "bringing wine!"

She was herself so far removed from the domestic furore that rose and fell round the recovering consciousness of Corporal Dick that she hardly commented on the fact that Rook said no word about *her* version of the episode in the garden. Rook was not the only perosn who heard the shots; nor was Rook the only person who knew of the Corporal's excited state of mind. Netta was once more, however, to become aware of how embattled a front the House of Ashover could turn to all outside interference.

Even when the gun itself was found, half-buried in the snow, it did not seem to occur to any one that the affair was a matter for official examination. The old feudal spirit, according to which in former days the Lords of Frome-side would have power of life and death over those within their gates, seemed to hover over every aspect of this unlucky incident.

But it was not only the alarums and excursions of domestic agitation that reached Netta, during the subsequent hours of that singular Christmas Day, through a dream-like mist. The attitude of each one of the family, their personal characteristic reactions, affected her with the same muffled remoteness.

It seemed to her half-unreal when she learnt that Corporal Dick was suffering from brain fever; still more unreal when she heard his voice, apparently perfectly sane and intelligible, demanding that he should be taken home; most of all unreal when it was decided that he *should* be taken—in Doctor Twickenham's closed carriage—to the gamekeeper's house.

It seemed to her exactly like an event in a dream when, after some talk with the doctor about a trained nurse, Lady Ann volunteered to sleep at the gamekeeper's and act that very part!

It was only when the church bells were ringing for the three o'clock afternoon service that this vaporous condition of Netta's mind was dissipated with an unpleasant and shocking suddenness.

The doctor had already carried off his patient, avoiding the snowdrifts in the narrower lanes, when it emerged as a settled arrangement that Rook was to escort Lady Ann across Battlefield and Dorsal to the house of Mr. Drool.

It was curious how bitterly Netta received this information as it was revealed to her during a rather strained and silent Christmas repast. On innumerable other occasions she had seen the cousins go off together without a qualm. But today, after her conversation with Lady Ann, she felt a sickening distaste at the thought of their association.

She was the one who had been shot at. She was the one who for Rook's sake had kept the thing a secret. It seemed an unnecessary stroke of irony that she should be just calmly set aside, and that all the drama of the event should centre in Cousin Ann's acting the heaven-sent trained nurse!

To Netta's simple mind an attempted murder was an attempted murder, a thing of bloody violence and notoriety, implying policemen and judges and law courts. There was something weird to her in the way Rook and Lady Ann could enjoy Mrs. Vabbin's mulled claret and mince pies and Pandie's chatter about the Corporal's craziness when, but for a stumble over a log, there would have been a dead body lying in the house—a body that would have been Netta herself!

How *could* Rook go off in such high spirits with Lady Ann at his side and Lion scattering the snow with flying leaps, when there was nothing for herself to do but put on her cloak and tam-o'-shanter again and set out to church—unless she wished to sit alone in her bedroom thinking of Mrs. Ashover sitting alone in *her* bedroom?

What her nature really craved at that moment was someone like Minnie or Florrie to whom she could tell the whole story; tell how she felt when she was running; tell how she felt when she saw the lighted windows; tell how she felt when she heard the shots; tell everything and have a good satisfying cry about everything—but instead of that, there were Pandie and Martha whispering over a belated meal in the kitchen and there was Mrs. Ashover upstairs with the Prayer Book on her lap—Netta could just see her!—reading about shepherds and Stars in the East and wishing that Corporal Dick had shot a little straighter while he was about it!

In the end she did slip out and hurry off to that afternoon service. She had never, since she was a child, missed altogether the Christmas Offices, and as she listened to Hastings's monotonous intonation mumbling over one of them now, like a great belated wasp in a forgotten apple loft, her indignant pity began to melt away.

It was no high supernatural consolation that came to her

there. It was simply as if she herself, Netta Page, moving in the wake of those unrealizable turbaned shepherds, with the sound of a gunshot in her ears and a pitiful purpose hugged to her heart, had stumbled upon the presence of an event, which—whether fabulous or not—had covered the sorry footprints of humanity as the snow covered the fields, with a mysterious inviolable beauty.

CHAPTER IX

ROOK'S high spirits did not diminish as, with Lion in front of him and Cousin Ann at his side, he struggled through the snow up the slope of Battlefield.

What Netta had interpreted as but another, darker example of that vein of inhuman detachment in him by which she had been so often hurt was in reality a feeling of immense relief that the Corporal had struck his threatened blow and that the blow had proved harmless. He had not breathed a hint to the girl of Uncle Dick's threats, but the thing had been a growing weight on his mind, the heavier because of its vagueness; and now that it was all over—for his instinct told him that the old man was henceforth *hors de combat*—his present sense of escape was proportionate to his former fears.

The darkness that came slowly upon them, as step by labouring step they struggled up the hill, was mingled for Rook with a warm, exhilarating consciousness of his cousin's proximity. The association of Netta's figure with complicated agitations threw him back with a peculiar relief, now Netta was safe and sound, to his old careless easy pleasure in Lady Ann's company.

He had always enjoyed being out in the fields with this warm-blooded creature of his own race, and to-night something in the character of the evening itself intensified that enjoyment.

It seemed to have a special quality of its own, the darkness that was falling about them now and isolating their two figures from the rest of the universe. It had a quality that was almost man-made, so burdened was it with ancient human consciousness of the ways of life upon the earth.

It seemed to carry with it an accumulated sense of the ending of days, of long, fate-charged days, that somehow or another *had* ended at last.

It was like a vast epitome of the various finalities, upshots, results, conclusions, that had descended, for better or for worse, upon all the eyelids that had ever closed, by sleep or by death, along that countryside!

Not a labourer, not a carter, not a shepherd, that had ever shuffled homeward after his day's work, but had left some residue of his patience and his resignation upon the burden of that darkness.

And it was a peculiarly English darkness. It was a darkness with an island roughness in it, where a faint tang of seashore fog blended with the breath of hidden moss and heavy mud and with the chill of the snow.

And withal it was saturated with history. Just such a twilight as this must have settled upon Pevensey or Sedgemoor after some great historic battle, when the alarums and excursions had died down!

It was not an easy matter, struggling up that hill through the soft unfrozen snow, between rabbit holes and molehills, between furze bushes and hornbeam stumps; and when at last they reached the top and found themselves among the great dark trunks of the Scotch firs, it was natural enough that they should lean against each other for a moment's breathing time before commencing the descent.

The touch of his cousin's cold cheek, the familiar associations aroused in him by the smell of the Irish-tweed jacket she wore, as they leant together against one of those rough tree trunks, plunged him into the irresponsible security of remembered things.

Between the enormous sky spaces above the trees, void of star or planet, and the heavy snow masses that had descended out of their gulfs, there must have been proceeding, all that evening, some magnetic affinity that in the end would result in still further visitations from those airy heights.

Some of these magnetic currents from the elements above the firmament must have passed through these two human bodies on their mysterious journey; for when after a while they began going down the hill on the Dorsal side, Rook became conscious that his former familiarities with his cousin had not blunted the edge of their attraction for each other.

As they descended into the valley hand in hand, there was that in the tones of both their voices that suggested the atmosphere of a reckless, unholy prank.

When they arrived at Mr. Drool's house they found that Corporal Dick was lying comfortably in his own bed, that the doctor had departed, and that Mrs. Drool had turned Binnory out of his especial room and had made the place presentable for Cousin Ann's reception.

The idiot boy was in a high state of excitement over all these developments. He watched his mother making up a cot for him by the kitchen fire with unbounded satisfaction, but he kept returning to the Corporal's room to tell the lady "who be going to sleep wi' I" what sounds and sights of the encompassing night were to be expected by his visitor.

The Corporal's room and Binnory's room were isolated from the rest of the house, so that Cousin Ann had no need to fear any difficulty or interruption in the performance of her nursing duties.

Uncle Dick was very quiet now, but Mrs. Drool told Rook that they had had considerable difficulty in keeping him in bed when they first got him undressed.

"Doctor told Drool," she said, "that we was to watch out for new sympterums in his sad state. He said Drool had to sit up wi' 'ee for fear 'ee'd do summat to hurt 'isself with his crazy old notions. What did he do up at house, Master Rook? There be a couple down this morning from Ash'ver

Old Pyke who do tell how Martha Vabbin wrastled wi' 'ee all night long, in backyard! They do say how he did shoot at she with's rabbit gun and how she did beat on's head to quiet 'un with a girt iron shovel!"

"Don't you worry, Mrs. Drool," the Squire of Ashover found himself saying in answer to this new version of recent events; and as he spoke he hesitated for a moment with that queer tightening of the nerves about the heart which indicates the forming of a subconscious resolution, of which the rational mind is only half aware. "Netta will understand," he said to himself. "She will know I have stayed up with the old man. I *could* send Drool over to tell them, but it's not a nice night for such a thing."

"Don't you worry, Mrs. Drool," he repeated. "I'll sit up with Mr. Richard myself. You and your husband can go to bed, just as usual. There *is* one thing, though, you might do for Lady Ann and me. You might send us up some sort of light supper—anything you have in the house—just on a tray, you know—let your son bring it up to us. We could have it in Mr. Richard's room if it isn't too much trouble."

The result of this suggestion was that a couple of hours later Rook and Ann sat down to a substantial meal of cold pheasant, home-made bread and Dorchester pale ale, while their low-voiced conversation attuned itself to the peaceful breathings of the invalid. They had scarcely begun their repast when Ann became conscious that the idiot was making some curious vocal attempts, in her room opposite, to imitate the voices of some carol singers or "waits" who had visited the gamekeeper's house earlier in the day. Binnory was practising a grotesque version of his own of the familiar ditty —"God rest you merry, gentlemen"; a version that seemed, as it reached her ears, to be mingled with a more questionable tavern catch, picked up from some less pious quarter.

Disturbed by this incongruous serenade, which the excitement of her nerves rendered the more noticeable, Cousin Ann got up, opened the door, and crossed the passage.

She found the idiot sitting on her bed while one of the pillows, decorated with her hat and cloak, was propped up horizontally against the wall beside him. "She be *you*, lady," said the boy with a certain obstinate sulkiness in his voice, "and I be Squire. Us be singing 'Born is the king' to them ghosties what do bide out there."

Lady Ann looked at the lad with a mixture of confusion and irritation. Then catching sight of her leather bag, open on a chair, with her heavy crimson dressing gown in it, she suddenly seemed to grow oblivious of the boy's presence and, as if she were quite alone, threw off her tweed jacket, slipped out of her tweed skirt, and hurriedly put her dressing gown on.

"You be different from *she* now," muttered Binnory, indicating the pillow with a jerk of his thumb.

Cousin Ann smiled at him as she had not often smiled at any one. The feeling of the soft garment against her limbs, in place of the other, made her suddenly vividly aware of that classic perfection of her form which had struck Netta so. The natural tingling of her relaxed muscles after their struggle through the snow increased this consciousness.

"Come in and have some supper with Mr. Ashover and me," she said. to the idiot gently. "And since I'm quite different now, we can put *her* back to bed, can't we?"

She removed the cloak and hat from the pillow and replaced it at the head of the bed, patting it smooth with her hand. Then she led the boy across the passage and into the Corporal's room where Rook had already disposed of half the great jug of Dorchester ale. Her thoughts, as she placed the boy between them and met Rook's clouded gaze of appreciation, were fatal and masterful in their recognition of her chance-given opportunity.

She had at first that sickening sense of inability to eat a mouthful which used to come over her at hunt breakfasts in her father's house before a great meet of Blackmore hounds; but it did not take more than a few sips of Mrs. Drool's jug to remove that inhibition, and very soon she found herself enjoying the meal with full youthful zest.

"And do you remember the night Aunt Edith found us in the hayloft?" Rook said suddenly, his heart warmed by the soft look in the girl's eyes. "How on earth did she get up the ladder, Coz? Or didn't she get up the ladder? And that evening you nearly fell through the ice on Abbotsbury Pond? *That* was a mad Christmas, eh? The time your father had to go to Paris, and you and I had the whole place to ourselves?"

"That'll larn 'ee to play the bitch in gentlemen's houses—that'll larn 'ee, ye sly baggage!"

The interruption came from the bed, but the old man turned over to the wall and once more his breathing was quiet and undisturbed.

"It's not only thik old owl-devil wot I do hear o' nights," threw in Binnory. "There be hosts and hosts o' them others, wot nobody but me take notice of."

"What others do you mean, Binnory?" enquired Cousin Ann, her face radiant with a heathen happiness that quite ensorcerized the lad, as if it had been the rich honey drink of Valhalla.

"I mean them hosts of girt gray boggles that go flapping over Dorsal, lady; same as can't bear to bide where Mister Pod do put 'em when they be deaded and shrouded."

"Goodness, Rook! Who puts these ideas in this child's head?" murmured Cousin Ann.

"Him as is over there, lady," replied Binnory, answering for himself. "Granfer Dick do tell I of everythink. 'A do tell of how babies be born wot bain't prayed over afore they be born, but be just dropped, like lambs at lambing-time.

'A do tell of babies that do cry like corncrakes after we, when us be up field-way or down river-way, till us dursn't bide in them places after dark be come. 'A do tell of how slimmity puss-cats, in shape of wimmings from Lunnon, do catch great folks round them's necks, and scrabbit them till they ain't no blood left in 'em!"

"Blood!" the voice came suddenly and startlingly from the bed. "I've 'a seen that bloody bitch quelled and quieted. I've 'a put the Lord's own lead in her."

Cousin Ann rose to her feet, but the old man with a commanding sweep of his hand waved her off. He raised himself up in bed and stared wildly at them, searching for words.

Binnory, too frightened to move or breathe, gazed at him with mouth and eyes open. Granfer Dick had always been more than human to the lad, and this burst of excitement in him was as though the eternal hills had begun to cry out.

Anxious not to increase the old man's excitement by unnecessary opposition, and not quite free from the fumes of the Dorchester ale, Rook remained passive in his seat, while his cousin leaned against the edge of his chair ready to spring over to the bed the moment the need arose.

It was at her that the Corporal now pointed his long gaunt arm, the white nightshirt clinging tight round the bony wrist, the forefinger outstretched.

"Where be the spirit of your people, Ann Poynings? Where be your love and your maiden beauty this bitter day? Have you no thought to put a hand out and stop this ruin of hopes and expectations; this crumbling down of what took a thousand years to build? What be your girl-pride and your lady-pride; your maidenhead-fears and your virgin-fears, compared with Ashover going down into a rumour of dust and dirt? Ay! Ay! Your cheeks are rosy-bright and your eyes shining. You do know what an old man would say but must forbear to say. You do know well enough! Ay! If ye be as comely in shift and smock as ye be in cramosin, he that be now sitting aside of 'ee would be a gowk and a gammon to let the ice freeze on the cold sheets!"

His arm sank down on the bed and his head fell back on the pillow.

Lady Ann went quickly over to him and pulled the bed-clothes up under his chin. He met her gaze with a look of beseeching intensity, the wild glare dying out from his face like the reflection of a blown-out torch from a murky pool.

Then to the girl's amazement one of his wrinkled eyelids closed in a fantastic goblinish wink and he heaved over against the wall and remained dead-still.

She stood by his side for a second or two, contemplating his giant frame under the chequered coverlet. The thoughts that passed at that moment through the head of Missy Sparrow-hawk would have been difficult to put into intelligible words.

She protracted her pose at the bedside longer than was necessary. When she did turn away from her now peacefully breathing patient, it was not at Rook she looked but at the boy.

"Better run down now, Binnory, and get into bed! Do you want the lady to come down and tuck you up? Very well, then! Be a good boy and undress yourself quietly and I'll come down and say good-night to you in five, six, seven, *ten* minutes."

The lad obeyed her without demur. He glanced reverently at the sleeping form, touched his forehead mechanically, as he had been taught to do when addressing the gentry, and slipped quietly down the stairs.

The cousins were left alone with the sleeping man. Rook got up and walked over to the window.

"Shall I open it a little?" he asked. The *soi-disant* trained nurse nodded.

He pulled the sash down.

The night outside was windless and hushed as a vast mausoleum, but before he pulled up the window again they both heard in the stillness the soft shuffling muted thud—snow upon snow—where some bowed-down branch was eased of its clinging load.

"It'll begin again before morning," said Rook, turning toward the girl. "Perhaps we shall be completely snowed up here! I hope the Drools have plenty more of that ale in the house."

He spoke casually and lightly to conceal his growing agitation. Vaguely in his mind he associated the great darkened mass of frozen cloud-stuff that covered the earth with the inevitableness of the fate that was gathering about him.

"I'll just run down to see that the boy's all right," said Cousin Ann, yielding to a little nervous shiver, "and then I'll go straight to bed. Good-night, Cousin." She made a slight movement toward him, and then, drawing herself up, lifted her half-extended hand to her own hair and adjusted its braids.

"Good-night, my dear," murmured Rook brusquely, emptying the last drop of ale into his glass and swallowing it at a gulp.

She closed the door. He heard her go downstairs and enter the front kitchen. He waited, listening intently, his knuckles pressed upon the table. Why should the ticking of the clock be echoed so ridiculously by the irrepressible beating of his heart?

He heard the shutting of the kitchen door and her quick rush up the stairs. Then her own door was shut; and the house was as silent as Antiger Great Knoll

An overpowering restlessness came upon him. He glanced round the Corporal's room, at the gilded clock on the mantelpiece, at the lithograph of the battle of Tel-el-Kebir, at the old man's Sunday clothes hanging on wooden pegs, at the mother-of-pearl shells on the little mahogany table, at the shiny horsehair armchair, at the spotted china dogs that glowered at each other from red-tasselled brackets. Finally he could stand it no more. "I'll have a breath of air," he said to himself. "A breath of air, Uncle Dick," he repeated aloud, apostrophizing the form on the bed.

"I hope she won't think I'm running away," he thought as he descended the creaking stairs. "But, no! She's a sensible girl and a man ought to cool his head after all that ale!"

The gamekeeper's backyard was no longer isolated from the surrounding planetary spaces. No mere fragmentary instalment of the inter-stellar darkness had lodged itself there. The whole weight of the great Opposite of Light, the whole volume of light's negation and antithesis, bore down upon him out of aërial infinitude. The superincumbent ocean of blackness, swallowing up all form, all colour, all past, all future, was indeed enough to drown fathom-deep every scruple left in his human brain.

He found himself recalling, as he stood there in the trodden snow, a particularly outrageous oracle of his brother Lexie, most mischievously germane to the matter in hand. He was on the point of turning to go in when a faint night wind, touching his face as it journeyed from nowhere to nowhere, seduced him into making a few further steps over the vegetable stumps and clumps of Mr. Drool's garden.

Peering through that blind opacity he could just make out the vague line of the garden hedge. The Antiger Woods were entirely invisible. The elm trees by the side of the lane showed themselves as vague pillars of darkness within the dome of darkness. It struck his mind as a strange thing, that, though all distinctions were blotted out, he still was conscious of the snow at his feet as being something white, rather than black or gray. Did human beings inherit some queer colour sense, quite apart from the vision of the eye; a *tactile* sense, perhaps; derived from some remote animal or even vegetable atavism?

Ah! Ah! what was that? . . .

A most uncanny sound, blood-curdling and shocking, came suddenly to his ears from the invisible heart of the snow-bound hills. He smiled to himself when it was repeated, for he was sceptical enough not to be startled a second time by any nocturnal terror.

He stood still, listening. The second time, however, proved to be the last time. Only once again until the hour of his death did Rook Ashover hear that sound; nor did he ever come to any rational conclusion as to that sound's origin.

Often and often after that night it was his destiny to wonder what that thing was. It was louder and more appalling than the cry of any wild creature. When Rook tried to describe it to Lexie lie emphasized the fact that it seemed to come to him through some heavy, remote intervening substance. The nearest description he seemed able to give of it was that it suggested the united exultation of a host of people buried underground.

The occurrence might have altered the course of events that night—for all his inhuman callousness—if it had not been that his wanderings through Mr. Drool's garden had brought him to that side of the house from which he could see his cousin's window.

There was her white figure standing in full candlelight against the small square panes!

Had she also heard the sound? Rook never knew. To her—for some subconscious reason—he always kept complete silence upon that mystery.

Whether she was even aware that he had gone out he never knew, any more than he knew whether the gamekeeper and his wife were conscious or unconscious of his nocturnal movements.

He did not stand there for long. He could see her turn

away from the window and blow out her candle, and that single natural gesture, more than all the other forces that were combining against him, stiffened the nerves of his resolution.

Back to the door and up the creaking steps, and once more he was in Corporal Dick's room!

The old man had apparently slept without any change of position.

Rook rapidly undressed, and putting on his overcoat as a dressing gown, lit a cigarette at the fire, using a torn letter from his pocket to transport the necessary flame.

He smiled to himself to see how his hand shook as he did this.

With hurried indrawing breaths he smoked about half of the cigarette, leaning against the mantelpiece. Then, throwing the rest of it on the coals, he moved to the door and went out into the passage.

As he left the room he heard the old man muttering in his sleep. He waited breathlessly for a moment, his hand on the door-knob.

"Die out? Never—never—I'll shoot the bitch like a rabbit first!"

The words were followed by an inarticulate moan and that again by dead silence. Rook left the Corporal's door open and moved silently across the landing.

Without knocking he turned the handle of the door opposite. It opened easily, and entering with a beating heart he left it ajar behind him.

The old man at least deserved that much consideration from the head of the family he had done so much to keep alive upon the earth!

CHAPTER X

IT WAS the morning of the last day of the year. Characteristic of so many winter days in Dorset the weather was neither warm nor cold nor wet nor dry. It was Laodicean weather, born, like the English Prayer Book, of a genius for compromise. If such weather had had a human soul, it would have been condemned by Dante as being "neither for God nor for His enemies"!

The sun was not sufficiently strong to throw a single shadow or to illumine a single blade of grass; and yet one could see its form up there behind filmy vapours, faint, wistful, like a pallid, age-worn coin, weak as the eye of a dying lion, at which any mongrel cur may bark.

After a breakfast with Netta and his cousin as neutral and colourless as was the sky outside, Rook was buttoning up his gaiters in the kitchen, his foot on a chair, when Pandie approached him with a look of gloating importance. No archaic herald carrying solemn messages from one monarch to another could have displayed more unctuous gravity than did this exile "from the banks of the Tone" in conveying to Rook the news that he was wanted by his mother.

As soon as his back was turned Pandie hurried to the elbow of Martha Vabbin and began eagerly speaking.

"Twasn't what the missus spoke aloud that made I know 'twere going to be bad for Squire; 'twere what Missus keepit locked up in her own besom. Missus be terrible sore about this fancy party for year's end what Master Lexie have prejicted for all o'n. She do want Squire to stay with she, decent and quiet-like, and not go hobby-horsing to brother's where there be no one to put cork in bottle save Gammer Bellamy, thik old trot!"

Martha Vabbin turned a large impassive face toward her excited colleague.

"Thee and me won't have nothink to complain of, woman, if folks be down village. Missus won't want more than her usual; and us can have Martin Pod up-along, same as us did five years agone, when them all was in London; only please God 'a won't have his rheumatics on him, the poor crotchety man!"

Pandie was unimpressed by the prospect of entertaining the cantankerous sexton. She retained her dramatic manner.

"Did 'ee see how much of thik brandy someone have drunk these last days? If someone do drink to-night like what she's a been drinking lately, up there by her lone self, Squire'll have to carry her home piggy-back, same as old Squire carried Nancy Cooper home the night of the eclipse."

Martha Vabbin tossed a bowlful of peeled potatoes into a pot of clean water and resettled the lid of another pot out of which came a fragrant steam.

"I can't see who's to object to a body having a nip between meals, even if she *be* living with a gentleman. Since Christmas, when she came in here and laid, side of my plate, that pearl and pansy brooch, I've 'a had a Christian forbearance for the poor sinner. What you wants to be, Pandie, is more 'vangelical, same as I. Fornication ain't the only thorn in the blessed Lord's flesh. This speaking evil of them that's soft as lambs be a terrible sharp prick for the dear Immanuel; which is to say 'God with us.'"

Pandie turned away and moved irritably toward the pantry. She knew too well what to expect when Mrs. Vabbin's voice assumed a certain pious tone, redolent of prayer meetings. "*I* won't be the one to give that Pod anythink to drink," she said to herself. "He do make Martha as high-falutin as 'isself."

The master of the house found his mother in a state of unusual tension. She had had a series of agitating interviews with Cousin Ann since the affair of the shooting and she had found the younger woman mysteriously reserved and unsympathetic.

"So I'm to be left alone to-night, Rook, it seems," she began, without rising from her armchair or lifting her eyes from her knitting.

The son did not risk a rebuff by attempting to kiss her. He shut the door and stood with his back to the fire, glancing round at the warm intimacies of the room.

"I don't see why Lexie should have a lonely New Year any more than you, Mother," he said slowly. "It's your own attitude you must blame and nobody else's."

The old lady sighed. "I don't blame anybody," she said querulously. "I'm past blaming anybody. I thought when you brought that woman here that things could not be worse. But they *are* worse. How you can find it in you to go on like this is beyond my comprehension. I only hope your dear father is protected from knowing what I've gone through. That's what puzzles me most of all, Rook; that you can bear to think of him looking down at us at this moment and seeing——"

"Stop, for God's sake, Mother; stop!"

She did stop and with trembling fingers unravelled several inches of her work.

"When you talk like that about my father 'looking down at us' it makes me feel absolutely sick! Aren't you ashamed of such plebeian sentimentality? It makes me feel as if Cousin Ann were right when she says that there's a streak of common blood in you, Mother. How *can* you say things like that? 'Looking down at us!' It's a disgusting phrase; worthy of a nonconformist minister; worthy of Martin Pod!"

The old lady met his angry look quite fearlessly, though

there was more unravelling of woollen threads in her black-silk lap.

Then the corners of her eyes and mouth began to wrinkle, and a smile that might have been called mischievous flickered across her face.

"Never mind about your father, then," she said. "You're a true Ashover, Rook, whatever Cousin Ann thinks of *me!* Come here, you troublesome boy, and give your old mother a kiss."

He went across to her and bent down.

"That's better," she said as he returned to the hearth. "Oh, Rook, Rook, if you could only once see things as they are. But there! I don't believe you men live in the same world as we do. I believe you all move about in some crazy unreality of your own fancy. Sometimes I wonder if you're not all a little bit mad! I teased you just now about your father. But, oh, dear! your father was just the same. Listen, Rook! Have I ever told you about his affair with Nancy Cooper the gipsy? No? But of course you've heard of it. You men always hear of those things. It's probably been tavern gossip for years and years! It was a New Year's night when he broke with her; found her in the arms of a tramp or something and never spoke to her again. He was easily shocked, was my poor dear John. And when once a thing was over, it *was* over!"

"I presume the story doesn't reveal what happened to Nancy?" said Rook with sombre sarcasm.

"Oh, yes, it does! She married a respectable market gardener. Her husband's potatoes were the best anywhere round here."

"Well, Mother, I've got to do endless things before lunch, so I must make a start. I have to run over to the Drools' to see if there's any change."

Mrs. Ashover sighed. A chilly wave of lonesomeness suddenly swept over her. She would miss Corporal Dick seriously.

"There won't be any change but the last," she said.

Rook nodded. "I'm afraid so," he murmured.

Mrs. Ashover gathered herself together for one more effort. She rose from her chair, holding the whole bundle of knitting in one of her hands.

"Cousin Ann thinks that if you ever *did* see your way to marry it would be no more than right to provide very liberally for Miss Page."

Rook looked at her with surprise. This was the first time she had shown the least inclination to recognize Netta's existence.

"I've been wanting to say something to you, Rook," she went on.

His eyes widened and his lips parted. Could it actually be that his mother was prepared to give up the struggle?

"It's this, Rook. I want you to know that I'm ready to make any sacrifice of comfort or income for the sake of seeing you happily settled. I would even be ready, if your wife didn't like my society, to leave the house altogether!"

These words went through Rook like a spear. From a long-suppressed well of feeling in him there arose a blind flood of tenderness for this little woman standing there before him fumbling with her magenta-coloured wools.

"Leave the house, Mother?" he muttered. "Why, you'd die in a week anywhere else than here!"

The tone of his voice broke down some obstinate inhibition in her, too. She moved a step toward him and a moment afterward he was holding her in his arms. It was the son rather than the mother who lost control just then. There was so much upon his mind. He was beset by so many complications.

She, too, as they clung together, almost yielded to an instinct which had not by any means been the dominant one of her life. Like so many women who exhaust what maternal feeling they possess upon lover or husband, her attitude to her children had fallen far short of anything resembling passion. She had never, for instance, manifested the least preference for one son over the other; nor had she ever felt any regrets at lacking a daughter.

Thus it was only natural that when Rook's emotion had subsided and he walked away to the fireplace his mother's habitual feeling toward him as the head of her house rather than as the child of her womb recovered its normal sway.

Following this return to her integral self it was also inevitable that with a woman's unscrupulousness she should make an instinctive attempt to exploit Rook's emotion to her own purpose.

"Don't you realize what all this means to me?" she cried, as soon as he turned a calm face toward her. "Don't you realize, Rook, that it's worse than death to me to think of you and Lexie being the last of our people? Will you never understand that I keep thinking day and night about this awful thing? Oh, Rook, my son, my son, don't be hard and blind! Give me what I ask of you, Rook! Give me a daughter whose children will be mine as well as yours; whose children will be your father's and *his* father's, and will save us all from dying from the earth!"

Rook was stirred more than she knew by this well-timed appeal, but he, too, began to feel a reaction from his momentary collapse. An obscure indignation in him rose up against this exploitation of his emotion. He spoke quite calmly now and even sternly.

"You mustn't say such things to me, Mother."

She lifted her eyebrows, shook her head sadly, and resumed her seat.

"Give me my knitting, Rook, please. And you'd better start now on your various engagements. I like a quiet morning and we've had a good talk."

He obeyed her in silence, but just as he had his hand on the handle of the door he suddenly turned round.

"Don't you love me at all, Mother, apart from the family? Don't you care whether I am happy or unhappy? Is the family so much to you that your son is nothing?"

She looked him straight in the eyes from where she sat, bolt upright, in her Chippendale chair. She removed her fingers from the magenta-coloured woolwork and let them slide along the chair arms till they clasped the two rounded ends tightly and fiercely, so that her knuckles showed white and sharp in the firelight.

"I have cared for you," she cried, "since you first walked and talked; but I would have seen you dead in your cradle if I could have had another son, a different son. You make me wish you'd never been born, Rook!"

He stared at her in sombre amazement. His whole world, his whole life illusion, heaved and rocked about his ears.

"Mother!" he blurted out.

The tone of that cry did for just the flicker of a second arrest the hardening of her heart, because it was the exact repetition of the tone of his indignant bewilderment when she had struck him as a child. But the accumulated tide of her anger rolled over the impression as a wave might drown a submerged rock.

"If only Lexie had been the sound one!" she wailed. "If only Lexie had been the sound one!"

Rook shrugged his shoulders, laughed a husky, miserable laugh, and left her as she was, staring desperately into the emptiness of the impossible.

Descending the stairs with a hopeless weight on his heart he found his cousin and Netta standing in the hall, the former holding a letter in her hand, the torn unstamped envelope of which lay on the ground.

"Oh, Rook, listen to this!" cried Lady Ann. "Nell invites us all to dine at Toll-Pike. She says Lexie has asked them, too, to drop in later and she says that William himself was anxious that Netta should come with us!"

Rook turned brusquely round. "Do *you* want to go?" he enquired harshly, addressing Netta.

"It's just as you and Cousin Ann like," replied the girl meekly.

"Very well," he said. "But I won't have Hastings patronizing you witH any of his confounded priestliness! Ann, you'll see to that, eh? I won't have Netta insulted by that chap's condescension. If he doesn't treat her exactly as he treats you, she shan't enter his house!"

A cold chill went through Netta's heart at these clumsy words. She looked down nervously at the envelope lying on the ground and longed to stoop and pick it up, so as to hide her face from them both.

Cousin Ann gave a quick protesting glance. "Of course," she said, "he'll behave as he ought to behave, since he's invited us. You don't intend to come yourself, then?"

He shook his head. "No. You'll find me at Lexie's. I'm going to the village now and I'll tell him. We haven't had a meal together for much too long."

"Where are you going now, Rook?" enquired Netta, making an obvious effort to speak lightly and casually.

"I?" replied Rook shortly. "I'm going first to the village and then over to Drools'. One of us *must* see Uncle Dick to-day."

What had been in her mind was the thought of having him to herself, for some little time anyhow, that last day of such an eventful year; but she let it pass humbly enough.

"I only thought you'd have to lunch somewhere, Rook. Wouldn't it be easier to come back here and then go to Antiger Lane afterward?"

"I don't *want* to come back here," he retorted sharply. "I must have a walk to-day."

"You're not very polite, Rook," said Cousin Ann. "I expect that what you've really got in your mind is a jug of

Mrs. Drool's ale. I expect he intends to lunch better than any of us. Don't you think so, Netta?"

Netta looked wearily from one to the other. She had not missed the glance that passed between them at the allusion to the ale.

"And what are you two going to do with yourselves this gray day? You're both so amiable that the only difficulty will be to find out what the other really wants!"

"Oh, we shall get on, sha'n't we, Netta?" said Cousin Ann, slipping her hand over the other's wrist.

Netta felt a wild plebeian desire to slap the handsome girl's face, but her shame at her own impulse gave her answer its appropriate lightness.

"Of course we shall, Rook. You needn't think that we can't get on without a man to amuse us, even though it *is* New Year's Eve!"

Rook looked at them, standing together there, and a sort of baffled moroseness took possession of him. What was this power in women that enabled them to carry things off with such disconcerting indifference? What was this mental fluidity that enabled them to enter into some strange subconscious alliance with one another from which a man was ejected like an alien, like a stranger?

With each of these two alone he had felt the thrill of possession. But now that they were together, he felt as if *all that* must have been an arrogant hallucination! He hated to see them together. It substituted femininity in the abstract—a thing he found almost repulsive—for the individual clinging arms which could carry him out of himself!

He moved off to the door into the kitchen, sulky and baffled.

"Well! Good-bye, till we meet at Lexie's!" he said, opening the door and sweeping them together in one weary dismissing gesture. "I hope Mrs. Bellamy mixes the punch as well as she did last New Year's Eve!"

Before that day was over there was a distinct alteration in the drab colourlessness of the weather. Little by little the puddles in the roads turned into cat's-ice. A faint film of solidification formed over the ponds at the meadow corners. Hieroglyphic patterns made themselves visible in the mud of secluded lanes. Wrinkled crisscross imprints appeared on the top of the new molehills, imprints made by lighter touches than the feet of mice or birds or the trail of worm or snail.

Dead leaves that had lain softly one upon another in the mouths of old enmossed fox holes or under clumps of fungi at the edges of woods were now soldered together, as if by tinkling metal, with a thin filigree of crisp white substance. The wet vapour distillations clinging to the yellow reeds down by the ditches began to transform themselves into minute icicles. Birds that had reassumed their natural thinness fluffed out their feathers again as they hopped about searching for sheltered roosting places. In every direction there were tiny rustlings and tightenings and crackings as the crust of the planet yielded to the windless constriction, crisp and crystalline, of a gathering hoar frost.

Nell Hastings had procured a young girl from the village to help her to make her preparations. She herself set the table for her little party; arranged the fruit and the nuts and the sweets; and even lit the four red candles half an hour before the time for the appearance of her guests.

When all was ready below stairs and she had placed her villager as sentinel over the various pots and pans in the kitchen, she ran up to her room to change her dress.

She found her husband seated on their bed, in his trousers and vest, struggling with an immaculate evening shirt. He had brushed his hair so carefully and was taking so much trouble with his clothes that for one moment Nell was aware of a wave of tenderness toward him. His profile, as she watched it furtively in the mirror, had really a certain Napoleonic majesty; and the naïve solemnity of his struggle with his evening clothes touched that particular chord in her woman's nature which must have responded to just such childish self-ornamentation of the preoccupied male for thousands and thousands of years.

She left the brushing of her own hair for a minute or two to hover over him with bare arms, her proffered assistance being itself a kind of subtle caress.

And woman-like she was not content to let this interlude just pass for what it was. She must needs exploit it. When they were both ready to go down she suddenly took his head in her hands and kissed him on the forehead.

"You see how happy we are now?" she said; "and how everything is all right again? That's because you've stopped writing that terrible book. Don't write it any more, William! I beg you! See, I beg you on my knees, in my best white dress, not to write another word of it!"

She actually did sink on her knees before him, clinging to the front of his coat and throwing back her head.

He could not have known, had he been as wise as Hermes Trismegistus, that the caressing abandonment of this gesture —apparently directed toward himself alone, and isolating the two of them from all the world by a sort of magical circle—was in reality entirely due to the girl's happy knowledge that she was going to see Rook Ashover that night. The power that all human nature has, of exploiting secret emotions in the interest of obvious emotions, is carried by women to a most delicate and extravagant excess. Even as she knelt before him with her head thrown back looking so provocatively and wistfully appealing, she was thinking of him and of his book with less than half her mind.

Had William Hastings possessed the cosmic clairvoyance of a Paracelsus he might still have been unable to fathom the motives of this thin figure, with bare shoulders, clinging so beseechingly to the buttons of his coat.

As a matter of fact, he made not the slightest attempt to fathom them. He replied to the unfairness of her woman's weapon by the unfairness of his man's weapon. He just pulled her up by physical force, and holding her more tightly and with more vicious concentration than he had done for many a long month, he took advantage of her instinctive, nervous yielding to snatch a moment of blind love-making, such as he might have snatched had they been complete strangers to each other.

The man had really been as much betrayed into their luckless marriage as had the girl. He had met her at her aunt's, an old priest-ridden fanatic, who at once set herself to curry favour with Eternity by handing over to its representative, as a menaced city might hand over its fairest virgin to a sea monster, the body and soul of her niece.

The girl had amused him at first, both by her idealizing devotion and by her neurotic moods. To the former he had responded by an attenuated strain of absentminded tenderness; to the latter he had responded by an ironic indulgence, as if her girlish perversities and caprices were the gambols of a half-human kitten.

It was not until her moods, her fits of crying, her childish obstinacies, her cravings for romance, had thoroughly wearied him and got on his nerves that he began to treat her with a studied callousness, hardening his heart against her, in an unphilosophic anger with her, for having ever crossed the threshold of his monastic cell.

It was a shock to the girl from which only her encounter with Rook saved her, when she first realized how little of natural warmth there was in the awkward tenderness which was Hastings's nearest approach to human passion; but even this new feeling, so satisfying to her suppressed craving for romance, did not obliterate the disastrous effect of that first revelation of what the sex instinct can sink into, in a personality dominated by the tyranny of thought.

It did make her cling, however, with a desperate and pathetic tenacity, to whatever romantic elements there were —and there were not many—in Rook's response to her infatuation. It was doubtless the fact that what the girl had so far never encountered, either in Hastings or in Rook, was just warm natural human amorousness that led to the contentment and complaisance with which she had received the shameless advances of the invalid Lexie. Lexie, with whom she had no responsible link of any kind, seemed the only one whose erotic proclivities left behind them no poison, no sting, no regret.

The ill-timed embrace between these two remote and alien human beings was interrupted by the sound of the door bell. They pulled themselves together at once, the girl smiling, the man grave, and after opening the door and listening for a moment to the colloquy below, they went downstairs side by side.

It was a wonder to watch Nell's little villager in cap and apron assume the airs of an experienced servant as she informed Cousin Ann and Netta that "Mrs. Hastings be expecting their ladyships; and please would they take off their cloaks and go straight into parlour."

Nell's dinner party, when it was once under way, proved successful beyond her utmost expectation. The thought that when it was over she was going to Lexie's to meet Rook gave animation and freedom to her chatter and something almost approaching loveliness to her thin face.

William Hastings, too, was in excellent spirits, and all went smoothly till the time came for the sweets and nuts.

Perhaps it was a glass of the Vicar's port wine that broke the spell and put mischief into the heart of Cousin Ann; for the little servant had scarcely retired to begin washing the dishes when that young woman said, turning to her host: "Have you got yet to the really exciting part of your book, Mr. Hastings?"

The look which the author of the work in question turned upon his guest startled even the daughter of Lord Poynings. It must have resembled the look with which the famous Dean Swift actually killed the unfortunate Vanessa.

"Has my wife been talking to you?" he asked in a tone that made Nell wish the ceiling would fall down on their heads. "Have you," he went on, "got the slightest idea of what my book means?"

"Means?" stammered Cousin Ann. "I understood you to imply that it was slightly heretical. But beyond that—I—I have no notion, of course. I've never heard you read a line of it!"

The countenance of Mr. Hastings expressed the passing within him of a terrific struggle. The veins in the man's neck stood out like whipcord. Beads of perspiration appeared on his forehead. His cheeks grew flushed and then very pale. His fingers, which were playing with the blade of a silver fruit knife, bent it back until it looked as though it would snap. He remained as if petrified in his seat; breathing heavily, like a person on the verge of some kind of fit.

The three women stared at him in dead silence. They all seemed to recognize that a chance spark might set off a terrific explosion. But, in their silence, their own whirling thoughts must have resembled, for any occult initiate, three differently coloured lighthouses, projecting upon a mysterious storm their divergent rays!

The enormous magnetism of the man, in the turmoil of his suppressed fury, stirred up all manner of latent emotions in these three feminine bosoms.

Cousin Ann thought to herself that if she *were* destined to conceive a child for Rook, she must be careful to avoid the risk of any more shocks of this kind.

Nell thought to herself how odd it was that when William's madness was directed toward others instead of toward her, she felt a queer perverted pride in him and even sympathy for him.

Netta was swept out, beyond the little room, beyond the four candles, beyond the convulsed countenance of the man opposite, into the bleak country of her own bitter resolution. "I'll do it to-night," she thought. "I'll drink to-night at Lexie's all I can, so that he won't be able to bear the sight of me when he comes!"

William Hastings rose from the table. He had got his emotion into control, and he held it down within him as a man holds a maddened horse with an iron bit.

"Well, young ladies," he said with a benevolent smile, "I expect we'd better start, if we're not going to disturb Mrs. Bellamy's arrangements."

A quarter of an hour later they were all four entering the village. The lamps from the cottage windows shone out upon the littered yards, with their pails and wood piles and pig troughs and chicken pens; out upon the disconsolate vegetable patches where forlorn potato stumps and melancholy cabbage stalks carried the crisp whiteness of the beginnings of a heavy hoar frost.

As they turned into the alley where Lexie's cottage stood, they could see, at the end of the narrow lane, the dark-stretching expanse of the water meadows.

"There's a new moon this evening," said Mr. Hastings. "I shouldn't be surprised if we could see it from the end of the lane. It may be behind the house at this moment."

"Let's go and see," cried Cousin Ann.

"No, no," said Nell. "We're late already. Mrs. Bellamy begged me not to be late."

"It's no distance," protested the other, "and it would be so wonderful to see it over the ditches! Let's go, Mr. Hastings!"

"You go in with Miss Page, then, Nell," said Hastings.

"Lady Ann and I won't be five minutes. You can tell them we are just coming."

The young girl obeyed with alacrity. She felt in a state of complete psychic sympathy with Netta and it was more than she had dared to hope for to meet Rook without either her husband or Cousin Ann!

These two unwanted ones walked rapidly together down to the end of the little road.

In a softer humour than usual, because of the pressure upon mind and body of the oldest interrogation-mark in the world, Cousin Ann was less oblivious than might have been expected to the recondite magic of that place and that hour.

The dark flat surface of a tall house by the edge of the fields rose above them like the bastion of an ancient city. Perhaps just because she felt herself at that moment on the verge of becoming a living bridge by which the Past might go over into the Future, she experienced the feeling that long ago, and even many times, she had come to a road's end like this, where was just such a dark-walled house, and just such a smell of muddy, reedy fens stretching away under the burden of hoar frost!

Coming round the corner of the wall they found themselves on the edge of a little deserted paddock, bordered by a fence of loose stones and extending clear down to the first of the ditches, over the dark surface of which hung, sideways and drooping, the heavy trunks of a couple of pollard willows.

"Look!" cried Cousin Ann. "There it is!" and she pointed to the extreme edge of the western horizon, above which, sure enough, floated the thinnest, frailest moon-sickle that she had ever seen!

Squadrons of vaporous clouds kept up a perpetual march across it; but there it was—"Astarte, Queen of Heaven, with crescent horns!"—and the power of its presence, like the presence of the youngest, most fragile daughter of an old tragic dynasty, reached them through the night and blended with the vague earthy smells that came floating up from the shadowy fens.

"I'm glad we came, aren't you?" the girl whispered, aware of a great leap of power and strength in the very depths of her being. "*You* thought of coming, though. I should never have done it alone."

She laid the tips of her fingers on her companion's sleeve, and the effect of this slight contact was enough to enhance to a point of magnetic intimacy her feeling of power.

"Tell me, now, will you; now we're alone here, what you really are saying in that book?"

William Hastings swung round as quickly as if he had been struck by an invisible arrow.

"What's that?" he cried hoarsely. "Leave *that*, please, Lady Ann Poynings!"

But the girl watched the horned and crescented mystery, cutting its path through the clouds, like a fairy scimitar through a froth of soapsuds, and she remorselessly went on.

"Why should I leave that, William Hastings? I'm intelligent enough to know that what you're doing is no trifle, is perhaps of the greatest importance to us all."

"No trifle and of great importance!" he repeated mockingly. But she could see he was yielding a little, and she laid her hand again on his coat sleeve.

"Do tell me! Do take me into your confidence!"

He was evidently impressed by her words. He looked round furtively as if to make sure there was no one within hearing.

"May I ask you a question, Lady Ann?" he said.

Cousin Ann smiled in the darkness. "Why not? Especially since I'm asking *you* such terrific impertinences!"

"Well, then, would you be good enough to tell me what is your motive for going on living in this disgusting world?"

"You mean for not committing suicide?"

"Not at all! I mean for wishing your life to continue; for

wishing the life of the world to continue; for wishing that life *as* life should conquer death *as* death."

"But it never can *completely* conquer death, can it?"

It was his turn now to snatch hold of her wrist in the darkness.

"Never completely. No; never completely! But it can conquer it very far. It can conquer it so far as to encourage men, beasts, birds, fishes, to go on with the huge stupidity! It can conquer it so far as to encourage intelligent women still to persist in bearing children!"

Ann Poynings extricated her wrist from his unconscious clutch. Was all this a mere bookworm's eccentricity, or was the man actually out of his wits?

"Well?" she pursued. "And your idea is to analyze the motives that make people go on living when they are sick of life? Is that it, Mr. Hastings?"

He suddenly threw out both his arms toward her, so that she started back with considerable alarm; but he laid his hands on her shoulders and spoke thick and fast.

"I've always known you weren't quite like the rest. I've always known I *could* tell you about it," he began. "The Ashovers are enslaved by their sensations. They live for their sensations. But you're different. You live for something else. They are all nothing to me, I tell you. No one is anything to me except as a proof of my discovery! It's like this. What I've found out is the original secret of Life-Destruction; the great anti-vital energy, the death energy! What I've found out is the thing that one of the old poets symbolized once as the Breath of Demogorgon. It is just as much an organic force, an actual magnetic force, as radium or electricity. But it is more powerful than these because it belongs to the soul."

He paused breathlessly and dropped his hands from her shoulders.

"I know," he began again, after another anxious glance

round, to make sure they were alone, "that what I've discovered is not a mere metaphysical theory. Do you know how I know it?"

His voice became lower and more furtive and he leaned close to her in the darkness.

"I know it by actual evidence here in Ashover! No—don't run away. They can wait. You *must* hear me out now I've begun to speak. Ever since I came to this place I have been conscious of the power the dead have to preserve something of themselves alive in the world! Old families, like these Ashovers, have this power; just as old planets, like Saturn and Uranus, have it. Now do you know what I am doing? I am thwarting these dead! *I am driving them back.* I say this to you so that you can bear witness to the truth. There'll be no more Ashovers born into Frome-side. Rook and Lexie are the last!"

Lady Ann instinctively pressed her hands against her body as if to assure herself of its material substantiality. There was something so sinister and ghastly in the man's tone, and something so formidable in the perverse power that emanated from him, that she felt for a moment actually weak and faint. What horrible instinct of a distorted brain made him say these things to *her* rather than to any one else?

She glanced across the hushed empty fields, lying dim and vague before them. She searched for that "miraculous crescent", but while they had looked away, it had been swallowed up by the clouds. Alone with this sombre figure of negation, hovering there like a great gray owl in front of her, in starched shirt and woolly overcoat, her mind clouded and darkened, she felt as if she were struggling with some hideous sort of nightmare. The whole scene—the blank wall, the dark forms of the willows, the hoar frost on the grass—all seemed unreal, fantastic, like something that must be broken to pieces by an effort of the will!

That she—Ann Poynings—should be spending New Year's Eve with a human being dominated by such woe-begotten fancies, rumoured out of the remote heathen Past with "Gorgons, Hydras, and Chimæras dire," seemed to suggest some mad hallucination. It must be, she thought, the troubled expectation in her nerves as to what might come of the affair with Rook that exposed her so to this lunatic's chatter. She would throw the crazy enchantment off, break it up, return to her normal vision!

With a gallant effort of all the forces of her strong and cynical youth she did turn upon him now with a forced lightness of tone that would have changed the whole temper of the conversation with any one but William Hastings.

"But what about the book, Mr. Hastings? The question as to whether it is better for old families to die out or not to die out does not seem to require a whole volume."

The change in her tone seemed quite lost upon him in his excitement, but he had built up such an edifice of secrecy about his thoughts that to express himself with any clearness had become impossible.

"My book?" he muttered. "My book? I can't explain it to you now. It goes too far, too deep. Some day all the world will know. When I am dead, Lady Ann; when I am dead! But I have written it all down; step by step I have made it all plain. Every page has that breath upon it which the old poet talks of, the breath of Demogorgon! And when I am dead and they understand what I've discovered, what a power I shall have put into the souls of men! I shall have given man the power to counteract the creativeness of God. And Man shall say, 'Let there be Darkness!' and there shall be Darkness."

His voice died away over the frozen meadows. "Let us go back. Let us go in," he said after a pause. "I don't suppose that any human creature has ever felt the disgusting loathsomeness of life more than I have. Too many horrible things! Too many horrible thoughts! Oh, what a day—what a day—when it is all absolutely wiped out!"

They turned back together up the lane and stopped at Lexie's house. They could see the illuminated figures of their friends between the curtains of the room upstairs.

Mr. Hastings opened the gate into the little garden for his companion to pass in before him.

"Look at that!" he whispered, pointing to the window above. "It's all futility and disgustingness. Poison and ratsbane! Nettles and snakes! Frog spawn and fœtus! And it's the same up in the sky as in that silly room!" And he turned his accusing face toward the three stars of Orion's Belt, which were all of the celestial luminaries at present visible through the overhanging clouds.

"Shut the gate and come in, Mr. Hastings," called Cousin Ann from the doorstep. She had already rung the bell and had heard Mrs. Bellamy approaching from the kitchen.

CHAPTER XI

THERE was about half an hour more of the old year to tick itself away on Lexie's clock. The company had arranged itself by a kind of selective felicity such as rarely emerges from the shuffling of the chance movements in a group of friends.

Nell Hastings, in a mood of radiant excitement, was seated by Rook's side, talking with a reckless abandonment that was probably the result of the ritualistic bowl of punch, mixed and stirred with exquisite care by their host's hand, which stood in the centre of the room.

Lexie himself seated on a hard-backed chair was reading aloud in a murmuring, chanting voice, from the Oxford Book of English Verse, while Cousin Ann and Mr. Hastings, from opposite ends of the rug-covered sofa, listened to him with an attention that was at once entranced and wandering; the sort of attention that strangers in a foreign temple might offer to an alien liturgy.

Netta, isolated from the rest even more than Cousin Ann was isolated from Mr. Hastings, sat in Lexie's especial armchair watching Rook and Nell with an inscrutable smile.

Every now and then, unnoticed by any of the others except Lady Ann, she moved across to the table and replenished her glass from the deep nutmeg-scented bowl, whose silvery depths seemed as misty as her own cloudy thoughts.

By degrees the intent look with which she regarded her protector and his young companion changed its character. Her fixed mysterious smile degenerated into a fatuous stare and that again into an expression which resembled the ostentatious restraint of a burst of silly giggling.

The clock on the mantelpiece had now reached a point indicative of there being only fifteen minutes left of the year that was sinking into the gulf.

Lexie was reading Shakespeare's "The Phoenix and the Turtle." One by one the richly cadenced quatrains of the mysterious poem, thrown into a solemn relief by the unction of his voice, accompanied by the slow swaying of his heavy head as the music of the words took possession of him, even as the Delphic vapours were wont to intoxicate the Oracular priestess, fell grandly and fatally upon the rushing surface of that tidal ebb of the river of time, so soon to be swallowed up:

> Let the bird of loudest lay
>   On the sole Arabian tree
>   Herald sad and trumpet be,
> To whose sound chaste wings obey.
> . . . .
> Here the anthem doth commence:—
>   Love and constancy is dead;
>   Phoenix and the turtle fled
> In a mutual flame from hence.
> . . . .
> So they loved, as love in twain
>   Had the essence but in one;
>   Two distincts, division none;
> Number there in love was slain.

Like the corpses of royal children, slain in some religious holocaust, wrapped up in cerements of gold, the slow, gnomic, litany-sad syllables, murmured in Lexie's deep hieratic voice, sank down into that flowing stream and disappeared for ever.

What planetary mystery, beyond the death dirge of human love, beyond the annihilation of human faith, had the great poet in his mind as he composed these extraordinary strophes?

The clock on the mantelpiece had reached the point of

three minutes to midnight now; and though Nell's low eager voice talking to Rook had not ceased, one could note that it kept breaking and hesitating, as if the girl has been spiritually aware, without being mentally conscious, that the death and birth of time itself were interchanging their unfathomable secrets above her head.

The poet's stanzas seemed actually to be trailing their black and golden vestments to the measure of "a defunctive music" whose full significance was deeper, wider, more beautiful, more tragic, than anything that was passing between those four walls.

Before the two hands of the clock had come together under the sign of twelve, Lexie had reached the "Threnos" of this mysterious Shakespearean psalmody:

> Death is now the phœnix' nest
> And the turtle's loyal breast
> To eternity doth rest,
>
> Leaving no posterity:
> 'Twas not their infirmity,
> It was married chastity.

Directly the clock began to strike they all lifted their eyes and remained motionless, staring at one another. There was a hush in the room when the thin reverberation died away, out of the heart of which it almost seemed as if they could hear the death rattle of some enormous winged creature, some huge space-moth, whose soft-feathered body was even then crumpling up, contorted and rigid, to sink down into the pools of Nothingness, a vast, lamentable, empty husk!

It was William Hastings who broke the silence.

"It's curious to think," he said, "that Time is a mere human invention, a mere illusion, without reality or substance beyond the fantastic and arbitrary interference of man."

"Nonsense!" broke in Rook. "Time moves at a different

rate for different types of consciousness. But it isn't an illusion. It's the very essence of reality! It pours forth, like the water of life, from every shape and form into which Space is divided. You can't think of Space without Time, but sometimes I almost feel as if I *could* think of Time without Space."

"How *do* you think of Time, Rook?" enquired Lexie, anxious as he always was to encourage his taciturn brother to express himself.

"I think of it as a great gray Serpent, perpetually uncoiling itself from a pile of coils that has no end and no beginning."

"You mean that it always comes round again, having swallowed its tail?" said Nell with a little self-conscious, youthful laugh at her own audacity.

"No, no—I don't mean that at all. I mean that it just uncoils itself and goes off into darkness; scale after scale of gray silveriness; and then lost to sight! I can see those coils uncurling their endless length independently of Space altogether."

William Hastings looked at him with the weary indifference with which professional philosophers regard the utterances of ordinary persons.

"You can't see *anything* without using both the great illusions, Ashover," he remarked drily. "But I sympathize with you in your condemnation of Space. Space has *too much in it*. But then, so has your Time! The whole business has gone too wide and far. The hour has struck for striking a blow at these miserable illusions, at this disgusting spectacle!"

He rose from the sofa as he spoke and began walking up and down the room. Lexie, who had been watching the face of Netta with a certain anxiety, left the mantelpiece and drew up a chair by her side, slipping his hand into hers as if to establish between them a warm human barrier against these desolate speculations.

"I tell you," went on Hastings, "the time has come to unwind the clock, to unravel the woof!"

"Mr. Hastings has some very interesting thoughts," said Cousin Ann, clipping her words like a youthful undergraduate anxious to prove his sobriety.

"Netta and I don't know what the devil he's talking about, do we, Netta?" put in Lexie. Netta made no answer. With a blank fatuous smile and wavering steps she moved across to the punch bowl and refilled her glass.

When she had reseated herself, Lexie once more possessed himself of her hand. He did this with a grave protective gesture while his corrugated, seamed, and leathery countenance, full of a formidable Cæsarean dignity, turned toward the excited ecclesiastic a quizzical and hostile eye.

"You mean, I suppose," said Rook, filling his own glass again, while Nell watched him from her corner with big, infatuated eyes, "that your thoughts have hurt themselves against the ultimate walls; and you want a world without walls? You'd better wait for death, Hastings. That's simpler than trying to change the universe."

William Hastings paused in his monotonous walk and drummed with one of his hands on the table.

"Death is no good!" he shouted. "What we want is to stop death from breeding life! What we have to do is to go behind both life and death and get our hands on the mainspring."

Netta began to laugh at this, an unpleasant tipsy laugh that drew Rook's attention to her for the first time that night.

"What's the matter, Netta?" he said brusquely. "Let her alone, Lexie."

Netta's laugh died away in a series of suppressed giggles.

"Let her alone yourself," replied the younger Ashover, glancing almost angrily at his brother.

"Come and sit down again," came in Nell's faint voice from the corner of the room. It was difficult to decide whether the young girl's appeal referred to Rook or to her husband, or to both of them. Neither of the men, however, paid the least attention to her.

"What are you laughing at, Netta?" said Rook, standing in front of the unhappy woman and staring at her as if she had been an entire stranger to him.

A complicated expression, difficult to analyze, flitted across her face. There was in it the hunted look of an animal at bay. There was in it a sullen obstinate look, as of a child who is bent on mischief. And in addition to these things there was a curious coarsening process observable there, as if another Netta were dragging and tugging at her consciousness.

"I've—got—to—laugh," she gasped out. "It's—all—so funny!"

There was a dead silence in the room. Everyone looked at the two of them. Everyone seemed to be conscious, in a sudden suspension of all other interest, that a fatal and epoch-making event was taking place.

Lexie rose from his chair at her side and moved back again to the fireplace.

"What's so funny? I don't know what you mean," said Rook sternly.

His voice seemed to come from such a region of cold, sober detachment that all the company, fuddled a little, as they all were, by the fumes of that silver bowl, experienced an uncomfortable and disturbing shock.

Rook had, as a matter of fact, drunk less than the rest; but, in any case, his tough, phlegmatic nature was not easily affected by liquor.

Netta stopped giggling and pointed at William Hastings, who now sat, gloomy and abstracted, on the sofa.

"He said the mainspring," she cried huskily. "Yes, you did. You can't deny it. You said the mainspring!"

Lexie intervened at this point.

"It's one of his metaphysical symbols, Netta dear. He could easily have said gammon and spinach. It's what these philosophers always do—use some havering jargon that might mean anything! You're perfectly right, Netta. It's the devil's own silliness."

"What do you say to *that*, Hastings?" cried Rook, turning away from the bewildered face in front of him and glaring at the clergyman.

"I leave you to answer your little brother," retorted the other.

"That's not fair," cried Cousin Ann in her rich flute-like voice. "Rook and Lexie are two different people. Aren't you, Rook? You're much nearer Mr. Hastings in your ideas. In fact, I've heard you say much the same sort of thing; only you never stay in the same mood long and you love contradicting yourself."

She looked around as if seeking for corroboration of her words. Her eyes caught those of Nell fixed upon her with a sort of frightened wonder.

"You understand what I mean, don't you, Nell?" she murmured.

"I certainly do," cried the young girl in eager excitement, her mouth quivering and her cheeks flushed. "I've always known that the real opposite to William was Lexie Ashover and not Rook Ashover."

Netta's voice at this point rang out thickly and discordantly.

"Opposite? Opposite? What do *you* know about Rook? Rook's a deep one; that's what Rook is—a deep one; and I'm the one to know it."

Her tone had that peculiar emphasis in it of a tipsy person who grows quarrelsome.

"I'm not arguing with you, Netta dear," cried Nell, rising from her seat and then sinking back again with a weary indecision. "I'm not arguing with her, am I, Rook? Perhaps I'm stupid and childish, but I judge things differently than by just the words people say. And you *can* judge things like that, can't you, Rook? Judge them by something in the air, I mean?"

She grew self-conscious and embarrassed when she felt the silence round her and the concentrated attention of the whole room. But her embarrassment only drove her on to further self-exposure.

"What I mean is this: There's something hateful in William—something wicked and cruel—that wants to destroy things. Rook doesn't want to destroy anything. He only wants to escape, to get away, to let everything go. Things are only half real to Rook; and people, too. They're real to William; and that's why he wants to blot them out."

She stopped, trembling and exhausted, and gazed at Netta like a child begging for shelter and comfort. Netta nodded her head with solemn approbation.

"Half real," she murmured. "Half real. That's what it is! Isn't she clever to have found that out about him? I never could have thought that out for myself."

Lexie left the fireside where he had been silently listening to all this, and going to the window pulled the curtains back and pushed down the sash.

"Come and look here, Nell," he said, almost commandingly. The girl cast a quick questioning look at her husband and at Rook and crossed the room to her host's side.

"Have you ever seen that before?" Lexie said.

"What do you mean?" she asked.

"The whole look of everything," he replied ambiguously, taking her wrist and making her lean out of the window with him, while Cousin Ann with gestures of exaggerated chilliness threw an antimacassar round her shoulders and moved up close to William Hastings as if to include him in the somewhat perilous intimacy into which the company showed signs of drifting.

Nell was not long in realizing what Lexie meant. By reason of some peculiar thinness in the atmosphere, following upon the precipitation into glittering hoar frost of every particle of vapour, the stars shone down upon the earth with extraordinary brilliance. So brilliant were they, and so large and clear, that the most casual observer, that night, could hardly have failed to be reduced to some kind of amazement. The startling fact that these remote suns were not all of the same simple luminosity but were red and green and orange, and even faintly blue, gave to their appearance a palpable reality, brought their identity home to human senses as a measurable wonder, in a way that could never have happened if they had all of them been just monotonous points of shining whiteness.

But the phenomenon which had struck Lexie and was now holding his companion spellbound was not the fact that the stars were red and orange and blue as well as white; it was the fact that certain atmospheric conditions, connected with the hoar frost, had given to the diffused starlight a quality that properly belonged to moonlight; in other words, had thrown into pallid and phantasmal emphasis objects and distances that were normally obscured by darkness.

"What's the matter, you two?" called out Rook at last.

"Nothing, my dear," answered Lexie, pulling the girl back into the room and closing the window.

"Nothing," echoed William Hastings hoarsely, removing his clasped hands and lifting up his face with an expression like that of an opium-eater returning miserably to normal consciousness.

Netta burst into a peal of plebeian laughter. Her countenance in its convulsed state was not pretty to look upon and Rook after one glance turned away with a shiver of repugnance.

"Nothing—nothing——" gasped Netta at last. "It's like a game. It's like hunt-the-slipper. It makes a person laugh." And once more a peal of merriment more suitable to a Southsea bar-room than to the sedate bookshelves of Lexie's classical retreat rang through the room.

"Look at Rook's face!" she gasped out, when her fit subsided. "He's angry with me. He's furious at me! And doesn't it make him look funny?" And she laughed again.

The discordant note had sunk so deeply by this time into the consciousness of them all that an uncomfortable silence filled the room; a silence that was more than a mere negation of sound; a brutal, malignant, positive silence, such as seemed to possess a tangible though an invisible body of its own.

The fire on the hearth was almost extinct; the great silver punch bowl was empty; most of the candles had guttered down till nothing but flimsy blue flames hovered like shapeless astral lights over the prostrate wicks and liquid grease.

The window curtains had been left open; and Lexie Ashover, who alone of them all retained his habitual alertness, was aware of the contrast between that shining galaxy of many-coloured worlds out there and these abashed, disordered representatives of the race who had dared to divide the universal flux, the motions of those immense orbits, into days and weeks and months and years.

He moved the empty bowl from the centre of the room and replaced it by a vase containing some sprigs of untimely born yellow jasmine that had, without rule or reason and by the haphazard of accident alone, started budding under his eaves.

It had pleased him to see these wayward children of life and chance, and he bent over them now and smelt them as if to draw from their unfrustratable sap encouragement and strength for himself.

Cousin Ann, seeing him thus employed, threw off the antimacassar from her neck and moved up to his side.

Rook had resumed his original place by Nell in the corner of the room, but he was not speaking to her; in fact, he seemed unconscious of her presence. He was staring in front of him with the expression of one who, in place of a vague undetermined future, finds himself suddenly confronted by the hooked horns of an implacable dilemma.

A mysterious flickering smile kept crossing the lips of Cousin Ann as she stood by Lexie's table, caressing the jasmine buds with her fingers and murmuring little mischievous nothings. She felt at that moment a sudden wave of exultant assurance, beyond all rational scrutiny, that she was already upon the path of becoming the mother of Rook's child.

Woman-like, she could glance at him now, as he sat scowling and abstracted by Nell's side, with a furtive possessive triumph in her eyes which was tolerant of everything! She had won in the life-and-death struggle between them! She held all the court cards—every one of them—in her firm hands, and the trump cards as well. She looked at Netta, who had begun to show signs of falling asleep. Strangely enough, instead of feeling remorse for the evil suggestion that had begun this business, and instead of feeling any admiration for the exalted heroism that underlay this pitiful *dégringolade*, she began actually to share Rook's ignorant repugnance, justifying to herself her betrayal of Netta on the ground that under the influence of drink the woman's real character displayed itself in its true colours.

Netta's appearance, as she began to give up struggling against the approach of what was really a drunken sleep, was certainly calculated to shock any sensitive nerves. Her hair was disordered, her dress ruffled, her forehead beaded with perspiration, and she kept pulling up her legs into her armchair and rearranging her petticoats with that maudlin air of exaggerated sex-consciousness which, of all things, is the most jarring and offensive to women.

"Oh, it's been a huge success, your party!" murmured Cousin Ann. "Don't you feel that yourself, my dear?"

Lexie looked at her sardonically and even went so far as to put out the tip of his tongue.

"Well? Hasn't it?" she continued, sweeping aside his humorous grimace.

The young man shrugged his shoulders. "We shan't know whether it's been a success or not until the year is over."

"Oh, that's it, is it?" she laughed. "Well, I've a strong presentiment it'll prove a success to *you!*"

The lower part of Lexie's face, the heavy Claudian contours of his cheeks and chin, stiffened, at her personal allusion, into panic-stricken apprehension. He positively pinched her arm in his agitation.

"Ann! How can you say such things? Don't you know that to talk of the luck of the year *after* twelve o'clock is the height of dangerous folly?"

Lady Ann was absolutely nonplussed as to whether she had committed a real *faux pas* or whether Lexie was fooling. His beautifully moulded lips, as classical as her own, did actually display vexation; but directly she met his eyes they seemed to be mocking her with a mischievous and reckless raillery. He changed the emphasis of her attention before she had solved this mystery.

"There isn't a person in this room, Ann, except you and me, whose soul has not been reduced to something pallid and drivelling by this party! I oughtn't to have put so much gin into the punch. Mrs. Bellamy was all for more rum and less gin. But I've always had a *penchant* for that turpentinish, bark-like taste, like the style of Dean Swift."

Cousin Ann looked round the room, and it really did seem to her as if the place were full of woebegone, abject wraiths—wraiths that floated, like stiff corpses, in front of the brains that had begotten them. At the end of any long entertainment between the same four walls there is something of this effect, with the forlornness of which the very furniture seems to conspire; as if the chaos in human brains had the power of ruffling the natural decorum of the inanimate and reducing it to a lamentable simulacrum of its own littered wretchedness.

The girl got no comfort from looking at the cold glittering sky through the uncurtained window. There certainly was something that night not only remote but actually unsympathetic about those points of fire.

She had put out her hand again and touched the yellow buds. She felt at that moment isolated from the rest of the world; menaced and threatened by a thousand perils. Nothing was clear to her as to the significance of this sorry end of a pleasant party; but she felt as if something hostile to the very essence of her happiness was abroad in that room. Cousin Ann did not often let her imagination run away with her; but at this moment, while she contemplated the inert misery that had fallen upon that group of people; when she saw the ungraceful sleep of Netta, the exposed infatuation of Nell, the morose lethargy of Rook, the suppressed malice of Hastings; she felt as if the place were a sort of hospital ward over which the high stars twinkled like the brilliant electric bulbs over an operating table.

She was just on the point of opening her lips to suggest their return home when, with a shock that made them all stare bewilderedly at each other, the door bell rang violently.

"What's that?" cried Rook, leaping to the window and leaning out. "Who's there?" he called, for the intruder was concealed by the porch.

"Mrs. Bellamy has gone to bed long ago," said Lexie. "Do you mind running down and seeing who it is, Rook?"

"I'll go," cried William Hastings who happened to be nearest the door.

As he went down there was an intense moment of expectancy. Even Netta, who had been waked from sleep, realized that there was something serious in the air.

Nell was visibly trembling. "I feel," she whispered to Rook, "as if a goose were walking over my grave."

They could all hear the door opened and shut, the sound being followed by the tones of a man's voice talking in a low, hurried murmur. Then there was the creaking of a hall chair as Hastings made the messenger sit down, and almost immediately the clergyman reappeared.

"It's Drool, from Antiger Lane," he said gravely. "Mr. Richard Ashover died two hours ago."

CHAPTER XII

More than three months had passed over the precincts of Ashover, and before this space of time had elapsed the greatest transfiguration possible to the life of the earth was already growing visible and audible. The passing of autumn into winter, for all its stark relief of bare branches and frozen hills, has nothing comparable to this miraculous reversion, taking place in the heart of the vegetable world, heralded from the yellow bills of blackbirds and from the throats of wind-tossed missel thrushes mating in the high trees.

The poignance of the change has slid into the very word we use to mark and note it, a word that seems to be itself the essence of this jargoning from brown and yellow beaks, this rising of bubbling freshets between green banks, this mounting of sticky sap in cool-growing stalks!

For there is something in our northern syllable "spring" which suggests, not only the vernal fragilities themselves, but all that damp, chilly, earthy, moss-scented world out of which these little emerald-coloured blades and sheaths and filmy spears pierce their path into the air.

Latinized words, like the word "primavera," have their own sophisticated allurement; but the word "spring," full as it is of the very greenness of hyacinth stalks, the very blueness of hedge-sparrows' eggs, the very glint of celandine petals, has a sadder, more human significance; has something that carries the mind back, beyond the suppliance of any particular spring sound or spring sight, into the dark rain-soaked background which gave all these things birth; into cold wet places where stinging hazel twigs switch the skin, where the ground is treacherous with hidden swamps, where young birds and young rabbits are devoured by hawks, where the winds bring a perilous relaxation and heart-hurting memories, where the beech drippings are black and poisonous, where the blackthorn buds are ominous with fate and sorrow and sudden death.

It was by a gate in Antiger Lane, as they were on their way, at the end of a long, rambling walk, to make some final arrangements as to Uncle Dick's scanty belongings, that Lady Ann revealed to Rook that she was destined to have a child.

The girl never forgot the tiniest aspect of the scene they looked at at that moment. Her condition seemed to have softened something in her; seemed to have made her sensitive, in a way she had never been sensitive before, to the little things of nature and life.

As they leaned now side by side upon this gate the faint, almost sickly smell of primroses stole over her senses and made it harder than ever to break the silence. She had a little bunch of them in her dress, loose pink-tinged stalks and diaphanous blooms mingled with large vegetable-like leaves.

She could see the crimson buds of a large pink campion hanging loosely down against a mass of dog mercury; and not far from it, at the edge of a fallen trunk spotted with fungi, she could make out what she imagined to be the fragile greenish-yellow petals of the little plant called moschatel.

The deeper interstices of the wood as she let her gaze wander into them were not of one uniform green. It was as if there were in Nature some living spirit of growth and life that trembled and wavered into one nuance of colour after another, from faint coral to elusive purple, according to the manner in which the filmy sheaths and coverings of the buds and the sap-filled tenuous twigs took the character of their particular tree. Something in the inmost nature of the young sycamores, for example, gave to their large, clumsy, sticky embryo leaves an embronzed glossiness that was as different from the diaphanous green of the beech buds flecked with translucent threads of moth-soft whiteness as was the delicate freshness of the larches, as if an emerald-coloured waterfall had splashed down upon them, from the sturdy outgrowths of the dogwood.

"I ought to tell you, Rook, that it is certain now. It's no good not telling you, is it?"

Some obstinate maliciousness in him made him refuse to let her off with this.

"What's certain now? What are you talking about?"

She knew that he knew perfectly well, but she was too much softened by the season and by her mood to answer his obstinacy in like coin. "I am talking about the fact that unless anything goes wrong I am to have a child, Rook."

As she spoke she looked straight into his face. Her gray eyes, a little distended, were solemn and almost infantile in their appeal.

"You're not angry, Rook, are you? You're pleased, Rook, aren't you?"

His obstinacy did melt at this and he kissed and embraced her in all tenderness.

"Yes—I suppose I am," he murmured, as he released her. "More than I like to admit to myself, I expect! But what the devil are we going to do now, my sweet Coz?"

"*Do*, Rook?"

The reproachfulness in her tone was obliterated for him by the droop in the corners of her mouth which had the look of a child who, whatever happens, must be brave and not weep, though it has "full cause for weeping."

He made the great decision quickly now. Probably he had really, in his unconscious nature, been gradually making it all through that warm, relaxed, balmy-breathed spring.

"We must be married at once, of course; without a moment's delay. I don't want to make use of Hastings. In fact, he's been so odd lately in his manner to me that he might easily refuse to have anything to do with us, and that would be the kind of thing we want to avoid just now. No! I'll run over to Tollminster, get a special license, and see my little friend Tishmarsh. He'd marry us like a shot and nothing said! There'd be no difficulty if we did it like that. You've not been married before and I've not been married before." He paused, and after a second found himself drawing a deep breath: "Heigh-ho!"

The sigh of the Master of Ashover floated away into the Antiger Woods and lost itself amid the chatterings of hedge sparrows and chittering of wrens. Cousin Ann bit her lip and repressed an instinctive rush of Poynings pride that might have altered the whole course of subsequent events if she had given way to it.

All she said was: "I shall put myself in your hands, Rook. You must do with me as you think best for us both."

He drew her arm within his own and they walked on silently together toward the gamekeeper's cottage.

Had any stranger approached them, as they loitered thoughtfully side by side, his first thought would have been: "What a splendid typical pair of English lovers!" His second thought, on catching sight of their faces, would have been: "Those people have quarrelled and neither of them is of the stuff to forgive!"

When they reached Mr. Drool's cottage Rook looked at his watch.

"I think," he said, "I'd better go straight back to the house, get the necessary funds, and make Twiney drive me over there before dark. It's four o'clock now and I should catch young Tishmarsh at his tea. Twiney's mare could easily run me over in half an hour."

She took in all this with a calm, inexpressive face. "What had I better do, then?" she asked him.

"Do you mind going over Uncle Richard's belongings?" he said. "There isn't much, but you might put aside the kind of things one would wish to keep and tell Mrs. Drool she can have the rest. Poor old chap! I think we owe something to him, eh, my dear?"

She smiled faintly. It gave her a queer sensation to think of standing in that room again, and in her heart she was conscious of a bitter disappointment that she was not to be with him there. She had had at the back of her mind during the whole length of their walk the image of a cozy little tea tray shared between them in that familiar place. But there it was! Better let him do what he had to do for them both while the mood was on him.

There was a moment, when, as he held her hand at the gamekeeper's gate and felt the warmth and pathos of her youth in its magnetic pressure, they both were conscious of a closer reciprocity than they had ever known before; but the peculiar quality of that moment did not outlast his vision of her figure passing slowly up the little garden path and disappearing into the house.

Her reluctance to leave him and his reluctance to go seemed based on a sad clairvoyant recognition in them both that chance had given them that one brief interim of understanding only to take it away again for ever; and when he did turn aside at last and clamber up through a certain gap in the hedge which he had known from childhood the nerves of his mind were so strung-out and taut that the briar thorns that pricked his hands and face were a sort of assuagement to its tension.

Beginning to ascend the uneven slope of Dorsal he was unable to prevent all the little aromatic tufts of ground ivy over which he stepped from associating themselves with his thought. The pale-green fronds of the bracken, too, like miniature motley-coloured giraffe necks transferred to the realm of vegetation, uncurled themselves amid the images of his brain, as if they had been so many motionless sea horses among dark-finned, swift-flashing fish.

And most of all did the peculiar fragrance of the yellow gorse pass into his troubled consciousness, bringing with it, as he avoided those piercing spikes, a sense of honey upon the air.

As he approached the fir trees on the summit Rook found himself gathering up the tangled threads of his consciousness into one ravelled wretched skein. A feeling of miserable self-reproach took possession of him, mixed with a helplessness in the presence of this rush of events. He looked back woefully to the days when he first inherited Ashover, to the days when all his available emotions were centred round the personality of Lexie; round the long, delicious, irresponsible conversations they had had together under sweet-flowering hedgerows, in hot cornfields, and by the banks of the river!

He remembered one particular June evening when, as he watched by his brother's side a great orange-bellied newt sink languidly down into the depth of a meadow pond, while the hum of the heavy mowing machine went round the field followed by the scent of newly cut clover and the flicker of careless-winged dragon-flies, he had responded to Lexie's expression of unruffled happiness by an ill-advised desire that "something new and strange should turn up."

It was only a twelvemonth after that ill-fated wish that he had first met Netta; and ay! what troubles, what troubles his restlessness had brought upon them all! He tried to analyze the weakness, nay! the deformity in his nature, that had betrayed him into this cul-de-sac. If only he had been capable of one natural simple human passion it would have been all so different! It was this accursed detachment of his brain, mingled with his particular kind of cold sensuality, that had rendered him so fatal an influence in the lives of all his friends. If only he had kept altogether clear of the love of women! His temperament must resemble, he thought, that of those mediaeval monks, for whom any feminine contact was an evil thing just because of this queer lack of genuine normal emotion.

Arrived at Heron's Ridge and standing motionless there under one of the Scotch firs with his eyes fixed on the fresh green shoots, moist and glossy, of a chance-sown patch of Lords-and-Ladies, Rook made a forlorn attempt, in a kind of weary desperation, to visualize his life in some sort of perspective.

He saw this cold, this saurian viciousness of his as present in every case. He saw his relation with Netta as viciousness mingled with pity; with Ann as viciousness and camaraderie; with Nell as viciousness and romance. Unconsciously taking note of the extraordinary shape of the queer plant at which he stared, he found himself associating his own ambiguity with the contours of its leaves, and Lexie's more direct and more wholesome nature with the shameless purple spear which those leaves encircled; and it came over him, as he stared at this wanton outgrowth of the huge indifferent universe, that he would have done far better to concentrate all his affection on Lexie alone, and satisfy his satyrishness, if it *had* to be satisfied, with chance encounters in the city streets!

It came over him that his whole relation with every one of these people, with Ann, with Netta, with Nell, was in reality a superficial thing, external to his inmost life illusion, external to the deep, subconscious link that bound him to Lexie.

And as he let his thoughts drift dangerously along this road there suddenly gathered about him a sickening, panic-stricken fear of life; a fear of life burdened and sharpened by the responsibilities he had incurred in regard to these three women. He felt as though he could lift up in that sweet spring air a howl like the howl of a trapped animal.

Why, oh! why had he got himself so miserably entangled? And then, like a bitter undertide, like salt sea water in the midst of an inland river, there swept over him the weight of these different human existences upon which he had so disastrously impinged. *Their* lives to them were as important as his own to himself; and yet he had presumed, in his blind selfishness, to treat them as he might have treated insensitive, inanimate objects. Oh, he deserved every inch of the iron which now pierced him through his bones! With cold clairvoyance he reviewed the stages of philosophic scepticism, of spiritual disillusionment, that had gradually made him so indifferent to what he did, so indifferent to work, to ambition, to any purpose in things at all. He recognized the fact now that it was this refusal to take the ultimate issues of life seriously that had laid him open to these disasters. Lexie, who was far more materialistic than he was, could never have got entangled so; because he treated life as a work of art, and was consequently sagacious, meticulous, cautious, in spite of his scandalous humour.

With a sigh that came from the depths of his soul the unfortunate man lifted his feet from the spot where the patch of Lords-and-Ladies had seemed to paralyze him, and proceeded to run down the slope of Battlefield, running with a certain rather awkward movement of his long legs, such as used to make Lexie laugh at him and tease him when they were boys together.

Something seemed to be turning a kind of screw inside him with a squeeze and a twinge that scraped upon the very parchment of his soul as a lead pencil upon a slate; and it is likely enough that nothing that Ann or Netta or Nell had ever suffered, or would suffer, because of him, quite equalled the cold, unmitigated misery that hounded him on then, down that hill, like a murderous ice dog!

Arrived at his house he entered it, as was his wont and the wont of his father before him, through the kitchen door. He told Pandie to put on her things and run down to the village to order Twiney and his mare.

"Have you taken up tea yet to Miss Page?" he asked.

Pandie hummed and hawed and hovered, doing the thing that Lexie always described as "standing on one foot." He saw that she had something on her mind beyond her courage to express, but he cut her short with a gesture.

"Have you taken the tea up yet, or haven't you?" he asked irritably.

Pandie looked helplessly at the broad back of Mrs. Vabbin, who had ostentatiously occupied herself at the stove, but whose whole figure radiated "eyes and ears." She muttered something about the door being locked.

"Locked!" he cried. "Well? What then? Haven't you got knuckles? Haven't you got a tongue?"

It might almost have been supposed that the wanderer from the county of Somerset had suffered paralysis in all her senses, for she remained rooted to the ground, staring at him as if she were looking at a ghost.

"Oh, be off, then, for heaven's sake!" he cried. "And make Twiney put his horse in at once and drive you back here. A breath of air may quicken your wits, my good girl!"

He left the kitchen and ran up the great 17th-century staircase, two steps at a time. He had heard enough to fill him with all manner of sinister forebodings.

The door of Netta's room was *not* locked, but the sight that met his eyes was worse than his worst presentiment. The room, facing south, was flooded with lovely spring sunshine. The window was wide open, and across the garden came the song of an invisible blackbird, that clear-throated gay-wistful song, which always seems to reach the mind from some mysterious pre-natal region, full of something sadder than human tears and happier than human laughter.

But what a travesty, what a farcical travesty of the first

romance of a man's life was the figure he found seated by that pleasant window! Netta sat there in her shift. Her hair, hanging loose and disordered on each side of her head, betrayed only too many gray streaks in its untidy brown masses; while her right arm, falling limp and inert to the floor, still held in its feeble clutch one of those small glass bottles of French brandy for which the Ashover cellar had formerly been famous!

Her face was flushed and not agreeably flushed, the lines in it being drawn tightly and harshly underneath the skin, while the skin itself was that of a person marked and sealed as belonging pitifully to a nature divested of the natural instincts of human self-respect.

Rook closed the door behind him and turned the lock. "The servants have known this for a long time," he thought to himself.

He crossed the room and stood by her side. Her breath, heavy with liquor, spoiled the scent of that divine air, which floated in upon him as if over thousands of leagues of newly sprouting grass.

He shook her by the shoulder; not roughly but quite without tenderness, for his heart at that moment felt dead within him beneath all the futilities of human existence.

She opened her eyes and stared at him wildly, appearing hardly conscious at first as to where she was. Then, with a natural impulse of concealment, as if—thought Rook bitterly—he had been a policeman in a raid, she pushed the bottle under her chair and made a pitiful movement to adjust her attire to the requirements of conventional modesty.

"So this is how you amuse yourself," he said. "Perhaps you'd like me to hand you your dressing gown?" he added, with a sarcasm in his tone which was as completely lost upon her as if it had been addressed to the lime tree in the garden.

She took the dressing gown he brought her and, holding out her arms as if she had been a doll, passively allowed him to help her into it. Then she rose unsteadily to her feet, clutching the folds of the garment against her breast with one hand and gathering up her hair with the other.

"Well?" he said in a low bitter tone.

She let her hair fall down again and put out her hand toward him with a helpless, deprecating gesture.

"Don't you love me at all, Rook?" she murmured huskily.

He disregarded both gesture and words and, stepping past her, closed the window with so much unnecessary violence that its panes rattled. Then he pulled the blind halfway down as if to shut out the unbearable loveliness of that spring day. But the slanting sunshine was kinder than he was, for it threw upon the floor under her feet a pool of yellow light in the midst of which she continued to stand, like a woebegone leaden statue in a fountain of gold.

"I did it for you! I did it for you!" she brought out recklessly, too unhappy under his rep oaches and too dazed in her mind to care what inmost secrets she betrayed.

He stared at her in sceptical bewilderment.

"I don't know what on earth you're talking about, Netta," he said; and then, fumbling awkwardly in his pocket for a cigarette, "Oh, do sit down!" he added, crossly and petulantly. "How can I talk to you when you're standing there like a petrified image?"

"Rook!" she said, moving a step toward him.

Something in her expression touched a chord of remorseful tenderness in him and he took her in his arms; but he had no sooner done this than the overpowering smell of liquor in her breath extinguished the impulse. So as not to hurt her feelings he continued to press her against his shoulder and to let her lean all her weight upon him; but it was with a cold, unhappy, weary eye, without warmth and without pity, that he took in, over her bowed head, the familiar aspects of the room and the great stream of sunlight, full of flickering dust motes, that wavered across the floor.

As he looked at those tiny illuminated specks he thought to himself how likely enough it was that each one of these atoms was itself an enormous world, a world that doubtless at that very beat of time—perhaps a whole year of it—contained many Rook Ashovers in the process of disentangling themselves from many Netta Pages!

And the immense misery and futility of the whole boundless spectacle drove itself into his brain. What suffering! What misunderstanding! What cruel dilemmas! And all issueless and meaningless as that dance of April sun motes!

He registered in his mind a deep, silent vow that he would never, whatever happened to him afterward, forgive the Power that was responsible for this fermenting-vat of misery. No conceivable rearrangements or renewals or redemptions should ever make up, to him, at any rate, for what certain sensitive organisms are compelled to endure while this particular sphere is turning upon its axis!

Though he retorted thus, with all the righteous anger at his command, at the shameless First Cause of human suffering, his own nature was such that it never occurred to him to ask her again what she meant by that obscure cry: "I did it for you! I did it for you!"

And she, recovering now, as she clung passionately to him, both her sobriety and her love, recovered simultaneously with these her original heroic resolution.

In the strength of nothing less than this she extricated herself at last from his embrace, and some blessed principle of chance ordained, in defiance of the malignity of fate, that she should not know how cold and perfunctory, how weary and without human pity, that embrace had been!

No sooner had she recovered her mental balance and moving across to the bed had stretched herself out on it, a natural and touching smile upon her face and her hands clasped behind her neck, than there came the sound of wheels upon the gravel of the front drive. Pandie had been extremely expeditious in her embassy, and Mr. Twiney and his horse were at Rook's disposal.

Netta was clear-witted enough now to understand from the look upon his face that there was something about the appearance of this conveyance at this moment that agitated and troubled him.

He moved to the window and stood there with his back to her, absorbed in miserable thought. Netta guessed shrewdly enough that he was suffering from the particular situation of all situations which he dreaded most: that of having to make a quick and momentous decision. She resolved to help him to make this mysterious choice at once, whatever the consequences might be.

"You've got an engagement, Rook," she said quietly. "So don't let me keep you. You needn't worry about me any more. I'm all right now. I'll ring for Pandie presently, when I'm dressed, and have my tea. Then I've got a nice story to read till you come back. Or I may go out. That's what I'll do," she added cheerfully and firmly. "I'll go out for a bit! So don't worry. I shall be here; and quite good and quiet, Rook dear, when you come back."

He found it the easiest thing to do at that moment, just to obey her; just to take advantage of the velvet cloak she snatched off her heart and spread out before him, covering the fissures that yawned under their feet, covering the mud, covering everything!

"I'll tell her about Ann and me to-night," he said to himself. "It'll be easier to tell her at night. Her mind is not calm enough yet."

His brain said other things to his heart, too, as he moved irresolutely toward the door, his eyes fixed on her face and his hands fumbling with the buttons of his overcoat. Had not her resolution held firm, with all the power of her love for him tightening the fibres of its cruel strength, had she collapsed again, or appealed to his feelings, or clung to him in the blind pathos of her helplessness, the probability is that he would not have found it in him to go.

But she did none of these things. She forced into her countenance that world-old smile, full of the bitter wisdom of centuries, the smile of Sarah, the smile of Mary, the smile wherewith the sons of men have been at once mocked and protected by the daughters of men since the beginning of the world.

"Good-bye, then," he murmured, something within him surging up in one last wild desire that she should implore him, that she should conjure him to stay with her. "Good-bye, then, Netta dear. Don't forget to ring for tea as soon as you are ready. See you again soon!"

The door opened, shut upon him, and he was gone.

A minute or two later she heard the sound of wheels upon gravel. He was gone; and she had done what she had taken upon herself to do. He was gone thinking of her *like that*, like the figure he had seen seated by the window when he first entered the room!

She did not move a muscle now. In exactly the position wherein he had left her, there she remained; but her mind, empty of every other thought, kept hovering round one particular thing: kept wishing that he had kissed her at the very last, just before he had gone, so that her heart could have given him, her cheek against his, its own secret, unrecognized, desperate farewell.

Rook had forgotten that one of the ways to Tollminster was by that very Antiger Lane where he had left his cousin. He remembered it just in time; just at the moment when Mr. Twiney's gig reduced itself to a walking pace to ascend the long tree-shaded hill known as Friday's Dip.

Halfway up this hill they came to a lane that left the road at right angles. An old signpost, lichen-covered and weather-stained, pointed a long exhausted arm toward this lane, bearing the single word "Gorm."

Rook clapped his hand on the driver's wrist.

"Go the Antiger way, will you, Mr. Twiney?"

"'Tis a deal longer round, Squire," replied the man. "And there be bad ruts on thik little road. The best way is the nat'ral way as you might 'spress it." And he indicated with his whip the long straight ascent before them.

Rook's next speech was perhaps as much of a surprise to himself as it was to Mr. Twiney.

"I have to pick up Lady Ann," he said, "at Drool's. We have an engagement together at Tollminster."

"Right you be, Squire!" returned the man cheerfully. "I reckon me wold horse can wamble on through more dirt than any dirt these folks have a-known. These roads be nothink to what I've a-seed down Stourbridge way. Illigant carriage drives they be, to them parts!'

He turned his mare in the desired direction as he spoke; and Rook, watching the gleaming celandines in the ditch as they jogged along, found himself repeating the word upon the signpost as if it were an incantation.

"What kind of a village is Gorm?" he inquired casually. "I've seen that signpost ever since I was a child, but I can't remember ever having seen any place corresponding to it. I know the hamlets so well, too, between here and Tollminster."

"'Tain't a village at all, Squire," answered his companion. "'Tis writ on thik signpost and that's all I do mind. Gippoo Cooper, same as your Dad were smitten wi', did used to say down to Black Pig that 'un were a girt devil's name, writ on thik board for to guide boggles and ghosties. I've always been a bit scared-like, in dirty weather, when I've a-seed thik sign; and me mare, too, stopped in's tracks one terrible wet night and turned 'un's head right round to I, same as a living Christian might, as much as to say, poor dumb beasty, 'This place bain't a place for neither thee nor me, mister!'"

The warm golden afternoon light had deepened to a rich

amber tint, falling upon hedge and copse and meadow, by the time they approached Drool's cottage.

Rook was reminded of that mysterious glow, seeming to come from all quarters of the horizon at once, such as forms the background to the delicate Tuscan leafiness in many an Old Master's picture. The very cuckoo-flowers in the damp margins of the fields had that curious allegorical look which all fresh spring growths sometimes assume, as if they were painted in the illuminated edges of old breviaries.

Twiney pulled up in front of the little garden, where not so many hours before the cousins had separated, and Rook hurried up to the door. He knocked sharply with the handle of his stick and waited impatiently for an answer.

As he waited the impression came over him, as impressions do on such occasions—our reasoning faculties not having altogether destroyed our intuitions—of something or another being seriously amiss. Made up of an accumulation of many converging little signs—silences where there would naturally be sounds; sounds where there would naturally be silence —there gathers suddenly upon the human heart at such moments a burden of prophetic misgiving.

He opened the door and entered the little entrance hall. As he did so he became aware of two simultaneous sounds, both of them sinister and disturbing. The louder of the two sounds was the high-pitched monotone of the idiot Binnory; and the words uttered by the lad, as Rook listened in breathless amazement, were more extraordinary than the sound itself.

"I do see 'ee! Binnory do see the fine lady what's been brought low! Loowhee! Loowhee! Loo wheel I do see through crack and chink! I do see through hole and cranny! I do see 'ee! Binnory do see 'ee. The fine lady, on the high horse, what our Squire have tumbled and towzled! 'Ee be left, all draggled and scanted, like a fine girt mallard with's wing shot off. And Squire be gone to London town and he'll never come back; never no more at all! And Binnory do see 'ee and do hear 'ee! You mid drive Binnory away but a'll come back. And you mid live now where Uncle Dick did live; and you mid tell Binnory stories and stories, like what Uncle Dick did tell. Loowhee! Loowhee! Binnory knows all that do befall in earth and in sky!"

The second sound that reached Rook's ears, simultaneously with the idiot's babble, was the low persistent crying of a girl in abandoned misery. *Could* that be his cousin? *Could* that faint pitiful whimper come from the heart of Lady Ann?

He waited to hear no more but rushed up the little staircase.

He found Binnory clinging to a hole in the wall, which he had evidently made for himself and through which he was peering into the room. Rook was too concerned now to bother about the boy; without even knocking at the door he burst straight in.

Lady Ann was lying with her face on the pillow, having exhausted herself to such a point that her crying was scarcely audible.

"*My dear!* What's the matter? For God's sake, what's the matter?" And Rook knelt by the bed and pulled the girl over toward him.

"Send him away, Rook! He's there still! Send him away, Rook, or I shall go mad!' And her voice began to rise to something like a scream.

Rook got upon his feet, rushed out into the passage, caught up the idiot under his arm and carrying him downstairs as if he were a bundle of hay, put him out of the front door and locked it from inside.

Then he went into Mrs. Drool's part of the house and locked the other door, too. There was no sign of the gamekeeper or his wife anywhere about the place.

When he returned to the room upstairs he was amazed at the change in Cousin Ann. It was just as if Binnory had really cast a spell over her, and that the moment he was disposed of she came entirely back to her normal self.

She had already got up from the bed and was smoothing out her ruffled hair at Uncle Dick's looking glass. When he entered she turned round to him, smiling; and Rook had his second lesson that day as to the variable nature of women's smiles.

This smile of Cousin Ann's was whimsically penitent, full of the deprecating cajolery of a child. She put her hands on Rook's shoulders and kissed him on the forehead.

"I couldn't help it, my dear," she said. "I was alone in the house with him and he teased me and teased me. I was doing what you told me—making a list of the things—but he wouldn't let me alone. He must have heard those people talking about us. I was feeling upset and I lost my temper. I hit him. It was dreadful of me; but that's what I did. I hit him! And after that he wouldn't go away but kept peeping at me through that hole in the wall. It was awful, Rook! It was like a nightmare. I kept dragging him away from that hole and pushing him downstairs. But he's so strong. He always came back, and then kept jeering at me. But you've locked him out now, have you? Oh, I am so glad!" And she sucked in her breath with a little gurgling sibilance, as if it were all she could do not to burst into a fit of unnatural laughter.

Her mood touched Rook's heart more than she realized. He had always associated her with such complete independence that to see her in this agitated state struck home at him through all his defences.

The vague intention which had formulated itself in his mind at the moment when he saw the word "Gorm" on the signpost now hardened into a definite resolution.

"Get your things on quickly, my dear," he said. "I'm going to take you with me to Tollminster."

More passive and docile than she had ever been in her

life, Cousin Ann allowed herself to be led down the stairs, hurried along the little garden path, and lifted into the cart. Rook placed her between himself and Mr. Twiney, and as they rattled through the muddy lanes and through the gathering spring twilight the girl abandoned herself without restraint to a delicious wave of voluptuous contentment which cradled and rocked her and obliterated all doubt and responsibility.

She had fallen into a kind of trance wherein all objects lost their substantiality and became porous and dream-like, when the lighted lamps of the cheerful High Street and the rough cobblestones of the inn yard made her realize that they had reached Tollminster.

Rook gave orders to Peter Twiney to meet them in that same inn yard later in the evening, and he and Cousin Ann made their way through the narrow old-fashioned streets to the lodging of his friend the curate.

The closing of spring days in an ancient country town has a glamour about it of a quality more delicate and penetrating than anything that can be reached in the leafiest and remotest solitudes. The sense of the open roads stretching out from the lighted thoroughfares into the embalmed darkness; the fragrance of lilac bushes from invisible walled gardens; the emerging of the impression of new-leafed greenness from behind the moss-covered gates of church precincts and almshouse precincts; the twilit presence of newly planted pansies and primulas in old Georgian window frames; all these things together, mingled with sudden breaths of mud-scented coolness coming up from river banks, where the great moist marigold buds are swelling and swelling in the darkness, give to the streets of such a town an enchantment that has the power to summon up and embody the rarest memories of our race consciousness.

The curate of Saint Mark's Church received his visitors with undissembled delight. Full of a youthful idolatry for the Squire of Ashover, in which a natural and innocent snobbishness mingled with a quaint personal hero worship, the young clergyman was quick enough to catch every emotional nuance of this unexpected visit.

"I'm proud to be the one to launch you," he kept repeating, as he dragged them out again, up Antiger Street, up South Street, until they reached the necessary office.

The place was closed; but the energetic curate, with his knowledge of local ways, was able to follow up the official trail to such excellent effect that when they returned to his lodging the desired special license was safe in Rook's possession.

What followed was even more dream-like to Lady Ann's irresponsible and reckless mood than was their drive through the muddy lanes. Mr. Tishmarsh rummaged up his sexton and his verger as witnesses; opened the little postern-gate of the dark Henry the Seventh church with his own private key, slipped on his vestments in the easy familiar manner of a disciple of the Bishop of Oxford, repeated his nervous formula: "I'm proud to be able to launch you!" so unconsciously that it struck the girl as falling into a sort of allotted rhythm amid the austere hieratic injunctions of the fatal service, and finally made them write their names in the parchment-bound book as man and wife, leaving both of them with a queer impression in their minds that they had been hypnotized by a romantic schoolboy.

"Couldn't have been worked like this for any one but you, Mr. Ashover," remarked the exultant little cleric as he escorted them toward the yard of the Red Lion. "Nor for any woman but yourself, Lady Ashover!" he hurried to add, fumbling in his confusion over the bride's new name.

Rook was exceedingly anxious to shake off the little man before they encountered their driver's inquisitive sympathy, but Mr. Tishmarsh had at least this in common with his professional enemy the Devil that, when once he had been made use of, it was not easy to get out of his clutches.

"I must help you into your vehicle, Lady Ashover," the youth announced. "That's only my right, isn't it, as I was the one to launch you?"

Rook found himself damning the kind little priest in his heart with vindictive fury out of all proportion to the slight occasion. His nerves, now the drastic step had actually been taken, were feeling the effects of the unnatural tension of this long day.

They were off at last, but not before Mr. Peter Twiney had thrown a most quizzical and knowing leer in the direction of the curate of Saint Mark's, left bare-headed and excited among the staring ostlers of the Red Lion.

It was nearly eleven o'clock when they reached Ashover House. Rook made Mr. Twiney drive round to the back door, so as not to disturb any one; but it soon appeared that this familiar precaution was, for once in the history of that quiet dwelling, ironically unnecessary.

The whole house was stirring with lights and voices and emotional confusion.

Pandie met them in the doorway; and not only Mr. Twiney, but also, it appeared, his long-necked horse as well, listened with an attention that suggested one of the rarest dramatic sensations in two blameless lives, while the white-faced servant, her apron and cap awry, and her hands waving in the air like the flappers of an unhappy penguin, explained that Miss Page had runned away unbeknown to any one; that in her own opinion, she had drownded herself in Saunders' Hole; while in the opinion of Mrs. Vabbin she had been kidnapped and ravaged by them murdering gippoos.

CHAPTER XIII

IT WAS almost as if the momentous event that had happened to Cousin Ann—that secret victory of the Ashover dust under the chancel floor—had laid a paralyzing finger upon the life-hating pen of William Hastings.

Nell awoke late on the morning after the events just described, awoke with a mysterious sense of some great load having been lifted from her life during her sleep. To her surprise she found a note from her husband, fixed to the pincushion in front of her looking-glass, telling her that he had had his breakfast and had gone off for the day to Bishop's Forley.

She knew why this had happened. A celebrated theologian from Germany, one of the few modern thinkers whose writings interested this lonely nihilist, had co me to stay with an expriest there; and it was at the invitation of this man that Hastings had gone.

Brushing her hair before the open window with the scent of the young leaves and the new-grown grass floating in upon her and the songs of thrushes and blackbirds answering each other across the road, the girl abandoned herself to a thrilling current of happiness that seemed composed of every magical sound and every ecstatic scent that the great reservoirs of life held in their hidden springs.

It was as though she could catch, behind the shrill bird notes and the arrowy odours, the very stir and movement of the green sap as it pressed upward to meet the warmth of the generative sun.

Out of the recesses of her nature where they had been so long hidden rose a thousand indescribable memories.

Pale-green cowslip stalks mingled, in these faint evocations, with the transparent lilac of cuckoo-flowers, with the unique thrill of the first purple crocuses against the brown earth mould, with the crimson-tipped petals of innumerable daisies on dew-wet mossy lawns. Sharp birth pangs at once jocund and poignant seemed to answer from the depths of her being the unsealings and unsheathings that were going on in wood and garden and field.

All her buried responses to Nature, responses that had seemed to come to her in the form of pure ecstasies of childish happiness but in reality were associated with quite definite impressions of warmth and coolness, of stalks and leaves, of earth mould and roots and moss, of sun-motes and shadows, now rushed upward to the level of her brain, flooding her with a rapture that was beyond human description.

She tied up her hair, put on her shift, and ran down, bare-armed as she was, to make the preparations for her breakfast, against the moment she should be washed and dressed. There was not much to be done, for Hastings had built up an excellent fire and had put both kettles on the stove.

Hurrying through her ablutions with the impatience of a child, delaying just long enough to open her trunk and take out therefrom a real spring dress, in an incredibly short time she was seated at the kitchen table, with the door into the garden open in front of her, eating bread and butter and drinking tea with a face so radiant that had a sub-human elemental wayfarer lingered on the threshold watching her it would have certainly thought that the lives of the daughters of men were the ones to be envied throughout all space!

It then came over her what she would do when she had washed up the breakfast things, made her bed, and watered the purple and pink hyacinths that were budding now under the south wall. She decided that she would cross the Ashover bridge, skirt the Ashover garden by a little path she knew well, and make her way over the hill to the Antiger

Woods. She would not let herself think of an encounter with Rook; in fact, she was by no means sure that she wished to see him that day; but she wished to associate him with her unusual mood; she wished to be near him, to feel the pulses of the spring in the locality haunted by his presence.

She was so impatient to get out of the house that in the end she forgot all about the hyacinths; and it was not until she had reached the entrance to the churchyard that, with a little funny smile on her twisted mouth, she remembered this omission.

Drawn, against her intention and against her will, by the memory of that afternoon in the darkened church, she lingeringly and slowly entered the enclosure and moved round toward the west door.

Her astonishment was great when, turning the corner of the building, she suddenly found herself faced by Rook's mother. Mrs. Ashover was standing by the grave of her husband. Nell got a quick glimpse of her before she was observed and she was amazed at the expression on her face.

The old woman looked like an exultant and malignant witch, who had come to confide some unholy triumph to the responsive bones of a heathen corpse. She showed herself disconcerted and annoyed at the apparition of Nell, but she did not make any effort to conceal the causes of her wicked satisfaction.

"You'd better know at once what has occurred, Mrs. Hastings," she said, "and then you can tell your husband, if Rook hasn't told him already."

Nell's face grew white. What blow was this, then, that had chosen this day of all days to fall upon her head?

"What?" she murmured, her mouth open and her eyes wide. "Has anything happened—to any one?"

"Happened? I should think things *have* happened! You may be interested to learn that my son and his cousin were married yesterday by special license in Tollminster; and that *that woman* has run away."

Mrs. Ashover fixed upon the girl, as she brought this out, a look of such evil exultation that Nell felt as though every secret of her own heart were stripped bare. She could only make a little gasping noise in her throat in response to this overwhelming information and instinctively she pressed her hand upon the late Squire's head-stone.

"What's the matter?" said the old lady, laying her gloved hand on the girl's wrist and retaining it in her nervous clutch. "Come, come. This won't do! Why, you're as white as a Wyandotte hen. Come into the church and sit down a minute. No! No! I'm not going to have you fainting here by my John." And she chuckled with a high-pitched quavering chuckle such as might have emerged from the leathery lungs of an agitated bat.

She dragged the girl with her into the building and they sat down side by side. As the blood began to come back to Nell's cheeks and she began to make an attempt to visualize Cousin Ann as Rook's wife, her deeper consciousness was aware of the Ashover tombs and of the difference between the way they looked now and the way they looked on that dark, misty evening.

"Where has Netta Page gone?" she whispered to her companion.

"Gone to the gutter!" was the unspoken response of the old woman. But what she actually said was: "We have no idea, child. Not Rook or any of us! They've been scouring the country all night; they've been to the police and they've been to the railway stations. Not a sign or trace anywhere! The curious thing about it is that she didn't take anything; nothing but her handbag; and *that*, from what my son says, must have been practically empty. I think myself that she took money, but Rook says not. If he's right *there*, it's because she's gone with someone, with some man or other with whom she's been keeping in touch all the time. You know they're like that! That's what they always do: go back to some lazy bully who takes all their earnings!"

As Nell listened to this tirade her disgust grew greater and greater. If it had not been for those tombs in the chancel, whose presence had never been more emphatic, she would have protested indignantly and rushed away. As it was she just leaned back with half-closed eyes, trying to imagine what Netta must have actually felt as she stole out of that unconscious house with her empty handbag. In her growing sympathy with Netta she began to feel calmer and less hurt under her own personal blow. After all, she had never let her thoughts or feelings wander off beyond the romance of the immediate present. With regard to Lady Ann she felt no individual jealousy; only a sickening weight of troubled concern as to what the whole thing must have meant for Rook.

"I shall leave them alone for a while."

Nell heard the old lady's voice through the thick screen of her own agitation, as if it came to her through a tapestried wall.

"Alone for a while. You can tell your husband that. And if Lady Ann would rather have the place to herself *after* that, I shall be all right. It'll kill me, very likely, if they find they can't put up with me here; but I shall die happy."

Mrs. Ashover lapsed into silence; and her gaze, as well as that of her youthful companion, wandered from the Voltairean lawyer to the melancholy Cavalier; and from the Cavalier to the austere Crusader.

"It's absolutely all right," she murmured aloud to these exacting spirits of the race she served. "It's absolutely all right."

There was something in the mere fact of Mrs. Ashover's revealing her thoughts in this way to a comparative stranger that startled and astonished the young girl. This insanity of devotion to so impersonal a thing as the survival of a family was so entirely outside Nell's own life illusion that she felt like a person who watches the clash of phantom armies upon a phantom shore. And yet she was intelligent enough not to miss the note of something almost sublime in the old woman's crazy loyalty.

"It'll kill me if they can't put up with me here." That desperate sentence kept repeating itself in the girl's brain like the beat of a drum that outlasts all the other sounds as the mêlée rolls itself away over the muffling hills.

Absorbed, each of them, in their own thoughts, the old woman and the young woman could hardly be expected to be aware of the full power of the occult influences that streamed forth on that enchanted spring day from the mouse-coloured dust underneath those marble slabs. It was as though the rejuvenative stirrings in earth and air had actually pierced through the slow dissolution of the centuries and roused some hidden vital force down there in the darkness, latent and potential, beyond all annihilation.

Some sort of obscure summoning from these tombs of the race she had saved must anyway have carried its exultant vibration into the nerves of the new mistress of Ashover; for, after a long lapse of silence between them, both the women seated there, with a pool of sunshine under their feet and a wavering stream of sunshine falling on their heads, became suddenly conscious that they were no longer alone in the church. They turned round simultaneously. They simultaneously stood up. And there was Lady Ann, erect and bareheaded in the doorway, regarding them with a blank, dazed, inexpressive face, like the face of a noctambulist.

They extricated themselves quickly from the narrow pew and walked down the aisle to meet her. She smiled faintly at Nell and held out her hand, but it was from behind the same impassive mask—the mask of a hypnotized sleepwalker—that she addressed her words to Mrs. Ashover.

"I came to tell you, Aunt, that Rook has got on the track of our lost lady. It appears she was seen, by someone who knew her, in Bishop's Forley last night. I know there's a great mass of slums round those glove factories. I've seen awful places down there—lodging houses and public houses and that sort of thing where any one of that kind might naturally go."

Mrs. Ashover glanced at Nell, her instinct as a woman of the world warning her that this was not the moment for any interchange of unholy triumph between herself and her new daughter. But Lady Ann seemed strangely oblivious just then to all the conventions.

"You're lucky to be able to enjoy a day like this with a clear mind," she said, looking Nell straight in the face with her formidable gray eyes. "You're lucky to be free of any contact with our crazy family."

"William is in Bishop's Forley to-day," murmured Mrs. Hastings.

"Perhaps he'll be the one, then, to find our lost sheep and bring her back!" responded Lady Ann with a joyless laugh. "Rook drove over there hours ago," she added.

Walking side by side the three women skirted the angle of the church wall and moved toward the gate leading to the road. They walked in silence, the old woman and the young woman on either side of the newcomer, whose personality seemed endowed at that moment with an immense passivity of weight and power, capable of reducing them both to the role of irrelevant supernumeraries.

The warm spring sunshine covered them, all three, with its fecund benediction, and gave to their silent association an almost biblical solemnity. It was as if they had been moving, in accordance with some preordained religious rite, from flower-strewn altar to flower-strewn altar! They seemed, all of them, relegated to subordinate yet essential parts in some vast mystery play, some vernal celebration, complicated and dumb, in honour of Persephone or her mother. The cawings of jackdaws, the chittering of sparrows, the harsh cries of a flock of starlings as they settled for a moment on the edge of the roof, did not disturb, any more than did the bleatings of some distant hurdled ewes, the almost supernatural seriousness with which those three figures moved to the entrance of the churchyard.

Were they subconsciously aware, just then, in that magnetic weather, of the invisible pressure of the countless spirits of the dead, rushing forward through the body of the half-formed nameless one, hid in the womb of a new mother of the generations, forward, forward, into the dim, uncreated future?

If it *were* so, if the sublime mystery of the continuity of human life, beautiful and terrible, withdrew from these three sensitive female frames on that fatal morning all power of individual resistance, all power of personal choice, it is easy enough to understand how it was that they moved so slowly toward the gate. Such is the clairvoyant link between all women in their knowledge of themselves as living channels between what was and is and is to come it is likely enough that the strange passivity that emanated from the nerves of one of them on this occasion passed insensibly into the nerves of the other two.

No sooner were they out of the consecrated enclosure, however, and on the sunlit road than the whole mental atmosphere about them changed.

"May I come with you as far as the bridle path?" said Nell. "I made up my mind this morning that I would go to Antiger Woods to look for primroses, and I think I shall still do that—unless," she added with a gentle glance at Cousin Ann, "I can be of any help to any one?"

Rook's wife and Rook's mother exchanged a quick significant look.

"I think, my dear," said the latter with a sudden sharp eagerness, "you may be of immense use to us a little later. If my son, for instance, succeeds in finding Miss Page, and brings her back here, as I'm afraid he's only too likely to do, it would be a blessed relief to all of us if you could—perhaps—for just a few days—till other arrangements were made—take her in at the cottage?"

Nell was unable to prevent the blood rushing to her cheeks. Had this aunt-mother and this niece-daughter, with their merciless aristocratic gray eyes, sounded her heart's secret to its uttermost depths? Were they bent upon punishing her for her temerity? Was this extraordinary suggestion their premeditated revenge?

"I am sure William and I will do everything we can to help you, Mrs. Ashover," the girl answered gravely. "I only trust no harm has come to Netta. I can't believe that she went to any of those dreadful places. I expect she just took the night train to Bristol. I know she's got people she knows there. Or she may have gone to London."

Mrs. Ashover had ceased to listen. A new thought had come into her mind.

"Will you walk back with us to the house, Nelly? There is something I'd be most grateful to you if you'd do for me. Something I want to send to Lexie."

The girl permitted herself to be led prisoner by these two dominant spirits and they all three crossed the bridge.

A few minutes later Nell found herself waiting alone in the great chilly unused drawing room whose spacious ceremoniousness seemed to embrace and envelop her as if she were just one more primrose or crocus or snowdrop to be "arranged" in a slender glass vase.

Never did the room look more stately, in its gilt and its whiteness, in its water colours and French prints; but the young visitor felt an intense and increasing hostility to the whole atmosphere there, as if the great room were consciously emphasizing a sort of victory over her and over all the wayward romance she represented.

She moved to the mantelpiece and stood silently regarding a little gold-framed miniature of Rook's father when a young child. The picture fascinated her by its resemblance to Rook, and a wave of overpowering pity for what she knew well enough he was going through during these agitated hours swept over her like a shivering ague fit.

The odd thing was, and she wondered at it herself, that she felt no anger, no bitterness against him. She longed to rise up against them all and do something—she knew not what—to clear his path for him; to make, as the Bible says, "his way smooth." She felt glad that she was to be sent on a message to Lexie. She wondered how much Lexie had been told of all that was happening. Had Lady Ann found time to send him news of her marriage, news of Netta's disappearance? What an irony if this "something" that she was to take to him were nothing less than this double-edged piece of overpowering intelligence!

She looked at the marble and gilt clock. It was already nearly one. Would she be forced to stay and eat lunch with this mother and this daughter?

The idea of such a thing was utterly repulsive to her. It would have been like eating with two judges while the executioner was at work upon the condemned!

A sudden sound of the opening and shutting of doors in the rear of the house made her stand transfixed on the faded hearthrug, her eyes hypnotized by its convoluted pattern, her ears listening, listening— In a moment she lifted her head and made one irrepressible movement toward the door. She had heard a familiar voice outside, engaged in a hurried low-toned dialogue with Pandie. Then there came his step in the passage and the door of the drawing room was flung open.

Nell stared at him for a moment in speechless dismay. He might have served, save for his English clothes, for a picture of Hamlet rushing in upon Ophelia. His clothes were muddy and untidy, his boots unpolished, his chin unshaven, his eyes bloodshot and sunk deep in their sockets as if after many nights of sleeplessness.

He shut the door with studied precaution and fixed a long nervous look upon the girl as if expecting some angry outburst from her. Then, advancing a step or two, he threw down his hat and stick upon the rosewood table and looked wildly round him like a hunted criminal seeking sanctuary.

Nell's paralyzed dismay melted into infinite tenderness when she saw how broken he was. She went straight up to him and threw her arms round his neck.

His face felt cold and clammy to her kiss, as if it had been something carved out of the pith of elder-wood, and the unshaven hairs upon his chin pricked her cheek.

"Hush," he whispered nervously. "Hush, for God's sake! They haven't any idea that I'm here. They're upstairs. Pandie told me you were alone. I've come back for money and my shaving things. Twiney's waiting for me in the road. I wouldn't let him drive up. Pandie's gone to my room to get everything. She won't breathe a word. So *you* mustn't either, my sweet Nell! Oh! I shall find her; I shall find her; or never come back here again!"

The young girl released his neck but clung still to his shoulders, gazing up into his face.

"You will find her, Rook dear. I know you'll find her! I never believed it for a moment when they said she'd gone to that dreadful place."

He took her hands gently from his shoulders and held her at arm's length away from him. In his excitement the grip of his fingers was so powerful that he bruised her flesh.

"You don't know what it is to feel as I feel, Nell," he muttered huskily. "It's like being a murderer."

"It was not your fault, Rook darling," she whispered "It was not your fault. I know all about it. I saw it all happening; but what could I do? Oh, Rook, my dear, dear love, what could I do?"

"It's like being a murderer, Nell," he repeated, gripping her thin arms so tightly that she could not refrain from a little smothered cry. "It's just as if I had deliberately killed her! And she was so good! Oh! Nell, I was all she had. And she was so dear and good!"

He loosed her arms and uttered a sigh that shook his bony frame to its centre.

"You will find her, Rook dear! You will find her!" the girl kept repeating; and then, feeling suddenly faint with the tension of this encounter, she sank down on one of the tall, embroidered, Louis Quatorze chairs, heart-shaped and gilded.

He fell on his knees at her side and taking her face in his hands kissed her pitifully and blindly. Under his kisses her colour came back and she leaned forward, her hands clasping his head.

"Rook, dear, dear Rook, you'll find her!" she chanted, in a kind of crooning monotone, swaying a little as if rocking an infant. "You'll find her, Rook. Have no fear! Something tells me that you and she will meet again."

He rose to his feet and glanced nervously at the door.

"If I do, Nell," he whispered, "you'll be my friend, won't you, and help me through with all this?"

She never knew what he really meant by this last appeal, for with a quick tap at the door Pandie put her head into the room and beckoned to him.

"I'm with you, Pandie," he cried. "Good-bye, Nell!"

And before she had found the strength to get up from the rose-embroidered chair with the stiff gilded arms, he had got out of the room and the door was shut.

Once upon her feet she felt her normal strength coming back; and with that strength she felt a certain strange deep happiness stirring in her heart, a happiness that was different from the happiness she had experienced earlier that morning, and yet was not, it may be, altogether remote from that! She bent down over a great shallow vase of primroses that stood in the middle of the table where Rook had thrown his hat and stick, and she buried her face in those pale virginal blooms.

She approached the verge, as she inhaled that penetrating sweetness, of nothing less than the open secret which "many prophets and kings" have died without knowing, namely, that when love passes a certain subjective barrier and flows outward over the life of the person loved, it liberates itself for that moment at least from the sting that is "cruel as the grave."

She was still smelling these flowers when Mrs. Ashover came in; carrying in her hand a folded note.

"Will you take this to Lexie for me, my dear?" she said. "I would have loved to keep you to lunch with us, but as you can see, everything is at sixes and sevens!"

For no reason at all except from an inherent and invincible capriciousness in the very texture of all terrestrial happenings, it was this silly phrase "sixes and sevens" rather than anything that any other human being had said to her that day that kept teasingly and mechanically forming itself upon her lips as she recrossed the two bridges over the river, on her way to be the first messenger to inform Lexie Ashover that his historic name was in less danger than it had been, two days ago, of disappearing altogether from the face of the earth!

CHAPTER XIV

EMERGING from the ex-priest's house at Bishop's Forley, the Reverend William Hastings, his head throbbing from the excitement of his metaphysical arguments with the German visitor, found himself walking, about six o'clock in the evening, through a street completely unknown to him in the poorer district of the rambling overcrowded town.

He had walked all the ten miles to the place that morning and when he left his confrères he announced his intention of walking all the way home; but the agitation of the arguments they had had in this singular meeting had left him so exhausted that he began to think he would give up all thought of getting back that night.

This point being settled he felt half inclined to return to his heretical colleague and ask for hospitality; but the memory of the wretchedly meagre quarters the man lived in, combined with a vision of the abnormal physical size of the foreign guest, made him shrink from such a step. He decided to dispatch a telegram to his wife and find a room in some lodging house or inn.

The hum and stir in his brain, reverberating and richocheting with dark and disturbing oracles, had driven him blindly on so far from the centre of the town that now, when he came to his senses and looked round for any sign of what he wanted, he found himself as much lost and confused as if he were in a completely strange country.

The sun had disappeared behind a bank of clouds, the edges of which wore that peculiar crimson zig-zag, so portentous and menacing, such as long ago the hawk-like eyes of Dante must have lit upon, as appropriate to the dusky walls of Dis!

This jagged torch flare in the west gave a yet more threatening and lurid aspect to the narrow poverty-stricken streets, abutting upon blackened sheds and upon desolate open spaces. There were shallow pools of rain water in some of these open spaces, pools whose metallic surface, livid and motionless, reflected this sunset glow.

Across the path of the sunset rose up certain dilapidated groups of melancholy and lamentable dwellings, from which a tall broken chimney here and a projected roof-corner there isolated themselves from their surroundings and stood out, black and ominous, against what looked like a vast bleeding wound in the ribs of the world.

Vaguely moving in the direction of the sunset, and falling back, as he went, so deeply into his wild cosmic speculations that he became oblivious of everything around him, it was not until he was right under the wall of a hideously recognizable building that he grew conscious once again of his human identity.

It was the Bishop's Forley Workhouse which he now was skirting, feeling obscurely aggrieved, even as a philosopher, at the rubbish heaps and smouldering rubble mounds that made of this place a sort of Golgotha. One particular spot struck with a vibration of horror the tough nerves of this lover of Nothingness.

It was a sort of local potter's field or pauper burying-ground, and it was entirely surrounded by iron railings some ten feet high. A fresh instalment of young nettles had come back with the coming of spring, but the old ones were there, too, interspersed with anonymous oblong mounds and with rusty tins and rain-drenched newspapers.

The look of the nettles between those tall iron railings presented itself to the mind of William Hastings in a sudden bleak objective light that was unusual with him. He stood still and stared in front of him.

On one side of the enclosure rose the blank wall of the Workhouse. There was only one iron-barred window in that forlorn expanse, and this window had caught from the afterglow in the western sky a certain greenish phosphorescent tint such as may be observed on the flesh of corpses.

On the other side of the enclosure were the roofless walls of a ruined factory: walls from which emanated that peculiar ghastliness of futility which only the work of men's hands, when it has fallen into desuetude, is able to evoke.

What came over the mind of the heretic priest at that moment was a certain day, years and years ago, when, in the wretched playground of a second-rate preparatory school, he had watched a couple of his companions throwing handfuls of cinders taken from a galvanized iron ash bin at the body of a dead rat. He had been the laughing stock of the school even before that day for his inability to conform to their standards, but after that day his loathing for every aspect of youthful high spirits hardened into a misanthropic mania.

His mind recalled the loveliness of the country through which he had passed on his way to this town. It recalled the elaborate patient defence of a certain "hope against hope" advocated by the man from Germany. And there arose in him a ferocious wish that he could take this abomination of desolation, standing here so real and tangible in the twilight, and plant it down among the gracious meadows and the plausible arguments, so that none should escape its terrible significance.

His thoughts were interrupted by the sound of approaching footsteps and he turned his back to the iron railings and waited, listening.

The steps came drifting along slowly, uneven, spasmodic, shuffling, and stumbling. When they came round the corner by the ruined factory he saw that the figure bearing down upon him was that of a woman. She came up to him, muttering as she came, one hand dragging after her a torn umbrella and one clinging tenaciously to a black bag that swung half-open against her side.

When she reached him she stopped short and looked him straight in the face with a long, puzzled, half-understanding stare. Hastings knew her at once. His own mind was so wrought upon by what he had been feeling that it was with something less than a startled shock and yet something more than a casual comprehension that he recognized her and realized what her state implied.

"I've left that place—I'm never going back," she said hurriedly; and then with a pitiable and almost infantile intonation: "You won't tell them, will you? You won't tell any one, will you?"

He sighed and made an awkward gesture as if shrugging his shoulders. The sight of her standing there with that wretched open bag and that trailing umbrella was something he had to deal with, to get into focus, to be drastic and practical about.

Like a slowly retreating wave, leaving only wisps of scattered spindrift behind it, to be blown at random hither and thither, his metaphysical thoughts fell back, fell away, displaying him, as the outside world generally found him, a quiet, self-controlled country priest.

What was this woman doing in the slums of Bishop's Forley? And since he had encountered her there what did it behove *him* to do? For the flicker of a second his instinct was just to bolt, just to leave her as she was; but a kind of aloof, weary pity, mixed with the mechanical habit of his trade, kept him from such an extreme of callousness.

"I can't take her back to Ashover to-night," he thought. "I suppose I must take her to some lodging house." He stood looking at her, as she let her vacant stare wander away from his face and drift along the wall of the Workhouse and over the Paupers' Cemetery.

"Will she come with me?" he wondered, "and if she does, will she behave properly and stay in the room I find for her? She looks as if she might refuse to remain in any one place to-night." And the man began to recall the various hopeless experiences he had had with women in this state.

While he hesitated and wondered what to do, Netta turned away from him and began to shuffle off down the road. This decided him. He stepped quickly after her and offered her his arm She leaned upon it at once with a hopeless docility like that of some dazed and bewildered animal that has lost all power of individual decision. She even permitted him to take from her the black bag, which he at once proceeded to shut, and then to retain in the same hand with which he held his stick.

He did not dare reverse the direction she was following, knowing by experience that such interference with a person's obscure desires is apt to cause any sort of outbreak or collapse. As a philosopher he let the whole thing take what course it would. As a clergyman he automatically assumed a kind of professional responsibility that remained on the alert for each new crisis as it might happen to arise.

They were soon outside the limits of the town. The deepening of the twilight about the solitary roadway, bordered by forlorn allotment patches and broken wooden palings, seemed rather to intensify than to diminish the dilemma of the exploited misanthrope.

It was Netta herself, as it happened, who was the first to bring them back to practical urgencies. The effect of whatever it was that she had been drinking began to wear off in the effort of physical movement and in the impact of the chilliness of approaching night.

"Where are we going?" she said suddenly, bringing him to a pause by a field gate through which they could see the dim shapes of a hurdled flock and catch the smell of turnips and damp straw and sheep's excrement.

"Do 'ee ask the dear gentleman where he be taking of 'ee?" came a startling voice out of the hedge.

Netta pressed instinctively closer to the clergyman's side; for the figure that followed the voice, from what seemed the very depths of a watery ditch, was strange enough to scare the most preoccupied mind.

It was that of a woman so old as to be almost beyond human recognition. Her face was not so much the colour of ashes as the colour of the inside of a white eggshell that has been exposed on the top of a rubbish heap for many weeks. Out of this face looked forth a pair of ghastly sunken eyes, colourless now in the darkness, but possessed of some kind of demonic vitality that made both Hastings and Netta shrink and draw back, as if from the presence of something malignant and dangerous.

"Betsy must have known 'ee was coming, dearie! What else was I nursing my old bones for on way home from town? 'Twas so when the gentleman from London brought his sweetheart this way fifteen years agone. These things be writ in the stars, sweet lady; they be writ in the stars. What else was it that made old Betsy bide in ditch for best of an hour, and her with her partners waiting for she at home? Well! Well! Ye've a-come, ye've a-come; and since this be so and partners be waiting, I reckon Betsy'll be getting home-along before 'tis dark."

She pulled out of the ditch as she spoke a heavy pedlar's basket upon which apparently she had been sitting. Netta still clung with obvious dismay to Hastings's arm and this seemed to arrest the crone's attention. Her sunken eyes, like those of a hundred-year-old weasel, examined every detail in the appearance of the two intruders. There was nothing in any casual inspection of William Hastings to suggest his profession. He was wearing a dark overcoat and a black cloth cap drawn low over his forehead. He might have been a land agent or a doctor or a well-to-do commercial traveller.

"Be the gentleman nice to 'ee, dearie?" said the woman, moving a little nearer.

Conscious of Netta's discomposure Hastings waved her off.

"Where do you live, granny?" he asked.

The question evidently put a new idea into the old trot's head.

"Me partners be waiting for I," she murmured; and then in a shrill eager voice, "But you mid come and see where old Betsy do bide. You mid come and see! Betsy'll tell the sweet lady's fortune and bring down wagonloads o' luck on both your pretty heads. So come along wi' I, young folk; and me and my partners will show you Cimmery Land in the girt wold crystal stone!"

Hastings and Netta looked at each other in the darkness. He could see she was expecting him to make a curt refusal to this apparition's suggestion. It was on his lips to do so and lead her away, but then he imaged to himself the long dreary road they had followed, the hopelessness of hunting for shelter in a district of the town completely unknown to him, and the possibility that even if he did find a lodging of some sort Netta would not settle down in it. The old woman's words suggested that the escape from their present uncertainty which she offered was not far to seek.

He cast his eyes round them. All was silent. All was obscure and dark. His philosophy was authentic enough to make it easy for him to be led, at a moment like this, by any chance-blown straw. It did not really matter! He was tired and hungry. His companion was near the end of her tether. Why not just resign themselves and see what happened?

He looked at Netta with a little shrug of his shoulders. She, too, was beginning to feel her powers of volition ebbing and sinking.

"Very well, Mother," he said to the old woman. "Let's see where you live."

The issue was more propitious than he could have hoped. Their guide led them forward not more than a few hundred paces, and while they were still, both of them, in a sort of exhausted daze, they found themselves clambering up the steps of a stationary caravan; and in an incredibly short while after that it seemed almost a natural thing in their bewilderment that they should be drinking better tea out of better cups and saucers than any that Hastings, at any rate, was accustomed to enjoy under his Nell's housekeeping!

The interior of the caravan was spotlessly clean and the old woman herself under the yellow lamplight presented a much less sinister appearance than when she had first materialized, like an evil spirit, at the gate by the sheepfold.

There was one moment when Netta began nervously looking round, as she stirred her tea, as if desirous of something else, that might have had an unfortunate issue; for Hastings, catching the look, enquired of their entertainer if she could give the girl a taste of brandy.

"Not if she askit me till Judgment Day!" cried the woman. "I bain't a soft-heart and I bain't one for blunt knives or silver bullets, but I be afeard of liquor as if it were a burning lake of adder's gall."

Netta had coloured with pitiful shamefacedness under the exposure of her companion's remark, but she exchanged a quick glance with him now.

"Why are you afraid of liquor, Granny?" said William Hastings.

"Because of *they* in there! Because of me partners!" answered the old woman.

Her repeated references to "partners" had already disturbed Netta's mind and she now looked with much uneasiness at a large Paisley shawl which hung down from an extended rope, concealing a corner of the caravan from view.

No more was said, however, until the gipsy's guests had finished their meal and the table had been dragged aside against the bed leaving a space in the centre of this curious interior empty and clear.

Then the old woman, with a furtive look at her visitors and a queer sort of inarticulate caressing murmur, such as a person might make to soothe the fears of some species of wild animal, drew aside a piece of the shawl and stood there, holding the fabric in her hand and clicking with her tongue. At first there was no response except a feeble scuffling in the darkness. Then to the horror of Netta and to the amazement of her companion there issued forth, holding each other's hands, a pair of creatures that it was difficult to regard as the progeny of the human race.

They were of the masculine sex and wore extravagant clothes; the sort of clothes that one sees on the bodies of dwarfs and midgets in circuses, but it was impossible for either Netta or Hastings to look at anything but their faces, which were more horrible to human sight than if they had been creatures of a monstrous nightmare.

It was only after a second or two that the full ghastliness of the deformity that dehumanized these beings entered the consciousness of the two spectators, but when it did so Netta clapped her hands over her own face and sprang to her feet.

"I can't bear it! I can't bear it!" she screamed. "Take them away! Let me go from here!"

The old woman placed herself between her "partners" and the terrified girl.

"It's all right, Missy," she mumbled, and then making once more the same sub-human caressing sound and the same clicking noise with her tongue, she shuffled the two unfortunates back again into their hiding place and let fall the covering.

It was several minutes before Hastings succeeded in pacifying Netta and persuading her to sit down again; and even after she was seated and was able to smile faintly at her own weakness, several involuntary spasms of shuddering ran through her frame.

"Didn't I tell 'ee?" the old woman triumphantly protested, taking her seat on the narrow bed. "Them's queer to look on and that's God's truth, dearie, but if it hadn't been for the drink, them 'ud be as natural-like as your own self."

"Who are they?" enquired Mr. Hastings, looking with a good deal of relief at Netta who had now overcome her shivering fit.

"Me partners," repeated the hag. "Them as has got old Betsy her poor living, day in, day out, these twenty years. 'Ee should see 'un dance, Mister. Them can dance same as real poppets."

"But who are they?" repeated the misanthrope, displaying more curiosity than Netta had ever seen in him before. She herself had now completely recovered her sober senses, and dimly through a turbid cloud of dream-like images there began to rise before her the vision of what she had run away from and the stark question of what she was to do next.

"Them be the childer of me own daughter, Mister," replied the woman. "Of me own daughter, Nancy Cooper, what Squire Ashover sweeted. When Squire broke with she, her married a decent market-man, what grew 'taties and such-like. But 'twas no use. Squire'd learned her to drink terrible; and 'twas along o' that she runned off wi' Colpepper Thomas the horse-dealer. He were the drunkenest brute between Exeter and London, and it was my own self who buried her. She left me her two, them as has been my partners for twenty years. She swore they were Squire's, and we got hundreds of pounds out of 'ee for they, unbeknown to his lady."

Old Betsy paused, and Netta, who had been staring at her in consternation ever since she began, now began stammering: "Do you mean that those poor things are—half-brothers—to—to—the present Mr. Ashover?"

"That's what old Betsy means and not a word less," chuckled the old woman. "We bain't gipsies, as folks do say; not a bit o't. We be a good Frome-side family same as Squire 'isself. Them Ashovers be Satan's own tribe, every one of them. There be old man Dick who went and hanged 'isself so I've a-heard. He was Squire John's brother. And now they say Squire Rook have got some doxy or other in house wi' 'ee. *He'd* look silly, would Squire Rook, if I askit he for a few hundred for me partners here!"

William Hastings was not surprised to notice that Netta avoided meeting his eye. He had summed up her situation pretty shrewdly by this time and was vaguely considering in his own mind what line of action he ought to take. What he did not feel sure of was whether she had left Ashover with its master's concurrence; or whether, out of sheer weariness of her equivocal position there, she had just drifted off.

Having relieved her feelings by her long confession Betsy Cooper now became taciturn and practical. She indicated that in return for a small sum of money she would retire for the night behind the Paisley shawl, leaving the rest of the interior of her retreat at the disposal of her guests.

"There be a horse-trough under hedge," she remarked, pointing at the door of the caravan, "if so be that either of 'ee want to wet your hands afore night."

The idea of setting out again to look for a more conventional shelter was appalling to Netta. She slipped down the caravan steps upon the roadside for a moment; and did dip her fingers in the receptacle described by the pseudo-gipsy; but the night was so dark and the air so chilly that she was glad enough to return to her seat by the stove. She would have given a great deal just then for a taste of what the old woman had designated as "adder's gall"; but her whole life seemed so broken up that she was thankful enough to have someone, even if it were only William Hastings, to cling to as a raft in that blind sea.

Hastings also made a temporary exit into the environs of their shelter with a view of collecting his thoughts and deciding upon his course of action. He made up his mind to accept this chance-given hospitality, leaving the problem of what to do next undecided till the morning. Netta had begun to look as if she longed for nothing so much as sleep. Well! Sleep would perhaps clear his own mind and give him the clue to the best course of action.

While the old woman herself was filling up her water jugs at a spring that adjoined the trough, Hastings contemplated his companion, who sat on the bed, her head buried in her hands, and wondered what the circumstances actually were that had led to this flight from peace and comfort.

"Netta!" he began, anxious to get some insight into her thoughts.

"Yes, Mr. Hastings."

"I don't want to hurt your feelings or be impertinent, but you must know what I feel, meeting you in a place like this, after knowing you as well as I have."

She looked at him with her forehead wrinkled in hesitation. Could she make a confidant of such a man? Something in her yearned to unburden itself in a torrent of pitiful words, but something else—a queer mixture of pride and timidity—made her feel as if it would be a sacrilege to speak to any living soul of what had happened. With the recovery of her normal self there rose up before her mind, as the one anchor to which she must cling, through ruin, through disaster, through blind misery, the fixed idea that she had effaced herself by her own will for the sake of her love.

"I don't think you know me *very* well, Mr. Hastings," she said, smiling.

He was curiously nonplussed by the ease and naturalness of her tone. Seeing her as he had seen her in the street that night he had forgotten how far she had gone in her acceptance of the light social tone of the Ashover circle.

"No—no! Of course not," he muttered hurriedly; but in his heart he thought: "Oh, these women! These women! One minute they fling themselves upon your neck and the next they take this society air and bow you out of the room."

"I mean it's difficult to explain everything to-night," she pleaded, not missing the clouded expression that had come over his face.

He remained silent for a moment; while she looked at him rather wistfully, wishing that he *was* the kind of person to whom it would be easy to unlock the secrets of her heart. Then he said suddenly: "You won't mind staying the night here with me, will you? I don't see what we can do except leave everything till the morning."

For the moment she misunderstood him and a deep indignant flush mounted into her cheeks, but his matter-of-fact air reassured her and she felt ashamed of herself.

"Don't think I'm ungrateful, Mr. Hastings. You've been most kind to me." And then she added as an afterthought: "But I shall hate taking the only bed in the place!"

Once more Hastings got that funny impression of something put on and artificial in her tone. But he let it pass and the return of Betsy Cooper brought their dialogue to a close.

The arrangements for the night were simple enough after all when they were actually made. Old Betsy retired behind the suspended shawl from the recesses of which emerged the most extraordinary succession of inhuman sounds that Hastings had ever heard in his life.

The clergyman himself, notwithstanding the libidinous leer to which the old woman treated him as she disappeared, a look that was made doubly significant by her manifest recognition of his profession, proceeded to wrap his overcoat round Netta's passive form as she lay on the bed and then, making himself as comfortable as he could in the wicker chair, prepared to spend the night in metaphysical reverie, his pipe lit, and his feet on the stove.

Netta's quiet breathing soon showed she was free from her troubles among the eidolons of sleep, and the man was left to his own thoughts.

Strange enough were his thoughts!

This lonely wheeled hut in the midst of the darkness seemed to him like a silent ship voyaging through the gulfs of immensity. He visualized the unspeakable deformities behind that curtain, sleeping against the lap of that old woman, like Phorkyads against the knees of Medusa; and it seemed to him as if that invisible group were a fitting enough symbol of all that this whole terrestrial ship carried, in *its* voyage, through the godless and measureless ether.

He recalled what Betsy had said of that "Cimmery Land" to be revealed by these pariahs in a "girt wold crystal stone"; and he smiled grimly to himself as he thought of how all over the county of Dorset men and women were moving in their dreams through just such an impossible country.

And then he thought of his book and of how during these last spring days he had neglected it; seduced a little, he could not tell why, by a certain quality in his wife he had not noticed before.

And then letting himself go upon the full stream of his misanthropic fancies, he imagined that this caravan, in which he sat, warming himself and smoking, contained all that was left alive in the whole stellar system. He imagined it transported through empty space; through space star-less, planet-less, moon-less; a vast "Cimmery Land" crystal, void of everything except the unconscious spirit of darkness.

And in the gray hollowness of that crystal, which he now saw as the very rondure of eternity, he was obscurely conscious of a projection of himself, of William Hastings; not the William Hastings who was on the verge of discovering the secret of universal death; but a William Hastings who was a little unhappy boy at school, persecuted by his companions and hating all the world, but able to *think the whole world away* and to sink back, back, far back, into the comfortable arms of the infinite Nothingness!

His last thought, before his pipe fell from his mouth and his head sank back in sleep, was that of the two creatures behind the Paisley shawl. He fancied he saw them emerge from their retreat. He fancied he saw them take each other's hands and dance a strange and monstrous dance, the dance of the Annihilation of All Life; the dance of *That* which was destined to take the place of Life; when the Caravan of the Universe touched at last the circumference of its voyage!

CHAPTER XV

THE day that broke over the five human heads—if Betsy Cooper's "partners" could be called human—domiciled in that fantastic shelter was one of those exceptional spring days that seem created by Nature to protect herself against the too exquisite intensity of her own birth pangs.

It was as if a tenuous film, composed of some aërial stuff more delicate than vapour or cloud, had been drawn like a floating veil between earth and sky.

Every palpable object by roadside or meadow seemed to emerge from a soft enveloping mist that was neither white nor yellow nor purple but resembled rather that mother-of-pearl opalescence which shimmers in the hollowness of certain seashells.

The mental atmosphere in the caravan was, however, as so often happens with our persecuted humanity, in direct and discordant opposition to the tender vaporousness of the relaxed weather outside.

It was an atmosphere of cold and obstinate resolution; disenchanted, joyless, weary, but rigid in its purposes, and defiant of all opposition.

The mood that dominated that small group as they talked over their bread and tea was the mood of Netta Page. So hopeless in its inflexible determination was this mood that it seemed to obsess and preoccupy the girl herself to the complete exclusion of her other normal faculties.

She manifested no more than the very faintest shrinking when, in the process of satisfying the needs of the deformed twins, the Paisley curtain was dragged completely aside.

What she had decided upon was to take the midday train

to London and just lose herself in the unsearchable depths of that great sea of tossing humanity.

Contrary to Cousin Ann's opinion, she had taken no more money when she left Ashover than the coins in her purse; and the appeal she now made to Hastings was that he should purchase her railway ticket for her before they separated.

Hastings refused for a long time even to consider such a thing. What he felt was that whatever may have been the reasons for her unaccountable flight it was incumbent upon him to plead for second thoughts; incumbent upon him to prevent any irrevocable step till Rook had seen her again. He was anxious to hire a conveyance and just take her back to the village, leaving it to herself and Ashover to settle their difficulties when they met. If he had had the least inkling of the fatal visit to Tollminster, it might have given him a clue as to how to act, but the situation being so dark and obscure, all he could think of was just to retard the rush of events.

It was unfortunately true, and he had had to confess this to the obstinate girl, that the bank he dealt with happened to be in Bishop's Forley, so that if he once agreed to lend her this money all they had to do was to wait till the hour for the building to open. She dragged this out of him by wild talk about pawning her cloak and rings, but he cursed himself for his candour when he found how ardently she jumped at it.

Old Betsy Cooper listened with intense interest to all this talk and hurried off with alacrity to find pencil and paper, when, the discussion concluded at last and Hastings conquered, Netta insisted upon writing a letter for him to take to Rook.

Had the clergyman been more of a man of the world, had he been less hopeless and disenchanted himself, he might have held out against her entreaties. But what could he do? He couldn't put her by force into a cart bound for Ashover; and to leave her to trail round in desperation through the pawnshops of this forlorn town seemed more heartless than to accede to her wishes.

A vague idea did for a moment cross his mind that he might leave her imprisoned in Betsy Cooper's care while he hurried back himself to Ashover; but even so abstracted a disciple of Paracelsus was too well acquainted with the tenacity of women when under the power of a fixed idea to give more than the attention of a second to such a scheme.

Another line of action that flashed through his mind was to send the old woman off to despatch a messenger or a message to Rook, while he while himself held Netta by force just where she was. But Netta's impatience, shut up with him there alone for half a day, in close propinquity to those Deformities, was more than he found himself prepared to face. Had she been a younger girl or a weaker girl, the thing would have been easier. He could have dominated her then by sheer official authority. But how could he dominate a self-possessed, reserved woman, her own mistress, knowing exactly what she wanted, and knowing exactly what she wanted of him?

The end of it was that with Netta's letter to Rook in his pocket and with all the money he had had on him transferred to Betsy's pocket, he started off with the girl through that vaporous spring haze on their way to Stockit's Dorset Bank.

He found no difficulty in drawing out the money from his small savings. The difficulty came when it was a question of giving her something beyond the actual price of the ticket so that she should not find herself penniless when she reached London.

Another woman perhaps would have been unpersuadable over this, too, but as long as the money she made use of was not Rook's money Netta's scruples were feeble and easily over-ridden. He had the satisfaction of knowing, before they separated, that what she finally accepted was enough to keep her alive for at least a month after she reached town, and even longer than that if she were very careful. But if she yielded on this point and seemed quite vague and uncertain as to whether the money were a loan or a gift, she became as rigid as adamant when Hastings asked for some address.

"London is enough address for any one," she said, with that peculiar society tone that Hastings found so difficult to put up with. "You'll hear of me, if I become a celebrated actress," she added more naturally.

Hastings had taken for granted that since he had made it possible for her to escape he was in a position to demand her address, and this point-blank refusal outraged his sense of justice. When he understood that she really intended to remain obdurate, he began to regret that he had not made this stipulation earlier, made it before the means to exact it had passed from his hands.

It was eleven o'clock when this conversation took place, and the London express left at noon. The girl entreated him to say good-bye to her before she actually went to the station. She was nervous, she said, lest someone should recognize him, even if she herself passed unnoticed.

Her umbrella was rolled up neatly now and her black bag looked eminently respectable. No one would have recognized in this quiet dignified woman the forlorn creature of last night's encounter.

They went together into a little dairy shop and had a luncheon of cocoa and halfpenny buns on a marble counter. It was then that, in a final attempt to change her resolution, he began to emphasize the unfairness of the course she was taking and its cruelty to Rook. The girl's reply to this was to break, without a moment's warning, into a passion of silent weeping. Her big tears, for it was a peculiarity of Netta's to shed very large tears when she wept, came literally splashing down upon the marble table and reduced all his arguments to silence. Even at this juncture, however, he was struck by the manner in which women can give way to mental anguish and yet retain their consciousness of practical exigencies. For even in the midst of her tears he saw her glance at the clock and begin feeling in her purse to make sure she had not mislaid the money he had given her.

It came over him like a sudden illumination, the tenacious power of life in human beings, this mysterious life, against which he was waging his insane metaphysical war!

For Netta pulled out of her pocket one of those tiny handkerchiefs, compressed into the shape of a small puff-ball by being clutched in the palm of a feverish hand, such as all the lovers and all the sons of women see so often *without seeing*, as if they were the handles of doors or the knobs of bedposts, and after rubbing her cheeks and adjusting her hair looked straight into his face with a spontaneous smile.

That smile, more pitiful and more heroic than anything Hastings was destined to witness for many a long day, returned to his mind more than once in the course of the next twenty-four hours. It followed him back to his cottage by the water meadows. It followed him to his supper table. It followed him to his bed. And when he was next seated at his desk, reassembling the dark threads of his devastating philosophy, it troubled his sentences and ruffled his thought in the same way that the discovery of a gleaming bracelet in an ash pit would disturb the occupation of a gatherer-up of cinders.

Though there was so little of a link between them, the mere sense of the fatality and finality of the step she was taking made it difficult for both of them to bring themselves to the irrevocable moment of saying good-bye. He walked with her lingeringly down the narrow street, with its rows of little greengrocers' and confectioners' shops, faintly hoping as they went along that even yet, at the last, she might draw back from her desperate plunge.

They passed a vulgar modern hostelry entitled the Antiger

Arms just before they reached the final turn to the station; and quite casually and with that peculiar kind of dull, sick, superficial curiosity, such as must often be the mood of condemned criminals as they are led to execution, the girl glanced into the little carriage yard of this place.

Her fingers clutched her companion's wrist.

"There's Mr. Twiney!" she whispered.

Hastings did not need to be told. With a rush of fierce relief, which showed how far below his misanthropic indifference his uneasiness at Netta's departure had gone, he recognized the familiar figure of the most affable of his parishioners.

Netta made now an instinctive movement to escape; but the priest held her arm tightly and pulled her into the yard after him, past the painted shafts and the muddy splashboards of a long line of farmers' gigs, till he had attracted Mr. Twiney's attention.

"Mr. Hastings! Lord 'a' mercy on us! And Miss Page! Well, I'll be blotted out of Book! Ay, won't Squire be glorified to see 'ee! A've been raging and carrying on like a ferret in a poke. It's been hither and thither with him and no mistake; no rest, no sleep you might say, since he drove wi' I to get tied up to's cousin. Ye've a-heard of *that* goings-on, I reckon? 'Tis all over Dorset. Tied up and married *he* be, safe and sound; but a's had no pleasure in't so far; only hither and thither, as a person might say. But a'll be a man again now, belike, the poor gentleman, now you've a-found this lady, Mister Hastings!"

The clergyman looked at Netta to see if she had caught the drift as unmistakably as he had done himself of Mr. Twiney's words.

Her head was rigid on her neck, but tilted a little to one side, like a flower-pot on the top of a dahlia stick.

"Mr. Ashover and Lady Ann are married, you say?" She repeated the words as if they were an echo of something else, of some other, quite different words that were resounding in her own ears.

Mr. Twiney looked at them now with an expression of grave concern upon his countenance. It came over him that he had "let his tongue hang out" as his wife Eliza was wont to express it.

"That be just how it be, miss," he answered solemnly. "But don't 'ee take on because of that, lady," he added anxiously. "Gents like our Squire do marry or not marry same as the likes of I do throw peelings to pigs. 'Tis a small matter to they, lady. Why, 'tis nothink at all! They sleeps the same; and they eats the same. 'Tis a kind of whimsy with they, and I'm blind sure Squire'll be as joyed to see 'ee as if he ain't never set eyes on that grand young woman what is now his lawful missus!"

Hastings slipped his hand into his waistcoat pocket and glanced at his watch. It was a quarter to twelve. In fifteen minutes the express would come in. In twenty minutes it would have come and gone.

He found himself looking nervously at the entrance to the yard. At any moment, he thought, Rook might appear on the scene and settle everything!

Netta might have easily noticed both these significant movements on the part of her indiscreet protector; but at the close of Mr. Twiney's speech she had produced a lead pencil and a bit of paper—legacies, both of them, from their night with Betsy—and had begun writing hurriedly and quickly. She held up the paper now toward William Hastings.

"That'll find me in London," she said. "But you must swear to me, by God's truth, that you won't show it to Mr. Ashover. Do you swear that?"

Confused and bewildered by the rapidity of her movement, and only anxious to retain her with him till the train had gone, Hastings gave her his promise.

"I shall want to know how he gets on," she murmured hurriedly, repossessing herself of her black bag which he had placed on the ground. And then with her hand on his arm: "But you swear you won't even tell him you've got an address? If you do, if you give him the least hint, remember you've broken your word!"

She need not have pressed her point so desperately. In the earlier hours of their contact the priest's consideration had been mostly for Rook, who, after all, was his patron if not his friend. But, as so often happens in these cases, when one enters an emotional imbroglio from one particular entrance it is likely enough that one comes out of it on quite the opposite side. Hastings had been swept so far into the tide of Netta's feelings that it was impossible for him to remain the neutral spectator he had been at the beginning. The mere fact that she had taken him into her confidence as she had done drew him to her side and compelled him to divide his loyalty.

As he took from her this little bit of paper he saw a look on her face which made him realize her identity as he had never done in the days at Ashover; realize it in the way human beings so seldom do realize these mysteries as they pass and repass in the casual encounters of life.

At the very moment, however, when this new perception broke the hard crust of the clergyman's sensibility, Mr. Twiney, who had been staring at the entrance to the yard, suddenly called out in stentorian tones: "There he do go! There he do go!"

Hastings looked up and saw the figure of the Squire of Ashover on the farther side of the road, running as fast as his legs could carry him in the direction opposite from that of the railway. Rook had made a point of being on the platform to see that particular express go; but a policeman in the station, of whom he asked the eternal question he had been asking all day and night, had reported that he had just seen a woman, exactly corresponding to the description given, eating with someone in a little dairy shop in the town. "But whether she's still there, Mr. Ashover, I can't inform you, sir."

If Mr. Hastings had been more of a strategist and less of a philosopher he would have clung to Netta at this crisis and made Mr. Twiney pursue his master. Instead of doing this he completely lost his head, bolted out of the yard into the road, and ran up the street after him, shouting: "Mr. Ashover! Mr. Ashover!" at the top of his voice.

A great brewery van nearly rolled over him as he tried to cross, and he had to draw back from under the very horses' heads; and when he did get over, Rook was already some twenty yards away, running at a great rate, entirely oblivious of the fact that any one was following.

The policeman's words had filled the unfortunate man with that sickening desperate hope that trembles, by its own extravagant impetus, on the verge of certainty. As he ran, he already saw Netta in the small shop; saw himself rushing in upon her there; saw himself hugging her savagely to his heart; saw the illuminated look with which she would greet him; felt a flood of sobbing, ecstatic relief, as if a dead body, loved beyond everything in the world, had been restored to life.

It came over him with a blinding rush of tragic certainty that if he let Netta slip out of his hands now at this moment she would disappear completely into the void. To find her, to speak to her, to hold her *now* was his one chance!

He was actually within a few paces of the very place where the girl and Hastings had had their hurried meal when the latter overtook him.

The priest was too breathless to do more for a moment than stand gasping. As he struggled to speak he could hear in the distance the unmistakable thunderous sound of the Great Western express rolling into the station.

"She's there!" he gasped. "Rook, she's there! She's got her ticket for London!"

The unhappy victim of the hunting dogs of remorse did not delay a minute. Like a leaf in the wind he turned his face; and breathing hard as an animal that reverses his track, he rushed off the way he had come, scattering the astonished pedestrians and making the drivers of market carts and trade wagons turn round to stare at him.

It had not been wasted, even on the indurated skull and irresponsive nerves of Mr. Twiney, that as the man ran so desperately north-northeast, the woman hurried with equal precipitation south-southwest.

He returned to the stable, and in order to be what the poet calls *utrumque paratus* (prepared for either event), he began harnessing his long-necked mare, expressing, as he did so, his own commentary upon these events into her cavernous ear.

"He've a-run *from* train and she've a-run *to* train! That's how things do go, Liza, me beauty. 'Tis a pity for man and beast, me lass, that 'tis so, but so 'tis and us has best reckon on't. He *that* way, she *this* way! 'Tis only to be trusted, me little hoss, that since World be round and Christmas be coming, this poor sorrowing gent and his sweetheart'll cuddle down yet, comfortable and sly, spite of all accidents."

Philosophers *may* have had, ere now, sufficient detachment from human feelings to contemplate the cruel tricks of time from the point of view of eternity; but though William Hastings, as he followed his desperate patron at a slower pace, endeavoured to regard these things with ironic equanimity he found himself listening with the most agitated attention to the distant puffing of the great green-painted engine as it waited in the station.

As for Rook, driven, as it might seem, by the Eumenides themselves, he had no strength left for any thought in his head except to reach that platform before the train moved out. On this return run he no longer visualized his encounter with Netta. His heart seemed on the point of bursting in his body, as he dashed along, keeping to the roadway in spite of the traffic, so as to be less impeded.

He did suffer from a vague impression as he ran that if he only could find breath in him to shout her name the girl would be bound to hear him and unfasten her carriage door, even if the train were moving. But, as it happens in dreams, his voice seemed to die away, ineffectually, in his throat. The nearer he came to the station the more clearly he could hear the heavy snorting of the locomotive, waiting like a great leashed hound to rush forth again upon its way.

He ran faster yet, and still faster, a strange enough figure in his long flapping ulster, his arms bent at the elbow, his fingers digging into the palms of his hands. Every second that passed seemed to him like something more living and terrible than just mere *time;* seemed to him like the pulse beat of a long-drawn-out gigantic arm—the invisible arm of his desire—the fingers of which were already clutching the door handle of Netta's compartment, at which the railway guard was standing now with his whistle at his lips.

The whole world was reduced to a very simple equation at that moment, to the coming together for ever, or to the rending apart for ever, of Netta Page and Rook Ashover. Nothing existed for him, as his breath came in gasps, but the formless outline of an unspoken cry, a cry that implied words and yet was never destined to be uttered in words; the cry, "Netta, stop! Netta, stop! Netta, it's all right!"

He actually heard the guard's whistle now and the louder responding whistle of the engine. He rushed blindly forward. He did not realize that he was shouting wildly as he ran. Afraid that he would not have time to force his way through the doors and the crowds of the waiting room, by an infernal piece of misjudgment, one of those fatal blunders that seem like the very hoof of a demon outstretched to trip a man up, he veered aside when he heard the train moving, and rushing round the corner of the building, saw himself jumping on to the platform of one of the last carriages, perhaps of the guard's van itself! God! There were high iron gates at this spot; gates to climb over which he would have had to be a veritable acrobat.

It was over. It was all over. He was too late.

He shook the iron bars of the gates with his hands, and out of his mouth came a hoarse frustrated howl.

The train was moving too fast now and his eyes were too blinded to see her face at the window; but she saw him, and a kind-hearted commercial traveller in the seat opposite her was horrified to see a quiet-looking, white-faced woman leap up and begin fumbling with the handle of the door. "Can't get out now, missy!" the worthy man protested; pulling her back with gentle firmness into her seat.

When William Hastings arrived at the station he was more disturbed than surprised to observe a small crowd of porters and cab drivers collected round the gates to the left of the waiting room. At his appearance on the scene they thinned themselves out and he was aware of the figure of Rook Ashover, seated on the ground with his back to some iron railings, gasping for breath and crying like an infant.

"Ashover! Rook Ashover!" murmured the clergyman, recovering his own breath in long deep sighs. "You'll see her again, Ashover! You can find her again!"

As he uttered the words he felt the silly futility of them, and the two pencil scrawls he had in his pocket, the letter and the address, seemed to possess pulses of their own which beat in unison with the beating of his heart.

He got Rook on his feet at last. The wretched man insisted upon going into the station and making enquiries about the next train to London. There was no train at all, it appeared, until six o'clock that night and *that* was a slow stopping train that did not reach town till after midnight.

Even Rook, distraught as he was, realized the folly of pursuing his friend any farther that day.

It was, however, only by degrees, only after they had walked slowly back to the Antiger Arms together, that the full stark hopelessness of the situation dawned upon the distracted man's mind. London! How could he possibly find her in London, whatever day he went, or whatever train he took?

While they were waiting in the hotel yard for Mr. Twiney, who had retired to the tap room, Hastings handed over to Rook the letter which Netta had given him. Rook opened this as he stood there and read it leaning against the wheel of the gig; while Hastings went discreetly off to call the driver.

The letter ran as follows:

DEAREST ROOK:

I beg you not to think hard of me because of the drink. I did it because I had to do it. Don't think hard of me, Rook, my dear, dear love. I did it for the best, but I can't stand it any longer. Don't worry about me. I shall be all right. Good-bye, dearest Rook. There's nothing for you to feel sorry about. . . .

NETTA.

With his eyes full of tears and his mouth drooping at the corners, in that grotesque twitching way in which a proud man struggles against breaking down, Rook folded up this letter and hid it carefully in his pocket.

He had recovered a good deal of his normal equanimity by the time Hastings brought Mr. Twiney back from the tap room; and that excellent man remarked to them both as they drove off, sitting side by side: "'Tis a wonder, gentlemen, 'tis a Bible wonder, how what do seem worse to we than dirty weather by thik old Gorm signpost do in the latter end when us turns about, seem Heaven's own blessings! 'Tis a wonder that so't should be. But so 'tis; and us has got to reckon wi't."

The long drive back to Ashover was broken by only one brief stop, when both Mr. Twiney and Hastings insisted upon Rook's drinking a glass of beer and eating a bit of cheese. The sky remained overcast all the way by that same strange filmy veil that Hastings had noted when he first awoke in the caravan.

They reached Ashover by the middle of the afternoon; but when they approached the house Rook commanded Mr. Twiney to stop the gig.

"Hastings!" he said, "would you do a good turn for me?"

The priest, who had been throughout their drive singularly divided in his mind between his loyalty to Netta and his obvious duty to Rook, expressed himself ready to do anything.

"Get out here, then, would you? And run into the house and ask for Lady Ann? You might tell her that I've driven on to the village with Mr. Twiney and that I rather think I shall stay the night with Lexie. Will you tell her that? Oh, and you might tell her, too"—he hesitated, conscious of the alert interest of Mr. Twiney—"you might tell her—well!—everything that's happened; just as it *did* happen! Will you do that for me?" And he helped the clergyman to descend from the cart, and then, calling upon the driver to drive on, got up again into his place.

CHAPTER XVI

IT WAS the third day of June, and Pandie, having "done" the occupied chambers of Ashover House, was busy cleaning the windows and brushing the floors of the two small rooms which opened upon the landing opposite the large front bedrooms.

The bedroom above the dining room looking out upon the linden tree was still used by Rook. Netta's bed was covered by the same counterpane. Netta's clothes still hung in the mahogany cupboard. Netta's modest cold-cream pots and bottles of eau de Cologne still stood on the old-fashioned washstand.

Lady Ann, too, now Lady Ann Ashover, had not moved out of the great "spare room" above the drawing room, which had been allotted to her from the moment she first arrived.

It had been a shock to Rook's mother and something approaching a scandal to the inhabitants of the kitchen when it became evident that the master and mistress of the house did not intend to share the same room. Martha spoke of it with hushed voice and gloomy solemnity to Pod, the evangelical sexton.

"It be contrary to nature, that's what I do say, Mr. Pod. Contrary to nature and contrary to the blessed Scriptures."

The sexton had no quarrel with this sentiment. Indeed he was prepared to go further than his friend in his reprobation of "these heathen ways what the gentry do pick up in their travels." He put the case to Mrs. Vabbin with convincing logic. "If the holy Lord had meant us to sleep single He would never have put it into our brains to hammer up these here double beds. Double beds means sleeping double. Any turnip can see that. And who would have thought of girt double beds if the Lord hadn't whispered into the patriarchs' ears them holy texts about the Woman being subject to the Man?"

Mrs. Vabbin's enormous countenance, with its little nose, little mouth, and little eyes, shone with a kind of interior lustre as she imbibed these oracles. "Pod be nothink to look at," she remarked to Pandie afterward, "but when he opens his mouth to speak, the Holy Spirit do fly out'n and make a person's heart grow weak, same as they girt drums down at Patchery Fair."

As April passed into May and May began to take upon itself the appearance of a summer month, Mrs. Ashover's concern over this unnatural behaviour of the Squire and his bride began to quiet down. As far as she could see, the two treated each other just exactly as they had done before; and the knowledge communicated to her by Ann—for the niece concealed nothing from her aunt—of the child the girl expected before that autumn was over, was so unspeakably gratifying that everything else sank into insignificance in comparison.

It was an infinite relief to her, too, that not for one second would Lady Ann consider the idea of her leaving Ashover. It was also a pleasant surprise to find that in the thousand and one details of managing the establishment, details passionately precious to the old lady's heart, she was not going to be interfered with in any way by her daughter-in-law.

The return upon the scene, gradual but sure, of the "county families" of the neighbourhood, was also a source of intense and secret satisfaction to the little woman. Lady Ann seemed ready to leave this aspect of her new life as completely as she had left the domestic side of things, entirely to her aunt. Mrs. Ashover found it difficult to persuade either Rook or her to take the least interest in the little society visits that began steadily increasing in number as it became more and more certain that *that woman* was gone for good.

For the aunt it was a new light on her niece's character to find that Lady Ann despised the "county families" and detested every sort of "society," being quite content to spend her days in long rambling walks alone with Rook's dog, or in just sitting on the seat under the linden listening to the thrushes. It was almost as if Netta's mania for unsocial solitude had been bequeathed to her successor; but the happy old lady was too preoccupied with the success of her grand scheme to bother her head very much over this new phase or to worry herself as to what it indicated regarding the relations between husband and wife.

The third day of June was Mrs. Ashover's birthday; and now, as Pandie went in and out of the two little rooms she was attending to, rooms kept scrupulously clean in a sort of contented emptiness, as if waiting to be turned into a day nursery and night nursery when the autumn came, it occurred to her mind that it was time to remove the old lady's breakfast things and receive her orders for the day.

Through the open windows and the open doors of that panelled landing the warm sunshine was pouring into the old house bringing with it the pleasant sound of the mowing machine and the sweet smell of cut grass.

Pandie hummed to herself as she went up the short flight of polished steps that led into the "new wing," as it was called, at the end of which, looking out upon the orchard and upon the yellow gorse and green bracken of Battlefield, was her own bedroom and that of her friend Martha.

Taking off her rough apron and tidying herself before the glass, preparatory to ascending to the third floor which was almost entirely taken up by Mrs. Ashover's long, low-ceilinged boudoir, the red-haired servant changed her humming into the erratic strain of an ancient Somersetshire song, such as in all probability had never been heard before in that Frome-side manor.

She moved to her open window, as she sang, tying up the strings of a spotlessly clean apron and rolling down her sleeves. Leaning out of the window she soon met the gaze of two elderly men resting at that moment in leisurely contentment from the not very arduous task of mowing the grass paths of the kitchen garden. It was the privilege of Mr. Twiney to steer the lawnmower, while Mr. Pod, acting the part of a human horse, marched in front, pulling the machine along by the aid of two slender cords.

Mr. Pod was now with the utmost deliberation emptying the box of the lawnmower into a wheelbarrow, which was already half full of velvet-soft dark-green grass.

Mr. Twiney was lighting his pipe. The two old cronies standing there in the early summer sunshine between the rows of immature green peas and immature sweet peas, between a border of yellow pansies and a hedge of pink and white peonies, gave an added sweetness to that ribald Sedgemoor song, as the hard-worked damsel trilled the lines like a great red-poll'd bird.

Both of the elderly men were arrested by her voice; but Mr. Pod only gave her a cursory glance and turned to his wheelbarrow. Mr. Twiney, however, jerked his thumb in the direction of his companion, as much as to say, "Don't 'ee mind *his* being there, me pretty maid; I be a-listening to 'ee!" and then made a deliberately gallant gesture, beckoning the wench to come down and speak to him.

Pandie did not hesitate. With one glance at the looking glass on the chest of drawers she ran down the stairs, slipped through the scullery unnoticed by Martha, and emerged from the back door.

Mr. Twiney, moving leisurely toward her in his shirt sleeves, had the air of one whose professional duty required him at that juncture to survey with care certain gooseberry bushes and certain rhubarb stalks and to pick off the blighted leaves of particular standard roses whose buds were still green.

Arriving at length, after many pauses, at a point opposite to the kitchen door he proceeded to greet the red-haired maiden with a gesture of dignified surprise; and, like a man interrupted in the preoccupation of a lifetime, began to unbend the austerity of his visage into a grave but indulgent urbanity.

"A fine morning, Pandie, me girl!" he exclaimed. "'Tis good growing weather for both beasties and roots. Them peas be wonderful well come on, and I've never seed they onions so high. 'Tis the same with me old mare down in village. She do put her old head out of winder and hollers to every think what traipses along. 'Tis real summer be come this season, same as it used to be when us were childer. Old Pod he be got his bit of mead, down by river, most ready for cutting; only it be so full of them sour weeds that 'twon't make good hay. Now there's me own little patch up by churchyard, maidie! Pod had dunged his mead with no-think but cow-dung, while all them dead folk, right down from King Charley's time, do make hay for I and me old mare!"

Pandie nodded her head sympathetically.

"You was always a lucky man, Mr. Twiney," she remarked. "Though they do say that grass what's nourished by corpses makes milk bad for butter. But maybe horses be different; though me old father used to say that horses be more human than we be. They *be* sensitive beasts, I reckon. But maybe your horse takes kind of natural to churchyard grass, Mr. Twiney?"

"Maybe she do. Maybe she don't," replied the gardener. "There be more sextons in my family, come to think of it, than there be in Pod's; though he did cut me out with the parson that is. Not that I grudge it to the poor man. If it weren't for what he gets for thik little job 'twould be workhouse for 'ee; and all the village do know it."

The two interlocutors stared gravely at each other, while over them both floated, on waves of aromatic sunshine, the scent of currant bushes and gooseberry bushes, the scent of heavy peony blooms, of the sun-warmed leaves of budding briar-roses and of the barrowful of cut grass.

Pandie pondered in her heart for some piece of news that would enhance her value in the eyes of her friend. She recalled the occasion when by a heaven-sent piece of luck Lady Ann had been so nervous and "beyond herself" that she had confided in the servant that this was the beginning of her fifth month of pregnancy.

How dearly would she have loved to reveal this fact to Mr. Twiney!

Still more powerfully was she tempted to speak of a matter that she and Martha Vabbin had been discussing for the last three months: the extraordinary change that had taken place in Lady Ann's own habits and ways; her long preoccupied silences under the linden, when she neither sewed nor read; her long hours of heavy thought at her own window, her long lonely walks with the dog.

But the most agitating urge of all, an urge that only the strongest inbred loyalty could have resisted, was the desire to make a confidant of Mr. Twiney concerning the two separate bedrooms and concerning certain inexplicable scenes that had taken place between the Squire and his new lady, scenes of which she had not even dared to speak to Mrs. Vabbin herself!

Suddenly the right inspiration came to her.

"'Tis Missus's birthday to-day—the old Missus's, I mean. And she've a-got in her head to do what she've a-always done on her birthdays; and that's to picnic out in Antiger High Mead. I'm a-going up now to her room to take her orders for what Martha have to pack in hampers; and pretty soon they'll be sending for thee own self about driving of them out there."

Pandie's face got as red as her hair as she made this announcement. She looked at the gardener with austere gravity, as much as to say: "You see before you the possessor and revealer of all hidden things."

But Mr. Twiney's composure was unshaken. "I've a-known all that these last two days, maidie," he replied, "and I've got somethink to tell 'ee what'll make 'ee stare like an owl to hear of! I heard tell of it from our policeman when he was last round here. It seems that that old bitch-wife Betsy Cooper, what folks call a gippoo though she be no more a gippoo than I be, have moved her cart up from Bishop's Forley to thik crossroad where Gorm Lane do meet Antiger Lane. 'Tis where the old bitch can snare all the rabbits she've a mind to and where there be a fresh-water spring. The place have naught to do with our Squire. All that belongs to he over thik way is that Antiger High Mead where I be to drive the Missus."

Pandie's face, which had been growing more and more downcast under this recital, which transferred the glory of knowledge from herself to Mr. Twiney, now brightened again.

"There be nothink in the move of a gippoo's cart to make an ado over," she murmured complacently.

"That'll be all thee do know on't," retorted the gardener. "It'll open your eyes a bit wider, me maidie, when I tell 'ee that Squire have gone and gived old Betsy two ten-pound notes for to clear out of thik lane; while she be biding where she be to get more from 'un! They say them innocents she do take money for be Squire John's by-throws; seeing as how he was so smitten wi' Nancy, what was their mother."

Pandie did indeed open her eyes at this. She even became a little pale. She had more than once heard this legend about Nancy Cooper, but the idea of her master being actually compelled to hand money over to Nancy's mother shocked and startled her feudal pride.

She opened her mouth to utter an indignant protest, when the voice of Martha from the scullery behind her put an abrupt end to the colloquy.

"Pandie, where Pandie, be 'ee? Missus be ringing for you, Pandie!" And then in a tone intended to be heard across the currant bushes as far as Mr. Pod's wheelbarrow: "What be come to 'ee, lass, that you go interrupting a man's work like that? Come into house, lazy-bones! Come into house!"

While the family's dependents were thus discussing affairs in the kitchen garden the new lady of the house was displaying signs of unusual agitation as she sat in her favourite place under the lime tree. The tree above her was in full blossom and the air hummed and murmured with the innumerable bees that hovered about it. All the sweetness of the early summer flowed in upon her senses, one little thing and then another bringing its own especial evocation of delicate memory. The sudden sound, and equally sudden cessation of sound, as a blue-bottle fly droned past her; the rich lazy movements of two tortoise-shell butterflies, the swifter flight of a great yellow brimstone butterfly; the gleam of the pearl-white blossoms of an elder bush in the shrubbery, held up like a cluster of filigreed chalices to catch the distilled quintessence of that golden morning; all these things and something beyond them all, something which might have been defined as the accumulated anonymous fragrance of all those flowers of the field that lack any definite scent and yet from their very number *must* fling some sort of essence of themselves upon the air, such as buttercups and moon daisies, flowed in upon the mind of Cousin Ann and blended themselves with her troubled thoughts.

Every now and then she would cast a nervous glance at the three windows of Mrs. Ashover's boudoir; windows which projected from the eaves of the house, above the level of her own and her husband's more spacious bedrooms. She seemed to shrink from the idea that the old lady was aware of the agitated state of her mind, to shrink from the thought of that erect little figure watching her inquisitively, anxiously, from one of those three windows!

She kept rising from her seat under the tree and making little impatient excursions, first to one flower bed and then to another, as if to assure herself that the green stalks of this or that plant of the later summer had not blossomed into sudden miraculous bloom. What a rush of turbulent thoughts whirled that morning through Lady Ann's brain! What troubled her most through it all was the agitating change that seemed to have taken place in her own nature. She had always regarded herself as being "in love" with her cousin; but, as she looked back on those early days of her association with him, the feelings she had then, compared with what she suffered from now, seemed a mere girlish fancy.

She would have supposed, from her own abrupt and straight-cut psychological insight, that the condition of being pregnant would have completely saved her from this miserable infatuation. She would have predicted, had the case been that of another woman, that the new interest, the looking forward to a new life, would have detached her from the child's father, numbed her emotional nerves, lulled her into a kind of lethargic trance and nourished her upon vague, sweet, half-animal dreams.

Nothing of the kind! She found herself wretchedly and shamefully in love with her husband, torn by the most humiliating of all forms of jealousy, jealousy for a rival whose personality she despised and whose existence had melted into air and become nothing.

She was jealous of a ghost, of a shadow, of a memory, of an unreal image conceived by pity and begotten by insane remorse.

Every incident in her new life with Rook hurt her to the inmost nerve of her personal pride. It was humiliating that he refused to share her room. It was gall and wormwood to her to see him day by day so submerged by his own fixed idea that he went to and fro like a man in a trance, seeing nothing, hearing nothing, noticing nothing; taking not the least interest in any of her projects, taking no interest at all in this child of theirs which was now so emphatically beginning to manifest its presence. She had broken down under the strain once or twice; and, as Pandie alone in that household knew, there had been some terrible and lacerating scenes between them.

But on the whole she had just suffered in silence; and she was at least thankful that the sagacious old mother remained, as far as she was able to detect, completely oblivious of what was going on.

What was preying on her nerves at that particular moment was not, as it happened, connected with Netta at all. It was connected with Nell. Rook that morning had carelessly announced that he had been invited to lunch at Toll-Pike Cottage. Well! There was nothing but what was perfectly natural in that! It was only by pure accident that she had that very morning, about half an hour ago, caught sight of William Hastings, mounted on his bicycle, riding at a steady speed in the direction of Bishop's Forley.

He might of course have been on his way to visit some outlying districts of their own estate. He might easily have been running over to Antiger Lane to call upon Mrs. Drool, to buy honey or eggs from her, or because Binnory had got into some trouble. At the thought of Binnory she instinctively shuddered, remembering the experiences of her wedding day. Her nerves were all jangled that fine June morning. The chances were surely all against the man's having set out on so long a ride.

And yet were they?

It was unusual for Hastings to go visiting in the morning. He generally wrote in the morning and went his rounds in the afternoon. Besides, Ann knew that he had a philosophical colleague in that squalid town.

She wished she could remember what the reply had been to Mrs. Ashover's invitation, asking the vicar and his wife to picnic with them in Antiger High Mead. Had Nell Hastings accepted for them both or only for herself?

The abnormal condition of Ann's nerves was proved by the fact that she actually got up now with the intention of going straight to Mrs. Ashover's room to satisfy her mind on this point; and then, no sooner had she reached the front door than she felt so invincible a repugnance at the thought of encountering the old lady that she reversed her steps and came hurriedly back to the shelter of the lime tree.

She had "The Bride of Lammermoor" with her in the old Ballantyne edition; but in vain she tried to forget the sting of her trouble in following the proud griefs of the unhappy Ravenswood! All she could do was to gaze absentmindedly on those quaint illustrations; too abstracted even to brush away the little ivory-coloured yellow-stamened blossoms that kept falling on the open pages.

The uncertainty of it all was the thing that seemed to hurt her most. She visualized the thin harassed face of Rook, as she had seen it that morning, as he perfunctorily kissed her cheek, preparatory to setting out on some too-long-delayed piece of business connected with his property. He had been growing steadily thinner, steadily sadder and quieter, ever since his marriage. He was invariably kind and considerate to her. The only violent scenes they had were scenes deliberately and wantonly brought on by herself in the irritation of her nerves.

Over and over again she had told herself to wait till the birth of her child. Then, surely, if it were a son—and she had made up her mind that it *would* be a son—Rook's interest in her, in life, in everything would come back!

All would be well if only this poisonous stabbing of jealousy would cease.

What a thing jealousy was!

It was like an actual sharp thorn pressing into her flesh; a thorn through which a little rankling stream of fermenting poison ran like a corrosive acid through her secretest veins.

Cousin Ann smiled bitterly and miserably with her beautiful full lips. How she would have mocked at herself half a year ago! How she would have sworn that such emotion as this was nothing but a silly female affectation! It was like a definite material malady. She could almost localize it; as if it were a malignant growth within her physical frame, counteracting with its persistent throb the sweet lethargy of pregnancy.

The thing was made worse for her—though she herself was unconscious of this—by the innate primitiveness of her nature. With all her social breeding Ann Gore was essentially an unsophisticated, natural, savagely simple creature of earth. Rook's ingrained cerebralism, those dehumanized ponderings upon life, into which he used to fall, even in the early days of their companionship, had never so much as penetrated the outer surface of her smooth feline skin.

But it was this uncertainty that maddened her most!

Was Rook unfaithful to her with this funny-looking little clergyman's wife, as well as with the ghost, the phantasm, the wraith of Netta?

She had felt so confident that if once she got hold of him, in complete intimacy, the spirit of her youth, her vitality, her strength would soon put an end to these aimless philanderings!

But there had been no intimacy! The ghost of Netta stood unappeased upon their bridal threshold holding them apart. And kept like this at a distance from him, all that was most formidable in her, the beauty and power of her body, the pathos of her pregnancy, the resilience of her spirit, remained unused, unexerted, disallowed.

She was like a strong and beautiful plant cut off from water and sunshine by some invisible yet insurmountable barrier.

The uncertainty, the miserable uncertainty! It was becoming more than she could bear. With a resolute movement, more obstinate than any she had yet made, she rose now from that sun-warmed seat, adjusted her summer hat, pulled her embroidered smock smoothly down over her rounded hips, picked up her long-handled parasol, and started off toward the entrance of the garden.

She emerged into the road and, with slow deliberate steps, without hurry or hesitation, proceeded to cross the bridge.

All that enchanted summer landscape quivered and vibrated around her in an air that was almost windless. The tall grasses of the ditches and hedges seemed like undulating ripples in a vast umbrageous sea, of which the deep-grassed hayfields, full of buttercups and red-stalked sorrel and white daisies, were the untraversed ocean floor, and the hills and copses and orchards the spray-flecked waves!

The Frome itself flowed high and strong that day between its banks, where tarnished marigold stalks and freshly sprouting rushes gave to the muddy roots of willow and alder the dignity of microscopic African swamps, with newts for alligators and tiny green frogs for hippopotami.

The fecundity of summer filled every little hollow and crevice in those banks with infinitesimal growths, nameless except to botanists, many of them the embryonic sproutings of plants destined to wait a couple of months, or even longer, for their time of flowering.

Crossing the bridge and following the familiar road, now white and dusty between its uncut grass borders, Lady Ann walked forward with a firmer, surer pace. She used her red parasol as a walking stick. Her summer hat, with a cluster of tulips beneath its wide brim, was held high and straight on her proud young head. Her mind, as she walked, was not oblivious of the singing of at least three invisible skylarks, out of a sky as blue as a Della Robbia plaque; and in the vigour of her youth, even against her conscious mood, her senses began to respond to the jocund pulse beat of a prodigal, lavish, irrepressible countryside!

It was about half-past twelve when she arrived at the wooden bridge near the sheep-washing pool which marked the halfway point between Ashover Church and Ashover village. Just beyond this bridge, on the side of the road opposite to the water meadows, there was a little field path which mounted slowly, through a couple of green barley fields, to the rough open country below the northern extremity of Heron's Ridge.

Cousin Ann climbed over the stile leading to this path and began slowly ascending the incline between the divided masses of immature green stalks. Skylarks trilled and trilled above her head, one song blending with another song in that peculiar timeless ecstasy which seems to have more in common with the scarlets and blues of some great Venetian picture than with any musical instrument.

She had crossed the first barley field and had reached a thickset hedge which was now a mass of new leafage mingled with a weight of dim, half-faded hawthorn blossoms. She turned to her right at this point and moving slowly through the feathery grasses between the green barley and the hedgerow advanced to a spot on that sloping hill from which she could look straight down to the back entrance to Toll-Pike Cottage.

All the wide stretch of the Frome valley lay before her, green and lovely in the quivering translucent noon heat of that summer day. Out of the level plain of the brook meadows the familiar outlines of the church and its gravestones stood like a reef of gray rocks in a green halcyon sea.

Between the excited woman and the mysterious power emanating from the mortality of that place there was a formidable and strange correspondence—a correspondence that did not rise to the level of the girl's mental consciousness, but affected her, none the less, and strengthened, so to speak, the despotism and magnetism of her will. Lady Ann had all the Ashover dead behind her; supporting her, sustaining her, protecting her; as if she were a faithful seaworthy ship into whose care they had entrusted their last forlorn hope.

The kitchen door of Toll-Pike Cottage stood wide open and from where she stood she fancied she could detect the form of Nell's enormous tabby cat asleep on the sun-warmed threshold.

She hesitated a little now; not for any emotional reason, but because her instinct as a landowner's daughter reluctated at the notion of crossing a field of corn that was already ankle-high.

She moved on a few hundred yards, searching for the faintest vestige of a path. The brown mould as she continued to thrust her parasol between those spears of diaphanous green was not yet so devoid of moisture as not to emit its own peculiar smell—the smell of the actual flesh of the earth—which mingled so naturally with the sharp sour scent of the growing stalks. In spite of the obstinate anger in her heart which was driving her forward, her whole physical being found itself responding to that immemorial contact, the contact of a woman who has conceived, with that which conceives and brings forth all life.

Suddenly her spirits rose in triumph. There *was* a little path!

From a gap in the hedge, evidently an ancient secretive way, for the sticks that had been twisted across it had burst into leaf, right down to Nell's very door, ran a narrow ribbon of brown soil dividing the expanse of barley.

Lady Ann hurried down this path, her skirts swishing

against the growing corn, her parasol grasped tightly in her hand. The back door of the house *was* wide open and Nell's great cat, the Marquis of Carabas, *was* fast asleep on the threshold. Cousin Ann with noiseless fingers unhooked a little wire gate which was there, and stepping over the ridges of William Hastings's potatoes, approached the door.

The thrill of action, of any kind of action, had so quickened the pulses of her energetic spirit that, strange though it may sound, she felt happier at that moment than she had actually felt since she came back from Tollminster on her wedding night. A situation that would have appalled a different type of woman seemed to rouse some ancestral fighting spirit in Cousin Ann; seemed, in fact, to assuage, with a sort of sporting or hunting recklessness, the lodged and rooted trouble within her. . . .

What was that?

She paused, listening, one hand pressed against the lintel of the door; the other stroking the Marquis with her parasol, as he rubbed his back against her ankles.

From within the little front dining room came the sound of the arranging of knives and forks, of plates and glasses; a sound which conveyed instantaneously to Cousin Ann's mind the fact that whoever they might be who were to partake of that meal, the meal itself was not ready.

And then, all suddenly, she heard Nell begin to sing as she put the finishing touches to her luncheon table. She sang the famous song of the exiled courtier in "As You Like It":

> Who doth ambition shun
> And loves to live i' the sun,
> Seeking the food he eats,
> And pleased with what he gets,
> Come hither, come hither, come hither
> Here shall he see
> No enemy
> But winter and rough weather.

The girl had no power of voice and no very good ear. She sang in a careless and irresponsible way, but the jealous heart of the listener did not fail to catch the strain of thrilling feminine happiness that underlay the notes of the old song.

"She is alone and she is expecting Rook," thought Lady Ann; and a sudden spasm of fierce anger took possession of her; an anger that caused the red parasol to tremble in her clutch as if it had been a deadly weapon.

Then in a flash it came over her what to do. In a far better trained and far richer voice than Nell's she burst out into the melancholy Jaques's bitter antiphony:

> If it do come to pass
> That any man turn ass,
> Leaving his wealth and ease
> A stubborn will to please,
> Ducdame, ducdame, ducdame!
> Here shall he see
> Gross fools . . .

She did not get any further; for Nell, who had stood for a minute with a plate of almonds and raisins in her hand, frozen helpless with panic, now came hurrying down the passage, her cheeks white, her mouth grotesquely open.

"Lady Ann! How you did startle me! Is anything the matter?"

Cousin Ann made no movement to meet her, no movement to cross the threshold. She waited till the girl came quite close.

In one second Cousin Ann became as calm and collected as if the two of them were casually meeting at a garden party at Antiger House.

"I'd no idea you had a voice, Nell," she said. "We must have you bring your songs up to the house one of these nights."

Nell bit her lip. The tone of that "we must have you"

was like the tone Lady Ann would have used to some pretty little girl in the village; to some child of Martin Pod or Mr. Twiney.

"Won't you come in?" The words were uttered mechanically. She had meant to say something altogether different.

"Oh, no, no! On no account!" Cousin Ann responded. "I'm lunching at home. It was so nice of you to ask Rook to join you and your husband. By the way, could I see Mr. Hastings? I've got a message for him from my aunt."

Nell's mouth opened and shut and her eyes looked as frightened as a hedge sparrow's when it hears the hunting call of the shrike.

"William isn't here," she murmured faintly. "He was suddenly called away and I thought—I thought it would be silly not to enjoy the pleasure of such an important guest. If I had had any one to send, I would have begged you to come, too; but I expect even then it would have been too hurried a notice. But now you *are* here, I do hope you will stay? And let me have the pleasure of getting a meal for you both?"

"My husband has not come yet, then?" enquired Lady Ann. Nell shook her head. "Well. Perhaps I will rest a little then, if I may?" And taking the other's consent for granted, and carrying it off with so natural an air that it was impossible for Nell to resist her, she moved hurriedly down the passage and went straight into the dining room.

There lay, betrayed and revealed to those jealous eyes, a pathetic little love feast prepared by the young girl for the man she idealized.

The two places had been laid opposite each other in the curve of the bow window. A great bowl of blue violas, light and delicate as butterflies' wings, more like wild flowers than garden flowers, stood in the middle of the table. At the side of one of the plates, evidently the one to be used by

Rook, lay three pansies, a purple one, a yellow one, and a black one.

Lady Ann surveyed this spectacle with a sudden indrawing of her breath. So this was the way the sad, remorseful, preoccupied Rook was taking his diversion. And he had lied to her, with the worst kind of lie, the treacherous half-lie of a coward. He had duped her, under the guise of conscience-stricken remorse. What hypocrisy, what calculated cold-blooded hypocrisy. And she, too, in the state in which she was.

Her indignation blotted Nell completely out of the picture. Her one desire now was to meet Rook face to face.

"How prettily you have set the table," she said with a smile. "I'm sure Mr. Ashover will be delighted when he sees what a charming welcome is awaiting him. Well, I must be off."

She moved back to the kitchen door, quite oblivious now of her pretended need of resting.

Nell was too miserable and bewildered to say one word in answer to this. All she could do was just to follow her visitor meekly down the passage.

"What a lovely cat," Cousin Ann now murmured, stooping down to stroke the Marquis of Carabas. "Oh, by the way, Nell, my aunt expects you to her picnic this afternoon. Will your husband's engagement prevent his being there, too? What shall I say to Mrs. Ashover?"

"It's very kind of you, Lady Ann, I'm sure. But William can't possibly come, I'm afraid."

"Well. Come yourself, anyway," cried Cousin Ann, picking up her parasol and passing out. "You don't happen to know from what direction Rook will descend upon you?" she added gaily as Nell waited in the doorway.

The girl shook her head.

"Because I'd like to ask him whether *he* intends to come to his mother's little party. But never mind. My aunt and

I will survive it, I daresay, even if we are the only people there. Good-bye." And without waiting to see the closing of the door—the door that was no longer to be left open for intruders—she retraced her steps by the same path she had followed to reach the house.

She knew that Rook's business that morning had taken him to the other side of Heron's Ridge, and her only impulse now was to walk quickly enough so as to intercept him while he was still out of sight of the cottage.

She was conscious of feeling a little tired and faint as she ascended the hill; but her anger, which now settled into a calm, cold fury, was strong enough to support and sustain her; and it was not long before she reached the stile into the second barley field, breathing heavily as she went.

Here again she came to a tall hawthorn hedge voluptuously scented with the richly perishing May blossoms. She forced her way through a half-open gate which must have remained exactly in the same position since the early spring, for the feathery grasses grew high and tall around it and several wisps of bindweed had encircled its lowest bar.

She had calculated her movements to a nicety. There, approaching her with swinging careless steps, down the rough slope of a gorse-grown incline, was the figure of her husband. He saw her in a moment; stood for a second as if confused at her appearance; and then came on resolutely to where she awaited him, her free hand pressed tightly against her waist, her face white and drawn.

"Ann! What are you doing here?"

She made a little gesture that kept him at a distance while she recovered her breath.

"I—thought—I—would like—a little stroll—but it—it has been rather too much for me."

She spoke in gasps, but she smiled quite naturally into his face and her tone was calm.

"You'd better come into Nell's with me," he said. "You

can't walk back in that state. She'll be able to look after you."

"I think—if you don't mind, Rook—I'd prefer to rest a little where I am."

As she spoke she sank down, easily and spontaneously, among the grasses of the hedge. Her movement disturbed several white butterflies which fluttered away along the edge of the field, while a scarlet-and-black cinnabar moth flew heavily from a tuft of clover to a patch of hedge parsley; where it paused, as if to regard the tulips in her hat, its wings drawn close against its body.

Rook knelt down anxiously by her side, his face sad and puzzled; his heart infinitely weary of the whole business of living. Above them, lost in the cerulean blue, not one lark, or two or three or four, but it might well have been a whole classic chorus of larks kept up that arrogant, brazen, importunate monotone of ecstasy, such as no instrument of string or pipe, no voice of man or woman, could lift from the earth; the very voice, so it might well seem, of the griefless, merciless, exultant sky, whose colour mocks all human passion by the impact of its appalling simplicity!

CHAPTER XVII

IT DID not need a long interlude under that June hedge to bring the colour back to Lady Ann's cheeks and a more even beat to her indignant heart.

The savage and primitive portion of her nature was soothed and satisfied by the fact that she was keeping Rook away from Nell; and something more subtle within her was quick enough to divine that Rook's attitude under this turn of events was not at all the attitude of a baffled and disappointed amorist.

He seemed just simply concerned and agitated at her own state and apparently took it for granted, without any other thought, that he would now have to support her back to Ashover.

He took her back there, indeed, leaning on his arm, by the very same path she herself had followed an hour ago; and his tenderness and solicitude were so obviously genuine that, though her anger against him still smouldered on in the depths, she confined its expression to nothing more serious than a few bitter sarcasms. It still remained possible that "everything," including that carefully prepared table, was on Nell's side; possible, after all, that Rook had not wilfully deceived her, that he had not, in fact, himself been aware of the convenient absence of Mr. Hastings.

Though she was feminine enough to derive a wicked satisfaction in the thought of that table left there without a guest; those yellow, purple, and black pansies lying unseen by any eye except her own, she was practical enough to insist on

Mr. Twiney's being sent back at once to the village with orders to call in at Toll-Pike Cottage on his way to his own house. "And put the back seat in, Twiney, please," she said, as they encountered the gardener on their return. "And don't forget to call for Mrs. Hastings as well as Mr. Lexie! I shall drive; so there will be just four people. Mr. Ashover will walk."

Perhaps even the outraged feelings of Lady Ann would have been subdued into pity if she could have seen the forlorn figure in Toll-Pike Cottage removing one by one the plates from the dining room and the dishes from the kitchen stove. Nell had seen from her bedroom, to which she had fled to escape the mocking sight of her preparations, the husband and wife making their way back across the fields; and the sight had filled her with a cold, miserable hopelessness and a bitter shame.

Lady Ann's intrusion had been particularly cruel because there had been a pitiable struggle in her own conscience over the whole affair. She had seen very little of Rook since the fatal day of Netta's flight. He had given her very few chances to see him. And though she had struggled heroically to keep up the level of her emotion to what she had felt when they met in that drawing room, there were occasions when, as in the case of this unfortunate lunch, her longing to be with him, to have him to herself alone, overpowered her conscientious scruples.

The fact that she had steadily struggled to efface every instinct of possessiveness from her feelings so as to be of genuine use to him as a friend made it all the bitterer and more shameful to be thus exposed in her lapse from her self-imposed standard by Lady Ann's appearance.

Nothing is harder to bear than a fall from one's own ideal when it is grossly interpreted. A portion of oneself ranges itself then on the side of the accuser and the rest of one's being writhes helplessly under a double shame.

By degrees she managed to calm herself enough so as to restore her house to its normal appearance. She hadn't the heart to taste any of the things she had prepared. Standing by the cleared and empty table she nibbled a few biscuits and drank a glass of milk. Of those three pansies, she slipped one without a smile into a little apple-green volume of Shelley and squeezed the other two into a vase of wild flowers.

She had just done this when she saw Mr. Twiney at the gate. She went out to meet him. He announced in a circuitous rigmarole that he had been ordered to call for her with his gig.

"'Tisn't as if me cart were a gentleman's cart; but the lady up there," and he jerked his thumb toward Ashover House, "be going to drive me mare, and she expects 'ee to sit on thik back-seat 'long wi' Mr. Lexie."

Nell was on the point of explaining to the man that she had not the least intention of coming to Antiger High Mead; but she suddenly changed her mind.

"I am going up to see Mr. Lexie in a minute or two," she said, "and I'll tell him to expect you."

She let Mr. Twiney depart then; and running back into the house and up into her room began to put on her walking shoes and her newest hat.

Half an hour later she was sitting in Lexie's little garden at the rear of his cottage; confessing everything that had occurred. The enclosure was a small one, defended on two sides by rough gray walls and divided from a small orchard at the back by a briar-rose hedge.

The girl sat opposite Lexie in a low deck chair; and as she talked to him from beneath the shady brim of her hat she kept pulling at the green blades and brittle daisy-stalks of the grass patch beneath them.

From one of the apple trees in the orchard came the sweet reiterated quinquapartite moan of a wood pigeon; and

Lexie, as he listened to what his guest was saying, found himself repeating the measured Shakespearean quatrain that he loved so well:

> Whereupon it made this threne
> To the phœnix and the dove,
> Co-supremes and stars of love,
> As chorus to their tragic scene.

"And so she came right into my room and saw how I was expecting your brother—saw everything. And I could tell just how it struck her, just what she thought." Nell sighed miserably and threw away a little handful of squeezed-up daisy-stalks which fell across the burnished golden face of a dandelion.

"She thought what was the truth," said Lexie, the leathery folds and humorous wrinkles about his eyes deepening into a hundred crevices and furrows as ruggedly emphatic as those on the bark of his favourite elm tree.

The girl lifted her chin and leaned forward. "You know it wasn't like that," she said. "You know I hadn't the least wish to make her feel badly. It just happened that William was out for the day and I thought it would be nice to cook a meal for him—for Rook, I mean. I hadn't talked quietly and properly to him for weeks and weeks."

Lexie did his best not to smile as if he were speaking to an irrational child. He was conscious of a certain irritation against his brother. How badly things were arranged in this world. Why couldn't all this romantic "havering" be concentrated on someone more fitted to appreciate it than this master of manias and inhibitions!

"And now I've really hurt her," Nell went on. "She'll think that there's something serious between Rook and me and be up in arms whenever we meet. I've made things worse for Rook, made them much worse; and there's actually nothing between us except what you know perfectly well—just what I happen to feel myself—which doesn't matter to Rook at all or to any one else!"

Lexie's half-conscious irritation against his brother betrayed itself now in spite of his humorous lightness of tone. "Tell me, Nell," he said, "are you in love with Rook?"

The outrageous directness of this question did not seem to annoy the young girl. For some curious reason those plain significant words gave her a kind of relief. She liked the way Lexie uttered them. She liked to hear them being uttered.

"In—love—with—Rook?" she repeated very slowly. "I wonder if it *is* as thrilling as that. I certainly have never been in love with my husband if 'in love' means the sort of feeling I have for your brother. And yet William has been much nicer to me lately. He's been steadily nicer and nicer since he stopped writing his book."

"Has he let it go altogether?" asked Lexie.

She shook her head doubtfully. "I wouldn't like to say that and I think it would be unlucky to say it. It might start him off at it to-morrow. But he certainly has not written a line—I know that for a fact—since the end of April. He wrote a little after Netta went away; and then he stopped. Why do you suppose he stopped?"

Lexie replied to this only by one of his characteristic grimaces.

"Don't you worry about Ann, my sweet Nell," he said. "She'll be just the same to you. And when she's talked to Rook about your lunch, and beaten him up a bit, she'll be the same to him, too! These things are not really so terrible as people think they are. There's a deal of conventional bluff in it."

"Women think a lot about things like that," murmured the girl feebly.

Lexie sawed the air with his hand; a trick of his when he

got excited. The gesture was peculiar to him and its nature resembled the movement a person might make when obstructed by tall reeds in a thick swamp.

"They don't really!" he cried with more emphasis than Nell had ever heard him use about anything. "It's all put into their heads by what they read and by what they hear and by what they think that other people think. Left to themselves women would take these things very easily and very naturally."

As he paused to take breath, for he had worked himself into a sincere agitation now and his gray eyes had become quite large and brilliant, the girl opposite him suddenly burst into a peal of unexpected laughter.

He looked at her with injured gravity, the naïveté of which made it harder for her to recover herself. His self-respect was genuinely outraged; but the graver and more discomposed he looked, the more difficult did she find it to stop laughing. It was as if Lexie had become a church, a funeral, a parliamentary debate, a meeting of scientists. She began to have what children call "a regular laughing fit." She put her hands to her face, and tears of merriment ran down her cheeks.

"What the devil's the matter with you?" he demanded, rising from his chair and approaching hers. His face wavered between sympathy for what might have been hysterical agitation and annoyance at what might have been childish rudeness.

His tone quieted her and she took her fingers from her face and searched about for her handkerchief.

"I'm so sorry," she said, "I'm so very sorry. It's silly of me—— You're a dear, Lexie—I love you very much." And she held out her hand to him.

He took it and refused to let it go.

"What was it that set you off just then?" he asked gravely. "Did I say anything especially ridiculous? Did I give myself away in some unpardonable fashion? Did what I said seem obvious and banal beyond words?"

"Dear Lexie!" murmured the girl, trying in vain to get her fingers out of the invalid's clutch in such a manner as might seem natural and unconscious. "Dear Lexie! Of course you didn't do anything of the kind! What you said was very sensible; and I daresay quite true. It was *because* it was so sensible that I laughed. I don't think sensible things, or even true things, are ever the right explanations when it comes to women!"

Lexie's countenance at that moment would have made an engaging study for some master painter; for some portraitist possessed of the psychological impressionism of Spain combined with the grandiose vitality of Venice. The little wrinkles in the skin of his cheeks indicated that his humour was tickled. An unusually concentrated frown in his heavy forehead suggested that his wits were piqued. While the way his drooping half-closed eyelids reduced his eyes—lately so wide open—to nothing but little narrow slits of amorousness denoted that the accidental imprisonment of a hand that desired to escape had already aroused the satyr in his blood.

"You sheered me off just now," he said, pressing the hand he held against the girl's slender neck, "when I asked you a definite question. I don't believe you're half as much of an idealist as you think you are, you sweet Nell. Why do you keep that hat on? You're not afraid of sunstroke, are you?"

As he spoke he used his free hand to pull out the one hatpin that the girl wore; and in a moment her head was bare. He stooped over her as if to follow up his advantage.

Nell's own sensations at the moment were terribly complicated. His warm knuckles pressed against her neck sent a faint luxurious relaxation through every nerve of her body. She was so full of shame at her recent lapse from her own ideal that a great weariness possessed her heart, a weariness that could easily have found a numbing relief in letting him do what he liked.

But simultaneously with these emotions there suddenly rose up within her, to her own surprise, a surging wave of anger against him. What right had he to behave in this way? What right had he to assume that she would let him make love to her? She freed her hand with a jerk and pushed him back so violently and unexpectedly that he staggered.

"What are you doing, Lexie?" she cried indignantly. "I've told you before I don't like this sort of thing!"

She didn't catch the expression upon his face at this rebuff. She only heard him mutter something under his breath as he moved off; and then she saw him go hurriedly to the flower bed under the wall and stoop down. He seemed to be looking for something among the green shoots of the unbudded delphiniums, something that required much fumbling and searching for, if it were to be found at all.

His body looked so thin and fragile as he stooped over the bed and his head so heavy, that a twinge of commiseration passed through her.

"What silly punctilious creatures girls are!" she thought to herself. "Why shouldn't I have let him kiss me if he wanted to? He's a much finer, a much more interesting human being than I am; and he's ill, too! What a brute one is with one's wretched pride and egotism!"

Lexie had found what he wanted now and came back smiling, his head held high, his hand extended. It was a single lavender-coloured, double French primrose, enfolded in its own large crumpled leaf.

"It's the last left," he said, handing it to her. "Fast-fading primroses covered up in leaves," he added, purposely misquoting; "only this isn't a real primrose. I never have been able to make out what mysterious old associations

I have with this flower. It always gives me a peculiar sensation unlike anything else. Don't you think, my sweet Nell, that there are certain memories in us that come straight down to us from our parents and through them from *their* parents? If it isn't like that, what is it? Memories of our childhood before we were conscious?"

He stopped and they both resumed their seats; he to light a cigarette, she to pin the flower very carefully upon the edge of her dress, against her neck—"exactly," she thought to herself, "where he touched me just now."

"No, no," he said, "don't you let that scene with Ann have any effect upon you at all. I give you my word of honour, Nell, that there's nothing in it—nothing, nothing. She'll be exactly the same to you when you see her next. Please, don't let's have any bourgeois 'not-speakings,' and so on, in our circle!"

"But. Lexie, I *can't* go to this picnic after what happened to-day! I can't face Ann after that! It goes against something in me which doesn't feel at all 'bourgeois,' something that seems just the opposite of 'bourgeois!'"

Lexie peered gravely at her through his cigarette smoke. "You're wrong, Nelly dear. I tell you you're wrong. It's the very best thing you could do; for Rook, for yourself, for Lady Ann, for everyone. It is, indeed!"

The girl bent her head, frowning. She felt an unconscionable longing to see Rook that day. It was a chance she might not have again for many days; and it would be amusing, sitting on the back seat of Mr. Twiney's gig with Lexie.

"How is Rook going to get over there himself?" she asked.

"He? Oh, he'll walk. *Do* come, Nell. Do be a spirited, civilized, sensible girl, and come. My mother will think it awfully funny if you don't. It's her birthday, you know; and rather an event in our family."

The girl looked at him dubiously. "I don't—feel—as if I *could* face her and—and talk to her as if nothing had happened. She must think that Rook and I have been seeing each other much more than we have."

Lexie got up and threw away his cigarette. It fell close to her feet and she put her foot on its thin wisp of smoke.

"Think what a meteorite that must seem," she said, "to the tiny grass-insects. Isn't it hard to realize, Lexie, how all that we feel is only like a little smoke in the grass?"

"What's that?" he rapped out, and moving up to her he took her by the wrists and looked threateningly into her face. "What's that? What's that? Like a smoke? Well, and if it *is*—you dear troubled Nell—that doesn't make it any the less important."

He let her go and remained silent and very grave, looking away from her, away from that sunlit garden, where the early afternoon shadow was just beginning to pass from the gravel path to the box border; away from that piece of dusty white road outside his gate, where that very morning he had picked a bit of yellow stonecrop from the wall and a bit of ground ivy from under the wall, crushing them in his hands and only relinquishing them when Mrs. Bellamy brought him his breakfast, and it came into his mind how perverted, how corrupt, how mad with the worst madness there is in life it was to diminish one jot or one tittle of the unique, the miraculous importance of these heavenly sensations. "Oh, let me live another year—two more years—*three* more years!" he prayed to that June air and those June odours.

It was almost as if it came like a sign of acceptance, of recognition, from some hidden heathen deity, still able to exert his power in that Dorset village, that even as the man and the girl looked into each other's eyes, there sounded from some neighbouring tree invisible to them both the world-old *Cuckoo! Cuckoo!* of the unconquerable augur of sweet mischief.

Lexie's faced relaxed into a smile of thrilling satisfaction; every wrinkle in it deepening and radiating, while he rubbed his hands together. "It hasn't changed its tune yet!" he cried. "The summer is only beginning."

"Very well, Lexie," said the girl with a deep sigh of submission. "I'll go with you. I should only be perfectly miserable if I went back now to the house." She paused, frowning. "I *must* have just a word with your brother. I couldn't endure William's coming back and this whole day being wasted. I don't hate William as much as I used to, Lexie," she added inconsequently.

"No one hates any one when his own life is all right," he said. "Come on, you sweet Nell, let's see if Mr. Twiney's outside. If he isn't, we might walk as far as that."

He moved toward the house. "One moment," he said. "I'll just run in and tell Mrs. Bellamy."

She watched him disappear.

Over her head flew the long-tailed bird, cuckooing as it flew. Awkward and yet rapid in its direct movement, it seemed to her, just then, as if it were no ordinary feathered creature; but rather a mysterious agent of the gods. She felt a sick repugnance at the thought of encountering Lady Ann again; but her desire to see Rook, to talk to him, to hear his voice, grew every moment more imperative.

Far away though it was now, she could still hear the voice of the cuckoo; and in some inscrutable manner the sound of it acted as an irritant to her nerves, making her restless and impatient, making every minute of delay seem fraught with some kind of vague danger to both herself and Rook.

At the very moment when the young girl was thus concerned about him, Rook himself, having eaten a hurried lunch, was walking quickly across Battlefield.

Before leaving the house he had opened his iron cash box and placed two five-pound notes in his pocket.

"I'll settle that business with Betsy," he thought, "on my way to High Mead."

As he passed the Drools' cottage he was observed by

Binnory, who promptly followed him into the lane and overtook him at a run.

"Squire Ash'ver!" cried the idiot breathlessly. "Take I with 'ee to see the gippoos! Take I with 'ee to see them two who be half beasties and half men! Take Binnory with 'ee, Squire Ash'ver, and he'll do summat for 'ee one day! So he will, too, summat 'ee never'd guess at! Take I with 'ee, Squire Ash'ver!"

Rook turned toward the excited boy with a look of positive hatred. He remembered his behaviour to Lady Ann. He associated him with Corporal Dick.

"Go home, Binnory!" he rapped out. "Get home with you, child!" And he quickened his pace to shake off this unwelcome attendant.

He had never been quite satisfied with the accepted version of the lad's paternity. In his heart he had more than once accused Uncle Dick of being his father; but that was at moments when this whole business of the "Ashover immorality" grew to the dimensions of an obsession.

They all had the same taint! His father with Nancy Cooper, Corporal Dick with this gamekeeper's wife, his grandfather with the Corporal's mother—they had all, in taking their pleasure, become the causes of hideous complications.

If he had let Netta alone, perhaps by this time she would have married some honest man and been as happy as women are; whereas now—— His thoughts recoiled from the fantastic abominations his imagination called forth.

"Squire Ash'ver! If I give 'ee them three girt blue her'n's eggs I've a-got hid away, will 'ee take I to see the half beasties?"

The lad was trotting by his side now, his mouth open, his eyes furtive and foxy. Rook began to lose his temper in earnest. There was something peculiarly irritating to his nerves just then in this encounter. It was bad enough to have to deal with old Betsy and her "partners." There came over him an unpleasant sense of being surrounded by crowds and crowds of Ashover bastards, each new one more repulsive than the rest. He felt like Macbeth, contemplating the interminable descendants of Banquo.

"Get away with you, can't you?" he cried angrily. "What do you mean by following me like this?"

"Don't 'ee talk to I like that, Squire Ash'ver," pleaded the boy, his tone wheedling and coaxing.

"Go home!" shouted Rook, and began to stride along even more quickly than before.

But the voice continued at his elbow; for the boy found no difficulty at all in keeping up with him.

"If you'll take I to see the half beasties, Squire," cried Binnory as he ran, "I'll show 'ee where 'tis said Witch Nancy were bedded when they two was born! 'Tis a dry pond up High Mead way, near-along where you be going to eat and drink present. I've a-seed 'un when I were little. 'Twas Granfer Dick showed 'un to I; and he'd a-say how wonderful it were that them things should be born'd, 'long wi' frogs and toads and hedge-pricklies what have their own lawful nature!"

Rook stopped and turned round upon the idiot, furious with a blind anger. He raised his stick as if to strike him a blow. Binnory seemed not the least disturbed by this gesture; indeed, he grinned in his face and did nothing but just skip back out of arm's reach.

Rook went so far as actually to pursue the boy for a stone's-throw or two, in the direction of his home; but when he came close up to him a great wave of weariness and disgust fell upon his spirit and made it impossible for him to lift a finger.

"Go home, I tell you!" was all he could say. But he might have been addressing his words to the elm trees in the hedge for all the effect they had. Whether Binnory had the wit to detect an artificial note in his threats, or whether he trusted in his own obstinate tenacity to get what he wanted in spite of the Squire's anger, his next move was a masterpiece of strategy.

He scrambled up the bank and pushed himself through the hedge into the wood. Once in the wood, he waited till Rook turned to go on again; and then proceeded to run parallel with his victim's advance, keeping the thickset hedge between them.

Under the smooth branches of the newly leafed beech trees he ran; under the darker foliage of the sycamores; under the stinging twigs of the green hazels; over dog-mercury, over pink campion, over the soft unbudded whitish-green spikes of foxglove and mullein. Feeble-winged currant moths flapped against his face as he ran. Greenish-coloured pollen from the stamens of entangled parasitic plants clung to his cap and to his hair. Swathes of pith twine tripped him up. The oozy stalks of half-dead bluebells bent and broke beneath his boots, staining them with sticky vegetable juice. Rook heard him groan now and again as the thorns pricked him or the twigs stung his cheeks; but he no longer uttered any words. All his energy seemed taken up in the effort of keeping pace with his unsympathetic companion.

At last the man could endure the situation no longer. It had begun to touch the limit both of his patience and of his sense of humour.

"Come here, you rascal!" he shouted. "Come here, Binnory, you rogue! If you can run like that over there, you'd better come back into the lane. I'll take you with me! You shall see your gippoos!"

He had hardly finished speaking when, like a rabbit from its burrow, pushing aside the prickly thickness of a holly tree in the hedge, the boy came tumbling and scuffling down the bank.

Rook moderated his pace after that; and the two curiously assorted companions, having made up their quarrel, proceeded on their way down that sweet-scented lane, amicably discussing the weasels, squirrels, and rabbits that kept crossing their path and the various bird notes that reached them from the wood.

They came at last to the grassy clearing, where the lane associated with the mysterious name of Gorm branched off from the other; and there, straight in front of them, under the hedge, was Betsy Cooper's caravan.

The old woman had erected a clothes-line as a sort of extempore tent; and behind a row of vividly coloured garments hanging between two posts the forms of the unfortunate "partners" were visible, seated opposite each other on the ground, their laps full of moon daisies and quaking grass.

Rook could see Betsy herself, a few hundred yards or so down the road, digging up dandelion roots with a knife.

He went straight toward her, leaving his companion to stare at the "half beasties" to his heart's content.

"Ay, Squire! So 'ee be come to I, then; so 'ee be come to Auntie Betsy, same as she told 'ee 'ee would. 'Tis good hearing to me wold ears to catch the sound of thee tongue and see thee wicked smiling eyes again! Thou'rt always welcome, Squire Ashover. Thou'rt always welcome."

"I've brought the money, Betsy," said Rook quietly, manifesting little tendency to respond to her familiar garrulousness. "And now I hope you'll keep your promise and move away."

He put his hand in his pocket as he spoke and produced the two five-pound notes. The old lady's countenance assumed a time-battered expression of senile imbecility, out of the depths of which, like the gaze of a snake peering through a sheep's skull, shone her tiny yellowish eyes.

"Come to cart, Squire Ashover; come to cart. I've got summat to show 'ee afore us puts thik bit of paper across wood and across iron."

Rook replaced the notes in his pocket and followed her submissively to her wheeled house. His chief anxiety now was to get his business done before Mr. Twiney's conveyance, bringing the rest of the party, should appear upon the scene.

The old woman manifested no surprise at seeing Binnory, who was now seated on the grass at a cautious distance from the dwarfs, regarding their infantile play with a mixture of suspicion and fascination.

"He be an innocent, same as they be," she chuckled, glancing furtively at Rook. "Dilly Drool should have come to I for a sip o' tiger-root when she were heavy. My Nancy never missed a morning without taking of it; and 'twould have given her as healthy a babe as maid could wish; only her old man couldn't keep his hands off her because of the drink."

Rook moved aside to let the woman go up the caravan steps in front of him. She turned her head as she reached the top.

"Thee Ashovers be sweet-spoken gents and I don't care who hears me say it; but ye be queer ones with the maids; and 'tis that what brings the thwartings and blightings upon 'ee; for 'tis a sure thing that them as handles ploughs when rye be green and goose-pods be sour finds nothink in meadow when 'a do come to harvest-time save toadstools and devils-bit!"

"What do you mean by 'goose-pods,' Betsy?" her guest enquired, mounting the steps behind her.

"I mean them things in pond-water what ain't water-lilies nor ain't long purples. But come 'ee in, Squire Ashover, come 'ee in; I've a-got summat to show 'ee!"

The old woman made him sit down on the narrow bed which was covered now by a patchwork quilt. She pulled the white curtains across the window, so that the hot afternoon light that poured into that small interior was softened and mellowed.

Then she placed a wooden table in front of him and on the table a curiously woven very old mat, of an unusual and enigmatical pattern.

Rook wondered vaguely what the preparations meant; but his thoughts wandered off to his fixed idea of his bad treatment of Netta and they only returned to his present surroundings when the sound of the steady trotting of Mr. Twiney's mare broke upon that summer stillness.

He listened intently, his face toward the door; but the dogcart passed by without stopping, its occupants apparently undisturbed by the sight of the dwarfs and Binnory.

Betsy Cooper gave no sign that she had even heard the quick trotting of the mare, as Lady Ann speeded it up with rein and whip. What she did now was to place upon the table a perfectly round clear crystal, about the size of a large apple, and so smooth and globular that it was only by putting it down with the utmost gentleness that she rendered it immobile.

"What's that?" said Rook. "Can you see fortunes in it, Betsy?"

"Fortunes!" snorted the crone contemptuously. "You can see the Will of God in it, Squire Ashover!"

The man bent down over this microcosmic symbol of the world he found so hard to handle, and stared fixedly and rigidly into its irised depths. Violet, indigo, blue, green, yellow, orange, red—they were all held in faint solution in the rondure of that prismatic orb.

Betsy stood in front of him, waiting patiently. She did not ask him "if he saw anything." She leaned her hands upon the table and half-closing her eyes swayed a little, backward and forward, humming some obscure gibberish underneath her breath.

Then Rook did actually begin to see something. Whether it was a phantom of the mind, "a false creation proceeding from the heat-oppressèd brain," or whether a flawless crystal of that particular kind *has* the power—as yet unverified by science—of reflecting thoughts as well as objects, the fact remains that he saw the figure of Netta bending over something.

What was it she was bending over? Her head was lowered so that he could not catch the expression on her face; but the feeling he got from what he did see of her was sad without being hopelessly unhappy. It was calm and quiet.

"What is she looking at?" he muttered aloud.

The old woman above him took no notice of his words; but her hummings and mumblings increased in volubility. Then he became aware of what it was that this image of his ill-used mistress gazed at so calmly. It was himself—the form of Rook Ashover—and it lay hushed and white and still in a coffin of dark-coloured wood.

For a second or two longer he looked at this picture in the crystal; and as he looked a great wave of unalterable peace and happiness passed over him.

So deep and convincing was this sensation that when the figures finally faded away and he lifted up his head he experienced that sense of irrational fretfulness and irritation such as people feel when they are awakened suddenly out of a restorative and dreamless sleep.

He pushed the table away and stretched himself. His very muscles felt as if he had just been aroused from a prolonged slumber. He yawned and scowled crossly; stretched out his arms again and muttered: "Ay! ay!" in an intonation of petulant querulousness.

Betsy Cooper took not the least notice of what he was doing. She removed the mat. She took down an old clay pipe from a bracket nailed to the wall and filling it with tobacco sat down upon a chair to smoke. A thin sun-moted stream of light that had found an entrance between curtain and window frame turned her mummy-like face into gleaming gold and the smoke of her pipe into pontifical incense.

Rook rose to his feet and stood over her. He felt drugged and stupid and absurdly childish.

"Where did you get that thing from?" he asked, in a fussy, matter-of-fact, disparaging tone.

Betsy took the pipe from her mouth and stared at him with the slow, patient, satiric stare of thousands of years of sun-burned, rain-bleached wisdom.

"'Tis the Cimmery stone," she murmured.

He began walking up and down that small interior like a wild animal in the presence of his tamer.

"What Cimmery stone?" he demanded abruptly, standing in front of her again.

"From Cimmery Land, Squire," she answered quietly. "And that be the land where folks do live like unborn babes. They don't see nothink, nor hear nothink, in thik place, except what be like the smoke of this 'ere pipe; and when them folks do talk 'mid theyselves it be like the turning of Miller Cory's girt wheel—mum, mum, mum—where us can hear the drumming of wonderful green water and where millstone be all moss-mumbled and wheel be all hart's-tongue ferns! 'Tis real wet rain, what's finer than corpse dust, them folks do live under; and they tell I it be wonderful strange to see 'un walk and talk . . . mum . . . mum . . . mum . . . and thik mist all slivery and dimsy round 'un."

As the old woman spoke Rook became quieter and his nerves less irritable. He could not catch the full import of what she said, but it soothed and calmed him. It was as though she were describing to him the god-like dwellers in some unearthly Limbo—some Elysian Fourth Dimension—out of Space and out of Time—where everything was, as it were, painted with gray upon gray; and where large and liberating thoughts moved to and fro over cool, wet grass like enormous swallows, easily, naturally, without any effort; thoughts that were made of memories and of hopes, and never of logic or of reason; thoughts that came and went under a thin, fine, incessant rain that itself was composed of the essence of memory, the memory of old defeated, long-forgotten gods whose only immortality was in this gray, cool, silent, sadly driven mist!

As he listened to the old woman and watched the smoke of her pipe floating up into the illuminated sun-ray where it broke at once into a hundred silver-blue undulations, it came over him that this Cimmery Land of which she spoke was the thing that he had so often vaguely dreamed of; dreamed of on lonely roads at twilight; dreamed of lying on his bed listening to the sounds of the morning; dreamed of under walls of old buildings in the quiet places of historic cities, when the noons fell hotly and the shadows fell darkly, and from hidden fountains came the splash of water.

Dreamed of! But never, until this moment, *felt* within his conscious brain, as something that out of the turbulent arena of life might actually emerge—emerge and establish itself—as this crystal had done, projected like a Bubble of Eternity from some great under-tide, beyond the reach of loss and longing and lust and loathing, beyond the reach of everything for which humanity has found a name.

His reverie was interrupted by strange sounds from the grass plot outside.

"Thik innocent be pestering me partners," said the old woman, rising stiffly to her feet. "Best gie I them banknotes afore ye leaves," she added, screwing up her eyes and swallowing her thin lips till her face resembled a Chinese idol.

Rook put his hand in his pocket and drew out the two notes. The old woman took a bit of wood out of the unlit stove and a plain steel knife out of a drawer. She laid both these things on the table where the crystal had been, the former on the top of the latter. Taking the notes in her hand, she spat three times on them and spread them out upon the wood-and-iron cross which she had thus constructed.

"I'll be off from troubling of thee any further, Squire Ashover," she said. "And if I bain't much mistaken thee and me will follow different ways here-to-come."

By the time Rook arrived at Antiger High Mead his mother's birthday picnic was in full swing.

The late afternoon sun cast long richly coloured shadows across that small hayfield. The haymakers had left their work to go to their tea and their half-filled wagon was standing under a large pale-leafed ash, its glossy chestnut-coloured horse, monumental as a statue in classic bronze, patiently munching a great heap of fragrant grass.

The three women were sitting with their backs to him so that Lexie, drinking his tea with epicurean satisfaction, his eyes missing nothing of the magic of that June day, was the first to see him approaching.

He came round from the western side of the field, so that his shadow, advancing before him, fell across the whole party and extended to the wheels of the wagon under the ash tree.

"There you are!" he cried in a half-jocose, half-reproachful voice, a voice that carried the nuance that they might have waited for him before actually beginning their repast.

"You're late, Rook," said his mother, turning her head and making room for him at her side.

"How is it we didn't pass you?" enquired Lady Ann. "Is there any other way? I thought you had to come by the road."

"So sorry I couldn't manage that lunch with you, Nell," he said, taking no notice of the questions asked him and putting out his hand for a cup of tea. "Ann has explained how it happened, I expect? She'd got farther afield than she ought and I had to take her home."

"Oh, Nell *perfectly* understands!" cried Lady Ann, selecting a water-cress sandwich from the basket beside her. "Your apologies are so belated, my dear, that they're really unnecessary. Aren't they, Nell? It's just like Rook, isn't it, to be so formal in his explanations? You might think that we were all strangers, instead of—what we are!"

Her rich flute-like laugh rang across the hayfield and, her gray eyes, full of voluptuous malice, played mischievously over both her victims.

"I think it's quite right for Rook to apologize," said Mrs. Ashover. "I'm sure that's the kind of thing I brought you up to do, isn't it, Rook?" The little old lady surveyed her eldest son with ironic complacency.

"You brought us up to nothing of the sort, Mother," remarked Lexie, holding out his cup to be refilled by Lady Ann and laying it carefully down by his side as he prepared to light a cigarette. "You put into our heads such an idea of the greatness of the family that every single thing we did was done as if an Ashover couldn't do wrong."

"I'm sure Mrs. Ashover never taught you anything of the sort," threw in Nell gently, smiling at Lexie with a clinging, lingering smile on her unclassical mouth, while every nerve in her body responded tremulously to Rook's closeness to her. "I'm sure the outside world regards you all as possessed of beautiful manners. Don't you think so, Lady Ann?"

"Is that a subtle suggestion that however much I may marry an Ashover I must always remain an outsider?" retorted the daughter of the diplomatist.

Nell blushed. This kind of equivocal badinage was always embarrassing to her; and she felt vaguely that Cousin Ann was in some indirect way trying to make a fool of her.

Rook, who had been drinking tea and eating bread and butter like a man in a trance, now put down his empty cup, glanced whimsically at his wife, and holding out his hand to Nell to help her to get up, said quietly and naturally: "Come for a stroll with me, Nell, then, will you? And we'll make up for our lost lunch by finding a wood-warbler's nest. There used to be a lot of birds in these woods. Do you remember the black-cap's eggs, Lexie? How we left two in the nest; and I broke all we took; and then got angry when you wanted to go back for one of the two we'd left?"

While he threw out these casual remarks to cover their retreat, Nell was struggling to regain her composure; struggling to get strength of mind enough to look Lady Ann in the face. The temptation to obey him and follow him was more than she could resist; but she knew well that his naïve masculine assumption that he was carrying off the situation by his flippant tone was entirely unjustified.

To Nell's consternation Lady Ann herself at that moment scrambled up from the grass. "Black-caps!" she cried. "Oh, Rook, I'd no idea you had black-caps so near Ashover! We used to have to go so far out into the woods to see one; and then you generally heard it without seeing it!"

Rook's mind at that moment sank down into a veritable gulf of misery. He saw himself for the rest of his life having to deal with this strong, capable, high-spirited woman, for whose personality at that moment, although she was the mother of his child, he felt not one single shred of love, but rather something that bordered very closely upon sheer hatred.

This occasion would probably be repeated again and again and again—the same difficulty in getting away; the same inevitable dissimulation; the same teasing contest. And yet he ought to have been gratified and thrilled at having the love of a girl as beautiful and distinguished as Ann Gore.

The truth was, he thought, as he let his brother Lexie take up his wife's challenge and talk about black-caps, the truth was that men didn't want the love of women, unless under circumstances that gratify a certain subtle craving in their *life illusion*, a certain subconscious *self-love*, which is deeper than any pride, or any vanity, or any conceit, or any lust! They want to love women themselves, in every possible kind of way, wickedly, tenderly, chastely, licentiously; but when it comes to a matter of *being loved*, they become harshly exacting and suffer from every sort of antipathy and repulsion unless in the one single case where their life illusion is satisfied.

The most immoral of men are monogamists in this sense. They are perfectly prepared to exploit the love that women give them and turn it to their own profligate account; but it rarely occurs to them that such love is in itself a rare and exquisite commodity. It presents itself rather as a tragic and burdensome appendage to a lovely and magical experience. It only becomes precious, as a thing in itself, when it answers the hunger of this mysterious life illusion which is deeper than possessiveness and stronger than sensuality.

Women, on the contrary, so Rook's troubled thoughts ran, regard their own "love" as so rare and so precious, that it fills them with a sense of intolerable grievance when the man they care for slights it or undervalues it. They are ready then to accuse such a man of every sort of meanness and baseness. With malicious inspiration they label him with just the particular faults that are most hateful to him, associating their indignation against him with everything in the world except the one thing for which he is really to be blamed; the fact, namely, that he was betrayed into speaking *their* language when he was using them in *his* fashion.

He remembered vividly the bitter taunts that his wife had levelled at him as they lingered together in the hall before he started. They were all unfair, unjust; beside the mark. And yet they hurt him just because they touched him where he was most sensitive.

She had accused him of having concealed from her what she called his "love affair with a little chit of a married schoolgirl." And as they watched his mother coming down the Jacobean staircase she had flung at him the taunt which she divined would pierce him the deepest.

"It's *her* blood in you, you know! That Gresham blood!"

While these thoughts passed through Rook's mind his eyes were fixed upon the corner of the hayfield where Mr. Twiney's horse had been tethered. They had taken him out of the shafts and he was nibbling now at the new honeysuckle shoots in the leafy hedge.

Great bushes of elder, crowded with flowery "patens" of ivory whiteness, stretched their branches down to the level of the cut grass; and the look of these heavy blossoms against the close-shaven ground gave to Rook a sharp sensation of some old childish memory that made his present sadness all the deeper.

The badinage that had been passing like an invisible shuttle-cock among that group of people subsided at last. "Don't break the black-cap's eggs this time," cried Lady Ann after them as Rook moved away with Nell toward the edge of the wood.

They were still within sight of the others and were examining the tiny crimson petals of the first wild rose they had yet seen really in bud when the girl murmured anxiously in his ear: "We must never do it again, Rook. We must be very, very good from now on! Your wife is very angry with me. She despises and hates me, and I can't stand it. Oh, Rook, how cruel it is for everything to be like that, when it's all so beautiful!"

He looked at her face vacantly as it was lifted up to him from under her broad-brimmed hat. Her mouth was twitching. Her eyes gazed at him through so much water of unfallen tears that he began absentmindedly to speculate—as if in the presence of a scientific problem—how it could be possible that they could remain as they were without brimming over and running down her cheeks.

"Come on," he said abruptly. "Let's get out of sight."

They moved forward a few yards, skirting the hedge. Nell trailed her fingers through some tall umbelliferous flowers that grew amid the uncut feathery grasses. She hung her head and her heart felt weary within her. Was he in a mood to disregard all she'd been saying—all she had been vowing to herself of renunciation and effacement? Was he going to take her into all that lovely freshly budded greenery, into all that mass of leaves and undergrowth, of ferns and moss and entangled branches, and just seize upon her without further scruple?

Her heart began to beat violently. A vibrant tremor of magnetic excitement rose from the very centre of her soul and, like a mounting stream of quicksilver, quivered through the nerves of her body. By anticipating his unscrupulousness, his reckless indifference to consequences, as something already present before her, she was conscious of a sudden responsive thrill of complete abandonment.

They came to a gap in the hedge. Her heart beat so wildly that she was afraid the man must hear it. Where had fled all her self-sacrificing vows, all her resolutions of effacement? Glancing round at the others before she let him pull her up to his side on the hedge bank, she saw Lady Ann had gone over to the place where she had tied the horse and was re-adjusting the bridle so as to give the animal more scope to feed. There was something in this simple and natural proceeding that struck the girl's mind with a sense of shame. She saw Mrs. Ashover, too, talking so quietly and happily with Lexie—both of them with their backs propped up against haycocks—that she felt as if there were something discordant, ill-considered, irrelevant in this ill-timed love of hers for this husband, this son, this brother, whose days might have stretched out so calmly before him in these pleasant places.

Rook helped her through the hedge, however, and led her straight into the wood. Above their heads the indefatigable little chiff-chaff repeated his two-syllabled monotone. From far up the woody slope, where the trees were taller and the undergrowth thinner, there sounded the *Caw—Caw—Caw* of the man's own ragged-winged namesakes.

Nell's skirts were stained with beech drippings, with the sticky amber-coloured tar of the spruce firs, with the brown oozings of patches of swamp ground, with the black moisture where accumulations of former rains had saturated the hollow interstices of elm roots and oak roots; with the dust of last year's funguses. Burr prickles clung to her thin stockings. Her hair, for she had snatched off her hat and carried it now in her hand, was loose and rumpled, and full of bits of twigs and shreds of moss.

They came to a little open space, covered with thick bent-grass of a vivid emerald green and surrounded by young sycamores. Here they sank down exhausted and silent: Rook with his back against one of the trees, Nell huddled up at his side, her head resting on his lap.

The physical effort which she had had to make, in forcing her way after him through so many obstacles, had exhausted her to such a point that her nerves were now in complete quiescence. The movement of his fingers as they disentangled the various little objects that had got caught in her hair increased her feeling of profound passivity.

His own thoughts were perhaps sadder than they had ever been in his life. The very quietness of the moment, the faint innumerable summer sounds that came and went; the rising and falling of a cloud of indolent sunlit gnats, each one of them a little dancing speck of intense consciousness; the sharp reiterated strokes of a woodpecker hidden somewhere above their heads; the swaying of the bent-grass in a wind that was gentler than the breath of sleep: all these things seemed only to enhance and emphasize the lamentable futility of human life, its confusions, its blunderings, its pitiful misunderstandings.

His heart ached for Netta. If only he knew that she was alive; that she was at least in no desperate straits, in no hopeless misery! But this absolute dead silence lay like a block of heavy quarried stone upon the well mouth of all his natural happiness.

Nell's voice broke the silence.

"It's lovely here, isn't it?" she said. "I'm very glad we came here, Rook. I shall never forget this afternoon. It was sweet of Lexie to make me come, wasn't it? If it hadn't been for him I never would have thought of it."

The man did not answer at once; or rather he answered with a reassuring movement of his hand.

His actual *thought* at that moment was rather to be concealed than revealed; for it was one of those thoughts that isolate a person's identity and put up a sort of invisible screen of malicious loneliness between oneself and one's companion.

He indulged in the fantastic wish, in fact, that some sudden electric disturbance, some insane magnetic current, might kill at one blow every kind of "love" toward him in his mother, in his wife, in Nell. He would like to be loved by only two people in the world: by Netta and by his brother!

"Yes, I am glad Lexie brought you," he said. "It would have been absurd not to have had you here. Ann is not really as jealous as she likes to pretend. But you know how it is with me these days! I can't think of anything. I can't concentrate on anything. I see Netta's face, I see certain expressions of quaint enjoyment, of funny bewilderment, that she used to have, and it just paralyses me! I'm only half alive all the time. And I hate everyone—well! not quite everyone, Nell—who interrupts my thinking about her! Wouldn't you suppose, Nell, that it would be possible by sheer *willing* to force a lost person to reveal his hiding place? It seems so grotesque, so mad, that she should be at this moment somewhere in London wanting to see me; and I should be here wanting to see her; and that we cannot communicate in *any* way!"

Nell rose suddenly to a sitting posture and turned toward

him. "Do you know, Rook," she said, "I sometimes fancy that William knows more about her than he has confessed."

"*What!*"—The word leapt out of Rook's throat like a bullet from a revolver. "*What* are you saying?"

He scrambled to his feet and pulled the girl up with him so violently that his fingers hurt her arm.

"Dear Rook!" she gasped. "I—don't—I—I mean—I don't suppose——"

The excitement in his face, the return of life to his eyes, the grip of his hand, revealed to her with fatal lucidity how little, in the deepest part of his nature, her own personality and all the romantic happiness that had passed between them really counted.

"Knows more about her? Hastings knows more about her? What do you mean? Has he said anything to you?"

"No—no—no—no," she stammered hurriedly. "It was just a silly thought of mine. It was just that now and then, when I've talked to him about Netta, I seemed to feel as if he were uneasy in some way. I hadn't thought of it seriously till this moment. Oh, Rook, dearest Rook, don't think too much of so little a thing!"

"I shall come over to-night and talk to him. Will he be at home? He isn't away for the night, is he? Let's get back! My mother will be worried. We mustn't keep them. We don't want them to drive off without us."

His words came to her ears one after another, like the rattle of musketry, heard from behind the torrent of some tremendous volume of falling water, some splashing Niagara of doom in her own mind. She had not realized till that second of time how far she had gone in her vague irrational hopes about the future, about a future in which he and she were, by some heavenly sorcery, linked together. Consciously it had been to her no more than an enchanted episode, "the perfume and suppliance of a minute"; but in the unconscious recesses of her mind—as happens with most women—she had been spinning, like an insatiable little silkworm, a subterranean cocoon of romantic inventions.

But it was over now; over for good and all; and she must get back to those self-effacing moods; those moods whose sweetness—though she had not guessed it at the time—must have been craftily nourished by these irrational wellsprings of hope, far, far below the surface.

She must get back to that feeling she had had, on the day in the Ashover drawing room, when he fell at her knees wounded, distraught, beside himself; and she became for the moment a calm healing spirit, without a single selfish desire of her own.

"They won't have gone, will they?" she murmured, as they pushed their way back through the entangling undergrowth by the way they had come.

"They'll have waited! They'll have waited!" he kept saying, as he hurried forward.

When they came to the place where the ground was swampy and their feet sank into a substance that was brown-black with the dissolution of bark and leaves and grass roots and ancient moss, he put his arm round her waist to lift her faster along.

It was not till they were close to the hedge dividing the wood from the hayfield that Rook realized, as he released her waist and let her pause to tidy herself up and put on her hat, how white her face had become and how dazed and numb her whole being was. But self-absorbed in the mania of his remorse, it did pierce the armour of his egoism to see the look in her eyes as she stood fumbling with her hair in front of him, her arms raised and her body flecked with the shadows of leaves and branches. He became conscious that she, too, this troubled figure with the sycamore shadows wavering upon her dress, was unhappy in the same sort of way he was unhappy and without his toughness to bear it.

For a moment they passed out together beyond the circle

of both their deep-bitten sorrows; and it was as if what he had felt as he gazed into Betsy's Cimmery Land crystal rose up again from beneath and beyond them and lifted them into a region outside the sphere of all human confusion.

"They've waited!" he whispered. "I can see Lexie and Mother. It's all right, Nell dear!"

She smiled in answer and instinctively held out her hand. He took it and held it for a moment. "You've been very good to me, Nell," he said. "I don't know what I should do if I hadn't got you."

These last words of his coming after her realization, that afternoon, as never before, of how little, after all, she really meant to him, sounded as hollow to her ears as the mocking rhetoric upon a tombstone.

She did not speak but dropped his hand as one who had come to the end of her endurance and whose only desire was to escape. Breaking away from him she pushed blindly through the hedge and walked across the field without looking back.

CHAPTER XVIII

IT WAS just ten o'clock on that same June evening. So late was the sun in sinking and so protracted was the twilight that even now, although the last yellowish-green spaces in the infinite horizon had faded into steely gray, there yet remained a pallid nebulosity in the air, a nebulosity that seemed to emanate from the surface of the earth, as if the earth were its own moon and had the power of holding back both the velvety invasion of darkness itself and the natural luminousness of the high stars.

Nell had gone to bed by that curious earth light without requiring a candle. She lay now in an exhausted and docile suspension of all her energies, letting the fragrant airs that floated in through the open window stir her hair faintly and lightly upon her forehead and become the accomplices of that abnormal twilight of twilight which made the planetary orb itself resemble a leaf-shadowed glowworm.

She listened for a while in motionless passivity to the murmur of men's voices in the study across the passage. She even smiled to herself a little as the fantastic notion crossed her mind that she might be a girl in Damascus or Antioch or Stamboul or in some place where women had nothing of the free initiative such as they possessed on the banks of the Frome.

With this fancy still in her brain and the large serenity of that June night lulling her senses, she turned over on her side toward the wall. There, in the pallid dimness, she stared passively at a little chance-drawn mark on the gray-plastered surface before her, a quaint little hieroglyph of the fingers of accident, which had come to take many strange shapes and be associated with many strange feelings during her life in that room. Before she slept on this occasion that little scrawl took the shape of Mr. Twiney's cart; and in the cart, erect and straight, stood the figure of Lady Ann, holding the reins, like a classic charioteer!

She had a vague feeling that she herself was fleeing from this equipage, fleeing down the glade of a deep, deep wood; and then, all in a moment, like the celestial clouds thrown about their favourites by the Homeric gods, a great friendly mist received her and enveloped her; and she fell into a dreamless sleep.

Meanwhile, in the room opposite, a momentous and peculiar dialogue was imprinting itself, like a disordered pattern under the hands of a drink-crazed artist, upon the ethereal stuff of that June night.

"She gave you no sign, no hint, then—not one of any kind—as to where she was going when she got to London?"

William Hastings shook his head. Far down in the priest's subconscious nature there stirred a malicious exultation at the fact that he was holding back Netta's secret from this rival of his.

During these last two months, parallel with the cessation of his writing, there had arisen within him a more possessive attitude toward his wife, an attitude that made it harder for him to endure the girl's attraction to Rook. By one of those inexplicable contrarieties which seem so inevitable an adjunct to all erotic emotions, instead of being tempted to reveal Netta's address to Rook and thus to side-track him away from Nell, he was fortified and strengthened in what he had come to regard as a sacred contract with the other woman.

It is likely enough that in any case he would have held fast by his oath to the runaway; but under the present circumstances this oath became more and more of a superstitious trust, a trust into which he flung not only what was obstinate and unyielding in his nature but what was malicious and revengeful.

His pride had been hurt far more than he himself had realized by his wife's infatuation. He must have divined, even while still at work on his book, a good deal more of what was going on than he had permitted either Rook or Nell to detect.

He was a man whose subconscious emotions worked their way to the surface slowly, and, as it were, by a process of infiltration. His first response to his wife's attraction to Rook had been philosophical and indulgent, just as his first response to Netta's flight had been a concern for Rook himself; but both these moods were easy and superficial, while all the while there was gradually stirring within him a dark unconscious anger against Rook which only required the impact of some external shock or encounter to bring to head.

Thus in the matter of Netta's address his feelings had become extremely complicated. He had begun by keeping her secret out of a vague loyalty to her but he found himself keeping it now out of a definite hostility to Rook.

"No," he repeated monotonously to every appeal. "No. She only gave me that letter, which I gave you. Beyond that, you know as much of what happened as I do."

"Hastings, you're not concealing something from me because you think that if I get hold of Netta again it'll make my wife and my mother miserable, and upset everything? If that's what's in your mind I give you my word I won't bring her back! I've no thought of bringing her back, anyhow. It's the last thing I want to do now. I only want to see her, to know where she is; to get rid of this awful sensation of blankness and emptiness."

"So you feel like that, do you?" said William Hastings, pushing the matchbox across the table and lighting a cigarette himself. "I have often wondered, Ashover, whether it was possible for you to feel a thing like this, simply and naturally, as an ordinary man would feel it."

"Did she mention," interjected Rook, "when she was talking to you, any names of her friends?"

"She spoke of someone called Minnie," answered the other.

"That was it! Minnie!" cried Rook eagerly. "Did she mention her surname? Did she mention what theatre she worked in? Did she mention what part of London she lived in?"

William Hastings drummed with his fingers carelessly on the table. He had given Rook his only easy chair; and he himself sat erect and nonchalant on the chair he used when he wrote.

"No. She mentioned no surname and no theatre. She talked of Minnie a great deal. She seemed very fond of Minnie. I began quite to visualize this remote young woman; not by her appearance exactly; but by the way Netta made you understand the sort of person she was. I got quite interested in Minnie, Ashover."

"You're sure she hasn't written to thank you for that money? That's the thing I *cannot* understand."

Hastings became aware that irony and sarcasm were entirely irrelevant at that moment.

"No. She hasn't written to me," he answered simply. "If she *did*, of course I would tell you at once. I expect she's got a place in some theatre. Has it occurred to you, Ashover, to go the round of the London theatres?"

Rook cast a puzzled, scowling look at his host. He became vaguely conscious that this little stubby dark-eyed man with the Napoleonic paunch was practising some derisive trick upon him.

"The round of the theatres? Good God, Hastings! what do you mean? Do you mean that I should enquire from every manager in London what people are on his list?"

The clergyman looked at him now with unmitigated malevolence. "Why don't you apply to some detective office, Ashover? Those people are trained like dogs for just this kind of thing. They would probably ferret her out in a very short time."

"I have thought of that," replied Rook, crossing his legs and lighting another cigarette. "The objection to my doing it is, I'm afraid, a ridiculously simple one; and you know what *that* is, Hastings!"

Hastings lifted his eyebrows and drummed on the table with his plump white hands. "I can guess," he said.

"I just haven't any cash," went on his visitor. "I mean, nothing approaching enough for a thing like that! And besides—I suppose you'll think it silly; but I have a sort of horror of using detectives to find Netta."

"Perhaps you don't *really* want to find her," said the clergyman.

Rook looked at him sharply from the depths of his armchair. He began to be much more conscious than he had been at first of the maliciousness in the man's tone.

"Why do you say just that, Hastings?" he asked drily; and if the priest had been more clairvoyant than he was he would have become aware of a sudden veering of the psychological weathercock.

It had begun to dawn upon Rook that this man was, in some secretive way he could not quite define, playing a game with him.

"Oh, I don't mean anything, Ashover. I understand well enough how you shrink from using those people. I only meant that sometimes one is unconscious of the real impulse behind one's actions."

"You're sure you didn't give her any more than those fifteen pounds?"

As he spoke Rook looked at the pale, plump face above

him with its heavy-lidded greenish-black eyes and became conscious of the fact that he had no more notion of what went on in this extraordinary person's mind than he had of what went on in the mind of some great toad hidden under a rhubarb leaf in Nell's little garden.

Rook had insisted upon returning to Hastings that particular sum; and the clergyman, unwilling to make an issue out of a point of that kind, had accepted the money in the spirit in which it was given.

"Not a penny more," repeated the man at the table, resting his chin upon his hands and staring at the oblong frame of grayness through which the scented night air came floating into the little room.

Rook uncrossed his legs and clutched the arms of his chair with angry, bony fingers. He scowled helplessly at the impassive countenance above him. There was something in the immense silence of that slowly descending etherealized darkness that seemed to render it a kind of brute stupidity in him not to be able to read his companion's thoughts. That impalpable summer air was like a condensation of the thoughts of the terrestrial globe itself, strange, dreamlike, non-human, such as rose and fell, fell and rose, with the rhythm of some vast, placid, elemental sea.

Rook longed to tell the man that it was Nell herself who had suggested that he knew more of Netta's plans than he had confessed; but even in his present harassed impatience he had not quite the cold-blooded cynicism to drag the young girl into their colloquy.

"Shall we have a light?" he remarked at last, when it seemed to him that Hastings was prepared to go on staring into the darkness without motion or change or limit.

The man did rise from his seat at this; moving stiffly, like a person whose soul has returned to its body after some long translunar journey. He lit a couple of candles and put them down on the table before him; where they bowed gently in that perfumed air, one after the other, like two grave acolytes in the presence of a dark altar.

"Hastings," said Rook all of a sudden when, with no change in his position, the theologian had resumed his mute dialogue with the wordless spaces.

"Well, Ashover?"

"If Netta, by any remote chance, *does* write to you, you won't fail to let me hear of it at once?"

Hastings smiled. "Of course I'll let you know of it, Ashover."

The curious thing at this moment was, that, by reason of some inherent duplicity and illusion-weaving power in Nature herself, the priest was actually fortified in his dissimulation by the great flow of honey-scented darkness which now flooded everything and drowned everything.

It was as if "the still small voice" of the very planet we live upon, when, in the absence of wind or storm, it makes itself felt from its inmost interior integrity, were saturated with some irremediable ultimate evasion. It was as though this old protean universe, when once you reached its native inherent character beneath all its masks and transformations, had its own secretive life illusion, its own eternal magic-bestowing falsehood, from which the subterfuges and equivocations of the human race drew living nourishment.

"Hastings," said Rook again. "If you *did* by any chance find out where Netta was, you haven't got any grievance against me, have you, that would make you want to hide it from me?"

Whatever may have been the reservoirs of planetary duplicity from which the priest was able to draw his support there was no need to use them just then; for an interruption occurred which saved him from any reply.

Two moths, of the species known to entomologists as yellow-underwings, flew into the room together and fluttered straight into one of the candles. Hastings gazed at them without moving; but Rook, springing up from his place, began a series of frantic efforts to catch them in his fingers. He stood by the table, making desperate clutching movements with his hands, while his companion, pushing back his chair a little, watched him gravely and silently.

One of the moths was caught at last, and going to the window Rook threw it, rather than released it, into the embalmed darkness outside. By the time he returned to the table, however, the other moth was lying singed and dead beside the candlestick.

"Why didn't you catch it?" he cried indignantly; and the sudden consciousness of what had really happened—of those two feathered amorists moving together over the dark currant bushes in a mysterious ecstasy; of their being drawn toward a flame that desired them not and indeed knew not of their existence; of their being separated with an absolute and final separation; of the one he had thrown out fumbling vaguely with its antennae in that immense darkness, from under the shadow of a peony leaf or a dock leaf; fumbling and uttering—who knows?—lamentations and moanings that would sound like the voice of Eros himself if there were ears that could hear it—struck like a spear into Rook's brain.

He went to the window, closed it with a violent gesture, and throwing himself down with a groan into the creaking cane chair, rubbed his face with his hands.

"It's getting too much for me, Hastings," he said. "It's getting altogether too much for me! What qualities ought one to have to be happy in a world like this? Ay? Ay? What has Lexie got, for instance? Courage? A lust for life? A mania for the wretchedest flicker of consciousness, as long as it *is* consciousness? Oh, I would like to escape from the whole thing! To escape out of it, I tell you, clear, clear out of it!"

Hastings surveyed the agitated man with a concentrated frown. This interview was beginning to break up the misty veil of more natural human feeling which of late had been forming, like an attenuated film, over the dark river of his thought. The plummet thrown out by Rook's pessimism reached the surface of that formidable undercurrent and stirred its waters.

"Why do you say 'escape'?" he asked sternly. "The longing to 'escape' is only the other side of the lust to enjoy. It's as old as the hills, that 'clear, clear out of it!' and it's as feeble as a baby's wail." He looked at Ashover more gently now, as he felt within him, rising up from the depths, the pride of his own life illusion as opposed to the other's.

Ashover, too, felt, man-like, the challenge of a conflicting system of metaphysicalized self-assertion, and a gleam of interest in their discussion broke the gloom of his mood.

"Well? What do *you* do, Hastings, when you feel the turn of the great screw?"

"I never feel its turn, Ashover! I have nothing in me to resist it and therefore I can't feel it. We're talking in different languages."

Rook smiled. "I've always wanted to ask you what that book of yours is really about. It seems to me that this is a moment when I *may* do that."

The theologian got up. He walked to the window and opened it wide. Then he came back to the table and blew out both the flames.

"We needn't burn any more moths," he said in a low voice. "You and I can see enough of each other without candles."

He resumed his seat and the two men sat silently in their places in that perfumed darkness. There was a syringa bush by the garden gate and the smell of its flowers mingled with the less definite scent of the wide-stretching hayfields. There was a faint dampness in the air from the neighbourhood of so many water brooks, but this only had the effect of making the darkness larger and cooler and more liberating.

William Hastings gathered up within him those obscure

magnetic forces to which human beings give the names of "will" and "thought" and "purpose." There flowed into the resultant complex of his energy, as the two sat silently there, a desire to undermine the very foundations of this proud, alien, inaccessible soul that lay chafing and fretting before him with this ridiculous wound in its heart. He felt no pity, no sympathy; but the obscure malice which had been slowly accumulating within him for many months took the form now of a longing to overcome the creature's remoteness and detachment, to invade it, to overwhelm it, to drown its rock base and carry it away on the torrent of his own stronger, more formidable identity.

With a movement of his fingers that was much more rapid and nervous than usual he struck a match with the mechanical intention of lighting a cigarette. The little burst of sulphurous flame illuminated his own bent head; and at the same time brought his companion's face up out of what seemed an abyss of nebulous darkness. He shook the flame into extinction and threw the match-end away.

"There's no pleasure in smoking when you can't see the smoke," he said.

"Well? Are you going to tell me about your book?" repeated the other.

There was a moment's deep silence between them that lay upon the filmy folds of the darkness like a dead child upon a woman's lap.

"*Ashover!*" The word seemed to come from a portion of the man's being that was behind and beyond his mere physical frame.

"Well? What is it?"

"Do you realize that there is a hidden struggle going on in the depths—an appalling struggle—between two Powers that are beyond man and beyond Nature?"

"I certainly do not," muttered Rook sullenly.

"One of these Powers is the life force," went on the

priest. "The other is the death force. And what I have come to realize lately is this: that just as man can put himself into the magnetic matrix of life and germinate new creations, so he can also unchain the cogwheel and break the mainspring in that ultimate darkness! In other words, Ashover, I have found out that the soul of man is a much more dangerous weapon than is usually imagined."

"All this sounds to me very like what I've heard in church," remarked Rook grimly.

"It *is* like that!" cried the priest. "It is! It is! But that only shows that what I've discovered answers to an indestructible instinct in the human race."

"The human race is not much of a criterion," grumbled the voice in the cane chair. "It swings east by north; and then it swings west by south. It's a bloody weathercock, your race instinct!"

"It hasn't swung much for the last five thousand years on *this* matter," retorted the other. "Against all the claptrap of science it has steadily maintained the one great appalling truth that men and gods and all the living things in nature are only pawns and dice and counters in a conflict between two equal and unfathomable antagonists! Haven't you yourself felt it, Ashover?" His voice dropped to a penetrating whisper which pierced the darkness like a conspirator's dagger. "Haven't you felt that everything you consciously thought and did had behind it *something else;* gave way into something; just as broken ice gives way? And haven't you felt that this something was sometimes life and sometimes death? Haven't you felt that kind of thing, Ashover?"

Rook's voice out of the darkness had the sort of tone a floating tree trunk might have had, as it knocked against another, on the dark tide of a swirling river.

"My good man," he said, "I've felt so often every kind of sickening sensation that I've lost the spirit to tabulate them.

I don't see why you should stop at this duality of yours. Why not take it for granted that the universe is crowded with levels, strata, planes, dimensions, altitudes, regions, all of them full of wretched sensitive beings like ourselves longing to escape?"

The intonation of weary scepticism in his voice seemed to have a peculiarly irritating effect on the priest's nerves.

"You're not serious, Ashover," he said. "No one who analyses his own feelings can get away from this great undertow of opposite tides—the death urge and the life urge. What I've discovered is that we can get behind the scene and *pull up the dam*, so that the death force can flood the whole field."

Rook's voice became more weary and detached than ever, as all the mysterious polarities in his nature focussed themselves in fierce secretive resistance to this vision that was invading and seeking to dominate his own.

"I think nothing of these forces of yours, Hastings," he retorted. "Why stop at life and death? Why not have a whole vortex of conflicting powers? Life and death are just words! All we know is a mad chaotic jumble of things that we call 'living' and things that we call 'dead.' What I feel is that the whole imbroglio may be a set of obscene dreams, a great concourse of phantasmagoric shadows, most of them disgusting; some of them magically lovely! And what I would like to do is to dive down into some lake of nothingness where you could forget that there ever were such horrors!"

Hastings became conscious of a definite feeling of anger toward this man. A vague throb in some old deep scar within him reverting to some half-forgotten outrage his pride had received, when he, a child of middle-class origin, had been insulted by these careless aristocrats, began to mingle now with a rationalist's natural indignation against merely fanciful speculations. These people never took these ultimate issues seriously. They were no more to them than the leap of fish in a mill pond! Phantasmagoric shadows! The great dark fragrant night about him, full of the odours of a real earth, pressed upon his brain with a sense of the thinness, of the irrelevancy, of these bodiless conjectures. Life? Did he not know its bitterness, its brutality only too well? Death? Was not this divine darkness a very symbol of the sweetness of the eternal sleep? He felt that if, at that moment, he could, by raising his hand, have plunged the whole stellar system into final destruction, he would willingly have raised it!

And this man, this Ashover, had now linked himself with a spirited, amorous girl who would soon—he knew it well enough!—satisfy this tenacious family's desire to continue alive upon the earth. And his own fragile neurotic Nell was obsessed by her girlish fancy for this indolent sceptic; this persifleur who, with his pools of nothingness, posed as a martyr of remorse because he had driven his mistress out of his house! What did the man know about "Dimensions, levels, regions"? Phrases of that kind, how hollow, how rhetorical they were, with this enchanted June night whispering to them of the realities of life and death!

Far off across the wide water meadows he could hear at intervals the husky cry of some lonely nocturnal bird, a night-jar, perhaps, or a bittern; and the sound came to him as something that fortified his drastic vision of things. Was he not, himself, a solitary nighthawk crying out aloud, in a language no man understood, as he felt the damp airs of the great flood coming up over the marshes?

"What I feel about all this"—it was Rook's voice speaking again, and more wearily, more indifferently than ever—"is that the true reality of things, the reality that we may wake up to when we die, is so completely different from life and death that it is a mere waste of time to argue about it. You say that my longing to escape is only the inverse of—well! of Lexie's mania for living. But what of your own mania for death and destruction, Hastings? Isn't that, too, with all the energy you throw into it, just the inverse of what you call the life urge? You are really just as dogmatic in your death-cult as Lexie in his life-cult! What I feel is that the whole thing is so mad and so chaotic that to dispute about it at all is to lend yourself to being fooled and deluded. Better let it alone; and just take each day as it comes."

Hastings began to experience one of the most discomforting sensations that the human soul can endure, the sensation of feeling his spiritual pride menaced by something alien. He gave his chair a jerk backward in the darkness and clenched the fingers of his right hand so tightly that the nails nearly pierced the flesh.

It was absolutely necessary to him at that moment to find himself stronger, more formidable, more *evil* even, than this man who carried the airy indifference of his class into the very gulfs! And the sophisticated trifler was loved by three women! The struggle between them had by this time become one of those primeval struggles between two horned animals, in which power over nature, power over women, and power over God are fantastically mingled as the elements of a war to the death.

It seemed to Hastings, at that second, as if their hostility to one another, this sullen obscure wrestling that was going on in the darkness, occupied an arena that sank down into the very navel of the earth.

He felt a desire to go to the window and lean out. From where he sat he could detect a group of little faint stars; and he tried feebly to recall what constellation it would be that at that particular hour looked down upon Toll-Pike Cottage. A vague uneasiness had begun to trouble his mind. Was it possible that this Pyrrhonian attitude of Rook's toward life, this careless, indolent, drifting "chaoticism," gave the man the same advantage over him in philosophy as he possessed in the material world? But how could a person so casual, so formless, so evasive, be as close to the open secret as one who was concentrated and knit together, with a deep hard purpose in his mind?

He suddenly began to get an impression that Rook was playing with him, *had* been playing with him during the whole of their talk! That was an old trick of these accursed "upper classes." You never knew where you were with them; you never knew where you "had" them! Like a cold finger of boreal ice pointing at his central nerve the abominable suspicion began to invade his mind that his whole system of philosophizing was only a weapon in a fierce personal struggle for recognition, for ascendancy. Apparently it was not necessary for an Ashover to have recourse to such weapons! *They* need not formulate their philosophy. *They* need not be logical or rational. *They* could play with the realities of life and death as they played with their dogs and their guns and their girls. *They* could just lie back upon themselves and be what they were and all the rest of the universe might go on as it pleased! "Chaoticism" indeed! That was exactly the word. To walk through the lanes and the woods; to enjoy his meals; to seduce a girl here and a girl there; and to hand on his name by a well-timed marriage to another generation, who would also lie back upon themselves and talk of chance and chaos; while he, William Hastings, who had put his whole life's blood into a book of crushing, deadly, annihilating power only existed as an object of quaint interest, set aside as a fantastic-brained country parson who was useful for reading pious homilies in the presence of Ashover monuments!

"You won't deceive me in any way over Netta, Hastings?" The words, coming from the other hidden countenance, in that midnight chamber, floated away out of the window toward the little, unknown group of stars.

"Deceive you? Why on earth should I deceive you?

I tell you you know everything there is to be known in the whole world!"

The man's voice took on at that point the peculiar quiver which indicates in highly strung nerves the approach of a collapse of all self-control.

"Why don't you apply to the detectives, Ashover!" he went on. "To the detectives!" And suddenly without the least intention he broke into a loud harsh rasping laugh. "The detectives!" he kept on gasping in a choking voice. "The detectives!"

It was Rook who felt a longing to go to the window now. That little room was becoming intolerable to him. He did, in fact, get up from his seat and stagger to the window sill, his legs numb and stiff; but Hastings was still rocking himself to and fro in such an alarming spasm of laughter that he remained leaning there with his face to the interior of the room.

The priest's sinister explosion died down at last and he lifted his head from his hands.

"So I suppose now," he said, addressing the dark figure that concealed so much of the starlit window frame, "you'll have an heir to your historic family."

Rook was too surprised by this rude remark to make any answer at all. He began to think the moment had arrived for bidding his host good-night. There evidently was nothing more to be got out of him with regard to Netta and he was in no mood for prolonging this scene.

But the ferment he had unwittingly aroused in Hastings's soul had not exhausted its vindictive ricochets. "And so it's a boy you're expecting, is it?" His voice became hoarse as he went on with unrestrained malice: "I saw Binnory Drool to-night. He talked about you and about Betsy and the others. You've seen the others, I suppose, Ashover?"

Rook struck a match now and advancing to the table lit one of the candles full in his host's face. He was so startled and shocked by the expression upon that suddenly illuminated countenance that he drew back with an unconscious exclamation of dismay.

"Ay! What's the matter, man? What's up? Are you angry with me about anything? What have I done?"

The priest jerked his chair farther back. "What was that word of yours?" he whispered huskily. "Phantasmagoric! A good word, phantasmagoric!"

Rook took up the other candle in his hand and lit it from the one that was already burning. The two small flames rose now between the two men like the horns of the ultimate Dilemma.

"Your people in the family vault must be in high feather these days, Ashover," the priest went on. "They've been working and working for this, for many a long year. They were getting quite anxious, down there under the stones! It would have been a pity to disappoint them, wouldn't it? I wonder what it feels like to have a long line of ancestors regulating one's private affairs? It must be an interesting feeling."

Rook looked round the room to see where he had put his hat and stick. He walked to the spot where they were and took them up. "Good-night, Hastings," he said. "I must be off now."

The priest rose to his feet like a man drunk or drugged.

"What would you have done," he said, "if I *had* known anything about Netta? Known, for instance, where her address was now? Would you have gone straight off to her? Would you have left your wife and have gone to live with her? Not a bit of it! You'd have given her a little flattery and a little money and come right back here to your walks and your meals and your 'phantasmagoric shadows'! Tell me this, Rook Ashover. How does a phantasmagoric shadow look when its female shadow has been decoyed away? Does it dance like a good obedient puppet on well-pulled wires? Does it, Ashover—does it?"

It must have happened then that some mysterious nerve in the man's inmost identity, some nerve which had been strained by his struggle with Rook to the breaking-point, did actually break at that moment, destroying the normal intellectual self-control that renders certain actions impossible. For what occurred seemed monstrous and fantastic when Rook recalled it afterward. Repeating the words: "Does it dance, does it, does it, does it?" the man skipped up toward Rook, his arms grotesquely stretched out, his face distorted into a goblinish leer, one leg bent and raised in the air, the other hopping along the floor.

Rook drew back in apprehension, thinking that Hastings would end by striking him; but instead of that what he did was to seize one of the brass candlesticks from the table and fling it with a wild swing of his arm against the door.

Rook made a half-defensive, half-protective movement toward him; but the gesture proved unnecessary. The man clapped his hands to his head, staggered across the room, and falling into the cane chair where the other had been sitting burst into a passionate fit of weeping.

Two things occurred one after the other then, that were afterward so closely associated together in Rook's mind that it was difficult to separate them. From the silence of the darkness outside there came suddenly to his ears, carried as it seemed from somewhere beyond the garden and beyond the immediate meadows, that same extraordinary sound which he had heard on the occasion of his night with Ann in the Drool cottage.

He had no time to analyze the nature of the sound, but there did flash across his consciousness a vague and irrational notion connecting it with the savage outburst with which this huddled and sobbing object in the chair had derided his unborn child. Had the prophet of annihilation been answered by a howl of counter-mockery from those silent tombs under the chancel slabs? Or was the whole thing a ghastly trick of his own disturbed brain, an auditory hallucination practised upon him by the agitation of that extraordinary encounter?

He had no time to question further this "supernatural soliciting," to use the Shakespearean word, when the door of the room opened silently and, by the light of the one candle that still burned upon the table, appeared the white figure of Nell, her hair loose about her shoulders, her feet bare.

She had been awakened from a deep sleep by the noise of the candlestick hurled against the door, and without any clear consciousness of where she was or what she was doing she had rushed blindly across the landing.

Rook, who had flung down his hat and stick upon Hastings's desk, now made a mechanical movement toward them, feeling that it was not the moment to intrude any longer upon these two people.

Nell stopped him with a quick gesture.

"Oh, what *is* the matter?" she cried. "No! No! I can't let you go like that until I know what's happened! What is it, Rook? What have you done to him? Have you two been quarrelling?"

There was no need for Rook to reply for Hastings himself got up from the chair.

"Go back to your room, Nelly dear," he said gently, but in a tone that made it difficult for the girl not to obey him. "I'll just see Mr. Ashover out and then I'll come. Have you got everything, Ashover? I don't think you'd anything but your stick, had you?"

Rook could do nothing but just press Nell's hand as he passed. Her eyes clung to his in that dim candlelight in a way he never forgot. He left her standing with the light in her hand at the top of the stairs.

"Good-night, Ashover. I'm afraid I lost my wits just now. I have quite got them back."

"Good-night, Hastings, and I beg you not to think any more about it or indeed about any of these things too much. It's better sometimes to wake up in the morning as if you were newly born."

He held out his hand as he spoke and Hastings, after a moment's hesitation, took it.

"Perhaps it's just as well once in a way to lose one's wits," he said. "Don't be afraid. If ever I hear from Netta I shall let you know. Good-night, Ashover." And he closed the door behind him with a faint recrudescence of his lost sense of formidableness.

At least he had not revealed to him Netta's secret. It was necessary to his very life, at this moment of the supreme wreck of his self-respect, that the simple chance-given vantage ground of having the girl's address in his hands should act as a counterpoise to his abasement.

The ultimate duplicity of the universe, whether it were logical or phantasmagorical, had at least given him one way of crying an incontestable "checkmate!" to the Squire of Ashover.

CHAPTER XIX

THE last day of June found most of the Frome-side hay fields cut and carried. Not only so, but the newly sprouting grass in nearly all of these peaceful enclosures had begun to assume that peculiarly rich shade of green, deeper than the first spring verdure and in a certain sense even fresher, by reason of the fact that at the earlier season the new shoots are surrounded by so many of the old winter-bleached blades and stalks, whereas, at this great midsummer solstice, between the time of the rains and the time of the coming of the roses, the mowing machines have made a clear field for that vivid aftermath.

The wild roses were out already, and in their glory; so were the cream-yellow clusters of honeysuckle; so also the first-born of the foxgloves. Field orchids and bird's-foot trefoil were taking the place of daisies and cowslips; and down in the water meadows ragged robin and marsh-woundwort were lifting their heads amid the innumerable spear points of the new-grown rushes.

Dragon-flies began to appear in greater numbers over the rain-filled cattle ponds and along the ditches; the most common kind being those whose bodies were as blue as king-fishers and their wings like quivering fans of quicksilver chequered with powdered jet dust.

All through that month, through the earlier days of sunshine and through the later days of turbulent rains, Rook had sullenly been groping in his mind for some clue to the almost triumphant malice with which Hastings treated him now whenever they met. He found it difficult to believe that it was simply due to jealousy over Nell; for of late he had hardly seen anything of the girl and when they did meet it was under conditions to which the most jealous husband could hardly take exception.

The fact that his absorbing remorse about Netta had destroyed all desire within him for other women produced the illusion in his mind that he was isolated, cut off, marooned and under a sort of curse. To himself he seemed a moral leper, doomed to produce unhappiness wherever he went or whatever he did; and so, as often happens with egoists of his kind, he took it for granted that others saw him exactly as he saw himself.

That it never occurred to him that he might be paying the penalty now for earlier irresponsibilities was due to the fact that in those first days of his encounters with Nell, Hastings had seemed so entirely removed from all mundane or human emotions. The man had not been exactly what the old books used to call a "wittold"; but he had certainly produced the impression that no romance in which his wife chose to be involved was likely to worry him very much. But all that was completely changed! He felt as if Hastings were watching him with the eye of a malignant raven; and though his own sensuality was as dead in him, just then, as if he had been swimming among icebergs, it was an intensification of his self-condemned loneliness not to have the balm of Nell's sympathy.

This last day of the month was a day of days. It was one of those sequences of twenty-four hours that seem in some way detached and isolated from the rest of the season. There was a mild steady wind blowing from the southwest, a wind that in its journey across the orchards and dairies of the west country seemed to have gathered up the sharp taste of green apples and of green corn, and to have mingled this more astringent essence with the rain-scented breath of heavy-uddered cattle and with the sweetness of old-fashioned rows of pinks in hot sunny borders, between brick paths and box hedges.

By one of those earth-obsessed intuitions which his growing malady seemed to render more intense and clarified every day, Lexie had predicted the occurrence of this halcyon weather and had arranged to have himself driven out by Mr. Twiney to a place called Comber's End, which lay on the farther side of the great stretch of water brooks and meadows on the edge of which the village of Ashover stood.

Comber's End itself was hardly a hamlet; its chief peculiarity being an old manorial farmhouse surrounded by a large pond or small lake, of considerable depth, at one extremity of which was an ancient water mill.

Rook was to meet his brother at the spot and they were to lunch together there, Lexie bringing the meal with him carefully packed in a basket by Mrs. Bellamy.

There was no road of any kind directly across the marshes. The best road for driving round them was several miles east of the village, while the way Rook had selected to walk, following narrower and rougher lanes, was nearly as far as that in the western direction.

It was indeed down a narrow grassy road that he found himself walking, in the mid-hours of that unusual morning, with the larks singing above his head, the warblers chattering in the hedges, and the lane itself stretching away in front of him, a long straight line of narrowing perspective bordered by pollard willows. He felt wearily, hopelessly sad, as he walked along, switching aimlessly with his stick the dock leaves and hemlock plants and rousing from their noon siesta, now a long-legged heron, and now a green snake, while the far-travelled wind rustling through the alders and the guelder bushes seemed to him like a trailing army of defeated sighs; sighs that died upon the air, one after another, and were replaced, one after another, by new fugitives from new fields of remote disaster.

Rook would have felt less sad if he could have regarded the impasse in which he was caught as a matter of blind destiny. The poison that rankled in him came from the thought that he could have escaped from the whole thing if only he had been sensible as Lexie was sensible, and had not just run headlong upon the shoals, like a ship with a mad pilot.

He felt responsible at that moment for the unhappiness of all the lives within his reach. His mother alone was free from the curse that seemed to have fallen upon him; his mother, and perhaps his unborn child; Even his love for Netta was not so much a craving for Netta's society as a wretched remorse at being the cause of her disappearance.

He examined his heart as he went along; and it was borne in upon him that he never had really, in all his life, loved a single human being except his brother. And now his brother was dying.

As he stared at the long lines of pollard willows on either side of the lane, their grotesque trunks, topped by what looked like thick upstanding panic-stricken hairs, became to him a silent avenue of Rook Ashovers, each of them born without a heart and each of them awaiting some kind of retributive judgment day! He wished he could walk along that road for ever and ever; or that, by walking along it till his knees tottered and his soul was sick to death, he might do penance for the misery he had caused.

He saw life at that moment in a different light from any that he had seen it in before. He saw it as a place where not to have become involved in any other existence was the only cause for real thankfulness to the gods; in any other existence than such as was organically linked with his own. For his relation with Lexie had brought only happiness to them both. So had his relation with his mother until she had imbibed this mania about his marriage.

The rest was all misery! Netta he had disappointed and thrown aside. Nell he had tantalized and thrown aside.

Ann he had provoked and humiliated beyond the point of forgiveness. What was there about him that made any intimate association with a woman dangerous and fatal? Not simply his selfishness. Plenty of selfish men enjoyed, after their fashion, eminently successful lives with the girls of their choice. There was something about himself, something about his *kind* of selfishness, that was as deadly to his happiness with these sensitive creatures as was catsbane to cats or wolfsbane to wolves!

He tried to imagine a world in which there were no women at all, or rather a world in which he himself had no dealings with women. Could he have lived, in harmonious and contented happiness, without any amorous dalliance? He remembered a certain day when someone or other, he forgot who the person was, had challenged him about his idleness, had suggested that to go on as the impoverished Squire of Ashover, doing nothing but walk and eat and sleep, was unworthy of a man with any spirit. He swung his stick into a bush of dogwood and chuckled aloud. God! he had intelligence enough to dispose of *that* indictment. What did it matter? The world was full enough of "honourable men" struggling frantically to get the advantage of one another in this race for success, for fame, for recognition, for achievement. What did it matter? Better, far better, to live harmlessly in some quiet untroubled place, watching season follow season, month follow month, aloof and detached; leaving the breathless procession of outward events to turn and twist upon itself like a wounded snake!

What did it matter? There was no "great Task-master" in the invisible world waiting to fall upon him with upbraidings and penalties. The opinions of his tribe, of his class, of the human race itself—what did they really amount to? His account was with the universe that had tossed him forth and that would receive him again. No! he could sink back deep enough into his own nature to let accusations of *that* kind fall harmless about him. It was not in *that* direction that his mistake lay. His mistake lay in not recognizing that unless a man has the stomach of a pirate it is better to give these tempting brigs and brigantines a wide berth; better to sail the high seas without meddling with any of them!

If only he had found out how fatally Nature had mingled the elements in him before he committed himself to Netta or Nell or Ann! This blending of an irresistible attraction to the feminine body and mind, with an absolute lack of emotional passion, was nothing less than a monstrous deformity! What kind of a heart *had* he, when he could find it in him to wish that he had never set eyes on any one of the three? His instincts were not perverted. They were only so capricious and elusive, so bloodless and non-human, that they flitted over the flower beds of life very much as those little blue butterflies he was watching now flitted from that patch of St. John's-wort to that patch of hawk-weed!

He began to walk more slowly and driftingly along that interminable lane. He felt as if he had already been following it for half a day; and it still stretched straight in front of him, without any sign of an end or of a turning. It seemed to melt into that leafy horizon as the moon-path across the sea on a moonlit night dips down over the rim of the world.

He felt utterly weary of himself and his familiar destiny. Yet he found it impossible even to conceive of any other. The idea of leaving Ashover and starting life afresh with any new ambition was as far from what his energy could compass as for a perch in Saunders' Hole to turn into one of the swallows that skimmed its surface.

What he craved, with all the desperation of a fox caught by wire netting in a fowl run, was just to be free; free to enjoy precisely such an excursion with Lexie as this one was, without feeling a dull throb in his secret conscience, like the throb of a malignant growth in the pit of his stomach!

He stopped for a while, leaning over a gate and gazing into the green slime of a cattle-trodden ditch, across which three orange-bodied dragon-flies were darting with as much arrogance as if it were a Venetian lagoon.

He had a feeling that some deep inarticulate grievance, much less clearly defined than these other causes of misery, was obscurely stirring within him. He tried to plumb the recesses of this emotion and he came to the conclusion that it was a blind repulsion at the idea of being married to Lady Ann. He suddenly found himself actually trembling with a convulsive fit of anger against his wife; and not only against his wife. It was as if he had never realized before how profoundly his life illusion was outraged by his marriage. The thought that he was irretrievably committed to this brilliant high-handed companion; the thought that his life was no longer to be a series of sweet solitary sensations, but a thing which was only half his own, stripped the magic from earth and air and sky!

And this was a trick that had been played upon him by a subtle conspiracy of all the persons in his entourage. His mother and Lady Ann had plotted for it. Netta had sacrificed herself for it. Nell had accepted it and condoned it. And most of all, that indestructible and accursed entity, the House of Ashover itself, had pushed him into it with urgent, unwearied, importunate hands, all the more powerful because they were invisible!

His mind began running up and down the events of his life. He had drifted into this cul-de-sac in a sort of anæsthetized trance. Something very deep in his nature had always preserved an absurd faith in his power of extricating himself from any trap. This faith no doubt depended on his emotional detachment; on those remote translunar journeys of his mind that seemed to reduce all human relations into a misty puppet show, seen through the smaller end of a telescope!

He cast about in his brain until his mind trailed its wings and sank huddled and drooping from sheer exhaustion in the attempt to find some outlet from his dilemma.

To and fro those orange-bodied dragon-flies darted. To and fro across the oozing footprints of the cattle, between great heaps of dung, clouds of infinitesimal midgets hovered and wavered; while in a corner of clear water a group of tiny black water beetles whirled round and round, as if they were trying to outpace their own small shadows which answered to their movement, down there on the sunlit mud, in queer radiated circles like little dark-rimmed moons.

The peculiar nature of Rook's intelligence did not permit him the pragmatic refuge of some drastic change in his system of life. His soul wilted and sagged but he felt no energy to cry: "Hold . . . enough!" to the cohorts of chance; or to deify them with ethical nicknames.

That the universe could be envisaged as a place where human characters were hammered and chiselled into some premeditated mould of valour or resignation never so much as crossed the threshold of his consciousness. His vision of things would go on to the very end drawing its quality from just such vignettes of the ways of nature as he was staring at at that moment—those casual heaps of cattle dung, those dancing midges, that green pond slime, those revolving jet-bright beetles!

He was sick and weary with the effort of thinking; of thinking round and round in the same circle. He was like a hunted gladiator who, in his blind race for life, keeps seeing the same impassive faces looking down upon the same heart-breaking circuit of the arena.

At that particular moment it began to dawn upon him that this numb, paralyzed, gray, horizonless state was worse, in the kind of misery it produced, than his furious self-accusations about Netta.

It was not the Netta trouble that was hurting him the deepest now, it was his reaction to his marriage; a reaction that seemed to menace the very essence of his identity, an essence that had winced and squirmed under the whip of his remorse but after all had been *there*, intact and integral in the darkness; *there* for good or for evil!

But his marriage seemed in some mysterious way to invade this precious untouchable essence, to swamp it, to blur it, to destroy its outlines. The truth was that the peculiar "formula" or illusory "symbol" of his especial kind of sensuality had always implied a very definite relation between himself and the object of its attraction, a relation according to which it was necessary for him to feel himself entirely independent and detached from the other person; necessary, in fact, that he should feel himself to be stronger, more formidable, more integrated than this other.

Under conditions of that kind, with every nuance of this "formula" satisfied, he could be tender, pitiful, and even clairvoyant; as he had been, almost to the last, in his feeling about Netta; but when this "formula," this symbolic projection of the realistic fact reflected in the distorting lens of his mind, was broken up by a differently adjusted balance of relations, in place of tenderness he was liable to feel a blind hostility, and in place of pity a cold-blooded vindictive malice.

His "love-making" with Cousin Ann had always been of a very light and a very superficial sort, from his side of the encounter; just because the strength of her nature precluded that protective or possessive thrill which his vice demanded; and now that he found himself actually married to her, nothing that her brilliance or her beauty or her grand manner could achieve gave him the faintest sensual pleasure.

Rook's was the kind of nature that derives no satisfaction from sensual emotion unless it is at liberty to disparage rather than to idealize; to pity rather than to admire; to possess rather than *be* possessed; and in every one of these requisites he was outraged and frustrated by his marriage with his cousin.

What he really required of life was not an impassioned love with an equal mate, but certain faint, vague, elusive ecstasies that were entirely unspiritual, entirely unemotional, and entirely de-personalized. Women were to him not human souls to be loved for themselves but just vibrant quivering telegraph wires, from which, as they stretched across land and river and hill in their long mysterious reach, the rain-scented winds of night and morning drew magical hummings and whisperings and wild sad prophecies!

Rook had never possessed any sense of proportion; and he was especially liable to let his moods become manias when they were associated with anything physiological. At that moment he got the sensation that his brain was going to burst like the seeds of a gorse-bush in hot weather, as he contemplated those jet-black beetles revolving in their unwearied circles.

He felt as if Lady Ann's personality were actually adhering to his own; and not only adhering to it, but sucking it up; as a whirlpool might suck up a paper boat!

His imagination got more and more unbalanced; ran riot more and more wildly; as he thought of himself in relation to this cousin-wife. He began to feel as if from henceforth to the day of his death he were destined to be deprived of all separate individual reality, destined to become a mere husk or shell, in the centre of which was nothing that could assert itself, or sink down into itself, but only something that had to reflect, reflect, reflect the thoughts of a completely alien person.

He felt as though this female creature, to whom he was now so indissolubly linked, were some sinister living growth, fungus-like and carnivorous, that devoured his flesh and drank his blood; something that it would be necessary to cut away from his inmost bones before he could breathe freely or take any natural pleasure in life again.

The feeling grew and grew upon him, as he stared at that

stagnant pond; till it seemed as if some actual magnetic power were menacing him with suffocation! And then, all in a moment, he found himself continuing his slow progress along that interminable pollard-bordered road.

For some reason or other connected with the tension in his brain, the hedges ceased to be green under that halcyon sky. They became gray, like the colour of wood-ashes. The trunks of the willows, too, became gray; and the lane itself under his feet, its deep clay-stiffened cart ruts and its margins of silverweed and feverfew, became gray as the face of some enormous dead creature upon which he was treading.

A paralysis of dizziness seized him, mingled with an abysmal loathing for he knew not what. He staggered as he walked and he found himself feebly shaking his head as if to make some overt protestation against a vision of things that his reason still assured him was unreal.

And then it was that a rider, mounted upon a tall gray horse, came cantering toward him and, pulling up when he reached him, turned his horse round and proceeded to ride by his side along the lane, talking to him as he rode. The horseman was a young man of singularly prepossessing appearance, and as he bent down over the animal's neck to bring his face nearer to the pedestrian, Rook received a vivid impression that something which had happened to him before was now going to happen again and in exactly the same way.

He was not in the least surprised to detect in his companion's face a certain unmistakable resemblance to his own, nor was he startled or in any way shocked when the youth addressed him as "Father."

"It is just dizziness," Rook found himself saying. "It has nothing to do with what I have been suffering."

"You must not suffer, Father," the youth said gently, stroking his horse's neck with a light hand.

"I thought just now," Rook retorted, "that there was no human being in the world unhappier than I am."

"Why are you unhappy, Daddy?" enquired the youthful rider.

"It's an indescribable horror," Rook answered. "Something that a lad like you had better not try to think about. I myself could hardly put it into words. But the effect it has upon me I *could* describe; only that would make you as miserable as I am."

He placed his hand on the edge of the rider's saddle and the boy laid his own upon it and began caressing it.

"There's no need for you to tell me, Daddy," he murmured. His voice became so low and faint just then that Rook glanced at him anxiously. And it was not only that his voice seemed to sink away like a wind that sighed itself into silence among feebly stirred grasses. His very form and face grew shadowy and indistinct.

Rook was conscious of making a quick desperate effort to hold both horse and rider near his side. He had the sense of clinging tenaciously to something that was falling back into fathoms of water. The very silence into which the boy's voice sank, the grayness into which his form dwindled and receded, seemed to be broken and troubled by a confused medley of hummings and murmurings, obscure, indistinct, unintelligible to the man's ears.

"I thought just now," Rook went on, holding tightly to the edge of the rider's saddle, "that there was no one in the world more cowardly, more contemptible than I am; no one in the world more treacherous, lecherous, and mean-hearted! And then I saw that the green slime was the green slime, that the cattle dung was the cattle dung; and it came into my head that a man has to accept himself for what he is; or if he can't do that just kill himself and end it!"

Kill himself and end it! The words seemed to drift away, over the flanks of the horse and over the pollard willows, as if they possessed some palpable body of their own that could not dissolve at once into the air. Rook heard them floating across the fields. Why didn't they sink into that mass of grayness that now began suffocating him again?

He made a convulsive clutch at his companion's fingers, and once more that fresh, fair youthful face leaned down close to his own.

"It must be the boy from Comber's End," he wanted to say to himself; but in place of saying "Comber's End" the word "Ashover" came into his mind.

And then again it seemed inevitable and natural that the youth should be murmuring: "It's all right, Daddy; it's absolutely all right."

"I must tell him about the green slime," Rook thought insistently. "I must make it clear to him about the cattle dung."

"There's a heron over there, Daddy," said the young horseman quietly, "and it hasn't a gray feather on it."

For some reason or other the sense of a heron having nothing gray, not one single feather of gray about it filled Rook with indescribable relief.

"Can it fly?" he whispered.

But the boy was silent again and once more both horse and rider seemed to recede and recede into an enveloping mist. Frantically Rook clung to those youthful fingers, and as he clung to them they grew warm and firm again under his touch.

"It was the green slime," the man began again, in a hurried husky voice, his brain full of the one obstinate desire to make a very difficult point clear. "And the cattle dung," he added, pressing the horseman's hand against his saddle.

"What they made me think was that no one who makes any effort to change his nature or to change any one else's nature has any right to be alive upon the earth." His voice subsided but he was still driven on by that desperate impatient sense that he *must* make everything plain before the lad cantered off.

"Slime—dung—not one gray feather——" he gasped

wildly; and then, in a sudden burst of exultant freedom: "No one is worthy to live," he cried with a loud voice, "who doesn't know—who doesn't know——"

"What, Daddy?" whispered the voice at his side.

He flung the words into the air now with a ringing triumphant voice.

"Who doesn't know that all Life asks of us is to be recognized and loved!"

The young rider suddenly snatched up the hand with which Rook had been so desperately retaining him and raised it to his lips. Then he gave him a smile the penetrating sweetness of which diffused itself through every fibre of the man's body.

"Good-bye, Daddy!" he murmured gently; and whispering some quick word to his horse he gave the bridle a shake and cantered away down the lane.

The sound of the retreating horse hooves subsided slowly into silence. The boy's face, so unmistakably resembling his own but with a beauty and power in it beyond anything he had ever approached, remained in his mind as an ineffaceable reality!

"Recognized and loved," he muttered; and there arose within him the feeling that it was for the creation of a being like this that all the suffering he had caused and all the horror he had endured found their solution. It was toward this that the invincible life purpose, reaching out from the buried dust of his ancestors to him, had been pushing him blindly forward, tearing a path for it, clearing a way for it, through all his confusions and calamities!

The rider's figure was out of sight, however, now; and the beat of his horse's hooves was quite silent. The feeling which had arisen from some subconscious recess in the man's nature died down with their vanishing. Rook surveyed the empty road in front of him with a vague, incredulous smile. Then he shook his head in the same feeble protesting manner as he had done before.

"Rook Ashover, you must look to your wits!" he muttered; and he struck at a tall patch of hog weed out of which fluttered a tortoise-shell butterfly.

All sorts of quite irrelevant and even ridiculous things came into his mind. He remembered a wooden sword that he had played with as a child and he saw distinctly the gray dilapidated mane of a hobbyhorse he used to ride. Then there came suddenly into his head the word "Gorm," written upon a ghostly signpost.

"That boy must be the boy from Comber's End," he repeated mechanically. But as soon as he had formulated the words he remembered that it was when he himself was a boy that he used to meet the farmer's son of that remote manor house.

The face of the countryside had retaken its natural colour from him now. The appalling grayness which had so mysteriously fallen upon it had completely vanished.

"I must have worried myself into some sort of fit," he thought. "I wonder if I fell down just now and have been lying on the road, as Mother used to say I did when I was a boy. God! I must be a bit more careful how I let my thoughts run away with me! I wonder if someone on horseback *did* pass me by, or pick me up? But what on earth could I have said to the chap? He must have thought I was drunk. God! I must have seemed perfectly mad to him! I talked to him as if he were Ann's child grown into a man. And *he* talked to me like that."

He pulled his hat down over his head and walked steadily forward, puzzled and disturbed. He could see the end of the lane now, about a quarter of a mile in front of him. It merged itself in a broad highway, the famous Roman road between Salisbury and Exeter, and at the point where it met the road stood a copse of larches, incredibly fresh and green against the southern sky.

Rook continued to review with a sullen puzzled obstinacy

his recent experience. What annoyed him was that he kept seeing that green slime and those trodden cattle droppings; and then completely losing the thread of everything. Had he fainted there by the pond and just dreamed about the rest? But when he came to his senses he was out of sight of the pond. He must have got up and walked on, still in a state of unconsciousness! He had heard of people doing that kind of thing. What did they call it? *Amnesia.* Well! He must stop letting his thoughts run on into these wretched manias. He had been worrying himself too much. Marriage? Well! Other men had made fools of themselves before, without falling into these morbid spasms of horror. Was he, deep down in his subconscious nerves, twisted in some way, unnatural, abnormal, without the ordinary masculine feelings about women? He knew that the excitement with which he was now hurrying to Comber's End was something beyond any emotion he had ever felt in awaiting a rendezvous with a woman.

Was that fainting-fit into which he had fallen just a mental reaction from some deep shock of physical aversion connected with his marriage to his cousin?

He stood quite still under the green clump of larches and pondered on this with a scowling brow.

What nonsense! He remembered how wonderful and lovely that night in Drools' cottage had been. Was it nothing but the heady fumes of that rich Dorchester ale, nothing but the sorcery of those snow-burdened midnight spaces, that had cast such a glamour over that encounter? Was he, down deep below all his love affairs, an indurated, an incorrigible misogynist? He shuddered a little as the memory of the nausea through which he had passed reapproached the threshold of his consciousness. He shook it off with a jerk of his head and a wave of his stick; and started at a swinging, resolute stride, northward, along the highway.

"I'm tough enough to survive these shocks," he thought to himself; "and I can drink my draught of Lethe and forget them all."

He looked around him now with a return of his natural de-personalized passion for that perpetually changing face of the Frome valley.

"Forget them all," he repeated to himself: and out of the depths of his soul he uttered a kind of inarticulate prayer to those green pastures, to those leafy woods, to those sailing clouds, that he might remain to the end their unperturbed, unaffrighted votary!

After a quarter of an hour's walking along the Roman road he came to a lane on his right which was as thickly overgrown with summer grass as if it had been a narrow elongated meadow. "To Comber's End" said the signpost at the corner; and Rook hastened down this propitious avenue of greenness with a nearer approximation to a light heart than he had known for many a long day.

After following the lane's winding course for some twenty minutes and getting, as it seemed, deeper and deeper into a maze of ancient orchards and dark-stemmed covers he came to a place where his path widened out into a kind of miniature parkland.

Acres of velvety grass dotted with thick-trunked oak trees lay spread out before him in the hot, shadowless noon sunshine, with a herd of brown-and-white cattle feeding on one side of it and a group of horses lying asleep on the other.

The scene had that peculiar monumental quality under the cloudless sun, such as does not often, even in the most privileged localities, arrest the traveller's attention. It struck Rook now as if it came to him with the weight of a whole series of complicated human impressions behind it. It seemed to summon him forth, as it must have summoned his ancestors before him, out of the cluttered distractions of the passing hour into some larger, nobler world, some world that lay all the while only just behind the familiar, the taken-for-granted, the common undistinguished face of crude reality!

He crossed the grass with a happy liberated step; passed close to the sleeping horses whose huge and sprawling abandonment had something so naked, so *animal* about it—their legs and hooves protruded so shamelessly from their round bellies!—that he felt as if he were some shadowy supernumerary come to life in the rich canvas of a Tintoretto or a Titian; one of those carelessly sketched anonymous figures whose business it is to stare modestly and self-effacingly at some great mythopœic event whose "persons" are gods and beasts and heroes.

Passing down an avenue of chestnut trees, whose branches made a flickering catafalque over his head, he came to the edge of the little lake on the farther side of which the Comber's End manor house stood.

The place was as majestic and undisturbed as if the centuries had passed over it like a flock of wild geese dropping nothing but a few gray feathers to mark their flight.

The kitchen garden of the manor farm was surrounded by a high brick wall, the eastern side of which abutted upon the lake, leaving only a narrow footpath, overgrown with tangled vegetation, between it and the actual water.

Rook, as he saw all this, was suddenly almost glad that he had not come bolt upon his brother! That peculiar thrill, unlike anything else in the world, that trembles through us when, quite alone, we arrive suddenly upon a scene that answers to our deepest æsthetic exigencies is quickly dissipated by the neighbourhood of even the most friendly alien personality.

It establishes itself, this feeling, as if it were a furtive, intimate understanding between ourselves and whatever scene it may be answers to our craving.

And such moments have another, a yet more subtle value;

namely, their power of linking themselves up in some mysterious way with all the other past moments of a similar nature that we have passed through in the course of our life. Toward these other moments the present one seems to gravitate by a natural affinity, taking its place among them and establishing itself among them, in such a way as to draw them out more clearly, more definitely, from their hidden retreats, and to make us more vividly aware of them.

It is then that we become conscious that in addition to the ordinary gregarious human life, led by us in contact with others and in the stress of our normal pursuits, there is another, a more intimate life, solitary and detached, that has its own days and months and years, such as are numbered by no measurings of common time, by no computation on any terrestrial almanac.

Underneath the procession of our normal days the visions of these solitary moments mingle and flow, making the dust and noise of the overt drama of our life seem crude and vulgar in comparison. They have nothing to do with the emotional or with the rational processes of our nature, these moments of vision. They are purely æsthetic. Yet they are not æsthetic in the sense of being entirely preoccupied with what is usually called beauty. The more definite and more suggestive word "magic" indicates better the quality to which they respond. For "magic" can be felt, both in landscapes and in other places, where there are few elements of those high mysterious values which we associate with the beautiful.

As Rook stood now on the edge of Comber's End Pond and watched the moor hens and coots and wild ducks floating upon water that was the colour of lapis-lazuli, it was not the beauty of the scene that carried his consciousnes down that strange interior river, under ancient bridges and by hushed gardens, past shadowy terraces and turreted towers, past lonely towpaths and long-stretching melancholy roads! It was something that might easily have worked its charm upon him had the place lacked almost all the gracious beauty it possessed; had it been no more than a couple of stunted pine trees staring down upon the raw edges of a deserted quarry!

Rook's own particular response to the accidental groupings of scenery was something that implied sometimes a vindictive malice against the richer forms of loveliness and an obstinate sullen preference for things that were abject, woebegone, god-forsaken. Thus were certain peculiar characteristics in his erotic life transferred to his æsthetic life; and the misery of his yearning to comfort the unhappy Netta found itself balanced by his malignant reaction from the brilliant Ann.

Suddenly to his immense astonishment he caught sight of his brother where least of all he had expected to find him; and as he chuckled to himself and waved his stick in the air he became for a moment a completely different human being.

Gone were all his dark manias and phobias. Gone were all the mystic ecstasies of his secretive personal life. In one great wave of joyous rejuvenation he became a boy again with the companion of his boyhood!

An aspen poplar, blighted by some long-forgotten thunderstorm, stretched a great dead leafless branch, bifurcated in the centre, right over the surface of the lake. Out upon this perilous projection the reckless invalid had managed to climb; and there he lay, in serene and triumphant complacency, his Cæsarean head propped against the blackened trunk and his thin bare legs dabbling in the water. He had been there all the while, watching Rook with a whimsical amusement, and all he did now, when his elder brother walked over to his retreat, was to greet him with such a satiric grimace that Rook felt the same disturbed boyish embarrassment that he used to feel in the very old days when Lexie took him to task for some piece of egoistic priggishness which he had hoped had passed unnoticed by that cynical eye.

"You don't expect me to join you out there, I hope,' said the elder Ashover, regarding his brother's position with some apprehension. "What have you done with poor Twiney and his cart?"

Lexie's only reply to this was to make a second grimace which crumpled up his classical countenance till it resembled one of those goblinish tailpieces with which 18th-century publishers used to adorn their more decorative quartos.

"Don't you worry about your lunch before the moment I've arranged for it, brother Rook," he remarked after a moment of silence; during which Rook seated himself upon the bank at the foot of the tree. "The amazing thing is that I've managed to get you here at all considering the way you've treated me these last weeks."

"Ay? What's that? Oh, you mean that I've been more often to Toll-Pike than to your place? What nonsense! I haven't seen Nell for the last fortnight and we've been together twice—no, three times!—in that time."

Lexie settled himself more comfortably in his seat, drew out of his pocket a small cardboard box, rattled it vigorously, opened it, shook the contents into the palm of his hand, and conveying it from there to his mouth, swallowed it at a gulp.

"What's that?" enquired Rook, lighting a cigarette and stretching out his legs in luxurious contentment.

"Morphia tablets," replied his brother with ironic brevity.

There was a touch of bitterness, of faint reproach even, in the tone with which those two sinister words were uttered, which Rook did not miss.

The two men looked for a moment into each other's eyes. Rook was the first to remove his gaze; and as he turned it upon the sunlit waters of that great placid pond that he and Lexie had visited together from their earliest childhood, a sharp pang, different in its nature from any he had been feeling before, went through his heart.

What *would* he do, how *could* he endure his life, when this brother of his had been driven from his last stronghold, from the bifurcated branch of Ygdrasil, the World Ash tree, and had slipped into a lake deeper than that of Comber's End?

CHAPTER XX

IT WAS under the heavy green of a midsummer chestnut tree, of all trees the one which takes to itself most completely the character of that umbrageous season, of that interlude in the year's progression, when the "primal burst" is over and the yellows and purples of the August efflorescence are still unbudded, that Rook and Lexie unpacked Mrs. Bellamy's basket and enjoyed the culminating hour of their *fête-champêtre*.

The chestnut's branches, with their huge, somnolent leafy fingers hovering above them like an indulgent episcopal benediction, stretched out over the smoothly running brook which fed the water mill at the eastern extremity of the lake. Here Rook ate his meal, seated with his back against the trunk of the tree; while his brother, with that invincible desire to give every passing moment some additional heightening, which the fatality of his illness had begun to accentuate to a point of actual recklessness, had succeeded in balancing himself on one of the great motionless spokes, covered now with moss and ferns, that in former times used to turn the machinery of the mill.

The younger Ashover had finished his lunch—his taste for food was growing steadily more capricious and fastidious—and was now smoking one cigarette after another, as he sat hunched up there above the stream with his knees beneath his chin.

"I hope that wheel won't suddenly begin to turn," said Rook. "How does it manage to stay still with the water flowing on underneath it?"

"It's not really flowing," said the other. "To make it

come with a proper rush, strong enough to move the wheel, they'd have to lift up some dam on the other side."

They both remained silent, listening to the monotonous ripple of the little brook as it eddied and gurgled round the stones in its shallow bed.

"There's a trout!" cried Lexie suddenly. "Did you see it? It went under that green stone. Do you remember how we used to catch them in a butterfly net by damming up the pools under the bank?"

Rook shook his head. "I'd forgotten that," he said. "But I remember how you always used to say that a fresh-caught trout, lying stone dead in a handful of grass, was one of the objects a person would remember most vividly if he had been transported to a different planet and was trying to recall the most characteristic and delicious things in his old earth life. The look of those silvery scales and purple spots, with the little bits of bright-green grass sticking to them, was only rivalled by one other thing in the world you used to say."

"What was that?" enquired Lexie.

"The smell of the inside of a pea's pod when you've just shred the peas?" pondered Rook gravely. "Or the smell of one of those squares of fresh turf in a wheelbarrow when someone's making a new lawn; or the smell of honeysuckle, when it's very yellow and a little faded? No! I don't believe it was the smell of anything! What *was* it that you used to put second to the trout?"

He mused for a minute or two in a silence that was full of the faint ripple of the stream and of the distant murmur of wood pigeons.

"I know!" he cried eagerly. "No; it wasn't a smell. It was the look of silver weeds, all covered with white dust, at the edge of a road that's just going over a hill from which you can see the sea!"

Lexie stared at him from his precarious seat on the mill

wheel with a strange, intent absorption; an absorption so deep that Rook became aware that his mind had wandered away from their conversation. His eyes as he stared grew larger and more wistful, and the elder brother became uneasy and in some way put to shame by their expression.

There came over him, as he met their unseeing gaze, a sensation of the most heartbreaking sadness; that sort of sadness which comes upon us when in the middle of some hot cornfield, between the singing of larks and the hum of the cutting machine, between yellow stalks and red poppies, we hear the tolling of the village bell and think of the raw, open oblong hole in that crowded enclosure and of the white surplice of the priest!

"I'm getting stiff sitting here," said Lexie breaking the spell. "Give me your stick a moment."

Rook held out to him the end of his stick and his brother pulled himself up by its assistance and jumped upon the bank. Here he lay down upon the sun-flecked moss, his head against the other's knees. Rook ran his fingers over the embossed corrugations and deep-dented furrows of the younger man's heavy forehead.

"I wish to the devil," he said abruptly, "that you and I were quite alone in the world! Think what it would be like," he went on, "if this evening I were coming back with you to Marsh Alley, and there were no one in Ashover House except complete strangers! Mrs. Bellamy could look after us both perfectly well; and we'd have nothing to think of—no worries, no responsibilities!—nothing but just to read and talk and walk and watch the changes of the weather."

"You might have done it if you'd really wanted to," said Lexie.

Rook's hand left his brother's forehead and made an impatient clutch at the moss and the dry rubble.

"That's a cruel thing to say; and you know very well it's a silly thing, too. I couldn't have left Mother alone. I might as well say to *you* that if you'd really wanted us to live together you'd have never gone off to Marsh Alley at all."

Lexie shifted his position a little so as to get his face into the sunshine.

"How could I live in that house with you and the old man cursing each other all day long? It was you who begged me to go off, so that we should have a place where we *could* be at peace!"

"Then why did you talk just now about my leaving Ashover and living with you? We *did* practically live together in those days. I was always coming over to you. You know I was, Lexie."

The younger man's tone softened. "I know it, Rook, I know it. It's only been this last year, since you brought your girl here, that we've been really separated. Why did you do it, Rook? Why did you do it?"

"I wish to the devil I hadn't done it!" cried the other fiercely. "It was only *that* that made Mother bring Ann here; and if *she* hadn't come, we might have been just as we were!"

"You'd have got some other girl; or *I* should," said Lexie. "No, it's no use blaming each other. It's all natural enough."

"It *isn't* natural," shouted Rook; and Lexie, though he couldn't see Rook's face, was only too well aware of the quivering and tightening of his upper lip and the protrusion of a vein in his forehead.

"It's a monstrous mania, this obsession we both have for young girls! It's inherited from the old man; just as *he* inherited it from *his* father! It was a beautiful piece of irony, just worthy of the way things work out, that it was Grandfather's bastard who landed me with Ann. And then the trouble I've had with Betsy; and with Nancy's luckless progeny! I tell you it's a monstrous obsession; that's what it is!"

Lexie got up and sat in a pool of flickering golden sunshine, hugging his knees.

"I cannot understand," he said, "how you can be what you are, with flashes of noble insight such as you have, and then fall back like this. When you talk as you've just been talking I feel only one thing for you, brother Rook."

"What thing?" enquired the other in a more normal tone.

"Contempt," was the younger Ashover's laconic answer.

"Lexie, that's not fair," protested the accused man with the peculiar expression of half-ironic, half-authentic humility which he always assumed under a frontal attack. "Why is it contemptible to call this thing an obsession?"

"Because you sing such a bloody song about it, and then go on exactly the same! Why can't you treat your girls as girls ought to be treated; and as, in their hearts, they like to be treated? Why can't you just enjoy them for what they are and let them know what *you* are; without making such a devil of a fuss about it? It was a piece of pure sentimentality to bring Netta here in the beginning. And then, to go and marry Ann just because you'd taken your pleasure——"

"But, good Lord!" Rook interrupted, "one can't get one's cousin, and a girl like Ann, too, into trouble and 'nothing said'!"

The invalid made one of his most goblin-like grimaces at this.

"*She* got her pleasure out of it as well as you, brother Rook, and as for the results—oh, well! It's no good going back on all that now. When is her child to be born?"

He flung out the question with as much nonchalance as if it had been of very small moment whether Ashover had an heir or not.

"In September, I suppose," answered the other. In the silence that followed this, Rook's mind wandered off to Netta and a miserable frown came upon his forehead as with his eyes watching the movements of a pair of green finches in a small hazel bush beyond the stream he wondered whether that drinking habit into which she had flung herself had gone from bad to worse. "I've done it for the best," ran the phrase in her letter. Did *that* refer to the drinking? And if so, what did she mean?

"What's the matter now?" enquired Lexie, and his elder brother began to explain how his remorse about Netta's disappearance was mixed with his fear of the effect of drink upon her.

"You know what it is," he said. "Men can drink heavily without its changing their life. I don't think women can do that. If once they get any real dependence on it, they're lost! Their whole nature seems to go to pieces."

Lexie nodded grimly.

"I can't think what started her drinking like that," Rook continued. "She never touched liquor when I first knew her; but since that New Year's Eve party of yours she got worse and worse. She used to drink in her room. I found a lot of bottles afterward; and I could see that Pandie knew about it."

Lexie opened his eyes very wide at these words. "You don't mean to say you didn't see what was at the bottom of that?" he cried in unfeigned astonishment. "I saw it like a map."

Rook stared at him blankly. "What are you talking about?"

"You don't mean to say you missed the piquancy of *that* little game," Lexie went on. "I don't know how much was due to your philanderings with Ann and Nell; but it was plain to me that Netta had got something on her mind that she was trying to drown; something that egged her on to be absolutely reckless."

Rook struggled awkwardly and stiffly to his feet.

"Did she say anything to you?" he cried harshly.

"Don't fly off at a tangent now. You couldn't have stopped her. It was natural enough."

"But she knew Ann and I were old friends. I told her so often. And she hadn't the least idea there was anything between Nell and me."

Lexie smiled complacently and pityingly. "It's amazing, Rook, how you can be so intuitive with women sometimes and so absolutely blind at other times! I don't say that your flirtations made her unhappy; but they were quite enough to make her a bit careless of appearances."

"Did any one else see what she was doing, do you suppose, except you and that little baggage Pandie?" Rook began swinging his stick as he asked this question. A troubled and nervous desire for some sort of action made it impossible for him to remain still.

"I have not the least doubt that everyone saw it—except you. I shouldn't be surprised if Cousin Ann saw it, even before I did."

"Why didn't she tell me, then? Why didn't *you* tell me?"

"Really, Rook, that's going a bit too far! Outsiders can hardly be expected to meddle between a man and his girl. Besides, nothing could suit Ann better than that Netta should make herself impossible!"

Rook let his stick fall to his side.

"You don't think she encouraged her in it, do you?" he said in a harsh whisper. "They were always together."

Lexie laughed. "There's a big gap between encouraging a person in a thing and making a fuss to stop them from it. I don't suppose Ann did anything about it at all. Just watched it going on, as I did, and *hoped for the best!*"

Rook's face was now convulsed with anger. "You were all against her!" he cried. "Every one of you! You all hated her and wanted her to clear out, while you kept me locked up and fed with penny buns like the bear in the Bristol Aquarium!"

Lexie chuckled with immense zest at this comparison. There *was* something, he thought to himself, very like a zoo animal about Rook's sulky restlessness. He got up from the ground and came over to his brother.

"Come," he said, "we won't quarrel over Netta. I would far rather live with Netta, drunk or sober, than be married to Cousin Ann! But don't look so miserable! If I *were* married to your wife I would soon put her in her place. And I'd dearly love to do it, too!" he added, with a leer that was at once dictatorial and satyrish. "I'd manage her, brother Rook. I'd tame her."

They gathered up the remains of their meal and tossed them into the basket.

"No, I'll carry it," said Rook, "and you take my arm! I can't have the doctor cursing me for tiring you out over this day's business. I want to have a lot more jaunts with you this summer."

They moved off together along the edge of the lake. For some reason or other Lexie's blunt, uncompromising attitude to Lady Ann gave Rook a feeling of relief. He felt less submerged, less invaded, less divided from himself with his brother at his side.

"Well!" he said presently. "This isn't the first time you and I have walked along this piece of grass. Oh, Lexie, Lexie, what things we have seen and felt together! I know that, wherever I am and whatever I see, there aren't many objects that catch my notice without my wanting to share them with you. I don't hold back much from you, Lexie."

The younger Ashover irreverently put out his tongue at this.

"Liar!" he said. "You know perfectly well that you're as reserved as the devil, even with me! I often feel that you have endless ideas and sensations that you hug to yourself and would hate my getting a hint of. But I do believe you love me, Rook, better than any one else. I think you'll feel queer, now and then, after I've been put by Mr. Pod under that elm tree."

Rook's reply to this was to hang his stick over his wrist and hug his brother tightly in his arms, kissing him repeatedly on cheeks, mouth, eyes, and forehead.

"Well!" he said breathlessly as he released him, "it's a good thing that you and I were born under the same roof. Think what it would have been like if we'd just casually glanced at each other on some railway platform or pavement and realized what we'd missed when the crowd divided us! No, no, Lexie. Nothing will make me believe that you won't live longer than I shall. These doctors are always making mistakes. There! I announce to you, this last day of June and by the edge of this blue lake, that we shall live to walk here together in twelve months' time, talking just as freely as we're talking now! Perhaps I shall have found Netta again by then."

They looked straight into each other's faces; and one of those moods that do not often fall upon human beings, unless brought about by the magic of sex, passed over both of them and blended with the noble and spacious purlieus of those manorial woods, with the deep blue of the water, with the brick towers and gray slate roofs of Comber's End.

They moved on then; and after walking round a bed of reeds, from which a moor hen and its half-grown family splashed out into the open pond raising a thousand iridescent ripples, they came to a pause by a low ornamental wall decorated at intervals by brick pilasters the capitals of which were covered with the white droppings of innumerable swallows who made them starting points for their flights over the lake.

The two Ashovers sat down upon the sun-warmed coping of this low wall, a pleasant relic of the times when the Lords of Comber's End were the feudal enemies of their own family. It gave Lexie, who was something of an antiquary in these historic matters, quite a complacent thrill to be able to remind Rook how long ago it was that the last of these hereditary foes had died childless. "It would have given *him* a shrewd slap in the eye," he grossly chuckled, "if he could have looked forward a couple of hundred years and seen *us* sitting here in ease and satisfaction."

Rook sighed. "Perhaps not," he said. "He may even be at this very moment anticipating the blow that's going to finish us off. How do we know that Ann's child won't turn out a girl? If it does, *that'll* end it! Comber's End and Ashover's End—there'll be nothing to choose between' em."

"Why do you say 'that'll end it'?" protested the other. "It looks to me as if my sister-in-law were good for more than one fling of this sort."

Rook was silent. Why *had* he said just that? The words had seemed to come from him with the smooth and suave fatality of speech which makes it difficult for poets to say "earth" without saying "green" and "sky" without saying "blue."

"Somehow," he contented himself with replying, "I can't imagine Ann not having a son for her first child."

He smiled at that moment to himself; for he thought how Lexie would have jumped out of his skin if he had answered him by saying that he had himself, that very morning, seen with his own eyes the boy that was to be born!

"By the way," he enquired casually, "do you know if there are any young people at the farm here now?"

Lexie looked at him significantly and quickly. "I've a good reason to know," he said; "but I was going to keep it from you for a bit longer. As a matter of fact, there's a very handsome youth there and a charming young girl. I know it because I had a companion with me when I drove out here this morning."

It was Rook's turn to show signs of agitation.

"What's this?" he flung out. "You don't mean to say——"

Lexie interrupted him. "It's Nell," he cried hurriedly.

"Don't get annoyed with me, Rook! I met her quite by chance and begged Twiney to stop and pick her up. She was setting out to see this youth and his sister on some parochial affair of Hastings's. Hastings puts lots of things of that kind off on her."

"Where is she now?" The words broke from the elder man with an impatience and eagerness that surprised himself.

"I don't know where she is now," answered Lexie, "I told her we'd call at the house and take her home late in the afternoon. I meant to keep it as a surprise for you, so, for God's sake, don't look so sick!"

Rook "sleeked over," as the poet says, his agitated expression; and picking up a loose piece of masonry from the wall beside him flung it into the water. The missile caused an enormous circle of ripples which enlarged and enlarged under their eyes.

"Do you remember how we used to play ducks and drakes in this pond?" he said. "I can't remember now where we got the stones."

"Under the house, over there," said the other. "You used to send me off to get them while you went on reading your book!"

Once more, deep down underneath the immediate agitation of Nell's presence between them, the old familiar thrill of their intimate association ran through Rook's soul. He watched the ripples that he had made in the water go on extending and extending toward the centre of the lake. "When Lexie and I are together," he thought, "it's as if a new personality were created that throws a glamour over the tiniest little thing that happens."

"Do you believe," he said aloud, "that there's *any* chance—any shadow of a shadow of a chance—that you and I will meet again after we're dead?"

Lexie's answer to this was not lacking in either emphasis or assurance.

"Not the faintest," he said with a smile. "While either of us is alive the other will, in a sense, go on living. But when we're both dead, we're both dead. Do *you* realize what to be dead actually means, brother Rook? I sometimes have the feeling that in *that* matter I have more imagination than you!"

When he turned to see the effect of his words upon his companion he saw Rook's gaze intently fixed on something on the lake which was obscured from his own sight by a tuft of reeds. But a moment later he, too, saw it—the form of an incredibly proud and majestic swan, paddling slowly toward them.

The bird was so beautiful that the vision of it passed beyond the point where either of them could share the feelings it excited with the other. It seemed to bring with it an overpowering sense of awe; for both the Ashovers regarded its advance in spellbound silence. It was as if it were floating on some mysterious inner lake that was, so to speak, the platonic idea, or the ethereal essence, of the actual lake which they were contemplating. It might have been swimming on an estuary that had suddenly projected itself into our terrestrial spaces from a purer level of existence, some tributary of the Eternal and the Undying, that flowed in for one ineffable second of time, converting the watery element it mingled with into its own ethereal substance.

The spell of its approach was broken as soon as the bird itself realized that the Ashover brothers were not two motionless tree-trunks, but alien and disturbing invaders. It swung round with a proud curve of its great neck and an eddy of the blue water about its white feathers, and sheered off toward the centre of the pond.

Rook and Lexie regarded its departure with concentrated interest; but now that the magical moment had passed they were able to note the almost humorous effect of the swan's attempts to retain his impassive dignity, to show appropriate indignation, and at the same time to put a good clear space of deep lake water between himself and the onlookers.

"Susannah and the Elders!" murmured Lexie with a chuckle. "But aren't they provocative and tantalizing? I wish we could hide ourselves in the reeds and see it making love to Leda. What a shame Nell isn't here!"

"It's its neck that's so arresting," said Rook. "That sense of incalculable power mixed with serpentine beauty!"

"I don't know about that," remarked Lexie, "but I would give a great deal to see Nell caressing it."

A heathen and classic wantonness descended upon both men. They began to feel an irritable desire to separate from each other and find, each for himself, a companion as beautiful and capricious as that proud bird.

"I don't see why we should wait till the end of the afternoon," said Lexie, "before getting hold of Nell. What do you feel about going straight up to the house now?"

"All right," Rook agreed. "Only you know what that means? It means we're bound to quarrel! Won't you admit now that this whole business is a mad obsession? Here we sit, you and I, in the very acme of our precious day; everything enchanting round us, everything doubly delicious because we're together; and the mere sight of that bird's neck sets us off on the old wretched will-o'-the-wisp hunt, 'over bog, over briar,' though we know perfectly well that the whole thing's an illusion!"

Lexie made a deprecatory grimace. "Not an illusion at all. That's one of those tiresome metaphysical tricks you're always indulging in. Besides, it doesn't mean any very great separation. We usually come back to each other pretty quick, good luck or bad luck! Do you remember in old days how we used to set out for a bit of sport to Tollminster Great Fair? Have you forgotten those fields down by the river at Bishop's Forley? Or those seats under the trees at Polberry Cross? *You* used to be much more excited than I was when we started off, after breakfast, on a fine August day. That's just what you double-faced metaphysicians are always up to! You want to run with the hare and hunt with the hounds. You want to call honest natural pleasure an illusion; and yet you're more frantic to get hold of it than any one else!"

Rook sighed heavily. His brother's words, bringing back the long summer days of that old, careless, irresponsible life, made him feel the full weight of all his present miseries. Oh, why couldn't one separate altogether the spirit of adventure in these things from the wretched entanglements that come in their train? The outrageous notion came into his head of how lovely it would be if these irresistible beings, who allured him so, were as heartless and emotionless as that clouded-yellow butterfly whose flight he was now observing! Why couldn't it have been arranged like that; emotion and attraction remaining absolutely distinct things? They *were* distinct in him! Why couldn't they be distinct in everyone? And then, as the image of Netta's face as she had turned toward him on that last day in their room rose up before his mind's eye, he knew that all this chatter about sport and pleasure was a mere ruffling of the surface of reality. How could one even dream of girls being like clouded-yellow butterflies, when that single look, terrible and beautiful "as an army with banners," in the face of *one* of them, was enough to take the taste out of all food and the sweetness out of all sunshine?

"Let's walk once across the field before we do anything else," he said sadly; and Lexie was far too sympathetic to the fitful moods of his brother, and far too sagacious, to utter a word of protest.

So, turning their backs to that blue water, they moved slowly side by side across the sunlit park land. The oaks were beginning to cast shadows now, short abrupt shadows, the hot shadows of an early summer afternoon, smelling of moss and the breath of cattle and of puff-ball funguses.

The horses, which Rook had passed earlier that day, stood crowded together in the shade; while the brown-and-white cows, beginning to grow restless at the approach of milking time, moved uneasily along the edge of the meadow palings, snuffing the air and lowing.

They crossed the whole expanse of the grass in silence, and when they reached the road Rook could see that Lexie showed signs of feeling his malady upon him. They sat down by the roadside under a beech tree, where the ground was covered with last year's leaves and the scattered husks of beech mast. Here Lexie produced his little box and swallowed the last two tablets which it contained.

"I must have another," he murmured. "He said I could take three."

He dropped the empty box on the ground beside them and produced an unopened one from his pocket. Out of this, when he had broken its wrapper, he extracted one more tablet and swallowed it hurriedly.

"Let's have a look!" cried Rook, taking the little box into his hands.

The strain of suffering passed very quickly out of the younger man's face; as if his faith in the beneficent drug had the power of anticipating its chemical and physical effect.

"Ten of those little things," he said, "would finish *you* off, Rook. I fancy it would need about fifteen to kill me, as I've become inured to it. Odd, isn't it? Think now—how simple it would be for both of us to gulp them down, one after another; and then just to light our last cigarettes and make ourselves ready for Eternity. We're in such a convenient place, too! Twiney would be bound to find us; and he could bundle us into the bottom of his cart as if we were venison. Nell would have to sit by his side with one foot on you and one foot on me. It would be quite a *cortège-macabre*. The whole village would turn out to see us go by. You know how the rumour of those things runs in front of the thing itself? 'The brothers Ashover, furtively but blamelessly pursuing their last journey into their native domains.' Can't you hear how Hastings would describe it to his friend in Bishop's Forley? Can't you catch the unctuous clerical humour enhancing the taste of the well-baked tea cakes on some little tennis-lawn?"

Rook, who was holding the box tightly in his fingers, looked at his brother with a scowl. "I think it's extremely wrong of Twickenham to let you have so many of these damned things! You might easily swallow them in your sleep; or even forget how many you'd taken and take an overdose. Really, Lexie; I mean what I say! It's not right. I don't like it. There! I'm cursed if I'll give them back to you!" And he proceeded to put the box into his own pocket.

"Give me those tablets, Rook, or I shall get angry! You needn't blame Twickenham. I only get the prescription from him. The chemist makes them up. He's an old friend of mine. You don't know him. He's a great fisherman and we talk of flies. He knows me too well to be afraid that I shall take one tablet more than the right amount. And no one but you would ever dream of a person taking morphia tablets in his sleep. Give them back, Rook, or I shall get very angry with you, and that *may* finish me off!"

His face became so agitated that Rook did grow afraid as to the effect such excitement might have, and drawing out the box he laid it down on the grass by the side of the empty one.

At that moment Lexie struggled hurriedly to his feet. "There's a White Admiral!" he cried in childish eagerness. And sure enough, clinging to a beech leaf on a bough that was just above their heads, its wings drawn back so that the translucent loveliness of their green-veined sides was revealed in full sunshine, swung this rare and exquisite butterfly.

Rook watched his brother standing there with his back to him, his arm extended and his hand moving slowly and tremblingly toward the unsuspecting creature, evidently, from its flawless freshness, just emerged from its chrysalis. How often had he surveyed in old days this familiar figure, stealing up toward some gorgeous hoverer, his whole being absorbed and rapt in the intensity of the chase.

There! Lexie had made his snatch at it, but the White Admiral had slipped away and was fanning its wings, wide-open now so that its proud black-and-white markings were distinctly visible, on another beech twig farther away.

Lexie moved toward it and once more stealthily lifted his hand.

It may have been that this familiar vision, redolent of old, sweet memories, brought to the elder brother's mind, in one unbearable rush of bitter thought, the feeling that henceforth he no longer possessed his own independent identity; or it may have been that ever since he first saw Lexie with that little box, the idea had been vaguely stirring within him that it would be wise to have such a key to final escape safely in his keeping! Whichever way it was, just at the moment when Lexie was most absorbed, Rook quickly opened the full box, emptied about twenty of the tablets into the other one and thrust the two boxes into different pockets.

Among the many movements made by the animals and the birds in the environs of Comber's End on that loveliest of midsummer days it was significant enough that the two most symbolic and expressive ones made by mortal men should have been a movement to capture one tremulous living creature and a movement to set free another; to capture a White Admiral butterfly, and to set free—*hospes comesque corporis*—a human soul, fooled to the top of its bent.

CHAPTER XXI

JULY passed and August came. The halcyon weather of the Comber's End day had not lasted very long. The latter half of July was gusty and cold. In many of the cornfields the wheat lay prostrate, beaten down and rain-sodden; while the hedge flowers, such as knapweed and scabious and ragwort, had that look of overweighted overgreen foliage and undersized rain-blighted blossoms such as indicates the absence of long hours of uninterrupted sunshine.

But with the coming of August all this changed. The prostrate corn lifted itself up a little. The roads grew dusty. The fairy rings on Battlefield turned pale green; the turf around them became bleached and yellowish; while the taller grasses at the edges of the fields assumed that shade of old mellow gold which answered to the ripening of the grain at their side.

The effect of the preceding stormy weather had been to produce an anticipation of autumn in certain aspects of that harvest season, in others to retard the autumn's approach with a kind of second midsummer. It was only on the higher uplands and on the slopes of the hills, where the soil was lighter and more gravelly, that the grass embrowned itself and lost its sap. In the valleys it remained moist, even after many long, hot days; and though groups of trees, here and there, that had been exposed to the rains and winds carried signs of their ill-usage, the more protected ones, in the depths of the Antiger Woods, for instance, were as richly green still as in the early days of June.

But a week of hot sun and sultry twilights soon manifested its effects. All along the banks of the Frome great spikes of purple loosestrife alternated with the ragged clumps of hemp agrimony and with the rose-coloured tufts of willow herb. The ditches of the water meadows were overgrown with meadowsweet; and under the crowded stems of the hazel copses the yellowing leaf spears of the dead bluebells were covered with masses of enchanter's nightshade.

But the real quality of these cloudless August days was to be found in the cornfields. Here amid the tall yellow stalks and the grain-swollen ears of wheat and barley rose up, as if over night, millions and millions of poppy flowers. Something about the texture of these filmy scarlet petals, as if they had been made of the blood of the earth itself, shed by hot sun kisses and staunched by hot sun breath, carried the very secret of that season from field to field and across the white haze-tremulous roads.

Little quivering vibrations in the air, waves of heat, would be seen floating now over the tops of thyme-scented banks or over the burnished metallic surface of the bracken. And as these flickering heat waves drew their faint purplish veil between one's eyes and the landscape, they brought with them the feeling, even in the midst of some brief stroll abroad after early tea, that one was upon a long, significant journey; a journey to a country quite unknown, to great dim cities with towers and spires, far off, over leagues and leagues of shimmering poppy-stained vapour!

And indeed, as one great spacious golden morning followed another, there did seem to grow upon the consciousness of more than one of the persons living in Ashover the feeling that they were being carried forward on some steady-keeled purple-sailed galleon toward the unknown marvels of an unknown harbour.

Lady Ann, now beginning the eighth month of her pregnancy, seldom left the garden. For hours she would sit on her chair under the linden tree, her hands idly clasped upon the book in her lap, her eyes fixed on the shadows on the grass.

Rook had become more considerate and more tender toward her as her time drew near; but he could not pretend to an excitement he did not feel; and for any sympathy in the paramount question that absorbed her—would her child prove to be a boy?—she was driven to the rather teasing and exhausting speculations of Mrs. Ashover, combined with the old lady's memories of the pre-natal peculiarities of her own sons.

It was the beginning of the second week in the month. The herbaceous borders of the Ashover garden had become like little tropical forests of heavily scented blooms to the bumble-bees and humming-bird moths that moved about among them. Round the high stalks of the delphiniums and the hollyhocks all manner of smaller flowers huddled themselves: petunias, verbenas, calceolarias mingling with every variety of campanula.

"How incredibly secure," thought Rook to himself, as at about two o'clock in the afternoon of a day that seemed even hotter than the preceding ones he strolled along the flower borders with the vague intention of taking the opportunity of a solitary walk while his mother and his wife both rested and the whole place was hushed in its noon siesta, "how incredibly secure and complacent you do look!" He surveyed half-enviously a small patch of blue lobelia that had got itself wedged in between two tufts of London Pride. "I suppose the life of a lobelia is entirely composed of long delicious passive sensations! I suppose a deep narcissistic ecstasy in its own Tyrian blueness is thrilling through it at this moment, combined with all sorts of mysterious *rapports* with the earth and air such as our animal senses have absolutely no idea of! I daresay it can even feel the movement of the planet itself; very likely blowing back a lovely freshness upon it, through all this heat, from airs outside any of the airs that we're conscious of! And it probably has the most subtle nuances of pleasure from its sense of the deep cool earth under its roots. I must tell Twiney to make sure he waters all these beds every evening now!"

He glanced at his wife's chair with her book and parasol left upon it; and it struck his mind how completely this girl of sport and adventure had submitted to her new rôle. He sighed heavily as he turned the corner of the house; for it was borne in upon him that he had made not the least attempt to penetrate the barrier of aristocratic reserve with which this mother of his child had guarded her feelings. She must have been having her panics and her disgusts; as well as her thrilling moments of mysterious pleasure! He certainly had made no attempt to arrive at any real intimacy with her, at any intelligent comprehension of what she was feeling at this crisis in her life.

What strange creatures human beings were! What obstinate, obdurate walls of egoism separated them from one another and substituted ignorant hostility for imaginative understanding! He walked round the house and down the kitchen-garden path where the rows of dahlias, tied to tall sticks, were still only masses of dark glossy foliage with chilly sour-looking globular buds that in their immaturity seemed to reject rather than welcome the noon heat. The difference between these sap-cold shining-leafed plants and the warm bloom of the peaches ripening so fast against the hot red bricks of the great garden wall fell in with his fatalistic thoughts; seemed to suggest the same insurmountable divergencies in the vegetable world as existed in human nerves!

But how infinitely shut away from vexations and tribulations the garden was, with its floating breaths from mint and rosemary, with its vague, sweet, diffused essence of ripening fruit under the hot, tarry netting, where the wasps buzzed and the white butterflies played!

The place seemed to hold up invisible barriers against everything in the world that was not gracious and time-mellowed. Mild ghosts of generations of placid gardeners seemed to bend over those well-weeded furrows of brown earth mould; seemed to raise old wrinkled sunburnt hands to the rusty nail heads and mouldering shreds of cloth which held the smooth twigs of the apricots; seemed to shuffle along those quiet paths carrying musk-scented geranium plants from "frame" to flower bed!

The spot seemed in some especial sense the accumulated retort of the human race to all the elements of chaos. Rook felt, as he loitered in it, as though the absence from his own days of the sort of patient diurnal labour which for generations had made all this possible was the central cause of his discontent.

He passed out at last into the orchard; and from the orchard into the open uplands. The slope of Battlefield as he made his way between gorse and bracken was sweet with the invisible scent of thyme. It was difficult not to tread upon tufts of euphrasia and milkwort; and when he reached the top of the hill the hot, windless suction of the noon's leonine mouth had filled the air so full with the odour of pine bark and turpentine and fir needles that he felt as if the trouble of human thoughts were a kind of foreign intrusion, an ill-mannered and irrelevant guest, amid the largesse of all this earth life.

Instead of exhausting him, the heat of that hour of the day seemed to put a sort of magnetic fever into his blood. He ran down the slope of Dorsal, sweating from every pore, but with an almost fierce exuberance of energy. Reaching Antiger Lane he turned to the right, away from the Drools' cottage, and began striding up the road at a great pace, swinging his stick as he walked. He soon passed the place where Ann had confessed to him just four months ago that she was with child, but even the sight of the hedge and bank and gate and trees at that particular point did not destroy the careless aplomb of his mood.

By degrees the nature of the scenery on the side of the lane facing the Antiger Woods changed its character. The hillside diminished to a gentle upward incline and by the time he arrived at a point parallel with the village of Ashover this slope became a field of ripe wheat.

What wind there was—an almost imperceptible breath from the east—reached his senses across this cornfield; and the smell of the ripe ears, like a quintessential airy diffusion of the bread of life itself, passed into his veins and increased the heathen exuberance of his blood. For the first time since he had seen that white swan's neck curving so provocatively at Comber's End, Rook immersed himself in the great undertide of the world's sensual life. All sorts of passing impressions, selected at random out of the things he had seen that day, conspired together to push him on into this fatal humour. The blue lobelia was there, the yellow wasps were there, the rusty nails in the scraps of cloth against the hot brick wall were there, the tonic fragrance of the fir trees; and now this sense of the bounty of the gods in the "living bread" of the generations!

There came over him the old mysterious classic acceptance of life upon the earth, of birth and death, of pleasure and sorrow, of love and the loss of love; and he had the feeling that whatever might be the issue of all these things for him, it was enough that they had been just as they had been. The horror that is never very far away, the loathing and the sick mad dread, seemed to fall off from his thoughts like scum from a boat's prow.

That immense noon heat, large and indolent and yellow pelted, like a great planetary lion, had licked up with its burning tongue all the poison and putridity.

He was immensely surprised, as he turned a corner of the lane, to encounter the redoubtable Mr. Twiney seated luxuriously in his familiar cart while his long-necked mare cropped the grass by the hedge.

Rook had no sooner caught sight of Mr. Twiney's face than he knew that something had ruffled the man's equanimity. The blue smoke from his pipe ascended in a thin spiral wisp and wavered among the thick sycamore leaves above his head as if it had been the tail of some dreamy feline ghost; but Mr. Twiney's tone did not correspond with the placidity of the smoke.

"Heigh! And what be Squire Ash'ver doing, then, this peevish-hot day? Ain't it enough to make man and beast sweat their selves into rain pipes; and grow as slippy as eels in pond mud?"

"It certainly is pretty hot, Twiney," said Rook, wiping his forehead. "How does your wife stand this kind of weather?"

Mr. Twiney sat erect at this and eyed him with a defensive and suspicious eye.

"Me old woman be snappish in winter, prickish in ploughing time, and all heads-and-tails in harvest. But come summer, same as us has now, and she be sweet as oil of Lebanon. I wish other folks were as well-spoken as my old woman be."

Rook undid the buttons of his waistcoat and tugged at his flannel shirt so as to let the air touch his skin.

"Who is it you're waiting for?" he enquired.

The owner of the mare gave the back of his grazing animal a gentle flick with his whip.

"Them sting flies be poisonous bad for horseflesh," he remarked meditatively. "What they do feed on when there ain't no horses where they do bide passes me comprehension."

"Twiney, who *are* you waiting for?" Rook repeated in a more abrupt tone.

The man looked at him rather dubiously. "I suppose I ain't giving away no lady's secrets nor no gentleman's either, when I tell 'ee, Squire, that 'tis thee own brother that I've a-brought here, long wi' Missy Hastings from Toll-Pike."

"Oh, naturally—quite right—very nice. I'm so glad."

These meaningless syllables fell from Rook's lips as if they had been over-ripe apples detaching themselves from a motionless bough on a windless night.

The man in the cart watched him closely, but the indolent and casual expression on Mr. Twiney's freckled face made him appear as one who while observing everything observed nothing.

"They be gone to Titty's Ring, Squire," he said pensively. "'Twere only a few minutes agone that they set out. I saw the tail o'n vanishing into wood by yon hedge gap. Don't 'ee be worritted, Squire! Master Lexie walked as upright as if he'd never had an illness in's life. I said to 'un, 'Don't 'ee kill yourself with exercise, Master Lexie!' and Missy Hastings she laughed in me face like a green yaffle. 'Let 'un lean on thee arm, as if thee was man and he were woman!' I said. And Mr. Lexie he answered me short and brusk-like, same as if I'd said somethink indecent. It doesn't do to speak to quiet men as your brother have spoke to me just now, Squire. All village do know he hasn't long to live. And maybe that's what makes 'un cranky. And we must be considerate with a nice gentleman, as he be. But I bain't one for brusky speeches, whether from the gentry or from me own wife. I likes to be bespoke soft and easy, Squire Ash'ver, as well as any man in England."

"I'm sure my brother meant no harm. And I'm sure Mrs. Hastings didn't mean to laugh in your face, Twiney. I can't imagine either of them doing such a thing. Well! Good-day to you! If I happen to meet them I'll tell them that you're still waiting."

He began to move off, but Mr. Twiney's indignation was not yet appeased.

"I think you ought to know it, Squire, though I'm not the one to tell you. But they do say down village that Mr. Lexie and Missy Hastings be up to no good in these goings on. I've a-driven them two into every lane and every cattle drive round these parts. I think it's only due to 'ee, Mr. Ash'ver, seeing as you're Squire and such-like, to let 'ee know how the wind be blowing!"

"All right, Twiney; I'm much obliged to you, Twiney; but you mustn't listen to the village gossip, you know. Good-day to you!" And with unctuous discretion on his tongue but black anger in his heart he strode down the lane.

So this was why he had been seeing so little of Lexie during the last fortnight! The rogue had stolen a march on him and had been up to serious mischief with that romantic little idiot! He found it impossible to see the thing in a reasonable or magnanimous light. A few weeks ago he would have shrugged his shoulders and washed his hands of the matter. Nell belonged to Hastings; not to him. She had never really belonged to him! Why was it, then, that he felt so maliciously angry with both her and his brother? He refused to attempt to analyze what he felt. He just gave himself up to a blind irrational grievance; to a sense of having been betrayed by his brother and fooled by the girl.

Every complicated and suppressed irritation he had ever harboured against Lexie rose to the surface. He felt as if he had wilfully allowed his remorse about Netta to tie his hands in a struggle with his brother which had been secretly going on for many months; a struggle as to whether he with his translunar lust, or Lexie, with his humorous satyrishness, should carry off this sensitive little being of the twisted mouth and the slender pliable limbs!

No sooner was he round the first corner and out of sight of Mr. Twiney than he stood stock still, staring at the woods in front of him. He knew well where Titty's Ring was. It was a clearing in the centre of the wood where the ground became level for a short distance and where in former times there had been a spring. Lexie had had from childhood a curious predilection for this particular spot; for the lusciousness of the long damp grass that grew there, for its complete isolation in the centre of so much undergrowth, for its cuckoo-flowers that were larger and of a deeper lilac there than down in the valley, while all the years he had known it there had been two grass snakes in that place, which every spring cast their spotted skins; of which skins he had collected quite a number, mysterious and unique objects, different in the feeling of their scaly texture from anything else in the whole world!

It was, in fact, as Rook well knew, a symbolic and significant fact that his brother had taken Nell to this favourite spot of his, and had taken her there, too, on an afternoon that seemed, as Lexie himself would have put it, "dedicated" to such a felicitous proceeding.

He approached the fence that separated him from the wood and began staring savagely into its umbrageous recesses. The wood itself became, as he gazed into its leafy shadows, an utterly different thing from what it had been before. It became a classic and Arcadian refuge, "dear to Pan and the Nymphs," in whose embowered hiding-places all the responsibilities of the world fell away and vanished.

Rook began to visualize the scene in Titty's Ring with an intensity that caused him a sick sinking sensation in the pit of his stomach. He made a faint troubled effort to remember the menace that overhung his brother's life; but even as he did this he found his own fingers fumbling at the little box containing those morphia tablets, the loss of which, when he returned the other one, Lexie had never discovered. No! He himself, as his mind became more and more morbid, might be driven to die, too. And that being so, the difference between their two fates was not so tremendous as to give him a cruel and outrageous advantage.

And after all, at the bottom of things, when it became a matter of two males fighting for a female, these questions of honour and justice and fairness and even decency, didn't they always go to the wall? Lexie had flung them over.

There had been a sort of tacit understanding between them about Nell; and though he had certainly allowed Lexie to think that he had withdrawn from the field, it was taking his withdrawal a little too literally, to act as if Nell were entirely fancy-free.

Rook's thoughts, as the August sun beat upon his head, growing even hotter as it sank a little from the zenith, were so wild and unbalanced as to resemble the thoughts of a person in a fever. The shock of what he had just heard and the vivid material images his mind kept conjuring up of what was going on at Titty's Ring stirred up a certain black mud of human maliciousness which lay dormant in one deep recess of his nature.

The most fantastic ideas entered his mind; the idea, for example, that he was the victim of a conspiracy of persecution, or at least of manipulation, in which everyone in his circle played a definite part, propitiating and managing him to ends that were theirs and not his.

He began to envisage Netta's disappearance as part of this conspiracy and it presented itself to him that his wife had probably encouraged Lexie in this more serious pursuit of Nell. And his mother, too! He recalled now how often in the last few weeks the old lady had held him at her side, no doubt to keep him away from Toll-Pike Cottage. He felt an angry sensation of being waylaid and humoured and manœuvred at every turn, of being surrounded by the pressure of soft, firm, strong hands that were regulating his life contrary to his deepest life illusion!

Once more he began to feel that in opposition to the free play of his identity all these terrible forces of tribal continuity and tribal self-assertion were using him for purposes utterly foreign to his own personal vision of existence. They intended that the family should have an inheritor; and in order that this should come to pass they were prepared to turn him, Rook Ashover, into a mere passive link in a chain that stretched back to the 13th Century and forward God knows how far!

The old blind vicious feeling came over him that he, a lonely, solitary, hunted figure, was engaged in a life-and-death struggle with "Thrones, Dominations, Principalities, and Powers," all conspiring to reduce his independent life to a meaningless cipher!

Well! He would fight them all; and if Lexie—the only human soul in the world that he really loved—went over to their side, he would fight him, too, whether he were a dying man or not! All the time that these extravagant thoughts whirled through his brain he held his cloth cap in his hand; and the early afternoon sun, full of the iron virulence which it possesses at that hour, intensified the fever that raged within him.

All at once, driven by a sudden irresistible impulse, he forced his way through the fence and plunged into the wood. Like Lexie he knew every stick and stone of that countryside; and it was not long before he hit upon one of the little mossy paths, formerly game drives but invaded now by every sort of vegetation, which intersected the thick undergrowth.

He followed this path with a stride that grew more and more rapid as he advanced; for he knew by the look of certain outstanding trees that he was not far from the piece of level ground where Titty's Ring and other smaller nameless expanses of open grass broke the leafy monotony.

Arrived at the first of these woodland greenswards he paused for a minute to take breath. Steady, unflickering shadows, dark as the hollow places in some immense sorrowful upturned face, lay in great silent pools on the deep-rooted grass. Faint vibrations of the air that could hardly be called winds lifted the feathery seed tops of hawkweed and dandelion; while out of the silence all around him came indescribable sighings and rustlings, as if an invisible population of elemental beings, lighter than air itself, were awakening from their noon siesta.

Wiping the sweat from his forehead with the cap he was still clutching in his fingers, he shook his head solemnly and gravely from side to side as if replying to some formidable argument of an unseen antagonist. He then moved away from this first clearing and took a path opposite to the path by which he had come.

A second greensward was followed by yet another, each one more magical in its shadowy seclusion; and Rook felt as if he were passing through a series of sacred groves, the leafy purlieus and outermost "lady-chapels," it might be, of some thrice-holy place, as yet unvisited by any human votary!

Hush! He was certain that he had heard voices. . . .

He stopped dead still, listening intently, cursing the loud chatter of a jay that broke the surrounding stillness.

It was those two! He knew their tones. He knew the amorousness in his brother's low chuckling laugh; he knew the faint broken protest—who would not know *that* if not he?—of Nell's timid and enchanting reluctance.

The path in which he waited now was narrowed and almost closed by several horn-beam bushes; and to the end of his life he remembered the look of those thick leaves, so olive-green on one side and so ivory-white on the other! One of these bushes had extended clear across the path; and unwilling to force his way noisily through its thick growth he sank down upon hands and knees and crept under it, still holding his cloth cap in one hand and his stick in the other.

A sour-sweet smell rose from the earth as his knuckles pressed against it, that peculiar smell which belongs to dry wood mould that has been so fed by fallen leaves and by the rubble of dead twigs as to become something far more organic than the soil of any ploughed-up open field.

In the midst of the blind turmoil of his blood his senses seemed preternaturally acute and alert. He saw the tiny gray cups of a little patch of moss, each cup decorated outside by infinitesimal scales and bosses, as if from the fingers of some fairy Hephæstus, and shining inside as though inlaid with opalescent enamel.

It was extraordinary how clear his mind was as he crept forward, the lower branches of the hornbeam switching the back of his head. He even stopped, for the flicker of a second, to lift up the bent stalk of a minute saxifrage which his hand, as if it had been the paw of an animal, had brushed heavily aside. As far as the sensations of that little cluster of pale green petals were concerned he might have been a love-crazed dinosaur, advancing to interrupt the pleasures of a brother dinosaur. A blind weight, a crushing bruise, and then a great mysterious uplifting! That was all that the saxifrage felt. How could it know that this miraculous uplifting was the result, achieved at a moment when the rest of the man was demented, of the existence of a pitifulness in human nature that was older than its earliest appearance in An tiger Great Wood?

There was a single moment, just before he saw them there in that sunlit glade, when a half-forgotten memory of some childish game with his brother in that very place became a living portion of the olive-green screen before him, a living film of affection, which had to be torn apart by a conscious movement of his will before he leapt out upon them.

But he lifted his head now, very gently, rising up on his knees; and what he saw, as he rose, seemed by its own power, independently of his will, to break that filmy screen of ancient association. Standing locked together in one another's arms, in the very centre of Titty's Ring, the long grass in the sunlight showing green as seaweed about their feet, Nell barely touching the ground upon which Lexie's heels were so masterfully planted, the two figures were swaying to and fro in an ecstasy of amorous enchantment. He rose upright, flung aside the last intervening branch of the hornbeam, and rushed out upon them.

His first impulse was to strike them both down. The accumulated irritations of many months would have been behind that blow; and behind it, too, would have been a deep, subterranean, occult jealousy of Lexie; not merely the immediate jealousy over Nell but a much more subtle thing: a jealousy of Lexie's sagacity and—who knows?—even of the mysterious advantage in these things that his very illness gave him! And mentally speaking, the blow *was* given. Rook had the feeling of giving it. He had the relief, the exhaustion, the relaxation of having given it. And yet in the course of his rush toward them, and of his approach till he stopped in front of them, he never so much as raised his hand.

Lexie was the one whose head was turned toward him and he at once loosened his hold upon the girl, who sank down upon the grass. Whiter than any human being had ever seen it was the younger Ashover's Claudian countenance as he moved forward a step or two, putting himself between his brother and the girl upon the ground. As for Nell, she gave one startled cry, stared at the intruder as if he had been a complete stranger, and then covered her face with her two hands.

"So this is it, is it?" said Rook hoarsely, confronting them with a look so menacing that Lexie made a little nervous deprecatory movement.

"Rook—I'm ashamed of you—to follow us like this—to frighten Nell like this—— What's up now? What's the matter with you? Nell and I have a perfect right to come out together if we want to on a fine August afternoon!"

His voice took on the old familiar tone of semi-badinage as he said this, and the colour began to come back to his face.

"So this is it!" repeated Rook, staring wildly at Nell who had now removed her hands from her face and was answering his look with a steady scrutinizing gaze that became more and more full of complicated significance.

"So this is how you have decided to treat me," he went on, throwing down both stick and cap upon the grass and rubbing his forehead as if to obliterate some evil dream. "It's the sort of thing one expects from Lexie," he continued bitterly; "but I'd fooled myself into thinking that *you* were different from the rest of them, Nell."

The younger Ashover began at this moment to display unmistakable signs of his malady. A quick spasm crossed his features; his mouth quivered; a convulsive tremor ran through him. "Sit down!" said Rook in a commanding tone. "No, you're perfectly right. I ought not to have come. But you needn't be afraid, you two; I won't interrupt your excursions a second time. Sit down, Lexie, can't you?"

His brother obeyed him and sinking on the ground by Nell's side hugged his knees with his arms.

"I thought you meant fisticuffs just now, Rook," he said, smiling. "What would *you* have done"—and he turned his head toward the young girl—"if Rook and I had started butting at each other like two roaring bulls? God! I'm glad you didn't go for me with that oak stick of yours, Rook. It looks like the very father of cudgels! Sit down yourself, for the Lord's sake; and don't stand on one leg any more."

But Rook did not change from his dazed, fixed stare at Nell. It was as if he had been some infuriated but puzzled savage, whose spirit was slowly being sapped by the power of a civilized eye.

"I'm sorry, Nell," he blurted out at last. "I'm very sorry I followed you."

But the girl rose quietly to her feet. "I think I'll walk home by myself," she said. "I've had enough of the Ashover family for one afternoon!"

Her tenuous sarcasm, obvious and simple though it was, carried a weight out of all proportion to its justification, by reason of its incongruity upon the lips that uttered it. Lexie made a grimace; and searching about in his pocket for what he wanted lit a cigarette with shaky fingers.

But Rook's face darkened into an angry frown. "You won't leave this spot, Nell," he said fiercely, "till you and I have come to an understanding!"

She made no answer to this challenge; but tossing her head and giving him one quick reproachful look she walked off toward the hornbeam path.

Both the brothers saw her forcing her way through the branch-covered aperture with swift impatient movements of her thin bare arms.

When she was out of sight Rook made a hesitating movement to follow her.

"Stop, you fool, stop!"

The affectionate roughness in Lexie's tone did more than all his whimsicalities to soothe away the elder brother's dangerous mood. Curiously enough, too, the mere fact that he had *seen* the worst, or what he convinced himself was the worst, of that amorous encounter, drew out the sharpest sting of his jealousy. And the girl had gone. Lexie and she were no longer together. And in her going she had reserved her indignation, her hurt pride, her revolt, her sense of shame, entirely for *him;* her mute reproaches entirely for him; her revenge entirely for him. That "I've had enough of you Ashovers" was a barbed dart that she must have known *he* would be the one to smart under! Lexie would not care. Lexie enjoyed a certain humorous gregariousness in his amours. "Enough of the Ashovers" was a hit at the elder of the Ashovers; and in these cases the one whom the woman wants to hurt the most is the one she loves the best!

So he argued with himself, applying the balm of convoluted reasoning to the wound he had received; a wound that all the while was healing from another cause . . . from the relief of a blow that had only been delivered on the astral plane! Restrained from following the girl by all these concerted withholdings, Rook himself sank down now on the grass of Titty's Ring by the side of his brother and accepted from his fingers a cigarette of peace.

"Think of all the hands through which this little white tube has passed," said Lexie, with a relaxed sententiousness, "only that it may burn itself out into thin air, between two quarrelling men, in the heart of a Dorset wood!"

He pulled out his little box as he spoke and swallowed a couple of the lozenge-shaped tablets. Rook was conscious of a faint sardonic malice as he let his own finger and thumb toy with the companion box in his waistcoat pocket.

They subsided into gloomy silence while the wood murmurs around them became a sighing echo of the great forward-rushing flood of Time, swallowing everything up.

"By the way, Lexie," Rook said after a pause, "doesn't it seem as if it were carrying things a trifle far, for us both to be making love so openly to the wife of the village priest? Hastings, of course, is too lost in his book to care what his girl does; but I did get a hint from Twiney just now that the village had begun to talk."

Lexie looked at him with narrowed, scre wed-up eyelids. Rook got a faint impression of something approaching a lewd wink; but Lexie's eyes had so many natural wrinkles around them that he may have been deceived.

"I notice," said the younger Ashover, "that it isn't until *your* particular star is suffering a momentary eclipse that this matter of propriety comes to the front. Good Lord! if we're to begin considering the feelings of the village we might as well give up having any pleasure at all. At least *I* might, who haven't been blessed with a mistress like Netta or a wife like Ann! Why! Do *you* realize that I haven't had any dalliance with any wench at all since those days when we used to go to Tollminster together?" His voice became high-pitched and even querulous. "I tell you it would be *monstrous* if I should go down to my grave without having known *any* pleasure!"

He fell into a fit of bottomless gloom from which his voice emerged again like the sound of a bumble-bee in a great foxglove bell.

"I adore them all!" he muttered. "I adore them all!"

Rook watched him with sympathy; but a mysterious meanness in himself at which he was both surprised and ashamed made the difference of their luck in this particular case not altogether disagreeable to his inmost mind. A very queer sort of vicious irritable malice, akin to the malice with which one regards the struggles of a mob at the ticket office of a theatre, took possession of him as he looked at Lexie's agitated face. He felt for one second as if it would give him a wicked delight to crowd Titty's Ring with the forms of sleeping mænads; and then, immediately afterward, to obliterate them with a wave of his hand!

His thoughts were interrupted by an unexpected remark from his brother.

"Nell is quite certain now," said Lexie gravely, "that Hastings *does* know where Netta is. She got it out of him last night that he knows. She told me to tell you."

The whole face of the surrounding scene changed in a moment for Rook Ashover. He rose and pulled his brother up by his hands.

"Damn the man!" he cried fiercely. "I thought there was something of that kind. Come on; let me get you down to the cart. Twiney's been waiting long enough." He took Lexie by the arm and held the hornbeam branches back while he passed through.

The sound of their footsteps, the rustling of leaves and cracking of twigs died away in the distance. The light wind lifted the grasses of Titty's Ring with an undulating airy softness that was neither melancholy nor cheerful, a remote softness that did not correspond with any emotions known to the human race.

Clouds of wavering gnats rose and fell, veered and drifted, across that sunlit space; and in their movements there was a sort of rhythm as if they were obeying some unseen fairy orchestration.

The two spotted green snakes, secure now of any interruption, came forth side by side. They might have been drawing the beechnut chariot of Titania herself; so carefully did they advance, every now and then lifting their purple-stained heads and darting out their tiny forked tongues. No other living thing appeared. Sunlight and shadow lay peacefully side by side; and silence fell upon silence like water upon water.

But nothing that stirs the magnetic currents between human beings, those waves of emotion that are like invisible harp strings and are so cruelly jarred, can be altogether lost in the atmosphere where it was begotten.

Something remains, some faint disturbance, some ghostly ripple, in that particular air, of which minds that are sensitive to such vibrations must for ever afterward be conscious.

Limned in that enclosure between woodland and woodland, some shadowy residue, some tenuous adumbration of those three human forms would thenceforth tremble there on the verge of visibility.

Long afterward when those three persons were dead and buried, the eidolons of what had happened to them in that agitated moment would be ready to resume their shape.

The rains might disfigure that spot and the storms dismantle it. Titania's snakes might reach their appointed sum of years and cast no more skins. It still would remain as an evidence of the potency of human passion that something in the quality of that place would never again be quite as it was before. Less palpable than any *revenant* of definite shape, these airy essences would only touch the nerves of such as were responsive enough to feel them. But as long as Titania's Ring did not lose altogether the character it held then there would be that upon its air that would not pass with the passing of any summer.

CHAPTER XXII

ALL through the rest of that hot August, night after night in the small book-littered room at Toll-Pike Cottage, Rook wrestled with William Hastings over the matter of Netta's address. The priest did not deny, on the contrary he quite openly admitted, that he knew where she was; but weeks passed and nothing that Rook could say or do was able to shake his obstinate resolution.

"I promised Miss Page not to betray her and I won't betray her."

They gradually became occasions of a curious and complicated perversity, these recurrent and prolonged conversations in that stuffy little room. Nell did not by any means always absent herself from the arguments between the two men; and her presence, when she joined them, added its own troubled implication to the increasing morbidity of these strange encounters.

In her reaction against both Rook and Lexie after that incident in Titty's Ring she had drawn insensibly closer to her husband. What had gone on in the depths of that entangled system of nervous susceptibilities which her slight frame enclosed would have required the elucidation of a book far nearer to the mysteries of life than that sinister manuscript in her husband's bureau now so seldom looked upon!

Her romantic devotion to Rook, already removed from the turmoil of her disturbed senses, sublimated itself during these hot August weeks into a passionate longing to do something, to do anything, to restore his peace of mind. She had begun to believe that if only she could bring Netta into his life again, that restless fever that seemed eating out his soul would be allayed and quieted.

Her unsatisfied craving for love, roused and irritated by days and days of feebler and feebler resistance to Lexie's ardour, turned now, in her reaction from her yielding mood of that one unfortunate afternoon, into a less fastidious and more complying attitude toward her legal companion.

Hastings himself began to be vaguely aware of unsuspected depths of perversity in his own feelings, especially in regard to his contest with Rook. He found himself deriving a vicious triumph from drawing out to further and further lengths the protracted struggle between them and he was even tempted sometimes to pretend to be weakening in his resistance in order that his opponent should not lose hope and retire in anger and disgust.

But if there were unsounded levels of morbidity in his desire that their strange duel should not end too quickly, there were still more furtive depths in his attitude to Rook and Nell when he had them together under his eye. He did not hesitate at these times to make the very utmost of the newly established relations between himself and his young wife, playing unscrupulously upon Nell's desperate desire that he should reveal his treasured secret and exploiting her touching attempts to persuade him.

Nell had not the remotest inkling of all that was going on in his mind. She herself, with a young girl's erotic egoism, was living just then in a sort of lingered-out trance of dreamy self-effacement. Had she known what ambiguous motives were mingling with his refusal to yield up Netta's secret she would have shrunk from his caresses as from those of a hooded snake. But her indignant disgust, as in so many similar cases, would not have been altogether just or fair. Hastings had, until that eventful summer, lived so completely in his metaphysical thoughts that he might be said to have had no normal human life at all; and now when, for the first time under the biting whip of jealousy, his natural self-assertion rose up and demanded satisfaction, it was only to find that this long-starved, long-delayed burgeoning was afflicted at the very root.

Against the corrosive poison of the humiliation he endured from the mere sight of Rook and Nell together his wounded vanity turned and turned upon itself, like an animal that turns against its own flesh; and by a strange obscure law, working in that dark inner world, he found his account in lacerating his own deep hurt still further; because, in so doing, he dragged the others down with him in a morbid complicity of shame.

As August drew to a close and the ninth month of Lady Ann's pregnancy approached, Rook felt himself becoming more and more of a lean, lifeless, motiveless shadow of the man he had formerly been. The preparations for his son's birth—for no one seemed for a moment to doubt the sex of the newcomer—caused him nothing but irritation. It was as though, as the infant came nearer and nearer to birth, it drew to itself every magnetic current of vitality that stirred in the air about it. The atmosphere of Ashover House seemed to exist for no other purpose than for nourishing this insatiable intruder; and Rook went to and fro among his people with a sense of seeing his most cherished fancies and illusions reduced to insignificant wind-wafted straws blown up and down the steps of the Capitolium in the path of a young Cæsar!

There were moments when that strange hallucination of the rider on the gray horse who had overtaken him on the road to Comber's End returned with a dim rebuking gesture at the excess of his pusillanimity; but for the most part he found himself shrinking away from the flushed triumphant languor of Lady Ann, from the nervous excitement of Mrs. Ashover, from the gloating whispers and glances of Pandie and Mrs. Vabbin.

It was indeed with the feeling of an escape from something that had grown well-nigh unbearable that he kept returning, every few days, to his attacks upon the secretive malignity of Mr. Hastings. To his conscious mind it was always of Netta that he thought; but in reality the mere neighbourhood of Nell's devotion, the mere propinquity of that supple youthful body and those clinging idealizing glances, was something that restored him to his lost place in the centre of his universe, something that transformed him back, from a negligible courtier mannikin in the train of his offspring, to an authentic protagonist in his own life tragedy, dealing with existence on equal terms!

The last day of August came and went; and with its departure the weather showed signs of changing. Gusty westerly winds, blowing up from the Bristol Channel across Sedgemoor and Blackmore, began troubling the sun-bleached trees and moaning disconsolately through the deserted stubble fields.

Rook had begun to grow conscious that lie was playing no very dignified part in this psychological chess game. He felt certain uneasy misgivings as to whether his determination to drag the secret at all costs out of the husband had resulted in anything more palpable than the distraction of his own troubled nerves by the society of the wife.

There came over him, too, as he began to recognize that Hastings had an obstinacy in him that no importunity and no persuasion could influence, an ugly and unpleasant sense of having been entangled in some equivocal spiritual orgy that was exercising a drug-like and sinister effect upon all three of them.

He felt ashamed that he had permitted this Toll-Pike obsession, whatever its nature might be, to interfere with the frequency of his visits to Lexie. Lexie had not been so well after that Titty's Ring excursion; and though whenever he and his brother did meet it was quite on the old unassailable footing, the younger Ashover could not help being conscious that the only permanent effect of the summer jaunts which he had found so sweet was to throw his timid companion back more unhesitatingly into the arms of her husband, more absorbingly into her platonic passion for Rook.

If Lexie could have pierced with his sagacious weather eye the mile or so of gusty autumn-smelling air and the few inches of brick and mortar which separated his candle-lit chamber from these nocturnal encounters at Toll-Pike Cottage, he would have made more than his usual grimace of disgust at the neurotic tricks of the human mind. It would have seemed to him that the very atmosphere of that room of Hastings's was penetrated with unnatural suppressions. He would have denounced every one of its three occupants as being engaged in spinning out, like so many demented silkworms, a thick unhealthy cocoon of meretricious emotion. He would have cast upon his brother one of those looks of indignant moral contempt such as a shrewd horse-dealer turns upon a showy but short-winded nag. And if he could have appeared before the three of them with an appropriate protest upon his tongue, it would have referred to the superiority of the most gross and the most unsophisticated bawdiness over this super-subtle mental dissipation!

As one rain-swept day followed another over the roofs of that Frome-side village the sense of expectancy, in the minds of all the persons with whom we are concerned, grew steadily heavier and heavier; until it became something that could hardly be borne.

This expectant mood, with the burden of gathering fate pressing upon it, is a natural enough phenomenon in all cases of child-birth. In this case, however, it went further. It affected Marsh Alley and Toll-Pike as well as Ashover House. It entered the innocent domicile of Mr. Pod. It sat down like a veiled figure upon the lintel of Mr. Twiney. It even seemed to visit the stable of the long-necked mare;

so ominous and plaintive were the whinnyings that proceeded from that square window abutting on the village street.

More than ten days of these September gusts had passed; when, one stormy night, Nell Hastings found herself suddenly and unaccountably wide awake in her bed. There was a waning half-moon observable through her window which kept throwing a pallid stream of light across her husband's sleeping head, before it was swallowed up once more by swift-travelling clouds.

The girl felt impelled to prop herself up on her elbows and stare out upon that patch of troubled changing sky. She had that uncomfortable sense of vast world-wide impending catastrophe which often comes to people, when, at some moment usually associated with oblivion, they catch the face of the world off-guard, so to speak, and in unsuspecting disarray.

She glanced over her shoulder at Hastings's face. Was it some movement, some muttering of his, that had roused her into this unnatural wakefulness? She looked at his watch on the little table beside them. It pointed to half-past two; just that particular hour of the night which Rook always maintained was associated with the lowest ebb of vitality in mortal pulses; the hour when ships sank, when wild geese failed in their flight, when old trees and old men turned cold, and when animals and children were stillborn.

Ah! It must have been Hastings who had disturbed her; for he was beginning to talk in his sleep now.

His words were broken and incoherent; fragments, it might well have seemed, and wind-tossed straws, of that troubled substance, the whole compact rondure of which seemed to be bearing them gustily through space, buffeted up—down—here—there—by winds that had no mercy and no purpose.

All at once she bent down above him and listened with every sense in her body; listened with the beatings of her heart above all; and with a cold tension of her muscles.

"I'll see you dead before I'll tell you!"

Her brain became one petrified conch of listening. It became a brittle shell through which some mysterious sound was destined to pass which it found almost unbearable.

But she had to bear it; and it did not fail to come in that commonplace, realistic, matter-of-fact manner characteristic of all true oracles.

"Thirteen Walpole Street" came the words from the sleeping man. "Walpole Street." And then there followed more incoherent mutterings and once again that ferocious sentence the words of which seemed to glow with a smouldering lava-like fury. "I'll see you dead before I'll tell you!"

He rambled on a little further after that; but his words carried no more significance to her ear than does the wash of the tide upon the pier-posts of a ferry when the traveller has once stepped ashore. She sank down again by his side in that wind-tossed half-moonlight and lay staring at the little squares of the window.

As so often happens with momentous human decisions, such as carry in their train drastic issues and devastating results, the first knowledge she had herself of the thing she was going to do seemed in some curious way to precede and antedate all the motives that subsequently accounted for it.

It was as if she were making a discovery in the mind of another person, the definite discovery, in fact, that this other person had decided, for reasons absolutely hidden from everyone, to bring Netta Page back to Ashover!

What she really discovered, as she stared at those window squares, was that she herself had irrevocably decided to bring Netta back; but this decision—based upon nothing that could be accounted for by any rational argument—required every kind of rational argument to support it and make it plausible!

What she felt within herself as she considered her plan—

this plan that she suddenly discovered to be already existing —was that, now she knew Netta's address, it would be impossible to hide it from Rook; and if Rook knew it he would take the next train for London! It seemed so much better for Netta to be the one to make the journey. If Rook went off in his present mood, God knows when he would come back. And obviously he would go. She knew him well enough to know *that* for an absolute certainty. Well, then, if she didn't want to think of him breaking away from everyone and staying on blindly with Netta in London, the only thing to do was to bring Netta to him.

She had begun to feel an unmitigated reaction against the morbid entanglement into which the existence of that secret had brought the three of them. She hated to think of her husband in that particular light. She hated to think of his having that advantage over Rook. To bring Netta herself upon the scene was to clear the air in every direction. She did feel a moment's qualm at the thought of doing it when Ann's child was so near birth. But Ann had never been considerate of *her* feelings or indeed of any one's. Ann had always struck out remorselessly for her own hand! So drastically had she done so that it seemed a kind of Quixotism to consider Ann in the matter at all. The person to be considered was Rook and as far as Rook was concerned, now that she knew where Netta was, there seemed to be only two conceivable alternatives: either to give him the address without comment, which would mean his going off pell-mell to London, to return God knew when; or to wire Netta straight away and send her the money to make the journey herself!

As to what would happen later on, as to what permanent arrangements Rook might wish to make, or Netta might be prepared to make, *that* must be left to the future to decide. She and William would have done their part, as soon as Netta and Rook had been brought together again! Her own desire was simply to reinstate her husband's dignity in Rook's eyes, and Rook's dignity in her husband's eyes; and to break up the unhealthy and sinister duel between them which had converted that August into one of the most morbid epochs in her life.

Of any deliberate revenge upon Lady Ann her mind was quite unconscious. She just ruled Lady Ann out of court as a person who could be trusted to strike out for herself, whatever happened. She had not forgotten the intrusion into her dining room, or the exposure of the plate with the three pansies beside it. That incident had made a dent upon her mind which the intervening months had not obliterated, but it played no part in what she felt now. The waves of thought that kept overleaping one another in her small oval-shaped head as she stared at the square panes, at the racing yellow-tinged clouds, at the formless moon, were almost all generous and romantic.

The most dominant and most recurrent of these thoughts if they had been translated into definite words would have run as follows: "Rook is pining for Netta, who will never understand him as *I* understand him. But he wants her; he is full of remorse about her. Left to Ann and Ann's child, he will eat his heart out in utter misery. *I* alone can save him by bringing Netta into his life again."

The day that dawned upon this eventful night was a dark and strange one even for that unusual September. It suggested rain; but it was not raining. It suggested thunder; but there was no thunder. Only, without the assistance of any frost or of any apparent wind, the first fluttering down of leaves took place in all manner of unexpected directions.

Even Hastings felt the influence of the day. "Don't you smell something queer in the air this morning, Nell?" he said to her at breakfast.

The girl nodded in silence, waiting for the right moment to make her momentous announcement.

"It's extraordinarily odd," he went on, "but I keep being conscious of some subtle smell—in this room—in the garden—in the road—that I haven't noticed since I was a child. It's not exactly a smell, either! It's more than that. It's a taste in the mouth and a strange indescribable feeling through every pore of the body."

Nell did begin to listen to him now, lifting up her chin between a vase of salpiglossis and a vase of cinerarias, both of them brought from the Ashover garden by Rook.

"I keep thinking of all sorts of little objects connected with my life when I was a child," Hastings continued. "I see the backs of certain volumes of the Latin classics my father used to read. My father was a cobbler, Nell. Have I ever told you that? But he had a mania for reading Latin. He was not a learned man. It was a sort of fantastic game with him. And there's something about the smell of this air that makes me think of London pavements and the peculiar feeling of the wet city mist on your face when you open a window into a room lit by gas and crowded with leather-bound books."

He sank into silence again; but his face bore such a happy, dreamy expression that Nell was quite shocked by his next words when, after a long pause, he looked across at her with a light in his eyes.

"I shall take my book up again this morning," he said. "I've been getting a new angle on it during these nights with Ashover. I've been tapping his brain without his knowing it—not for ideas exactly—but to get my own thoughts into focus."

He rose from the table as he spoke and going to the window opened it a little farther.

"There's the smell of something more than rain out there," he said. "If you want to know what I really think, Nell, I think there's a terrific thunderstorm coming up! Perhaps it's *that* which brings what I have to write next in my book—

my chapter of all chapters, Nell!—with such a mad rush into my mind."

He moved back to his chair, but instead of reseating himself, he leant against it, keeping his eyes fixed upon her and growing more and more excited.

"I believe I could finish the whole thing if I really got started to-day, Nell. I've only four more chapters. But they're the difficult ones. That's why I've been letting it go lately. They're the ones that explain the actual process of cosmic unravelling. They're the ones that give the clue to the unwinding of the clock!"

She looked at his illuminated and disturbed face with a scrutinizing eye. Had he the natural human intelligence to grasp all she meant to do by having Netta here? One could never tell with him! There was an obstinate wilfulness in the man that might sheer off at any tangent, at any moment. "Shall I speak to him now?" she thought. "Or shall I wait?"

Her decision, like so many human decisions, was brought to a head by something entirely outside her control. She caught sight of the village postman passing their gate, an occurrence that meant that in the space of about half an hour, giving him time to reach Ashover House and return, he would be passing it again and consequently be at hand to enable her to carry out her precipitate plan.

She moved straight up to her husband, and in a low, hurried, eager voice confessed what she had overheard and what she wished to do.

The criss-cross currents that tossed themselves into spray within the depths of the priest's mind took two main directions as he listened to her breathless suggestion.

The first of these tidal currents was full of a heavy sulkiness at being betrayed into giving up his secret; a secret which had become a sort of fetish with him as being the symbol of his malignant advantage over Rook Ashover.

It was just because those harmless syllables, "Thirteen Walpole Street," had become a kind of mania with the man that he had been overheard muttering them in his sleep; and now Nell was in possession of them!

But the second of these two mental tides contradicted the mood of the first. By having Nell and Rook so often recently under his eye his jealousy had gathered momentum; while the perverse forms of malignity which at the start had supplied an antidote to this jealousy were beginning to lose their savour and to grow tiresome and insipid.

There were several reasons why Nell's surprising suggestion did not altogether displease him. For one thing he felt sure it would mean the end of this platonic philandering between his wife and Ashover. Rook could hardly make use of Toll-Pike Cottage as a rendezvous for two love affairs! In the second place, it would cause definite and emphatic annoyance to Lady Ann; for whom, ever since he had learnt that she was to be a mother, he had nourished one of his queer half-neurotic, half-metaphysical aversions.

As Nell talked to him now she could see from his expression that his feelings were not by any means simple. She had recourse therefore to a grand feminine *coup*, which came to her by a sort of inspiration.

"You know what you have so often felt," she pleaded, "with regard to all our friends here? Well—*that*, at any rate, will be quite different when you've asserted yourself between Netta and Rook."

He stared at her in clouded bewilderment. What on earth did she mean? He could not believe that she saw quite as clearly as her hint implied the gaping depths of the hurt to his self-love which his position as the priest of the village had worked in him.

"You mean?" he murmured tentatively.

She looked straight at him now; and, like so many essentially honest and unscheming women, she found that the very integrity of her nature gave her a power, when she *was* embarked on a campaign of diplomacy, far more effective than any actual cunning in argument.

"I mean that it'll be more of a relief to me than I can tell you for you to be worthy of yourself and in the open over Mr. Ashover. I can't explain to you what it'll mean to me, William, to be free of this horrid sense that you're doing something shameful and unkind, like this hiding up Netta's address! It's made a difference to me already—just our talking freely like this about it! And if we send our telegram and have Netta here I shall feel still happier! I *do* think, William dear, that none of them have looked to you for your help and advice in their lives, as they naturally might have done, considering, after all, that you *are* the vicar of the place!"

She watched him anxiously; and a glow of excitement came into her face when she saw that her words had not been without their effect.

"You mustn't think," she went on, "that my friendship with Mr. Ashover prevents my seeing how coolly, to say the least of it, both he and Lexie treat you in your position as priest. It's the one thing about them that I've never understood." She stopped and glanced quickly at him, wondering whether she had let herself go too far.

"I'm glad to have been able to tell you this, William," she added. "Because I feel so much that it only wants a little more respect on both sides for you and Mr. Ashover to get on splendidly together."

She had won her point. She knew it as clearly as if he had thrown up both his hands and cried out: "I yield!" Her victory was almost as unexpected as it was complete. She did not estimate, because it was outside her knowledge of the man's metaphysical mania, the part played in his yielding by his mysterious hostility to Rook's wife. Still less did she realize how much of it was due to a certain queer tenderness which he had come to feel for Netta herself, a tenderness that was, in the last resort, a kind of sympathy of pariah for pariah, of one child of the people for another child of the people.

"Then I can write the telegram?" she cried impulsively. And making a swift childish clutch at one of Hastings's hands she raised it to her mouth.

It was this gesture more than anything that she had done which reconciled him to her victory. There is nothing in the world more calculated to establish a man in his own esteem than to feel the lips of a young girl against his ringers! The psychological effect of such a thing, reverting to dim, far-off pre-Homeric times, carries a magic along with it capable of seducing the coldest-blooded philosopher.

Hastings watched her scribbling the telegram on a piece of paper. He heard her muttering aloud those familiar syllables: "Thirteen Walpole Street," which he had himself been so malignantly and triumphantly whispering under his breath for the last half year. He derived a peculiar physical relief, like the drawing of a piece of rusty iron out of his flesh, at the mere sound of those words on another's lips, and while his wife rushed out with the telegram to the postman he found himself running up the stairs to his room with a clearer mind and a more lively desire to continue his life's work than he had felt since the day of Netta's flight.

The woman had been more on his mind than he had acknowledged to himself; and his recondite revenge upon Rook, by refusing her address, had been a severer strain upon his nerves than he had calculated upon. Well! He was clear of it. He would have the whip hand of them all now. He would henceforth be in a position to assert himself as the formidable spiritual director of all these people!

He sat down at his table and drew out his manuscript. The sight of these closely written impassioned pages changed the current of his thoughts once more. What did it matter whether these people treated him properly or not? What did it matter whether he was an effective parish priest or not? What did it matter whether his gentle Nell kissed his hand or not? Long, long years after he was dust in dust, after there was no longer any living creature who remembered him, his work would still be exercising its effect upon the universe; the wonder of the disillusioned, the terror of the illusioned!

For the rest of that day Hastings worked silently, passionately, upon his book. When he came down to lunch he was like a different man. Nell had never known him in such high spirits. He gossiped about the village people. He told her stories about his early struggles, his desperate youthful attempts to get an adequate education, his experiences at various theological colleges.

The girl thought to herself, "If he'd been like this a year ago, I would never have gone out so much with Lexie." Had Nell been more superstitious than she was she would have felt uneasy in the presence of this unnatural exuberance. An occult-minded person would have watched William Hastings very closely at that juncture and would perhaps have endeavoured to calm and allay this stream of excited talk. But Nell's own spirits were so exalted just then at the despatching of the telegram and the idea of Netta's arrival that she responded to his mood with a mood of like kind. Never had Toll-Pike Cottage heard such voices and such laughter. It would have taught the evasive Rook something he did not know as to the nature of women could he have seen the apparently complete and radiant accord that existed between these two. All through the afternoon, until teatime, Hastings worked on; writing with scarcely a glance out of the window or away from the page; as if it were necessary to finish the book that very day.

After one of the happiest teas they had ever had since they were married, Nell announced that she intended to make

Mr. Twiney drive her down to Bishop's Forley station; so that, in case Netta had been at home when the telegram reached her and had started at once by the first train, she might not be left stranded.

Hastings shook his head. "You're assuming too much, young lady," he remarked. "The chances are all against her being in the house when your message arrives. And why should she start in such a hurry? The natural thing would be to give herself at least a night to think over it."

Nell looked at him significantly. "*That* shows how little you know about women," she said. "There's probably not been a day since she left when she hasn't imagined herself rushing off back again just like this! What I said in the telegram was that we both thought that she ought to come, that it was important she should come. That would bring *me* without waiting overnight, if *I* were in her place!"

Hastings smiled grimly. "You and Netta are different people, Nell. And there's another thing, too. You seem to assume that she's got the money to come. I must say I think *that's* a rather big assumption."

Nell's face crinkled itself into a fit of giggling at this.

"How funny you are, William," she gasped. "Didn't you see me go to my chest of drawers just now? I gave the postman five pounds to telegraph with the message!"

Hastings stared at her. "Five pounds? Where did you get that from, Nell?"

She laughed still more at this.

"Where—do—you—suppose I get—money—from?" she murmured. "Do you think someone gives it to me?"

"I give it up completely," he cried. "You're too much for me to-day, young woman."

She made the shadow of a childish grimace at him, more in the manner of a daughter than a wife; a look that if Rook had caught he would have felt a malicious suspicion that all the romantic glamour he had come to associate with her was in some sort of way a trick that had been played upon him.

It is doubtful whether there is any man in the world who, if he saw all the flickers of expression in the face he is enamoured of, would not be shocked to the foundations of his being; and both Rook and Hastings were such megalomaniacal subjectivists, that as far as they were concerned there really were two quite distinct Nells who doubtless inhabited the same slender frame! It was doubtless Lexie who came nearer than either of them to see the girl as she actually was.

"It's your own money!" she cried radiantly. "Well! We'll see whether you're right or I'm right about her coming to-day. But I'm going to meet this train, anyhow!"

She was going out of the room when he stopped her with a new tone in his voice.

"Have you given a single thought to the future?" he began. "I mean have you considered what's going to become of Netta after we *have* got her here?"

Nell made an impatient little gesture with her slender fingers.

"That's just like a man!" she cried. "Always calculating and weighing. How do we know anything about the future? We may none of us live beyond this autumn!"

The priest lifted his eyebrows and let it go. After all, whatever the upshot of all this was to be, it was a matter for Rook and Netta to settle between themselves. And it did seem to him clear that any issue would be better than the present uncertainty and misunderstanding.

He withdrew to his room and launching out once more upon the dark tide of his impassioned logic, forgot Nell, Netta, Rook, and all terrestrial happenings in that unique absorption in the pure pleasure of laying thought upon thought, speculation upon speculation, which can give, to those who abandon themselves to its fascination, a delight that surpasses every sensual happiness.

It was nearly ten o'clock that night when he heard through his open window the wheels of Twiney's conveyance stopping at the garden gate.

He listened. Two women's voices! So Nell *had* been right in her premonition, and Netta had come! He pushed his papers aside and ran down the stairs to welcome them at the door.

He had no time at the moment to do more than shake hands with the newcomer; for he had to help Mr. Twiney carry up her trunk to the attic room; but a few minutes later, when they were all three together in the parlour, he received his first intimation of how little they either of them knew of what was going on in their visitor's mind.

"I'm so glad you came, Netta," he said in a kindly, almost paternal tone. "What Nell thought was that something *had* to be done! She was afraid that Mr. Ashover was working himself into such agitation about you that it was cruel to keep you hidden away any more. Though I did obey you, didn't I, in holding your secret tight?"

"I knew you," broke in Nell, "better than William. He thought you'd wait till to-morrow. But I was sure you'd come to-day."

They both surveyed their silent visitor with friendly curiosity. Netta was quietly and unassumingly dressed. In general appearance, when she pushed up her veil, she looked quite unchanged. But there was something about her manner that made it hard to talk as naturally and openly as they expected to do as soon as Mr. Twiney's back was turned.

"Mr. Ashover is not ill, I hope?" she asked in a low voice.

"Ill?" cried Hastings. "I should think not! And it's Nell, not I, who's got this idea of his being so worried. Besides, it's not only about our Netta that he's been worrying. I suppose you've heard——"

He stopped suddenly, catching a quick warning look on his wife's face.

"When is the child to be born?" asked Netta quietly.

"Oh, pretty soon now, so they tell me," Hastings replied. "I daresay it's the kind of thing that Mr. Ashover finds especially trying," he added. "But I'm sure he'll be so thankful to have his mind set at rest about you that he'll be a different person to-morrow."

"I sha'n't be a burden on you long," said Netta. "I've told Nell that it's only a very short little visit." She made an affectionate movement toward her hostess and laid her hand upon her arm. "I can't let Nell's hospitality make me a trouble to you," she went on, "and I won't let it either!" she added with a smile.

Hastings drew back, baffled and puzzled. Netta had teased him before with a certain society air which he regarded as an affectation; but her present tone was different from that. It was the tone of a person who has a definite and unalterable plan in his own mind and who is just diplomatically sparring to gain time. There was something about Netta's reserve, something in her manner and in the expression of her eyes, that thoroughly puzzled him.

There was no more real conversation between them during the light supper which Nell now brought in upon a tray; but as soon as the visitor had retired to her attic bedroom her hosts exchanged their impressions.

"I don't believe she's drinking any more," said Nell. "That's the great thing to be thankful for."

Hastings shook his head.

"And yet there's something queer about her," the girl went on, "that scares me somehow. Did you notice it? A sort of unnatural quietness?"

Hastings nodded

"Of course, she always was quiet," Nell continued, "and very likely we've forgotten *how* quiet she was. But I can't help feeling it's more serious than that. I don't know what to make of it! She talks naturally enough and listens to what you say. But one has the feeling all the time that her mind is only half in the room with you."

Nell rubbed her face violently with her hands; an habitual gesture with her when she was cornered and bewildered.

"She frightens me!" she burst out. "You don't suppose she's taken to drugs, do you, William?"

He shook his head.

"She seemed to realize about Lady Ann's child," the girl added, "without being told. I couldn't stop Twiney talking about it. But it didn't seem news to her. Perhaps she'd heard about it on the journey. Twiney said, by the way, that Pandie had told *him* that the child might be born any day now!"

Hastings protruded his under-lip in the manner characteristic of him when any of his manias were touched upon. "It would not trouble *me* very much," he said grimly, "if after all this fuss it turned out to be a girl!"

The unwitting cause of this midnight discussion in Toll-Pike Cottage lay awake in her attic bed long after her hosts had wandered off into the paths of sleep.

Strange enough was it to find herself once more on the banks of the Frome! Strange and, in a sense that she was not able herself to analyze, sad with a sadness beyond anything she had ever known.

Vainly she tried to envisage what form her reëncounter with Rook would take. As she watched the rolling banks of whitish-yellow clouds crossing and recrossing that sickly, shapeless object, so distorted, so disfigured, that she knew to be the waning moon, a very curious and disturbing mental experience took possession of her. She had the feeling that some great passage of time had elapsed, some half-century of the journeying years, and that she alone of all the people she had known in Ashover was alive on that September night. She felt vividly conscious of being a solitary disembodied spirit, without desire, without hope, without regret, without any faintest wish to change anything or to alter anything; indeed, with no emotion at all except an infinite sadness.

Why she should be so sad she could not tell. Rook, Lexie, Hastings, Nell, Lady Ann—were they not all lying in absolute quiescence in that enclosure by the water meadows? A new race of men and women filled their places, who cared nothing for them, nothing for their memories, nothing for their names!

Her mind seemed to revert, with a cold, responsive weariness, to the inscrutable melancholy that used to puzzle her upon the face of Sir Robert; and it seemed to her, as she watched that bulging, unhappy, deformed moon, cringing before the clouds, that she now understood the secret of his sadness. It was a sadness that only a certain type of sentiency in this world ever responded to or touched the fringe of, a sadness that had something to do with what the undying elements must feel—the earth, the air, the water—as they submit in their patience to the eternal process; and watch the human generations coming and going and leaving behind so faint a trace!

And then, without any warning, a queer thing happened to Netta Page. She grew suddenly conscious that an actual human face was peering in upon her from outside the window; not pressing itself against the window pane, but regarding her with fixed intentness out of that heart-sick moonlight, its eyes looking straight into her eyes with an expression in them that gathered up and held in suspense the diffused woefulness that filled the great sky tent.

Long years afterward Netta could recall that look. And the curious thing about it was that she never hesitated as to the identity that hovered behind it, out there, in the sick, gusty night!

She knew it for the face of Sir Robert Ashover; and so deep an impression had that portrait of the Cavalier made upon her mind that even, now, as she felt a vivid consciousness of his actual presence, it was with no trace of fear but rather with a sort of emotional recognition that she met his gaze. Hardly conscious of what she did she stretched out her arms toward the window; and it seemed to her as if that sorrowful phantom countenance smiled gently and reassuringly at her as it faded away.

When it was gone and she was once more lying back upon her pillow she found herself silently crying; not with bitter self-pitying tears, but with the sort of tears that belong to the winnowed and de-personalized spirit of the human race itself as it draws back from the confused arena of its sufferings and catches the sounds of disaster and calamity, faint and muffled, and almost mellowed as they rise up above the roof tops of the world.

She made up her mind that when she did meet Rook on the ensuing day she would make him take her into the church, to that marble image of the Cavalier there! How strange it was, she thought, as her tears dried upon her cheeks, that the mind of a person dead and buried more than two hundred years should still retain its power to influence and to console! Was it that something actually survived, of such a person's subtler, more sensitive consciousness, among the places where it had moved in its lifetime? Or was there, behind all the dream stuff of the whole tragic scene, some imperishable cistern or reservoir of superhuman pity into which these nobler, these more imaginative responses sank, as the years moved round, adding always something to this great protest?

Netta's nature was too simple, her beliefs and half-beliefs too vague and unformed, to be conscious of more than the crudest outlines of these open questions; but the things she had suffered and the things she had done, combined with the pressure upon her mind of her return to a place of so many memories, stirred up within her thoughts and speculations corresponding with these and corresponding with that troubled night sky.

The face at her window may have been a creation of her over-excited nerves; but before she fell asleep at last, in the early dawn, she had immersed all the recent impressions of her London life in these earlier associations; associations saturated with the sights and sounds of the country, and full of a sadness that was more wistful, if not less bruising, than the kind of wretchedness she had superimposed upon it.

The faint light of the dawn as it filled the small attic window with a cold, pale, watery blueness, like the blueness of polished steel, merged with the great concentrated secret thought which had been sustaining her all that agitating day.

She dreaded her meeting with Rook more for his sake than for her own. What *would* his reaction be to what she had to make him understand? Why, oh, why, she thought, did things that were so clear, so simple, so indisputable, to one human mind, become so strange, so foreign, so insane, when communicated to another?

With something more than the hard bones of ivory skulls were human beings divided, each from each! And she flung out against the pallid, bluish dawn a last desperate prayer that that particular queer-shaped skull that had so often lain by her side should not prove impervious to what she had to communicate to the consciousness within it!

CHAPTER XXIII

IT WAS the last day of September. The Ashover brothers were seated side by side under Lexie's elm tree in the churchyard, the back of the younger propped up against the trunk, that of the elder against an anonymous tombstone.

The day was misty and warm. The early afternoon shadows had that purplish haze and dew-wet mistiness over their dark outlines on the grass which dwellers in the west of England have long learnt to associate with the red berries of traveller's joy and the white clusters of old-man's-beard! It was one of those days when the filmy seeds of dandelions move at random, without the stirring of a breath, from resting place to resting place; when the purple tufts of knapweed reveal the hard globulous husk below the petals; when the ragwort droops heavily over the mole heaps; when the dominant odour upon the air seems to be a blending of burning weeds and rain-soaked funguses.

"Are you sure she told you all she told me?" Rook was saying, in a voice that seemed as if it might have been the very epitome of that autumnal season, so languid and spiritless did it sound.

"Good Lord, Rook! How can I tell what she told you?" rapped out the other. "The thing is clear enough, anyhow. Those Anglican fathers must have got hold of her soon after she disappeared. She's had more than six months of their confounded chatter. The wonder is that they haven't spoilt her more than they have. You know what I'm like over these things; how tough and hard to be fooled I am? And though I can't forgive them for putting their nonsense into the mind of a sweet creature like that, I have to admit that it's the genuine thing with her. And I expect, too, it *has* given her a new interest." He paused and frowned meditatively. "I expect it's been for the best, Rook," he added gravely.

"Did she say anything to you about wanting to join some order?" asked the elder brother.

"She mentioned it as a possibility. But as far as I could make out, these Fathers, whoever they are, weren't encouraging it. I suppose they want her for other purposes. Oh, I don't like it—I don't like it, Rook!"

Rook recalled his own recent talk with Netta in Toll-Pike Cottage; and he also felt that he "didn't like it." Indeed, that was putting what he had gone through during that interview very much too mildly.

The encounter had been to him like a draught of coloquintida. It had been one of the master ironies of his life. He had rushed to greet his former mistress with an exultant sense of reconciliation and recovery. He had met her with a glowing wave of tenderness; and then in place of the answering tide of renewed loyalty, in place of the clinging and pathetic affection he had expected, he had been received by a completely different Netta; a Netta who treated their former life as if it had been sin; a Netta who took it for granted that thenceforth to the end of his days he was going to be faithful to Lady Ann!

The situation had been made doubly ironical by the fact that it had been impossible to conceal from his wife that the girl had come back. He had brought the news out boldly and frankly and there had been a distressing scene between them about it; a scene that had been repeated afterward with even more unpleasant nuances of misunderstanding when he had tried to explain the new and unexpected attitude toward him in which his mistress had returned.

Ann had never been more hard, more unyielding, more brutally cynical. She took the line, or pretended to take the line, that the whole thing was an elaborate pretence or pose on Netta's part. She treated him as if he were a clumsy and conceited victim of a masterpiece of calculated cajolery from an astute adventuress. She flatly refused to see Netta or to listen to any further explanations of her return. "*C'est fini! C'est fini!*" she had said with a wave of her hand when he brought the matter up for the third time.

"I saw Nell yesterday for a moment——"

Rook's thoughts had been wandering so far that he felt as if these words of his brother's had been spoken hours ago instead of a minute since.

"It was Nell who got her address out of him and wired to her to come," said Rook. "Just think of it! It seems difficult to believe that all these things have happened since you and I talked in this very place last November."

"That great full moon!" responded the other. "And I thought I shouldn't last out to the end of the summer; and here we are nearly in October! God! I'm glad to be still alive in this world; able to eat a tasty bit of pigeon pie as well as another; and to bustle over for a bit of back-chat with brother Rook of a fine autumn afternoon! By the way, Twickenham maintains that I must be getting a mania for morphia. He says I finished my last box a couple of weeks too soon!"

The elder Ashover's fingers instinctively pressed a little cardboard object in his waistcoat pocket; but all he said was: "I hope you'll need those things less and less as time goes on."

"I've had to go a bit slow on cigarettes this last month," remarked Lexie, striking a match and lighting one as he spoke with more than his usual deliberation. "My bill with Twiney was terrible, as you may imagine," he added, watching the heavy-scented circles of smoke ascend into the thick autumnal air.

Rook glanced at him with sardonic solicitude. "I could

just manage to lend you five or six pounds," he muttered, "but of course it's really Lady Ann's money."

"Oh, I shall get on," chuckled the other. "You'll want every penny you've got when this child of hers appears. Have you decided upon a nurse yet?"

Rook sighed heavily and looked away over the familiar water meadows, over that level plain of grass and reeds which had been so often "a bank and shoal of time" for his mind's escape. There came over him a grievous sense of being divided from his brother as they had never been divided before. This new responsibility, even if it *were* his wife's money that dealt with the material side of it, was something that in a subtle and invisible manner ended his old bachelor association with Lexie. His life with Netta had not impinged upon *that* at all; had been, in fact, only a more extravagant case of the amorous adventures that in the old days had consolidated their friendship, giving it that heathen predatory touch which adds quality and piquancy and substance, as if they were fellow huntsmen in the same perilous jungle! But this allusion to the nurse of his child, carrying the implication that thenceforward he was bound up with deep traditional issues independent of Lexie altogether, seemed to signify the definite end of something and the definite beginning of something else, seemed to stand out like a great ambiguous signpost in his days—like that obscure "Gorm" signpost; meaning nothing, yet meaning everything!

He looked at Lexie's face as the younger man puffed out those spirals of blue smoke into an air that was thick with diffused colour, like the palette of some planetary Tiepolo; and it came over him that the real mistake of his life was in having departed, one stone's throw, from the calm epicurean existence of those first years after their father's death.

What had made him depart from that unruffled backwater, that earthly paradise of equanimity? Well! Just his viciousness; just that desire to round off his life with some feminine person or other who would satisfy those insatiable instincts that in the nature of the case his brother could not satisfy!

Oh! Could he only have foreseen, could he only have foreseen!—If he'd been tough and hard and callous he would have been able to whistle them all down the wind. In *that* case he would have made love to Ann and kept her at a distance; love to Nell and kept her at a distance; love to Netta and kept her at a distance! It was this fatal mixture in him of viciousness and pitiful sympathy that had ruined his life.

For his life *was* ruined. He knew *that* as definitely as if he had seen himself like a dead horse in a field, with Lady Ann and her beautiful offspring battening upon his flesh like two resplendent-winged dragon-flies!

Another person would have considered him the fortunate possessor of a distinguished wife and—he felt sure it would be so—of a distinguished heir to his name. Outwardly, at this moment, especially now that Netta was off his conscience and independent of him, he was a man any one might reasonably envy. Yet here he was, looking yearningly at Lexie's seamed and weather-stained face, as he might have looked his last at some lovely enchanted island from which a fatal vessel was irrevocably bearing him away!

Ay! Ay! A human being's life was not a thing of outward possessions, of outward circumstances. It was a thing of a certain secret abiding life illusion, that *must* be in some measure satisfied or all was lost! *His* life illusion implied his freedom from every sort of responsibility, except the responsibility of being a good son and a good brother. He was a man born to make women unhappy if he so much as approached them! And yet, how *not* to approach them, being obsessed, as he was, with this insane impersonal desire? What a dilemma! Why wasn't it possible to have love affairs with trees, with the elements, as those old classical personages used to have?

Oh, how intensely he loved his brother as he looked at him now! If only he could have exchanged with Lexie; he to be the sick one, the doomed one, and Lexie to be the husband of Lady Ann!

"How did Twickenham say you were when he examined you yesterday?" he asked at length, bringing to an end his prolonged melancholy silence.

"Oh, I thought I'd told you," replied Lexie eagerly. "He was very pleased—really surprised, you know! He seemed to indicate that I might go on quite comfortably through another year. My peculiar trouble seems to lend itself to these prolongations and postponements. And in my own secret mind—though I don't want to say the words—I have a sort of instinct that if I *do* last out one other year, it'll be damnably hard to unloose my hold upon life!"

Rook looked at him with infinite sympathy. He looked at the enormous size of Lexie's head, at the depths below depths of life energy in his glaucous coloured eyes, at the sweet, rich, almost feminine curves of his sensitive mouth.

"Lexie," he began, and stopped suddenly.

"Well, Rook, what is it?"

"I oughtn't to say a thing like that, I suppose. It's one of those absolutely outrageous things that Nature lets people think, but that no decent person could possibly bring himself to say!"

"What is it? What is it, Rook?"

"Well, I was just thinking how many lives I would offer up, and *whose* lives, if the gods would make me absolutely assured that yours would go on for thirty more years!"

Lexie threw away his cigarette and made a face at him. "I wouldn't have the least objection to this holocaust of yours if I didn't know for a certainty that, no sooner had you done it you'd begin regretting it! You're a funny person and I doubt if you realize how far your queerness goes."

He got up from the ground and yawned. When Lexie

yawned he did so with the earthy shamelessness of a wild animal.

"Let's walk back to my place together, Rook," he said. "We could stop at Toll-Pike on the way, maybe, and see if either of the girls is in! Old Hastings, Nell tells me, has started off like a maniac at that book of his. She says he writes day and night now; and hardly stops to eat his meals. It's lucky for her that she *has* got Netta with her."

They crossed the graveyard together. "Well! Well!" Lexie continued, "It's something that you and I are still walking on a good gravel path side by side. I might so easily be now lying under that elm trunk with the beard growing on my chin and evil-smelling rheum running out of my eyes and nostrils! Yet here we are, looking forward to an excellent tea with black-currant jam among my phloxes, and very likely a couple of sweet-natured wenches to enjoy it with us! How any one can ever worry himself about the shuffling of the cards, as long as there are any cards to shuffle—that's what I cannot understand, brother Rook."

They emerged into the road and proceeded to wander slowly through its white dust watching the heavy-winged tarnished peacock butterflies flutter before them from silver-weed to silverweed.

"Think what it would be like," said Lexie, "if every human being left a thin silvery trail behind him like the slime of a snail! Think of such a trail crossing and recrossing its tracks from where it first leaves its perambulator to where it climbs into bed for the last time! *Our* tracks must pretty often have gone over the same ground, side by side along this road. And yet it is an absolute and irrevocable certainty that one of these walks together will be our last."

Rook's thoughts were preoccupied at that moment with the stark question, a question that gave him the sensation of looking into a gaping wound which had begun to fester, as to what kind of a tilt or twist or secret palliative he could administer to this truculent life illusion of his, so as to endure Netta's conversion, his child's birth, his mother's senile jubilation, and this indescribable separation from Lexie which Lexie seemed too egoistic and self-absorbed even to notice!

"One of these walks will be our last," his brother was saying. Didn't he have the wit to recognize that this "last" had already happened?

They approached the clump of alders that overhung the sheep-washing pool. This was the point where the river turned sharply to the right, heading for the water meadows, and was crossed by a wooden bridge bordered by the same kind of whitewashed railings as skirted the preceding strip of road.

In the centre of this bridge the two brothers came to a pause, leaning against the railing and looking away over the barley fields, now a misty expanse of golden stubble, which sloped up toward Heron's Ridge.

"Do you remember how we used to call this bridge 'Foulden's Bridge,' for no reason except that we had a nursery-maid called 'Foulden' who used to meet that old villain Pod here of a fine summer's evening?"

Lexie chuckled as he uttered these words with an unctuous comprehensive historic chuckle which "flew low," so to speak, like a great flopping mallard, over all the days of all the years of both their lives!

Rook did not trouble himself to answer this particular remark. The two brothers were so content in each other's society that they had a way of thinking aloud; each one pursuing his own deep-indented furrow of contemplation; quite satisfied if now and again these isolated trails crossed one another, like Lexie's silvery snail tracks!

"I think the most delicious moments of my life," said Rook dreamily, "if I put aside the very best of our excursions together, have come when I've been walking by myself along some road I've never seen before. Are you listening, Lexie?"

His brother bent over the railing to watch the course of a bit of wood which he had flung into the water. He lifted up his head presently. "One minute!" he remarked. "Don't forget what you were going to tell me; but I want to see"—and he flung another piece of wood after the first—"I want to see whether it's Rook or Lexie who gets safe under the bridge!"

Rook leaned over the white-washed railing by his side. The Frome ran shallow and weedy just there. A few slender dace, with their heads upstream, were letting the current carry them languidly backward; while at the side of the river, where the water ran over clear sunlit pebbles, a great shoal of minnows were hovering and darting, like little tongues of quicksilver.

"There we go!" cried Lexie, giving his brother one of those looks of complicated naïveté and subtlety which always troubled Rook's mind, as if with the tantalizing proximity of some dimension of human goodness and sweetness which was only offered to be snatched away. "There we go!" And he ran across "Foulden Bridge" to the other side. Rook followed him, puzzled at the eagerness with which he himself, too, awaited the issue of this childish contest.

"I'm out! I'm safe!" cried the younger Ashover, pointing with his stick. Then in a moment his face assumed a most curious mixture of condolence and triumph. "But you're stuck fast under there! You're done for, Rook!"

The elder man did at that second of time undergo an unusual and very unexpected sensation, a perfectly direct and unmitigated shock of self-pity, as if he had been suddenly condemned to leave a world full of beauty and happiness.

"Well? Shall we go on?" said Lexie. "I'm glad it was you and not I who sank, because that means that we *shall* be together this time next year."

They moved on across the bridge. The road stretched straight in front of them with nothing but the small white square of Toll-Pike Cottage, far away on the left, to break its perspective till it lost itself in the dim autumnal blur, haze-wrapped and purple-shadowed, of Ashover village.

They moved very slowly now, arm-in-arm, scattering the dust with their feet. Each time they prodded the ground with their sticks little white clouds arose, that subsided patiently and sadly after they passed, like the sighs of disappointed watchers.

"What a place in the imagination," said Rook suddenly, "has come to be taken by *dust*. Doesn't it always return to your mind, that scene in Syria, when the Lord stopped and wrote in the dust?"

Lexie swung round. "You mean when He spat in the dust and made clay! It certainly is strange how every incident of that life falls in with the commonest omens of any walk you go. What were you just going to say on the bridge, Rook, when I interrupted you?"

The elder brother frowned. "Oh, nothing," he said crossly; but after a pause and in an abstracted tone, "I was wanting to clear up a thing that's always puzzled me. What is it you feel when you're alone on a strange road, especially when it leads up over a bare hill? Do you suppose it's an atavistic memory from times when people were more nomadic and more isolated than they are to-day? Or do you think that all the feelings of solitude, accumulated from many generations, are gathered up then; as if there were a person in each of us who was like a kind of Wandering Jew, with a consciousness entirely made up of the vague, faint, half-human impressions of loneliness, a person whose whole long mysterious life, reaching through many centuries, were one solitary journey?"

In place of answering him Lexie pulled him round by the arm and they stood for a while looking back. All the familiar objects that they looked at then—the wooden bridge with its white palings, the dark-green alders by the sheep wash, the square tower of the church, the gray-stone bridge, the clump of thick-foliaged trees that hid Ashover House—all these things that each of them had known from childhood fell into a new and unfamiliar setting, as if they had been discovered off-guard, in some secretive mood that they had been at pains to conceal.

"Don't you feel," said Rook, "that we might be at this moment two characters in one of Grimms' fairy stories? Haven't you got that odd feeling, that you get in those stories, as if there were nothing really vulgar or banal in the whole world? As if we might see an old woman driving a goose over that first bridge and a man with a pack on his back crossing this second bridge, and every door in the village ready to open to the cooking of magic cakes and the purring of great wise all-knowing cats! It's what comes from living in the same spot all one's life and then suddenly seeing everything as if you'd never seen it before. The only way to escape from vulgarity and commonness is to live all one's days in a place like Ashover." He stopped and drew a long breath. "I don't think I really should care very much," he added, "if I should never go ten miles away from here until I died!"

They turned their faces once more toward the village and walked on together without further speech till they came to Toll-Pike Cottage.

Lexie's anticipations were justified. They found Netta and Nell seated together in the little front garden. They were able to observe the two girls several seconds before they were themselves seen or heard owing to the muffling softness of the white dust and the fact that the women were engaged in an intimate and agitating conversation.

As the brothers watched them across the fence there came into Lexie's mind that peculiar sense of the passing of time which so often seized and arrested him. That he and Rook on this particular day of September should catch sight of those two, Nell in her white summer frock and Netta in black, talking so earnestly and anxiously, with the little round bed of red geraniums in front of them and the window of Hastings's study open above their heads, seemed to be one of those events that, common enough in themselves, are yet pregnant in some peculiar way with an unforgettable significance.

"Rook is right," thought Lexie, "about living in Ashover. It's the fact of one's knowing every stick and stone in the background of events that gives to events their heightened value. To get the passing of time one has to possess a dial, as it were, on which the hours are marked!" They opened the gate and entered the garden.

Lexie found it piquant to watch this meeting between Netta and his brother. "*There* are those two," he thought, "solemnly shaking hands and gravely discussing some indifferent matter, when a year ago they were sharing the same room and using the same water jug."

His thoughts were impinged upon by a very serious communication from Nell.

"We're worried about William to-day," she said. "He's been writing at that book of his without cessation for the last twelve hours. He got up early this morning, before I was awake, and we haven't been able to persuade him to come to any meals."

"Has he eaten anything?" enquired Lexie.

"Hardly anything. I took him some milk and biscuits. He hasn't locked the door. But when I go in he looks so wild and haggard and gets so angry at being disturbed that I daren't stop more than a minute. I'm afraid for his mind if he goes on like this. He sat up till three or four this morning. He couldn't have slept more than two hours. And I didn't like what he said when I went in."

"What did he say?"

"It was about Lady Ann and her child. It was awful, Lexie! I can't think how a sane man can think such appalling thoughts. I don't believe he *is* quite sane," she breathed.

"Can you see him from here?" enquired Lexie, speaking in the tone he might have used if Hastings had been a dangerous otter or badger.

"No. You see? The window's open but he's got the blind down. Come here, Lexie. I don't want Rook to hear us." They moved away to the other side of the geranium bed.

"Netta, you can't mean that you're going back to London without letting me see you once more alone?" Rook spoke these words wistfully and pleadingly but there was an undertone of indignant sullenness in his voice and his eyes had an angry glint.

The girl's face was very pale; a pallor which the golden September light clinging to her brown hair threw into touching relief. She seemed as Rook looked at her, standing there resolute and sad in her loose black dress, to be thinner and more girlish than in former times.

She was aware that his look had in it a recognition of her physical desirableness; the half-conscious non-mental renewal of an ancient magnetism. She knew that he was recalling with a certain tantalized sulkiness his former possession of her.

"I cannot bear it, Rook dear," she said gently. "I could bear it if I didn't love you. But I love you far too well. Don't make it harder for me, Rook, than it is already!"

He glanced gloomily round; but Lexie and Nell had seated themselves on a wooden bench under the hedge, their eyes directed, not toward himself and Netta, but toward the window of Hastings's room.

"Come into the house," he said brusquely, taking her by the shoulder.

She felt so strong in her sadness and in her pity that she

allowed him to take her into Nell's little parlour and shut the door upon them; but her instinctive response to the familiar touch of his hands surprised her by its independence of her conscious mind.

The very moment they were alone the room began to assume that cunning, furtive, pandar-like look that rooms take on when human skeletons of opposite sexes stand in one another's presence, silent, obsessed, with beating pulses and hammering hearts! Rook's eyes mechanically noted a grotesquely sentimental picture of Nell as a little girl which stood on the mantelpiece and then without regarding her feeble protests he took Netta in his arms.

Those two human bodies seemed to rush together in a strange complicity of contempt for what was happening to those minds or to those wills. The man pressed his mouth so savagely upon the girl's mouth that before their kiss was over her lips had parted in helpless abandonment.

He had sworn in his anger that she was "like all women" and she knew in her heart that she had proved herself like many among them in the manner in which she yielded at that moment without really yielding at all. She just let him do with her as he pleased because her body already belonged to his body and seemed to return to its possessor with the inevitableness of a compass needle. And yet not for one second did she deviate or collapse from her mental resolution.

As soon as he had removed his mouth from her mouth and had begun to kiss her chin and her neck, this unseduced spirit in her revolted and flung him off. He became suddenly conscious that he was holding a l mp, cold, unresponsive husk in his arms, something whose essence was not there at all, a stiff, lifeless simulacrum of the real Netta. He let her sink down into Nell's one available armchair, the very chair in which she had sat nearly a year ago, when on that day of torrential autumn rain she had come into the room with Cousin Ann.

"There . . . you see!" he gasped breathlessly. "All this mania of yours is just a morbid fancy that you've fallen into by living too much alone. You're my same Netta . . . you'll always be my Netta . . . nothing that can possibly happen can change that!"

An expression of pitiable sadness came into her face. She looked not only very pale but actually old and haggard at that moment. With the sunlight gone from her hair and her hair itself ruffled by their embrace the gray streaks in its heavy masses became lamentably apparent.

"When you say that it's wrong for you to live with me any more, does that mean that you and I are to be as if we'd never lived as we have?"

She made an effort to answer him, but it was too much. Those big tears, the sight of which brought back the pathos of her personality more than anything else could have done, those tears as big as the eggs of golden-crested wrens, began one by one to run down her cheeks. She made no effort to dry them. She seemed unconscious of their presence. Nor did the lines of her countenance distort themselves as most people's faces do when they cry. Her eyes remained wide open and fixed upon his own. Her mouth, too, remained strangely untremulous, its quiet curves set fast in an expression of weary composure.

Very slowly she shook her head; and then, after making some little swallowing movements in her throat, she spoke to him firmly and gently.

"I shall never love any one but you, Rook," she said, "but I must go back where I came from. The Fathers have been very kind to me and they've found me work to do. I've got my life to lead somehow, Rook dear. And they've been very good to me. I owe them everything, everything!"

In her desire to explain she had touched just the one chord whose vibration was calculated to hurt him most.

"Everything, Netta?" he repeated with bitter sarcasm.

For it was just *that*, that she should have turned in her despair to other comforters, to other responses, to a different refuge than anything he could supply which hit him to the depths of his nature.

It seemed to him as if what she had done was something worse than ingratitude. She had taken their love, which was the expression of all that had been best and tenderest and most delicate in him, and had treated it as something evil and sinful. He had given her a pity, an understanding, a recognition, that went beyond anything those priests could give her; and now she was capable of this enthusiastic cry: "I owe them everything!"

The window of the room was wide open to the garden and there floated in upon them the distant murmur of Lexie's and Nell's voices and the musky scent of geraniums.

Rook found that he had counted much more upon Netta's attitude to him than he had until that moment realized. It was not that he had anything to offer her; any reasonable alternative to this new life she had found for herself. If there had been anything definite in his mind he could have dealt with this blow more effectively, have found an antidote for its smart. He was standing before her there, pleading angrily and helplessly for something that had no shape, no substance, no form. He was pleading with her to have pity upon his life illusion, pity upon his soul's inmost self, pity upon that ultimate reflection of himself before himself which lay in the abysmal mirror of his self-deception as the sky lies in a mirage of water above arid sands! He was pleading with her to save from destruction something that was so tenuous that he himself could hardly define it. Like a thin film of autumn mist his self-love wavered and undulated between them in that geranium-scented air. It became a drooping filament of unreal vapour. It faded; it hovered; it sank. A sense of intolerable emptiness came over him. Netta's Fathers had saved *her* soul; but they had stricken his.

But how could *she* know that? How could she know that his feeling for her was the one affair of his life that exactly lent itself to that morbid peculiarity in the depths of his being, his desire to love a person who in some way was dependent upon him, helpless before him, different from what he was by some impassable gulf?

Along with the emptiness that filled his soul there came the sting of a peculiarly masculine resentment; the resentment which arises when a woman with whom one has dropped one's mask and put aside one's reserve suddenly reassumes *her* mask and *her* reserve at the very moment when one is most unarmed and at her mercy!

"And so your Fathers have taught you to look back upon our life together as *sin?*" His tone was strained and harsh; and the girl saw clearly that he was on the verge of breaking out into a torrent of indignant words, bitter, corrosive, capable of leaving behind them scars that would never be effaced.

She must stop him. She must explain to him. She must make him realize what she had been feeling when she deliberately began drinking in order to degrade herself in his eyes. It was intolerable to her that he should take her present mood, her new life, and make of it something that diminished the value of all that had been between them. What she wanted to make him understand was that never from her—never, never from her!—could come any diminishing, any undervaluing of their love or of all that that love had meant. And if she could not make him see this without saying what was too hard to say, well, she must say it!

Woman-like, what hurt her most was that she should have blurred the image of herself that their love had created in his mind, nay, spoilt his response to that image by giving him the idea that it was possible for her to have changed so much as to be ready to betray their past together, to blaspheme against what they had shared.

She looked at him with that expressive look with which one human being beats at the closed shutters of another's conciousness, like a starving traveller whose language is so remote, so foreign, that it might be mistaken for the wind in the trees, for the rain on the porch! What she wanted to lay before him was nothing less than the full measure of her love. That he should accuse her of not recognizing the worth of their days together or the value of the sympathy he had given her—it was blind, unfair, distorted, mad!

That was what men were always doing in this world; they were laying stress on external, outward, logical aspects of relations between people and missing the one thing needful! They were always working themselves up into rational indignation about aspects of love that were accidental, occasional, relative; whereas, all the while, Love Himself, absolute and immeasurable, remained dumb and inarticulate on the threshold!

As she looked at him now with this mystery lying unspoken, unspeakable, at the heart of her existence, and that turmoil of wild accusation trembling upon his tongue, it came over her what a tragic chasm it was that separated the love of a woman from the love of a man.

"It is thus. It is so. There are these evidences. There is this proof," cries the exacting reason of the one. "I love you! Can't you see that I love you?" answers the blind instinct of the other. Netta began to feel heart-sick and dizzy as she watched him, standing there like a judge; waiting, waiting, till some self-betraying murmur on her part brought down on her head the already formulated sentence. She seemed to herself to be beating back with her hands a clamour of discordant voices, of confused inexplicable sounds. Why did those steps keep marching up and down, up and down, in the room above? Or were they, too, only the beating of her heart? Surely that must be Lexie and Nell just outside the door! But their murmurings reached her as if they were not human at all; as if Rook's pulses full of unjust anger had acquired some horrid goblin speech and were rushing upon her like an infuriated mob——

And then, without any reason for it, she saw with incredible clearness a little thin gold ring that the "Father" had worn on his finger when she was first pouring out to him the misery of her shame, of her loneliness; and as that vision disappeared, mingling strangely with a fierce red spot on Rook's lowering forehead, she found herself experiencing that lightning-rapid panorama of her whole previous existence, such as, people had told her, persons underwent when, in drowning, they sank for the third time.

She certainly had begun to feel actually faint. What was Rook doing standing there, so funnily stern, in front of her? What was it she had to make him understand? Something that a person could do when he loved another person very much—but something that it was impossible to speak of!

"Rook!" she brought out with a kind of gasp.

At that moment the door flew open and Lexie and Nell precipitated themselves into the room. They both showed signs of extreme agitation and they both began speaking at once.

"Pandie is out there——"

"Pandie has come to say that——"

Rook turned pale. Had the moment arrived? Was he even now the father of an heir to Ashover?

Netta rose to her feet, also very white and trembling.

"Is it Lady Ann?" she asked.

Lexie was the one to explain; for Nell's attention was distracted at that moment by the sound of her husband's steps moving backward and forward in his room above.

"Pandie is at the gate," said Lexie hurriedly. "She says your wife can't be found."

The first feeling that Rook had under the shock of this unexpected news was—strangely enough—a queer spasm of relief! For some profound subconscious reason anything seemed more tolerable to him just then than to hear that his child had come into the world.

"Can't be found?" he repeated. And then, taking advantage of the strangeness of the communication to give vent to his unnatural emotion in the form of blind anger against the messenger: "What does the little fool come running here for?" he cried sternly. "Why doesn't she look about in the garden, in the kitchen garden, in the orchard, up Battlefield, even? Ann has been walking quite far some of these days. She's taken into her head to go a farther stroll than usual, that's all! What's the use of coming here to tell us a thing like that? Let me see her." And he made a step toward the open door, where Nell was still standing, nervously preoccupied by the sounds overhead. "Let me see her! Let me talk to her!"

But Lexie intervened and stopped him. "It's more serious than you think, Rook," he said gravely. "For God's sake keep your wits about you! They've searched the garden *and* the orchard already. Pandie says they've been everywhere. Mother has been herself to the top of Heron's Ridge looking for her. God knows what may not have happened! Women are apt to go crazy at these times and do the maddest things. Pandie says old Betsy Cooper has turned up, dragging the idiot Binnory after her, with some wild story about having seen her in Antiger Lane near Drool's cottage. Martha Vabbin has gone to get Drool himself; and to see if by some lucky chance she just went in there to rest. But from what Betsy and the idiot say she didn't go into the cottage at all——" He broke off suddenly, disturbed by the sight of Nell rushing wildly up the stairs.

"There's something wrong up there, too," he added, with a shrug of his shoulders.

Rook without a word hurried into the garden. He found Pandie standing on the gravel path like a comic image of desperation, her head bare and her hand clutching an enormous garden rake.

"Oh, Master Rook, Master Rook! What have come upon our heads to-day?" cried the distracted servant. "Missus says I was to fetch 'ee to come home at once; and Mr. Lexie, too, if he were well enough to walk on his feet. And she says you was to fetch Mr. Twiney and Mr. Pod up along! And she says you was to summon the police; and I reckon myself 'twould be only right, considering how them gippoos be abroad, to send to Forley Barracks for the Military. Lord alive! Lord alive! That I should be the woman to tell the Squire of Ashover that his lady be gone to find a hole in the river deep enough to commit 'fanticide in!"

Rook was too bewildered by this time even to smile at these aberrations of the native of Somersetshire.

"What have you got that rake for, Pandie?" he asked.

"For to drag the ponds and ditches with, Master Rook! They say that when a body's expecting, like as your lady be, there ain't no pond water near or far that Providence don't tempt 'un with. 'Tis a pity her legs bain't swelled up! When their legs be swelled up they can't go suiciding and such-like. 'Tis a dispensation of Nature!"

Rook turned away from her.

"Lexie! Nell! Netta!" he called out. "I'm off to the house!"

He strode to the gate. "You go on to the village, Pandie," he cried, "and get Twiney and Pod and bring them back with you in Twiney's cart and don't go shouting all this nonsense to everyone you meet. I expect I shall find Lady Ann safe at home when I get back!"

He was already in the road when he heard his brother's voice calling him by name. He turned and met Lexie at the gate.

"Nell has just come down from talking to that beggar upstairs," said the younger man, "and she says she's had the greatest difficulty in quieting him. I couldn't get the drift of what the trouble was; but he's got his confounded book mixed up with your child. The chap seems to have gone all to pieces. I'm glad Netta *is* with them. Nell oughtn't to be left alone with him." He laid his hand on his brother's arm. "You're not letting this fuss about Ann upset you, Rook, are you? This day seems dedicated to one agitation after another! But don't you worry, dear Rook. Ann's probably turned up by now."

Rook suddenly bent forward, took his brother's grave and anxious countenance between his hands and kissed him rapidly. "I shall look in at the church," he said. "That's just the place none of them would think of! But, as you say, she's probably safe back in her room by now. There's something about this day that seems to make everyone nervous. I've noticed it before. Whenever the wind drops dead in Ashover and the air is absolutely still, something's sure to happen with us. We're a funny family. The gods must be perfectly sick of us. Well, I'm off! Don't leave Nell alone with Hastings, I beg you, Lexie!"

He strode off down the road.

Lexie saw Pandie staring up at Hastings's window as if she had been mesmerized. With one hand on her rake she was mechanically moving it about among the geraniums. Whether in that waking dream she imagined she was dredging a pond to find Ann's body or whether she was reverting to some childish memory of helping her father amid the rich loam of Sedgemoor, no one will ever know. There are instinctive actions and gestures of human beings, especially at some great crisis of drastic events such as was then gathering about these people, which will always retain an element of the grotesque and the inexplicable.

"I'll come with you to the village, Pandie," said the young man, breaking in upon her trance. "Here! For God's sake drop that rake of yours and pull yourself together! What's the matter with you, woman?"

The red-haired servant turned toward him a face that was distorted with emotion.

"She told I we be all flummoxed by thik parson up there."

"*Who* told you?" cried Lexie impatiently; and then, catching sight of Netta at the door, "Don't you leave Nell alone with that chap, will you? Pandie and I are going to the village."

Netta made a sign that she understood him and returned into the house. Lexie took the rake from Pandie's unconscious hands and led her into the road.

"Who told you?" he repeated as they moved off together.

"That gippoo bitch, Bet Cooper, 'twere what warned I of 'ee. 'Twas for that she be come, so 'a did say. She'd a-seen thik parson murdering our Squire, or summat o' that, in a girt wold crystal-stone, what she have stoled from some foreign scollard! I did tell thee mother what she did say; but not a thought would she give to it. Your mother's not one to attend to God his wone self when she be put about."

Lexie found his strength barely sufficient to reach the first house in the village, which by good luck happened to be that of Mr. Pod, the Sexton. Here he decided to rest, sending Pandie on to find Mr. Twiney.

Sitting in Mr. Pod's little kitchen through which not a breath of air passed, either by door or window, he could not help recalling his brother's words about these days when the wind was dead in Ashover.

"I don't like it," he said to himself. "I don't like it! Things are beginning to get out of control; and I can't tell what the upshot will be."

CHAPTER XXIV

THE inviolable stillness of that last day of September prevented Lady Ann from enjoying her usual rest in the afternoon. An unaccountable malaise came upon her, a sense of suffocation, of being shut in, imprisoned, sepulchred, buried alive. She had suffered from the same species of nervousness once or twice before, but never so badly as now.

She went to the window of her room and looked out.

Everything was hushed and death-still in the somnolent garden. The branches of the great cedar swam motionless upon the air and seemed borne up by vibrant aërial waves of soft blue mist.

"I'll go for a walk," she said to herself. "I'll take Lion."

She put on her prettiest summer hat, threw a thin loose dust-coloured cloak round her shoulders and slipped quietly down the stairs. Very cautiously, so as not to arouse any one's attention, she let herself out of the front door and walked round to the rear of the house.

She knew that Rook was out with Lexie somewhere and she knew that Mrs. Ashover was resting in her big upstairs room. As she came past the kitchen door she was met by that peculiar complicated odour which in English houses of the Ashover sort seems synonymous with two o'clock in the afternoon, might indeed be the very smell of the gamboge-coloured hide of two o'clock, that enemy of romance and all delicate joy! It was an odour in which the "washing-up" beginning in the scullery mingled with the servants' dinner ending in the kitchen and both of these with the indescribable sense of the crowding together of the various house pets, canine and feline, who had "followed the dishes out."

Lady Ann had not been able to eat much lunch and this two-o'clock smell made her feel for a moment a little dizzy and sick. But the great point was that nobody about the place saw her as she hurried past. Lion was neither at the kitchen door nor in his kennel by the stable. "Oh, I forgot!" she said to herself. "I told them to take him down to Drool's." She had vexed herself lately about the dog; feeling that, now her own walks were curtailed, it didn't get enough exercise, Rook being teased rather than entertained by the animal's company.

Her momentary malaise passed off after she had crossed the orchard and got clear away on the slope of Battlefield, and when she reached the top of Heron's Ridge she felt better than she had felt for several weeks.

She felt happier, too. That rich, indolent, windless autumn day was profoundly adapted to her mood. The sense of the apples and pears growing riper and mellower every day among those lichen-covered branches, of the hazelnuts growing browner and plumper among their crumpled leaves, of the mushrooms in the lush grass meadows appearing so suddenly and so quickly, that even those who knew their privileged haunts would wonder at their coming; the sense of all these things around and about her seemed to soothe her mind and liberate her spirit, as if the immense fecundity of Nature were something she could draw upon to enlarge and replenish her own vitality.

She had not been as far as Drool's cottage for several weeks; but to-day it seemed to her that it would be very nice to pay a visit to the place. She felt a queer emotional craving to stand once more, whatever might be the result of what she had soon to go through, in that little room of Binnory's. And besides, she would greatly love to catch a final glimpse of the dog, her one completely faithful and loyal supporter, before she entered upon this life-and-death struggle.

There were many feelings in her proud young heart that she had always found it easier to confide to horses and dogs than to her own species; and with Lion especially she had come to find a satisfying sense of dropping her reserve and giving way to this or that primitive and even savage emotion such as her stoical training had taught her to suppress in the presence of her own race.

She came down the Dorsal side of the hill with a gayer and more light-hearted tread than she had used for many a long day in her diurnal strolls. She watched the rabbits with the eye of a sportsman, at once sympathetic and predatory. She snuffed the air, at one big clump of bracken, catching the familiar taint of a fox in that misty windless atmosphere; and she stopped more than once to place her foot on the loose up-flung trail of earth mould which marked the movement of a burrowing mole. A few of her husband's black namesake birds kept up a perpetual clamour above the high tops of the trees as if to make sure that no invading jay or magpie should interfere with the return of their tribe when later in the afternoon they "made wing to the rooky wood," while the whirring headlong flight of more than one family of partridges made her forget her obligation to her own offspring!

It was only when she was quite close to the cottage at the foot of the hill that her mood veered. It was as if the master of the vessel of her mind had suddenly come on deck and given orders to swing sheer round, from larboard to starboard. It was a quick instinctive rush of anger against Rook that decided her.

"I'll turn round and go straight back," she thought. "That room is nothing to me now; and Lion will only want to go home with me if he sees me."

She was so close to the gap in the hedge, however, by which the lane was reached, a little to the right of the cottage, that she was led on, by that curious and childish instinct which demands that the most drifting of human walks should have some sort of goal, to struggle cautiously down the bank to the familiar road.

Once in the lane it occurred to her that the most sensible way home would be round by the barley fields; for Heron's Ridge was much less of an eminence there, and she could stroll back at leisure by the village road and the two bridges.

She turned to the right accordingly at this point, and soon found herself opposite the gate into the wood where she had first revealed to Rook that she was with child. An unpleasantly familiar voice came suddenly to her ears from the other side of this gate. She moved a step toward it; and there, under the brushwood, she saw Binnory.

Nor was the idiot alone. Occupied, beneath his fascinated scrutiny, in collecting some especial herbalist's plant—which may even have been, for all Ann knew about such things, the famous classical hellebore—the old trot, Betsy Cooper herself, turned toward her the sort of menacing scrutiny that a sinister sorceress of ancient times might have turned toward some Eurynome or Dione, big with the child of an Olympian.

"Save us and help us if it ain't her ladyship's own self!" cried the crone, rising from her knees and coming forward.

"'Tis my pretty leddy! 'Tis *my* pretty leddy!" ejaculated the idiot, approaching the gate with still more alacrity. "Have 'ee been to Lunnon to find Squire Ash'ver, what rumpled thee fine feathers for 'ee unbeknownst to any but poor Binnory?"

Lady Ann instinctively drew away from these two discomfortable figures, retreating, as she pulled her cloak around her, toward the middle of the lane. Here she stopped and faced them; but neither the old woman nor the boy made any attempt to come farther than the gate.

"Thee best get up along over Hern's Top as quickly as thee may," said Betsy Cooper. "'Twere only last night when I be cleaning me horse-cart, out where us do bide now, and me partners were quiet-like and 'twere all still as churchyard stones, that a voice inside me belly said to I, 'Look i' thik wold crystal, Betsy lass; look i' thik wold crystal!' And no sooner did I do what 'un did say than, Lord bless us and keep us! There was that black parson of yours a-murderin' of poor dear Squire!"

She stopped to take breath and Lady Ann moved as if to go on down the lane.

"It's true as God's dear blood, your ladyship!" screamed the old woman, making a feeble attempt to open the gate. "Get home with you, you owdacious turleypin!" This was addressed to Binnory, who was staring at the girl in the road as if he meditated a wild rush toward her.

"I can't listen to you now," said Lady Ann calmly. "But if you'd like to come up to the house later I'm sure you'll be made welcome."

She spoke in the tone she habitually used to poor people, the tone that was at once easy and distant. What it implied was: "I have no time now to chatter with picturesque vagabonds; but my servants will be charmed to give you tea in the kitchen!"

Betsy Cooper by no means missed the quality of this rebuff; but she was too excited to enter into personal adjustments just then; besides, beyond all her eccentricity, she was saturated with a feudal respect for the house of Ashover.

"Don't 'ee take on, your ladyship," she pleaded. "Don't 'ee take on! 'Twere after I'd a-seen that murderin' parson in Cimmery stone that I heard a voice out of one of me partner's mouths. They innocents *do* talk if it *be* talking, your ladyship; and it's what me partner said that do most bide in me mind. 'A said a terrible queer word, Lady Ash'ver; and it's as true as God's dear blood what I be telling thee."

The idiot, who had now climbed to the top of the gate and

was balancing himself there like a demonic gargoyle, burst in with an exultant cry at this point.

"I do know what the half beastie did say, pretty leddy! Binnory do know what the half beastie did say to Granny Cooper!"

"I can't listen to you now," repeated Lady Ann sternly. "Come up to the house later; and you, too, Binnory, if you like. Good-afternoon to you both!" And she swept off down the lane with all a grand lady's indifference as to whether the populace commented on her condition or held their peace.

She did not put her hands to her ears, however, as many prospective mothers of heroes and demigods have been driven ere now to do; and for that reason it was impossible not to hear what the old woman shouted after her.

"Till book be burned no child'll be borned!"

The idiot, who had now scrambled over the gate, ran after her down the lane. "Till book be burned no child'll be borned!" he screamed in his shrill voice; and it was only after Lady Ann had turned twice round, threatening him with her parasol, that he desisted and drifted back to his companion.

Even when she was out of all sight and hearing of these two troublesome beings and had rounded the corner at the point opposite Titty's Ring she still seemed to hear that ominous and fantastic oracle. The magpies chattered it; the green finches chittered it; the very rooks themselves, who now began to gather in larger numbers, seemed echoing it with their rueful cawings. The whole incident was peculiarly distasteful to the girl's mind; but the first effect it had upon her was doubtless an excellent one. It roused to full flood her gallant fighting spirit. What impertinence! What intolerable impertinence! And then her invincible youthfulness came to her aid. There was something that tickled her realistic sense of humour about the whole thing. "It's just a trick to get money out of us," she thought. "That fool Hastings has probably been telling everybody what he told me on New Year's night, about his abominable theories. No doubt when he spent that day in the caravan with Netta Page the old woman listened to his mad talk. The dwarfs probably heard him, too! In fact, the chances are that our absurd clergyman and his insane fancies are the common gossip of the whole neighbourhood."

Had Lady Ann been a more neurotic or a weaker person this agitating encounter would have been actually dangerous to her. As it was, so robust was her constitution and so defiant her temper, it seemed rather to hearten her and steady her than to do her any harm.

It did cross her mind as she left the lane and made her way through the stubble fields toward the village that she was at that crisis in her life singularly alone. Her own parents were dead. Mrs. Ashover was her nearest relative; and the girl was far too sagacious not to know that it was in the rôle of a mother of future Ashovers rather than in the rôle of a daughter to herself that the old tribal fanatic cherished her.

Alone. Well? What of that? Many a Norse ancestor of hers had been alone ere now, both on land and sea, and *that* fact had not weakened the strength of his arm or blurred his clear, unclouded glance into the shifty eyes of Fate!

Besides, she was not alone! Rook might have a cold and fickle heart. His mother might be obsessed by the family. Very well! Let them go. She carried *her* champion, *her* supporter, *her* ally, here in her own vitals!

She was at the top of the ridge now and beginning to feel exhausted. That young Viking in her belly was displaying his strength—and his sex, too—how sure she was of *that!*— by certain familiar thumpings and stirrings.

It must be getting on toward tea-time. The autumn sun already rested, red and glowing, like a vast eye-socket veiled in titanic sorrow, on the treetops behind the Drools' cottage.

The church and churchyard down there in the valley were gathered now in thick woolly mists, and as she looked at them she remembered the peculiar psychic support which more than once those dead people there had seemed capable of giving her.

Well! Weary though she was, she was so mysteriously self-subsistent at that moment that she felt strong enough to steer her vessel onward without assistance, or even sympathy, from any quarter.

As she came slowly down the stubble field with its faint strawy smell and its little tufts of fumitory and small wild yellow pansies she had a strange fierce longing for the unknown travail that was to come upon her. She felt associated so closely with her child in this struggle that it was almost as if two lovers, of proud Spartan breed, were preparing for an engagement with a barbarous enemy!

Never for one second did she contemplate the possibility of her death. The life force in her seemed so inexhaustible, so potent, that it tossed such thoughts aside, as a racehorse might toss the foam from his mouth and nostrils.

She soon reached the hawthorn hedge where she had met Rook on the occasion of her visit to Toll-Pike. She smiled faintly as she thought of that unenjoyed lunch! And she said to herself with stark sincerity, "How *can* Rook and Lexie find anything to attract them in that sentimental, funny-looking little thing?"

She sat down to rest on the identical spot where she had rested before. The hedge protected her from the rising mists, and the ground was still warm except where the longer grass had caught the dew. With her cloak wrapped round her she sank luxuriously back against the furrow of sweet-smelling earth mould. The largeness of that autumn day, its indrawn breath, its immense passivity, lulled her into a delicious relaxation.

She lay there for nearly an hour, living intensely and absorbingly in the great parturient process that was going on within her. Then, at last, feeling the approach of the evening chill, she rose to her feet, and, rested and comforted in mind and body, pushed open the ancient ramshackle gate into the remembered barley field.

It was then that quite suddenly, and, as it were, quite naturally, that tiresome, ungrammatical refrain, "Till book be burned no child'll be borned," repeated itself in her ears as if someone at her very side had whispered it.

Lady Ann became grave and stood motionless, like a beautiful animal scenting some species of ambiguous danger. "What's up with me?" she thought to herself. "Is this nerves? Or am I growing superstitious?"

And then without reasoning about it at all she suddenly felt an irresistible instinct driving her to go straight down to Toll-Pike Cottage and face this life-hating conjurer whose sorcery was so inimical to herself and her child.

She tried to find, for her own justification, some quite reasonable motive for stopping at Toll-Pike Cottage just then; nor was such a motive very difficult to find. She felt not the slightest embarrassment at being seen either by Nell or Hastings in her present condition. As for Netta's presence there, she did not permit it to affect her one way or the other. Her attitude to both these rivals of hers was that of an indifferent conqueror of superior race, whose caprices may be indulged to the furthest limit in sublime contempt for any reaction, favourable or unfavourable, that they might produce on the vanquished.

It did not take her long to reach the cottage. This time there was no Marquis of Carabas lying on the back porch. But Lady Ann did not intend to enter in that unconventional manner this time. She walked round to the front door and rang the bell. To her surprise she heard excited and agitated voices in the room above.

She waited. No one seemed to have noticed her ring. There was evidently something serious going on upstairs.

Was this crazy priest quarrelling with these two women? Was he ill-using them, perhaps? All her social instincts as a member of the English ruling class rose up in indignation. It was no more to her then that Rook had taken his pleasure with these girls than if they had been daughters of Twiney or of Pod! What was unpardonable was that in the village of Ashover, within a mile of Ashover House, an English clergyman should be behaving like a drunken blacksmith. For it *was* that. She was not country-born for nothing. She had heard so often that particular mingling of female clamour with masculine threats from under the eaves of thatched cottages, as she rode home, dreamy and content, through Sturminster, through Shaftesbury, through Stalbridge, from a successful hunt with the Blackmore pack!

With her practical and realistic mind she came to the prompt conclusion that in "his weakness and his melancholy" this hedge priest of theirs had taken to drink. Accustomed from her earliest childhood to high-handed interference, and entirely free from any physical apprehensions on her own behalf, the intrepid girl boldly turned the handle of the door, entered the little hallway, and walked resolutely and unflinchingly up the narrow staircase.

Her steps on the stairs were no more audible to the persons in that room than had been the sound of her ring. She heard scuffling and struggling in there as well as this turmoil of voices.

With a quick movement of her strong young wrist she turned the handle of the door and swung it wide open. The sight that met her eyes was disturbing enough; though it was not quite on a par with the violent ruffianism she had been imagining. Like all people of her kind she lumped the middle classes and the proletariat together, and took for granted that any of them might at any moment break all laws of decency and self-respect.

She was not surprised, therefore, to see William Hastings with a white distorted countenance struggling to release himself from the arms of Mr. Pod, who, very red in the face and obviously much embarrassed at being found in such a situation, was holding the priest down on a sofa-bed.

This article of furniture must have been recently dragged in from the room opposite, for it was placed awkwardly and grotesquely between the philosopher's desk and the round table in the centre of the chamber.

On one side of this makeshift bed stood Netta, evidently doing her best to soothe the afflicted man; while at its foot, leaning across it so as to touch her husband's hands with her own, was the slender form of Nell, from whose eyes the tears were streaming and whose whole body was trembling with agitation and concern.

"Lordy! Your Ladyship did give I a start!" cried the breathless sexton, relaxing his hold upon the man on the bed. "Us all thought as you was drownded in sheep wash or summat!"

"Thank God, you're all right, Lady Ann," said Netta gravely, glancing anxiously down at the man beneath her to see that he did not take advantage of this new apparition to make a fresh struggle to escape.

But Hastings was staring at Ann with wild intensity, every line in his face expressive of the passing of one complicated emotion after another across the clouded mirror of his mind. He had worked at the completion of his book so passionately that now it was finished the actual volume itself, its leather binding, its ink-stained pages, had become to his unsettled brain a magical engine of destruction, a nihilistic catapult as it were, that it now behoved him to hurl at the citadels of life!

Two of these life ramparts had got themselves lodged in his mind as especially challenging to his campaign—those Ashover tombs in the church chancel, and the living body of Lady Ann Ashover! From those tombs, Hastings had come to be obstinately convinced, emanated the very essence of this unscrupulous life force, which in its relentless strivings disturbed the placid pools of non-existence. And here was Lady Ann herself, now standing before him, the incarnation of the remorseless urge! With the extravagant fanaticism of a mad logician, Hastings formulated, even as he looked at the woman, a monstrous and diabolic project. He would make her herself hug to her heart his "Book of Annihilation" and carry it to the place of those living dead.

To his distorted vision this hurling of his book among his enemies presented itself as the supreme stroke in an abysmal spiritual warfare whereof he was the protagonist and this woman, big with child, the antagonist.

The man's intellectual magnetism was so great that as he sat up there in bed with the veins in his forehead distended and his face quivering with conflicting emotion the four persons in that room remained awed and silent. When he did speak it was with a mingling of insane cunning and disordered impetuousness.

"They won't let me take it and hide it!" he cried. "I want to hide it under those chancel slabs . . . I could easily get up those stones and put it there; but they won't let me! And now you've come and you'll join with them. If you hadn't come I'd have done it. Wouldn't I have done it, fellow?" And he turned his distracted glance upon the embarrassed Mr. Pod, who stood watching him with one of his great fists ostentatiously clenched, as if Hastings were a troublesome bullock at Tollminster Fair.

"'Tis true enough, your ladyship, what Parson do say," acquiesced the sexton. "'A would have rinned all the way to church and have scrabbled with's own hands at they paving stones! 'A would have done that; and maybe heaved up some of they ancient Squires what do bide under them moniments! 'Tis God's truth what 'a do say, your ladyship. 'A be a terrible strong man, and there be none to hold 'un but only I and these two young leddies!"

Lady Ann became suddenly aware of the actual presence of Hastings's book. The manuscript occupied a large leather bound volume as big as a business ledger, and it lay on the priest's desk just above his bed. She knew the look of the book, as she had seen it in his hands before; and she surveyed it now with a peculiar and unusual interest.

Nell, who was standing at the foot of the bed, caught the direction of the visitor's glance.

"My husband had just finished his last chapter, Lady Ann, when this idea of hiding it in the church came into his head. You feel better now, William, don't you? You won't frighten us again, will you, William?"

The man rose a little higher on the bed, straightening his legs and propping himself up on his two hands. He stared at Nell's face with that pathetic and puzzled frown with which people whose mental processes have grown jangled become for a moment aware of something wrong and unusual.

It was as if he were peering helplessly at the young girl through the entangled boughs of his own obscuring delusion. Fancying that he did hear her and understand her Nell flung herself down on her knees at his side and began chafing one of his hands.

Lady Ann exchanged glances with Netta; but neither of them, nor indeed Mr. Pod himself, who looked as if he would be thankful if the floor sank beneath him, seemed anxious to intervene between these two.

Lady Ann's thoughts wandered off to all that buried dust under the church pavement which seemed to be so persistent an influence in the movement of events in this place. She recalled the man's wild discourse to her on New Year's Eve, at the end of Marsh Alley, and how he had associated, even then, the negations of his ferocious logic with the extinction of the House of Ashover. He was disarmed and innocuous enough now; but she, in her sanity, began just then, as she saw the book lying there within her reach, to be betrayed into the same illusion as the one which this madman held, namely, that this mysterious destructive force had actually passed from the living man's intellect into the inanimate potency of the work he had just completed.

Once more that jingle of Betsy's—"Till book be burned no child'll be borned"—sounded in her brain with the appalling distinctness of a warning sea bell rocked by rising waves.

Nell was keeping up, in a kind of crooning tone, a sort of lullaby to the man on the bed. She seemed to forget the presence of the others.

Suddenly Hastings bent forward, stretched out his arm, and possessed himself of the volume on the desk. He turned over some of its pages with a sort of malignant awe; while a moment later with a glance at Lady Ann that had a flicker of demonic subtlety in it, he tossed the book down at the foot of the bed.

Then it seemed as if he forgot its existence; for he began to talk incoherently of certain early memories of his in the slums of London. He mentioned names that were completely strange to them all; and with those names he mixed the names of Latin writers and the titles of Latin books. And he talked of the lily pond in Kew Gardens, which must have been the objective of some thrilling childish excursion. And then he muttered something about park railings, with deer behind them. "Let me feed them, Mother! Let *me* feed them!" he cried out in a loud voice; and then, without any apparent connection, he began reciting the old grammar-school tag:

> "Common are to either sex
> Artifex and oppifex,
> Conviva, vates, advena,
> Testis, civis, incola,
> Parens, sacerdos, custos, vindex,
> Adolescens, infans, index,
> Judex, haeres, comes, dux,
> Princeps, municeps, conjux!"

Mr. Pod manifested considerable apprehension when he heard these strange syllables. He looked from one to another of the three ladies as if he expected them to call upon him to clap his great hand over the mouth of the delirious man.

"This do come of praying and preaching," he whispered in an awestruck voice. "Parson be calling upon the Lord in Greek and Hebrew, same as 'tis writ the Blessed Saviour did. 'Tis enough to make a man's wits turn to have to say 'Dearly Beloved' and 'Scripture moveth us in sundry places' every seventh day, wet *or* fine! 'Tis a wonder more on 'em don't start hollerin' and forgetting theyselves!"

Lady Ann heard these words of the sexton with the sort of attention a starving man on a raft might give to the screaming of a sea gull while his companions were casting lots as to which of them should die first.

The sight of that volume lying at the foot of the bed obsessed her with an irresistible fascination. Suddenly she could endure it no longer; and, without a word said, she just slipped forward a couple of steps, snatched up the volume, thrust it under her arm beneath her cloak and moved quickly back to the open door.

The voice of the delirious man went on mumbling inanely the classic doggerel:

> "Auctor, exsul, and with these
> Bos . . . tigris . . . interpres . . .
> Canis and anguis . . . serpens . . . sus."

It was as though, having completed his categorical Domesday Book of all life's progeny, he were waiting in sardonic expectation for the explosion of his train of dynamite.

Nell and Netta both made instinctive movements toward her. There was something treacherous and outrageous to their minds in this arbitrary despoiling of an unconscious man.

"What are you doing, Lady Ann?" cried Netta. "You're not going to take his book really away, are you?"

"Give it back. . . . Give it back. . . . Oh, how *dare* you?" protested Nell.

There was, however, at that moment such a dangerous light in the eyes of the girl in the doorway that neither of them had the courage to approach her. In any case, so tightly was she holding the book, it could not have been taken from her without a struggle; and the idea of anything of that sort, in the condition in which she was and under the eyes of Hastings, was inconceivable.

"Take it and good luck to 'ee, marm," threw in Mr. Pod. "And if 'ee *do* bury it, same as parson did tell 'ee to, me own girt pick what I do use in hard weather be lying under one of they stone seats in porch. I reckon 'twere a good deed if more of them books be put under sod! 'Tis this book-writing what do worrit quiet-lived folks more'n the worst god-danged ale in Dorchester!"

"You're not too . . . too tired . . . to walk home . . . Lady Ann . . . are you?" murmured Netta. "Because . . . I could go and get someone——" She stopped abruptly in the presence of the cold stare which the girl gave her from the door; but she added gallantly, "We are all so thankful to see that you're safe."

Ann replied to this only with a general and easy "Goodnight," and descending the stairs with the air of one who has paid a natural and normal visit let herself out into the garden.

A quarter of an hour later and Hastings's mood had changed again for the worse. The unfortunate man seemed to forget that he himself had wished to give his "Praise of Death" into the arms of a pregnant woman. He began to renew his efforts to break loose from Mr. Pod's restraining hands. So distressing was it to Nell to see his struggles that she enquired of Netta in a low voice whether it wouldn't be better to humour him and let him get out into the air.

"There would be no harm as long as we all went with him," she whispered.

But Netta opposed this suggestion with stern common sense.

"Nell, it's impossible," she retorted. "It's impossible. He'll be quieter presently. But if he isn't you'd better go to the village and get more help."

The girl's words were soon justified. Exhausted by his own violence the unhappy philosopher fell at last into a sort of comatose quiescence; and though, as the evening wore on, their hope that he would fall asleep was not fulfilled, there seemed no likelihood that he would make any further attempt that night to get out of the house.

He refused, however, to let Nell undress him; and she had to content herself with seeing him lying, pale and silent, his eyes fixed on the darkening window; while Mr. Pod, seated on a chair by his side, watched over him with respectful patience.

The twilight of that last day of September seemed loth to lose itself in the finality of night. All the various familiar sounds which that particular hour seems to evoke upon a country road—the lowing of cattle, the crying of nocturnal birds, the intermittent barking of a farmyard dog or of a fox in the furze covers—followed on her journey home the solitary figure of Lady Ann, with that closely written volume held tightly under her cloak.

As she walked slowly between the darkening water meadows and the misty stubble fields she became aware, more acutely than was usual with her, of the phantasmal quality of an autumn evening of this kind. The remote fluidity, as if they were being looked at through the windows of a sea king's palace, of the trees and gates and weir dams which she passed struck her with a sense of beauty that she had never in that particular way experienced before.

She had a queer, vague impression that she was feeling

these things not only for herself but for the child within her; and, as this feeling grew upon her, a deep mysterious gratitude to life itself; not to any power beyond life—for she was a woman almost completely devoid of the religious sense—but just to life, life as it was, with everything that it entailed, rose up in her heart so overpoweringly that she actually hummed to herself as she walked along.

She felt chilly, however, as she crossed the wooden bridge and inhaled the mud-scented mist that rose from its surface; and once more that oracular jingle came into her head. "It's all nonsense," she thought, "to imagine that those Deformities I saw by the caravan that day uttered a thing like that! Betsy Cooper must have invented it herself. It's the sort of abracadabra she *would* think of; especially after listening to that fool of a parson. I sha'n't say a word of this to Rook or any one!"

By this time she did begin to feel the effects of her long walk; but she was a girl of immense intrepidity and she struggled on gallantly until, crossing the stone bridge by the churchyard, she found herself at her own drive gate.

As it happened there was a pile of burning weeds just outside this gate, one of the growing evidences of Rook's absent-minded submission to the indolence and carelessness of his dependents. She was still thinking of that "Till-book-be-burned" catch of the pseudo-gipsy when her eyes fell upon the great red heart of this smoking heap, glowing with a crimson glow in the damp windless obscurity.

Once more acting on a sudden unpremeditated impulse she removed the volume from beneath her cloak and flung it into the centre of the smouldering heap.

Having done the thing, it was with a fierce and primitive satisfaction that she prodded its pages open with the end of her parasol and watched the ruddy flames leap up and devour them. So bright were these flames as the pages really began shrivelling that she could actually catch a word or two in

Hastings's meticulously clear hand, as they were thus illuminated in their vanishing. She caught the word "nothingness" and the word "equilibrium" and some other word that might have been "dissolution" or "devolution"; and then there were no more intelligible pages left of the life work of the Reverend William Hastings!

She was interested, however, to observe that before falling into dust the last of these pages remained as thin blackened ghosts within the licking tongues of the fire; ghosts of written sheets, upon which she still could trace unreadable hieroglyphs and indecipherable signs; signs that were the bodiless *revenants* of those irrefutable arguments with which the theologian had demolished the universe that begat him, hieroglyphs that were like long-necked cormorants flying over a gulf into which Time and Space had sunk.

She left the heap of burning weeds and moved slowly, very slowly, toward the house. She began to be aware that the exhaustion, which made her body feel like something that was made of pulseless wool but at the same time was as heavy as sods of turf, was now accompanied by other, more disturbing symptoms.

Lady Ann bit her lip and stood for a moment quite still. Then, moving on steadily and quietly across the lawn, she mounted the familiar steps of the entrance to the house and opened the door into the hall.

Here she swayed and staggered; and finally fell half-fainting into one of the great mahogany hall chairs inscribed with the armorial bearings of the House of Ashover!

CHAPTER XXV

BY GOOD fortune Mr. Twiney and his gig were both in the Ashover stable, when on Lady Ann's recovery from her collapse it became plain that her confinement was at hand. The man was despatched at once to fetch Doctor Twickenham, whose house was some three miles away, on the Tollminster Road.

It was Mrs. Ashover herself who discovered the girl, white and foredone, on that hard mahogany chair in the panelled hall. The old lady displayed as much energy in this crisis as she had done on previous agitating occasions; and it was not long before, with Rook's help, she had got the girl safely undressed and in bed, in the pleasant room she had used since her arrival on the scene more than a year ago.

Left alone at last with his wife, whose sufferings were at present very intermittent, Rook found himself quite differently affected and much more affected than he had anticipated. He was a man to whom the immediate presence of physical distress was more impressive than any mental or emotional appeal. Something peculiarly responsive and sensitive in him was stirred and troubled as he watched those quick spasms crossing the girl's flushed face.

"Ann," he muttered as he bent down over her. "Ann, my sweet Ann!"

She smiled at him stoically, but he could not help noticing that there was a remoteness and detachment at the back of her eyes, as if she were a duellist with drawn rapier saluting her opponent while she spoke lightly and casually to the friend at her side.

"You *will* get through it all right, Ann? You feel you'll be all right?"

It seemed natural enough to her that she should be the one to supply comfort at that moment rather than to receive it.

"Of course I'll get through it, Rook," she said. "Don't you fret yourself about me. Go for a walk and keep safe away till it's all over. And don't let your mother or any one else worry you about me. I shall be all right."

She clenched her fingers tightly as a recurrent spasm overtook her; but as soon as it passed she smiled at him again.

"He'll be born on the first of October," she said confidently.

There was a moment's silence between them while he wondered whether it would annoy her, or whether she would think it an unreal and sentimental thing to do, if he took hold of one of her hands.

To his utter astonishment she suddenly plucked both her arms out from beneath the sheet and flung them round his neck.

"Kiss me, Rook," she sobbed. "I love you! I do love you so much!"

He bent down; and for the first time in the lives of these two proud creatures there were salt tears mingled with the embrace they exchanged.

A hurried knock at the door made the man rise up erect and composed.

"Open it, dear," she gasped; and with a smile more obviously strained than any she had yet given him, "and go for a good long walk—but not *too* long!"

He opened the door and there stood his mother. The little lady had the demeanour of some military conqueror in an old print who stands amid dying men and horses with the complacency of a successful horticulturist.

"We mustn't exhaust her by talking," she said; and Rook felt inclined to take the triumphant old woman by the shoulders and shake her violently, while he bawled in her ears: "It's wicked! It's wicked! It's wrong! It's wrong! It's wrong!" What he did say was: "I'm going out for a while, Mother. Twickenham will be here in a moment."

"But—Rook"—and Mrs. Ashover showed signs of puzzled irritation—"she may ask for you presently. She may want you. They often feel like that!"

He pushed past her without replying and ran downstairs.

His overcoat lay on the hall table and he pulled it on, shivering. For some reason he felt at that moment deadly cold. As he did this Pandie came running out of the kitchen.

"Master Rook! How be my Lady? Be it really begun, then? 'Tis best for all when't do come quick and fast. Missus said I were to bide in kitchen and not come nigh to she; but 'tis terrible hard to stand afore thik old sink and act natural-like when my Lady be brought to bed. Martha, she do say 'tis the Lord wi' healing in His wings what us best to pray to; but *I* says, and they was my very words, Master Rook, *I* says, I'll just run out and ask Squire hisself. Maybe he'll say 'tis tempting of Providence for I to bide in kitchen! Maybe he'll say 'twere best for she and best for the blessed babe that I bide upstairs near thik door so's to be ready and waiting. Martha can open for doctor. She be one who can act natural when all be topsy-turvied! But I weren't born holy and hushed. I were born trembly and human-hearted. So don't 'ee tell I to bide in kitchen, Master Rook, when my Lady be brought to bed. 'Tisn't in nature that I should do the like o' that, whatever Missus do say!"

Rook hardly caught the drift of this torrent of speech, but a sickening pity came over him for that lonely figure in the room upstairs; and at the same time the feeling deepened upon him that he must get away—away—away.

He moved to the door; but the red-haired servant in her excitement clung to his coat sleeve.

"Thee aren't going out, Master, be 'ee? Oh, don't 'ee go

out, Master, don't 'ee go out! I've a-heard four girt thunderclaps already as I were trying to scrape thik old silver coffeepot what thee mother must have clean though sky do fall! Don't 'ee go out, Squire Ash'ver, don't 'ee go out, Master Rook! Doctor'll be here present; and 'tisn't in nature for 'ee to go!"

He flung her off and rushed bareheaded into the garden, slamming the great Georgian door behind him. It was with an indescribable feeling of relief, when he found himself outside the drive gate and in the road, that he felt heavy splashes of rain upon his face.

There was no sound of thunder; and indeed it may well have been that those four thunderclaps had no existence except in Pandie's head, but before he had gone many steps a torrential volume of rain descended upon him.

It was like the breaking of some vast taut hawser by which the very planetary ship itself was roped to its cosmic dock; so that the earth vessel now, free of all restraint, unpiloted, masterless, lampless, drifted, with all its dark, wet, silent decks and rigging, into a chaos of water, wherein the waters "that are above the firmament" mingled with the waters "that are beneath the firmament!"

When Rook reached the middle of the stone bridge he turned round, hearing the sound of wheels. Very faintly, like two watery marsh fires, phosphorescent and fitful, he could see the lights of Twiney's cart as it stopped at the drive gate. So the mare had been persuaded, somehow, in spite of this waterspout of rain, to pass the "Gorm" signpost; and the doctor had come to Ashover House, for the first time, for *this* purpose, since he came to assist at the birth of Lexie!

Rook leaned upon the cold parapet of the bridge from the surface of which the rain splashed into the darkness. As he stared down into the murmuring obscurity beneath him he remembered how the river had looked on that moonlit night when Lexie came over from Marsh Alley to meet him in the churchyard. That was the first time his brother had told him about his desire to be buried underneath the elm.

He clutched the cold edge of the stonework with both his hands and bent forward, listening to the gurgling noises made by the flowing water and to the hissing sound of the rain as it struck the river's surface.

The rain beat down upon his bare head with a force that made him wonder if it were not going to change to hail. But it was much too warm a night for that; and he recognized that it was the unusual size of the individual raindrops and the torrential force with which their massed volume hit his skull, which gave him that particular impression.

He bowed his head still lower over the parapet, deriving a fierce pleasure from thus yielding himself up to the mysterious caprice of the blind, soulless, formless element which knew no difference between a living human skeleton and the inanimate blocks of smooth quarried stone. His mind, always abnormally sensitive to physical sensations, began to detach itself from any definite train of thought; began to disembody itself and unsheathe itself, until it seemed to arrive at a naked airy freedom which enabled it to mingle with the dark flow of that invisible gurgling water and with the seething downpour of that inundating deluge.

Drowning! That was the ultimate sensation he craved; drowning in these vast inhuman elements that obeyed no master and had no purpose or object or obligation; but only drifted and drifted, on and on, up and down, as the unknown reservoirs of subhuman force sucked them in.

Oh, with what happiness he could imagine himself floating—dead—dead—dead—down that current of dark swollen water! No more responsibilities, no more decisions, no more miserable remorse!

That mysterious country of the underworld of which the Greek wanderer had his vision, coming to it at last through those Cimmerian mists, may after all have held a shadowy correspondence with something that really did exist!

If so, it was surely there, surely under those gray willows and among those tall grasses, that the land of untroubled twilight awaited him, whose margins he had so often approached, caught in quick strange glimpses, along the Frome-side roads and the green Frome-side lanes!

He stood erect and looked about him. The rain began rapidly to diminish now, moving away over the valley toward the east with the same capricious suddenness as that with which it had first arrived.

He crossed the bridge and walked on to the entrance into the churchyard.

He hesitated here for a while, his mind returning to his wife and to that devastating sense of a woman's absolute loneliness at these hours which had driven him forth by a kind of shame. How wicked it was, how dark, how heathen, that mock sympathy which his mother and Pandie had displayed! How horrible this deep, blind, pitiless understanding that women had of one another at such moments—an understanding that was not tenderness or pity but something else; something that came to the surface at these times from the subterranean abysses of nature.

"Ann—my dear sweet Ann—bear it a little longer, just a very little longer, and you'll be happier than you ever dreamed was possible!"

So he said in his heart, making of his craving to relieve her in her travail a sort of desperate conscious prayer, directed to no deity and to no demon, but to the vast night itself, oldest of all divinities, accomplice alike of the birth of grass blades in the wet dew of Titty's Ring and of the birth of planets in the cold emptiness of space.

Then it occurred to him that he would like, on this night of the birth of his first-born, to go for a moment to where his father—"the old man" with whom he had had a lifelong feud—lay stretched out under his six feet of clay.

This irrational yielding to the very tradition against which he had struggled so long came upon him without warning; came upon him as if in reply to an actual summons. He hesitated for a moment longer, shaking his head from side to side and pulling his drenched overcoat tightly round him, while with a grim, rather ghastly smile he stared at the dark roof in front of him, from which the water was now audibly dripping.

He became suddenly conscious, as never before, of the appalling finality of human decisions, even in the least important matter. The water dripped, dripped, dripped, from that sloping roof, upon the enmossed slabs of some enclosed tombstone; and it seemed to him as if it dripped from the eternal wound in the heart of the universe, the wound that nothing could staunch or heal, the original blunder of the gods, the free will of life to *will against life*.

Shivering now a little, though the rain had quite ceased, and lifting his feet very heavily and with difficulty, as if they were subjected in some special way just then to the law of gravitation, Rook moved up the gravel path and rounded the corner of the building.

There before him, visible in spite of the darkness, was the familiar white headstone; there, too, the well-known trunk of Lexie's elm. But what struck his mind with a shock of abrupt amazement, struck it with the sort of chill that comes over us when something occurs which resembles the intrusion of the abnormal or supernatural, was the emerging from the church porch of a human figure. He moved forward boldly, however, in pursuit of this figure which proceeded to cross the churchyard to its remote end under the broken wall. There, as he approached it, it assumed the appearance of a woman, a woman who took up a spade which she had left on the ground and began to dig with animal-like rapidity and concentration, throwing the loose earth upon a growing heap at her side.

It was clear she must have been at her task for some while before the rain interrupted her; for the heap of earth at the edge of the hole she was digging showed large and unmistakable in the darkness.

He recognized her now. She was Betsy Cooper. And well enough did he apprehend what she was at; for it had been one of the scandals of the village in his boyhood that Nancy Cooper, his father's favourite, had been buried somewhere in that quarter without a tombstone; and that even the mound that indicated the place had been flattened out in some orderly but impious tidying up of that particular spot.

He walked straight across to where the old woman was digging. She did not hear him approach and lie came close up to her before he spoke.

"Betsy!"

She leaped up at the sound, and drew away trembling, dropping her spade into the hole. When she saw who it was her face became transfigured with wild concern.

"Get 'ee back into house, Squire Ash'ver! Get 'ee back into house while there be time! What be 'ee doing traipsin' in churchyard when thee's wife be brought to bed? Get 'ee back, Squire Rook, lest some girt blow fall on 'ee! Hist—hist—dear Squire alive! There be terrible mischief abroad this blessed night for thee and thine. I do know it and I've a-told them maidies in kitchen what I do know! Dursn't one of all thy folk up and tell 'ee what I did say to they afore this same sundown? I'd a-told it to thee wold mother but naught of it and naught of poor Betsy would *she* bide. Wahay! Wahoh! And that none should heed! Wahoh! And that thee own self should be traipsin' here, none withholding! Get thee back to house, for the sake of thy own flesh and blood, Squire Ash'ver! Get thee back for Christes' sake afore 'tis too late!"

The old woman's agitation was so extreme that she actually waved both her thin arms in the air, while her face assumed the look of some inspired prophetess.

Rook looked at her with grave attention. But, as in the case of a greater than he, there were powers and influences abroad that rendered him obstinately obdurate to her clamour.

"So you're trying to find Nancy?" he said sternly and quietly, looking down into the hole she had digged.

And as he looked, a sharp spasm came over him and a strange emotion gripped his vitals. In one single flash he got a vision of the whole tragic pity of the human race—these mothers, these children! He saw his own delicately nurtured Ann alone in that bed. He saw this old woman wrestling with the very earth, if so be that she might touch the bones of her child dead twenty, thirty years ago.

"Let my Nancy bide where she be!" cried the hag in desperation. "Look to thee own self, Squire Ash'ver! Look to thee own self and get back to house!"

He turned away, unwilling to drive the woman to further extremes of supplication; but as he left her there he said compassionately and gently, but with a certain sternness: "If you do find your girl to-night, Betsy, or on any other night, I will see to it that she has a proper tombstone."

He passed his father's grave this time with a shrug of his shoulders. Was the late Squire himself responsible for the abominable neglect that was the cause of Betsy's nocturnal piety? Were those "half beasties," as Binnory called them, his own half brothers?

He walked rapidly out of the churchyard into the road.

Once more that leaden feeling in his legs, as if the law of gravitation had suddenly doubled its centripetal pull!

Once more that accursed sense of enormous importance in the making of trivial, unessential decisions!

"Ann didn't need me there," he thought, "till it's all over. It's the least I can do for her to obey her literally. She doesn't want any more of these mock-sympathetic watchers!" And he visualized with such appalling distinctness the red-haired Pandie, obsessed with gloating sentiment, clinging to the banisters or listening at the door, that he plucked at his heavy feet as if they had been two obdurate roots, and strode resolutely off toward Foulden Bridge.

It was then, out there between the river bank and the open meadows, that the quality of the sky above his head began to change. The waning moon was still below the horizon; but a gentle wind had risen from the west and had swept the clouds before it, so that Rook was able to discern at least one or two of the constellations with which he was familiar.

He could see the great outstretched wings of Cygnus, like the wings of some vast emissary of fate despatched by one demiurge to another, flying across the fields of space.

He could see a star that he fancied must be Aldebaran; and another that he noted to himself, with that pathetic satisfaction with which creatures of a day find respite from their nothingness in the mere *naming* of the immortals, as a luminary that might be, only his memory always failed him, that favourite sky mark of his brother Lexie, Vega in Lyra.

Lit by the stars as if by far-off candle flames the wide water meadows stretched away to his left; and beyond the river and beyond the barley fields rose dark and blurred, like a great bastion of some invisible fortress, the vague outline of Heron's Ridge.

Certain stars, watery and faint, as if they had been the drowned but not quite extinguished bodies of glowworms, lay silent and deep-buried in the muddy water of a ditch at the roadside. Bits of broken reed stalk and wind-blown twigs from willow trees and alders floated between the images of these fallen stars, as if they floated above a crevice in the terrestrial orb itself which sank down into antipodal gulfs.

Calmed and soothed by the largeness of the night about him the Squire of Ashover began to recover the equipoise of his perturbed spirit.

Ashover? Ashover? What was Ashover between the hovering wings of Cygnus and the stretching out of the chords of Lyra?

He suddenly began to feel strangely, exultantly happy; happier than he had been for more than twelve months; happier than he had been since those irresponsible days just after his father's death.

Every person he thought of at that moment intensified rather than diminished his happiness. Round all the people of his life there seemed to float a sort of ideal luminosity, enhancing their dignity, their beauty, their originality, their human worth.

He felt a sense of inexpressible gratitude to the gods that he had ever known these people of his life, his brother, his mother, his wife, Netta, and Nell. Some actual chemical fluid, wonderful, magical, as if those high stars had been melted in some enchanted forest pool to which he had pressed his lips, seemed to flow round the figures of these people as they gathered there in his mind, and to harmonize for ever his relations with them.

Under the healing flow of this magical fluid, which seemed actually at that moment flooding every cell of his brain, the knots of the nerves that were jangled there unloosed themselves and expanded freely; expanded like the floating tendrils of dry seaweed when the twilight tide covers it, after a hot day!

In the ecstasy of what he felt just then it seemed to him that he could live happily by Ann's side for the rest of his life. It seemed to him that even if her love were far more predatory and possessive than it ever *had* been he still could live with her, live with her and her child, without any of that abominable illusion of being suffocated, divided, impinged upon, from which he had suffered so horribly in times past.

And the same thing applied to all the other people of his life. Something had happened to those knotted nerves in his soul that had untied them completely, that had spread them out beautifully and freely like crumpled mosses that have been washed by rain and can now hold the sun in their leafy cups without withering.

As he came near to Foulden Bridge his happiness grew to such a pitch that he actually skipped a step or two with those feet of his that just now were so leaden and heavy.

The alders by the sheep wash, if they possessed any conscious interest in the human figures of their environment, must have been struck by the sight of a bony, hatless, middle-aged man, skipping with his feet as if they were the hooves of an escaped goat!

All at once Rook became aware—without warning, without premonition—of that same young rider upon the gray horse moving silently along by his side.

Instinctively, as before, he clutched at the youth's saddle; and as before, the boy laid his warm youthful fingers caressingly upon his hand.

"I told her I'd have a tombstone put up as soon as she found her," he discovered himself saying, as if in answer to some reproach which the boy had made. "And I've obeyed Ann to-night quite literally. She told me to walk to Foulden Bridge."

Why he said just this, when Ann had never once mentioned the word "Foulden," is one of those queer incidents in a man's life destined to remain to the end of time hidden away unsolved in the limbo of the irrelevant.

But what troubled Rook then was that the youth did not respond to his self-justifying speeches. All he did was to press the hand upon his saddle with still more tender solicitude. Rook wanted him to speak. His longing that he should speak was the first interruption he had suffered to that strange happiness which still hung about him.

But the boy rode slowly on and remained silent. Suddenly Rook felt those fingers grow cold. And it was not only that they grew cold. They seemed to melt away; they seemed to become lighter and more insubstantial than mist!

He looked up. Ah! that figure was receding, horse and rider together, receding and receding; growing dim and faint, dimmer and fainter, until there was no more left of them than a troubled shadow, limned as it were in a great withdrawing wave, rolling back down a shelving beach.

And as they vanished from the man's sight there came to his ears what seemed like a lamentable sigh:

"Daddy! Daddy! Daddy!"

And though with his reason he knew it was only the rising of the wind and its tremulous passage across the shaken reeds, to his heart it seemed an appeal and a warning and a farewell; but what was most strange of all to him just then was the fact that simultaneously with the sinking away of that forlorn sigh across the wet fields, he became absolutely certain, beyond doubt or dispute, that in her bed in Ashover House his wife had been delivered of a son.

So certain was he of this that a rush of quick irrepressible tears came to the back of his eye sockets, and though not a tear actually fell he was conscious enough that he, too, Rook of Ashover, was experiencing now, for all his sceptical disillusionment, the most primitive emotion of the human race: that immemorial exultation, older than the tents of Abraham, older than the tents of Achilles, the joy that a man child is born into the world!

For the third time that night he stood hesitating. He would have liked to go straight home, run at top speed home, leap up the staircase, push Pandie and his mother aside, and embrace his wife and the new-born.

But at that moment another instinct in him contended

with the desire to retrace his steps; namely, the instinct just to rush over to Marsh Alley and be the first to bring the news of his son's birth to Lexie.

Oh, he must do that. Lexie had been associated with every crisis in his life; and now—in the medley of events that had occurred since he left him at Toll-Pike—he had made no sign. To let this night of all nights pass by without seeing Lexie, would it not be something that he would regret to the end of his days? Lexie would laugh at him—he could see at this moment the face he would make—but he would be touched and pleased, all the same, at this disordered midnight visit. He could hear his voice rallying him: "So brother Rook is all 'alive-oh' at last!" That was the way he would fool him; that was the way he would send him back post-haste; utterly refusing, no doubt, to believe that the child *was* yet born; scolding him even for being so superstitious!

It was characteristic of Rook Ashover that at this particular moment of his life he should be hesitating between these two quite irrational appeals: the tug at his heart that pulled him toward a brother who would only tease him when he appeared, and the tug at his heart that pulled him toward a child whose very existence was entirely problematical!

For the third time he brought his hesitation to an end. For the third time he plucked at those earthbound feet of his and strode forward.

"I'll throw stones at his window," he thought, "if he's gone to bed." And he walked rapidly on to the centre of Foulden Bridge.

While these events were proceeding in the lives of the Squire and Lady Ann, matters were not much more quiescent or peaceful within the narrow walls of Toll-Pike Cottage.

With the help of the muscular arms of Mr. Pod the two girls had succeeded in restraining the violent excitement of the unfortunate philosopher. His thoughts still full of his book, his mind full of wild fancies, the fixed idea had taken possession of him that it was to deliver his precious work into the hands of his enemy, Rook, that Lady Ann had stolen it.

Helpless under the sturdy guardianship of his sexton gaoler the poor wretch had relapsed into that sort of petrified passivity into which rabbits and hares are wont to sink when some immense danger menaces their life.

The girls, who kept opening the door to see how he was, became more and more reassured as night drew on, believing —because it was just *that* they especially wanted to believe— that he had fallen into a calm, refreshing sleep, from which he would finally awake, cured of his temporary dementia.

So reassured did they become that they even prepared for themselves a little supper in Nell's kitchen and sat talking together there in low voices, while every now and then Netta would replenish a plate on the floor from which the Marquis of Carabas licked up the morsels his fastidious heart loved.

"We should have heard if she'd been seriously upset by going so far," Nell was saying in reply to some remark of Netta.

The other shook her head. "I'm afraid a good many things could happen in Ashover House and we remain in the dark about them here. To tell you the truth, Nell, I feel as if anything might happen to any of us to-night!"

She moved her chair a little as she spoke, so as to get it away from the window, against which the rain had now begun to beat with extraordinary violence. Both the girls turned their heads toward the streaming pane; and there fell upon them that tremulous and not always unpleasant shudder such as children experience in large shadowy gardens when they play at hide-and-seek.

"If William isn't better when he wakes up," said Nell presently, "I shall ask Pod to stay the night. There's no earthly reason why he shouldn't do that. One of us can go round and tell his wife."

Netta nodded. "I hope Lexie is safe home," she said suddenly, turning quickly round with a new trouble in her eyes. "Pod says he left him in his cottage when he came here, too exhausted to walk any farther."

Nell's mouth opened pitifully and she clapped her hands together. "Oh, Netta," she cried, "we forgot Lexie completely! How could we do that? Oh . . . oh . . . oh. . . ." And she rose from her chair and looked helplessly at the flood of rain which made the window seem as if it were a porthole in a wave-deluged ship.

"There's nothing we could have done, anyhow," said Netta soothingly. "I don't think Mrs. Pod would let him go unless he really felt better."

Nell looked scrutinizingly at her, as a child looks at an older person, doubtful whether it is being honestly or treacherously comforted.

"I hope you are right," she murmured, resuming her seat. "It would be horrible if anything happened to Lexie from our thoughtlessness. But I *can't* believe it will! Oh, Netta, oughtn't one of us to go to Ashover House and get William's book? I don't like to think of his waking up and wanting it and not finding it!" And once more she rose from her chair.

"Nell, sit down!"

The elder woman spoke with an authority far more weighty and unhesitating than would have been possible to the Netta of five months before. She had come to exercise, even in that short time, a sort of protective domination over the young girl.

"Don't let's work ourselves up into unnecessary agitation," she said, smiling. "Not that I don't feel just as you do," she added a moment later. "It's as if we two were locked up together in a fortress, isn't it? With some great battle going on outside, in which all our people are engaged, on one side or the other!" She looked at her companion thoughtfully and sighed heavily. "My whole life has been a sort of waiting," she murmured in a low voice. "But *that's* at an end now."

Nell hardly heard what she was saying. A nervous restlessness, beyond what she could quite account for, made her fidgety and preoccupied.

"I can just see Lexie describing his evening with Mrs. Pod, can't you?" went on Netta. "Can't you see him shutting first one eye and then the other in the way he does when he's done something he's pleased with? There's nothing in the world delights him more than listening to the opinions of people like Mrs. Pod."

"Why is it that I feel so funny and nervous, then?" demanded Nell. "I *know* it's not about William. I can't tell you just how I know; but I do know. . . . It's about the others." And she looked at her friend with an expression of puzzled exasperation, as if it were a sort of unkindness on Netta's part not to relieve her anxiety.

"Hush! Didn't you hear something?"

It was Netta who rose to her feet this time. She went to the door into the passage and opened it.

"I thought I heard the gate clicking," she said.

Nell jumped up hastily and pushing past her ran upstairs.

A minute later Netta heard her voice calling her by name from the room above.

"Netta! Netta! Come here!"

It hardly surprised her when she did stand by her friend's side in that littered room to see the figure of Mr. Pod lying fast asleep in the wicker chair, while the couch they had brought in for Hastings was untenanted and empty.

"He must have slipped out in his stockings!" whispered Nell. The girl was trembling from head to foot and her face was as white as the face of the marble clock on the mantelpiece which did nothing but point to half-past eleven with a malignant emphasis.

Netta bent over the sleeping man and shook him indignantly by the shoulder.

"Where be I? What be doing to I? Let a man bide where 'a be, can't 'ee?"

"You've gone to sleep," was the girl's somewhat hopeless answer to these murmurings. "Mr. Hastings has got out of the house and we must go after him! Get your things on, Nell, quick as you can! There's nothing else to do. We must all go and look for him. He's probably gone to Ashover House with the idea of getting his book back!"

"Be parson rinned off, then?" muttered the bewildered sexton, rising with some embarrassment to his feet and staring feebly at the bookcase as if he suspected his prisoner to be ensconced behind it. "'A were there right enough, not two minutes agone! Do 'ee think 'a be hiding somewheres about, lady? 'A be a terrible crafty gentleman, when's wits be working."

"Nonsense, Mr. Pod," said Netta severely, pulling on her hat and gloves and shoes, while Nell did the same in her bedroom. "Any one would think you'd been drinking. A reliable man *you* are, Mr. Pod; to go to sleep when we trusted you so implicitly! You don't know what harm mayn't come of this criminal neglect of yours!"

It is always a relief in any great human crisis to find a scapegoat; and the staring imbecility of the poor man at that moment certainly did lend itself to such treatment.

"Aren't you ready yet, Nell?" the impatient girl cried, adjusting her cloak between the two open doors. "The rain has stopped now, so we needn't bother *what* we put on! The great thing is to catch him before he gets to the bridge."

Why she used the word "bridge" at that moment she herself could never have explained. "We've got to catch him before he gets to the bridge!" She remembered that phrase afterward with a certain superstitious shudder.

Mr. Pod, meanwhile, was defending himself volubly.

"No need to be scolding of I, missy. *I* be ready to go along. 'Tis the other young leddy what's keeping us. I've a-laid out too many precious corpses in me time not to be up and lively for any think."

Nell did appear now, at the head of the stairs, still very white and trembling. She seemed so helpless and so nervous that her agitation communicated itself to her friend.

"For God's sake, let's start." The elder woman's voice had caught the quiver of suspense with which the whole atmosphere of that house of open doors was now vibrating.

They all three descended the stairs together and passed out into the garden.

It had indeed been a chance for "a crafty gentleman" to exercise his wit, that stealthy escape of William Hastings! He had achieved it with the supernatural cunning of a madman, that cunning which seems to be instinctive and subhuman; as though, with the atrophy of his reason, a man's mind were able to draw freely upon the magnetic duplicity of birds and fishes.

Passing the rain-drenched geranium bed, from which emanated an odour musky and sweet, as if from an enclosed conservatory, he picked up from the ground the great, heavy, iron-tipped garden rake which Pandie had dropped there early the same afternoon.

It was by reason of being burdened with this grotesque weapon that he allowed the gate to click as he went through, a sound that, in the silence of their suspense in the kitchen, had actually reached the ears of one of the girls.

The anger which the loss of his book had roused in him had now crystallized in his demented brain into a cold, murderous fury against the Squire of Ashover.

Hastings's passion at that crisis was to his own mind a pure irrevocable physical necessity. It was *necessary* that he should find Rook Ashover—even if he had to break into his house—and it was *necessary* that he should kill him. Behind this necessity swirled and seethed and fermented all his suppressed jealousy, all his accumulated life hatred, all his desire to "crack Nature's moulds" and bring back the original chaos!

Hurrying along the grass at the edge of the rain-soaked road without overcoat or shoes, the garden rake clutched tightly in his hand, he soon became aware that another figure, also bareheaded, was advancing toward him.

He was separated from this figure by scarcely more than the length of Foulden Bridge; but by the accident of his following the grass path rather than the open road he himself was a far less noticeable object to the other than the other was to him.

The coming together of these two figures, with the river and the white-railinged bridge between them, might easily have seemed like one single man encountering his own image, or even meeting a phantom of himself, as Goethe once did on an unfrequented road; but no such fancy as that crossed the mind of William Hastings. Whether in the whirl of his thoughts he paused to note the strangeness of this accident, that the man he was seeking was coming straight toward him, no one will ever know. Frozen stiff with excitement he savagely clutched his weapon in both hands and crouched down behind the woodwork of the bridge where it joined the road.

Rook came on with rapid strides to the centre of the bridge. What he saw was not the white railing at his side, or the swollen river beneath him, or the dim perspective of the road in front of him; least of all did he see that crouching figure.

He saw Lexie's face at the open window. He saw that expression of mock consternation which he knew so well. He heard his voice: "Is all well with the child? Is all well with Ann? What are you in such a 'toss' for, brother Rook?"

And then, before he had time to do more than make that

spasmodic mental jerk with which the mind passes from one region of reality to another, Hastings was upon him. With a terrific swing of that fantastic weapon the priest struck him full on the side of the head; the arm which Rook instinctively raised to protect himself coming in contact with no more than the handle of the instrument.

Stunned and unconscious the wounded man fell heavily back against one of the two solitary railings which formed the double balustrade of the wooden bridge.

The impact of so massive and bony a frame was too much for that weather-weakened plank; and with a sinister crashing sound it broke and fell outward, precipitating the unconscious man into the stream below. Face downward in that swift-rushing current floated now, limp and unresisting, what was speedily no more than the shape, the form, the image of a *homo sapiens*. First to one side of the river it drifted; then to the other; the weeds brushing against its face, and the Frome water, embrowned by the rain, splashing and gurgling round its unheeding ears.

It was quite out of sight in the darkness—it would have been perhaps out of sight in full daylight—when William Hastings flung his weapon down and returned to consciousness from the petrified trance he had fallen into after striking his blow.

He occupied himself for a while, with an absorbed and vacant concentration, in the task of breaking off and throwing into the river bits of the broken rail that still hung loose and uneven over the water. Then wearily and slowly he turned back the way he had come.

Exhausted by the storm of passion in his brain and by the physical stress of what he had gone through that day he did not get very far. Long before he reached the gate of Toll-Pike Cottage he sank down by the wayside, a huddled, shivering, half-dazed creature, who was quickly passing from all conscious memory of his identity.

Here they found him after the lapse of barely an hour; and when they had carried him back into his room and had undressed him and got him into bed it was clear that his incoherent murmurings were something different from his former insanity.

Before morning he was in a raging fever; and the doctor when he finally appeared, between eleven and twelve of this first noonday of the month of October, was able to say no more than that nothing could be done for him beyond what Netta and Nell had already done.

He died at two o'clock in the afternoon of the following day, recognizing no one, aware of no human feeling, returning, as he had so often wished to return, to whatever "equilibrium," it may be, beyond the difference between life and death, beyond the difference between space and time, smoothes away the outrage of consciousness and the "whips and scorns" of memory.

Some thirty-five years ago the wife of a classical-minded cobbler in east London had given birth to an unhealthily sensitive child; had nourished him with milk from breasts that were themselves ill-nourished; had lulled him to sleep with songs to which no feet had ever danced, with which no airs from green grass or from yellow sand had ever mingled; had washed him, clothed him, wondered at him, worshipped him. . . . Dead, stone-dead was that woman now; dead, and in a grave marked with no more than her name and the number of her few and evil years! She had died in absolute certainty that her son would be a famous thinker, known from the Hebrides to Land's End. But she had not been able even to lift so much as a finger to help him when the work of his lifetime was being thrust into a bonfire of weeds! And where was she now, that mother, when to a rush of girlish tears that were more than half for another man, her worshipped son, a thick-set, heavy-jowled image of lamentable mortality, was lowered into the earth, with a Mr. Pod at his head and a Mr. Twiney at his feet?

Rook Ashover was buried a couple of days later than the man who brought to an end his Pyrrhonian scepticism with a garden rake.

That harmless horticultural tool was picked up on the first of October by none other than Binnory, whose instinct for disaster brought him to Foulden Bridge before the wings of rumour had scarcely begun to flutter.

It interested Binnory to decipher on its handle the name of an ironmonger in Bishop's Forley. The name was Lovejoy; and Binnory got pleasure from speaking of the rake as if it possessed itself that sonorous appellation. He ran off with it across the hill and hid it under an elder bush on the edge of Titty's Ring. Here he would go, when the leaves began to fall, and rake them together with it; pretending that the elder bush was his house and that he was tidying up his drive "like Mr. Twiney at Ash'ver do"; and he would mutter his wildest fancies quite freely to this product of the Bishop's Forley shop, going so far in his weak-headedness as to treat it as a kind of living fetish. Once he even carried his treasure trove several miles down the lane to display it with pride to the "half beasties," whose caravan still remained in the neighbourhood.

Thus it happened that while the Squire of Ashover and the Priest of Ashover became less and less endowed with the illusion of personality, the rake "Lovejoy" gathered to itself more and more of this ambiguous value.

A hundred Octobers hence some pair of nameless lovers, seeking refuge from the inquisitive and the frivolous, may very likely stumble upon a rusty piece of iron and a worm-eaten staff, may very likely use them to clean the mud from their shoes, without the least notion of the part played by these objects in a long-forgotten Frome-side story.

No one knew what passed through Lady Ann's mind as she

lay pale and silent hour by long hour with her new-born child by her side; the child that *was*, after all, a son. Never had the proud girl kept her feelings more completely to herself. To whom, indeed, should she reveal them? Her father was dead. Her mother was dead. Mrs. Ashover's grief at her son's death was so mitigated by her sense of escape from a far greater disaster, the tragedy of the family's extinction, that she could not have responded, even had Ann been entirely unreserved, to the girl's craving for response. Lexie had always been critical and suspicious of her, his vanity piqued by her preference for his brother, his taste offended by her philistinism.

Missy Sparrow-Hawk was not made for submission to circumstance. She was made to control circumstance. But like many another shrewd diplomatist in this chaotic world she found herself baffled and beaten by that element of pure chance which even a Poynings could not outwit.

She had calculated her moves with the most perfect nicety. She had counted on this. She had discounted that. What she had not foreseen was the intrusion upon the stage of events of the rake "Lovejoy." She had felt so sure that in the end she would bring Rook round. Her child was her final master stroke. But no master stroke could bring the dead back to life.

Lady Ann was outwitted, outmanœuvred, beaten. As she lay in her bed listening to the wind in the autumn trees she looked steadily, unflinchingly, at the lonely years in front of her. She would live, of course. She would cherish Rook's child. But whatever happened in the long future she would never again be the same Cousin Ann who had put on that crimson dressing gown in the gamekeeper's cottage!

Well, there it was! She was twenty-six and she had her child. And yet in her unflinching realism she knew that she was beaten. The mouse-coloured dust in Ashover Church might exult in the continuance of its race. *It* had gained its end. *It* was victorious. But the human bridge by which that indestructible life urge had hurled itself into the future carried from henceforth a hurt, a scar, a mark, from which it would never quite recover!

Cousin Ann's beautiful lips closed upon her secret. She would be a proud and competent mistress of a rejuvenated House. But as her heart hardened itself to envisage her defeat, she stared with her gray eyes into Something that at certain hours, when for instance the branches of the cedar creaked and the branches of the lime rustled, was not very far removed from what less stoical persons than Ann Wentworth Gore would have named despair.

At any rate, she did not protest, nor indeed did any other member of that household, when, by the reiterated importunity of the remorseless old dowager, the boy was christened John after his grandfather. Lexie in his heart was glad of his mother's choice. Let the name of Rook disappear from the face of the earth! Let no other human being ever carry it, or be called to bed or board by its familiar sound!

But it was a blubbered and ravaged countenance, emptied of all zest for life, robbed of its most characteristic folds and creases, haggard and woebegone, like the knight-at-arms in "La Belle Dame," that the younger brother—who would, except for this infant, have been the new Squire of Ashover—turned toward the dishes prepared for him by Mrs. Bellamy and toward the books and trees and flower beds and sunrises and sunsets of his accustomed life. He saw, not felt, how beautiful those halcyon days of October were. He went to and fro in a blank and hollow trance, a trance scooped out and scraped dry of all rich and joyous aplomb, of all pleasant chat, of all mellow and wanton sallies.

When November came and Lady Ann's child was more than a month old Lexie began slowly to regain something of his old humour. The curious thing about it was that his health, Instead of suffering any collapse by Rook's death, took a decided turn for the better. It was as if, by passing so suddenly into the dim underworld, the elder Ashover had transferred some actual psychic magnetism into the nerves of his companion. Their life together had been so intimate and so involved that it is easy to imagine the existence of a sort of common cistern of energy flowing between them; drawn upon by both of them; and deriving its source from the indestructible vitality of their ancestors! Such a reservoir would naturally flow with its own independent pulse; and the fact that there was only one of them left to draw upon it would double the influx of its power as soon as the first shock of separation had lost its violence.

The first outward indication of this *vita nuova* in the sick man was the frequency of his visits to Toll-Pike Cottage where Netta was still staying on as Nell's guest. More than once Nell came alone to share some meal with him in his own house; and by the time the first two weeks of November were over, there had been some very uncomfortable scenes with Mrs. Bellamy, who passionately resented these unconventional entertainments.

In the middle of November there happened to fall upon Frome-side a long unaccountable spell of gusty westerly wind. It was a peculiar wind that thus came to that Dorset valley over the orchards and moors of Somersetshire. It was an intermittent wind, with wild spurts of incredibly thin rain, rain so fine and vapoury that it soaked to the core whatever it approached and made man and beast, and even the trees of the field, bend and bow and sway and crouch, when its chilly gusts swept over them and enveloped them.

It was at the close of one of the worst of these persecuted days that Netta Page came to bid farewell to her buried friend.

The rain had ceased with the fall of twilight, but not one flower upon the grave she came to greet had that persistent wind left intact. What disfigured wreaths did remain on the mound of disturbed loam were reduced to shapeless tangles of string and stalks.

The wind kept blowing her hair loose from under her hat. It swept her cloak against her figure. It whirled round her in eddies and spirals. It blew leaves and twigs against her face and made it difficult for her to breathe as it beat furiously against her mouth and nostrils. She kept forming words in her throat; and it was to herself as if she uttered them. But whether any real sound would have come forth from her lips, even if this tempest had ceased, is more than doubtful.

But she was talking to the shrouded form beneath her; and, coherent or incoherent, her words had their relief for her own soul. . . .

"You needn't fret any more about him or her or me or any one! It's all right, Rook dear. Everything is all right."

The force of the wind made her lift both hands to her rain-drenched hat; but even that movement did not prevent two long wisps of hair from detaching themselves from the rest and blowing like tattered streamers behind her. Hurriedly she sank down on her knees and pressed her face against the soaked clay.

The descending darkness swept over her and covered her, separating her from the rest of the world.

Over Antiger Woods, over Dorsal, over Battlefield, like some enormous arrow-stricken dying bird, that darkness came upon her; and though her mind was too absorbed in her grief to be conscious of anything external it is likely enough that the swallowing up of all shapes and contours and colours in the one great wave of blackness made it easier for her to feel that she and what lay down there beneath her were for that moment undivided.

So dependent are the minds of human beings upon these outward tokens, so pitiably do they cling to the least vestige of any "real presence" of what they have loved, that the worst pang of loss that Netta was ever destined to know came when at last, stiff and shivering, she moved away from that spot.

It is significant that these holes dug in churchyard clay are not refilled and covered up, so as to be left just level with the surrounding sod! For it is these tragic hillocks, themselves so nearly resembling enshrouded human shapes, that give us the last illusion of our sorrow, the idea that they actually wrap up and enfold that form which in reality lies so far below!

Netta stumbled several times in the darkness over other graves, graves that were no more to her mind than so many ridges of obstructing turf clods; but she reached the road at last; and when she did reach it and began to make her way with heavy dragging steps back to the cottage, though the storm of her grief had exhausted itself, what took its place was a cold, dull, inert recognition of that unbridgeable gulf between the living and the dead which the assuaging ritual of all the centuries leaves still exposed—yawning, gaping, uncrossed.

She found the door of the cottage left open to admit her; but the fire was almost out in the little parlour and the house was empty.

As she went to and fro among the deserted rooms, making weary and half-mechanical preparations for her own and her companion's evening meal, she fancied she heard the sound of loud harsh music coming from the direction of the village. She opened the kitchen door and listened. Certainly there *was* something going on. Oh! This was the worst of it; that a human soul is not even allowed to live in quiet with its own loss. Life must be rushing, jerking, trailing, dancing, howling forward, just the same; and forever deriding the least attempt to hold it back, to strike it into silence!

"It sounds like a whirligig," she thought as she closed the door. "I didn't know they had whirligigs in the country." When the meal was prepared and all was ready for Nell's return she sat down listlessly on a chair in the kitchen, listening to that harsh music in the distance, to the purring of the Marquis of Carabas, to the ticking of the clock. Once she started, fancying she heard a sound on the floor above. She thought how queer it was that rooms where people had died should be endowed with more life than other rooms; and that the very boards should creak and the very soot fall down the chimney with a sort of intense and solemn self-consciousness!

She wanted to concentrate her mind on a hundred little incidents of her life with Rook; but instead of being able to do this she was compelled, as if by an inner command, to listen intently to hear whether another board would creak up there in Hastings's room. . . .

Netta was not the only one who had heard the strains of music that November evening. A couple of hours before, just after she had taken her hat and cloak and gone out into the twilight, the unexpected sound had reached the ears of her two friends as they sat together in the very place where she was sitting now.

"Listen!" cried Lexie eagerly, leaping to his feet and running out into the back garden. The girl followed and he turned to her with an expression of childish delight. "It's a roundabout!" he chuckled. "Who would have thought it possible as late in the year as this and on a night like this? I've known them to come in October on their way to London; but never in November!"

He looked round him. It was nearly dark now; and, although the rain had stopped, the wind was moaning disconsolately in the trees above the wall and was tossing the bare stalks of the raspberry canes against the posts of the empty clothes line.

It was one of those evenings in which foot travellers on country roads lean for a while over some wet stile or gate and survey the faint whitish glimmer in the sad west, and listen to the splash of raindrops from some tall elm above their heads as a disturbed starling or pigeon tumbles out of sight.

"When was the last merry-go-round *you* saw, Nell?" he asked. And there was a tone in his voice as if he were deliberately defying the forlornness of earth and air and sky.

"I've never seen one in Ashover, Lexie," she answered.

"Well, you *shall* see one!" he cried. "For I'll show you one. I can take a girl to a circus of a cold November night as well as another!"

"But, Lexie——" she began.

He swept aside her objections. "Come!" he cried. "Get your things on! It'll do us good to have a bit of sport."

He hurried her back into the house and made her put on her cape and hat, both of them composed of new mourning black, bought at a shop in Tollminster.

As he held her cloak for her, she was struck by the manner in which the faded tweed suit he wore had grown by daily use to become a kind of animal's skin. No human being's clothes, seen without the wearer, could be more characteristic, more living, than Lexie Ashover's! The effect was enhanced by the perpetual presence of some dead hedge weed or another left in his buttonhole as it might have been left on the shaft of a cart or at the bottom of a wicker basket.

He put on a heavy muffler and overcoat and took his stick in his hand. This stick, a round-handled ash stick, was worn as smooth and glossy by long use as the carved pew of a monk or a hermit's spade.

Once out in the road they were aware that this stormy night had its own peculiar spirit, a spirit that had something reckless and magnetic in it, disturbing to human nerves. Neither the man nor the girl glanced back toward the white railings of Foulden Bridge, railings which had not yet been mended. Lexie kept talking and gesticulating; pointing with his hand in the direction from which the sound seemed to proceed; and laughing in his deep, chuckling, almost leonine manner over the strange fantasy of this belated showman in coming to such a place in the month of November.

He led his companion at a quick pace, past the house of Mr. Pod, past the entrance to Marsh Alley, until he brought her to a small enclosed field on the north of the village where such entertainers were wont to encamp when they visited that district.

The sound of the music increased in volume as they approached and was combined with spasmodic shrieks from the primitive engine that worked the roundabout, with the noisy shouts of young men, the laughter and giggling of girls, and the cries of children.

The wind was still blowing so violently that the rough naphtha-lighted tent, in the midst of which the wooden horses gyrated, shook and shivered and tugged at its supports to such an alarming degree that the older villagers hesitated to enter for fear of having the whole thing come down about their ears.

Lexie led Nell to the rear of a little crowd of wind-blown spectators who were standing at the entrance to the tent.

"It's late in the year, isn't it, for this kind of thing?" he remarked to a sturdily built stranger who was bending over one of the tent pegs, making the rope more secure.

"Late? I should think it was late," replied the man in a surly tone. Then, when he took in the personality of Lexie: "We're due in Bishop's Forley to-night, sir," he added, "and we stay there for the winter. I said myself 'twere a fool thing to stop here with the weather so bad; but he *would* have it so; and so here we are!"

"I've never known a merry-go-round in Ashover later than October," repeated Lexie gravely, moving forward with Nell into the tent.

The engine happened to stop at that moment, and as the boys and girls who had been riding clambered down, and another instalment prepared to mount, a quick whisper ran round among them and many eyes were turned upon the couple.

Nell pulled him by the arm. "Let's get away," she whispered. "They're noticing us."

But it chanced that a particularly grotesque piebald horse had stopped just in front of Lexie. This horse possessed an unscrupulous and world-embracing eye, an eye upon whose yellow-tinted orb the flame of the naphtha lamps shone luridly, giving it an almost Cyclopean look.

"One minute!" the young man said. And leaving his companion standing there alone, white-faced and disconcerted, he climbed up with careful deliberation upon the animal's back.

The music soon recommenced; and the fantastic circle of horses and riders revolved once more, to a pandemonium of raucous sounds.

"Looksee! Looksee!" cried one of the children. "There be Master Lexie, a-ride-a-cock-horsin' same as we!"

Nell, in her black dress and black hat, was the cynosure of many astonished eyes. She knew them all, but she carefully avoided meeting the glance of any one in particular. No one in the tent was bold enough to address her; the older people moving discreetly away to the farther side of the engine, the children crowding up as near to her as they dared but only whispering to each other in low tones that were drowned in the noise of the brazen din.

She herself stared helplessly at Lexie's figure, in its frayed overcoat and blue muffler, appearing and disappearing with punctual regularity, like some sign of the Zodiac in a clock-work heaven.

The piebald horse he rode lost most of its individual character in that whirling revolution; but Nell could still catch the staring voracity of its insatiable eye, an eye that remained fixed upon her with an expression that was neither sympathetic nor derisive; an expression of simple devouring interest.

As to Lexie himself, his own lineaments were composed into a fixed and smiling mask of infantile complacence. One of his eyelids was lifted a little higher than the other in a kind of ecstasy of ironic roguery; but the glance he directed toward his companion as he passed her by in his gyrations had in it a sublime acceptance of destiny worthy of the animal on whose back he rode.

The noise in the young man's ears was deafening; and as he listened to it, giving himself up to the motion, his mind began wandering off to other sounds of a less artificial character that were at that moment rising up toward the cloud-covered sky from his native Frome-side.

He thought of the way the branches were creaking even now among the Scotch firs on Heron's Ridge. He imagined the grunt of a badger as it trotted in the moaning wind across Titty's Ring. He heard the cattle stirring drowsily in their bartons. He heard the splash of a perch in Saunders' Hole and the cry of a stray mallard drifting across the marshes toward Comber's End. Out of the heart of that brazen clamour he seemed to be listening to the tiny German clock ticking the hour in his mother's bedroom. He even fancied he could hear the quiet breathing in its guarded cradle of the small head of his House, the young new Squire of Ashover. And then suddenly, as in his fantasy he counted up these unnoticed sounds of the night, it seemed to him that he could actually catch the whirring of owl wings hovering about his elm tree in the churchyard, as they had done in the moonlight, just a year ago, when he met his brother at that place.

Before the music stopped or the rotation of the wheel of horses and riders came to a standstill, Lexie jumped down on the ground by Nell's side. He took her by the arm and led her out of the tent where they were met in the darkness by that familiar smell of an enclosure of grass trodden by men and beasts, the precise savour of which none know who have not been to fairs and circuses in country villages.

"The hobbyhorse is forgot!" he muttered; and the girl was bewildered by the fierce intensity of his grip upon her arm. The wind seemed to blow against his face at that moment with an ice-cold menace, as of some breath from the outer spaces. He gathered his forces together to resist this threat; and instinctively, in so doing, he let his arm in the darkness enclose Nell's waist.

"Don't let's go back just yet," he pleaded. "Netta won't mind waiting a little for supper."

The girl was so startled and shocked by the change in his manner as they came out of the tent that, in her pity for him, she did not have the heart to resist. But the touch of her warm young body, as he pressed her against him, soon restored him.

He led her down a grassy rain-soaked lane; one of those lanes on the outskirts of a village that usually end in nothing more hospitable than some isolated group of cattle sheds or pigsties.

What in this case they stumbled upon, however, was an open barn; and Lexie was enchanted beyond measure to detect in its cavernous obscurity a mass of sweet-smelling piled-up hay.

But Nell hesitated now and drew back when, with an exclamation of unashamed delight, he pulled at her hand to lead her forward into this shrine of Demeter.

"Let's go home, Lexie," she begged. "My shoes and stockings are soaking, and I'm sure yours must be! We really oughtn't to keep Netta waiting any longer."

But it was not easy to resist the wistful and humorous appeals, some of them almost querulous in their childishness, with which he implored her; and she yielded at last.

From outside in the darkness they could hear the shrieks and snorts of the merry-go-round and the wild music of a country jig that might have been the very tune to which the

West Saxons first invaded Frome-side, so heathen and barbaric did it sound.

Neither of them could have told how long they were there together, with that sweet penetrating smell of the hay about them, and the scent of the dark, rain-drenched fields blown in through the door. But when they stood at last on the threshold of their hiding place, and while Lexie's countenance was illuminated for a moment by the light of the match with which he lit a cigarette, Nell noticed to her consternation a look upon his face like the look of a child outraged and lost.

"What is it, Lexie?" she asked anxiously.

But he threw the match away without answering. His mind, like a blind home-turning mole whose moving tunnel escapes all prevention, though its course can be traced by the upheaved turf, reverted to that six-foot-deep hole in the churchyard.

"Come along," he said brusquely; but a minute later, offering her his arm to lean upon, "I do hope you won't be the worse for this, Nell. It would be a shame if you were; for you're a brave and generous little girl. Do your feet feel *very* wet? If they don't *feel* wet I expect you'll get no harm."

This time it was the girl who made no answer. When they reached the field where the tent had been, they found the showmen in the process of packing up and departing. The wind made the lamps by which they laboured flare and smoke like the fires of some wild bivouac; and the figures of the men, showing dark and sinister in the tossing shadows, seemed as alien to the hedges and gates and trees as if they had been brought there by evil wizardry.

There was a group of two or three farm lads still lingering about the show wagons; and when Lexie and Nell had passed they heard behind them shouts of ribald laughter. Lexie felt his companion's hand tremble on his arm and a wave of anger, out of all proportion to the incident, passed through his frame.

"What brutes they are!" he muttered aloud.

And then in his secret thoughts he lamented the innumerable obstacles and difficulties by which the simplest and most natural attempts to be just ordinarily happy are surrounded and hemmed in.

"Something has given this human society a twist in the wrong direction," he said to himself. And even as he said it a shameful subterranean thankfulness that it was not he who was lying in that six-foot hole took possession of him.

"Nell, my dear, you're not angry with me, are you?"

She pressed his arm gently; and the wordless tenderness of that response touched him more than any words could have done.

"How sweet and lovely a girl can be!" he thought; and then in a kind of inward ecstasy, "I am alive! I am alive!" he cried to his own heart.

But a moment later, quite unknown to the girl at his side, "the form," to use a biblical phrase, "of his visage" changed. "Oh, Rook! Oh, my brother, my brother!"

Nell never quite understood why it was that just then he stopped dead still in the road and dropped the arm that was supporting her.

But he had gone down in his remorse among those who "lie in hell like sheep." He, the life amorist, the worshipper of the sun and the sweet air and the grain-bearing earth, was up to his knees at that moment in waters deeper and colder than the waters of the Frome.

But even there, though his face in the darkness had the injured, bewildered look of an outraged child, he held the dead man tightly, protectively against his heart. He did not budge an inch from the integrity of his nature. But his love, like a spear driven into the bed of a swollen river, stood up erect and defiant, visible through the driving mist to all such as might come that way, a signpost in the night, a signal, a token, a witness that would at least outlast his own days, even though it did not outlast the Scotch firs on Heron's Ridge or the linden tree and the cedar tree on the lawn of Ashover House.

THE END